“Every [illegible] iew in this novel i[illegible] ı, dialogue, pacing, [illegible] llent.”

[illegible] Oklahoman

“The consistent qua[illegible] tions in this alphabet series justify all the praise these books have received over the past thirty-five years.”

—*The Wall Street Journal*

“I’m going to miss Kinsey Millhone. Ever since the first of Sue Grafton’s Alphabet mysteries, *A is for Alibi*, came out in 1982, Kinsey has been a good friend and the very model of an independent woman, a gutsy Californian PI rocking a traditional man’s job. . . . It’s Kinsey herself who keeps this series so warm and welcoming. She’s smart, she’s resourceful, and she’s tough enough to be sensitive on the right occasions.”

—*The New York Times Book Review*

“This will leave readers both relishing another masterful entry and ruing the near-end of this series. Prime Grafton.” —*Booklist*, starred review

“Grafton once again proves herself a superb storyteller.” —*Publishers Weekly*

“The series may be coming to a close, but Grafton (*W is for Wasted*) constructs an intricate plot following two time lines with at least a dozen characters in play while rarely slowing the pace.” —*Library Journal*

"Sue Grafton is one of the most creative crime writers of our times. She breaks established rules of the mystery and crime novel and establishes new ones. Kinsey Millhone will be the new model for mystery and crime novels for several generations. Each new addition to the series is better than the previous ones. *Y is for Yesterday* will keep your heart pounding more than the previous twenty-four novels in the series. It is everything all her twenty-four previous novels were and much more."

—*Washington Book Review*

"Y is for Yes, you should read Grafton's latest novel"

—*Santa Barbara News-Press*

"The lively, engrossing *Y is for Yesterday* demonstrates that she hasn't lost her touch over the years. . . . Grafton is in sure command of Kinsey's wise-cracking but warm voice and of a many-layered plot that moves back and forth over events of a decade. *Y is for Yesterday* might make you wish the alphabet had a few more letters."

—*Tampa Bay Times*

"[A]n accomplished and disturbing tale of decay and dysfunction, one informed by the full force of Grafton's talents and illuminated by her profound sense of decency."

—*Richmond Times-Dispatch*

Praise for Sue Grafton

"I've come to believe that Grafton is not only the most talented woman writing crime fiction today but also that regardless of gender, her Millhone books are among the five or six best series any American has ever written."
—*The Washington Post*

"Grafton purposively begins with a standard situation . . . and then sets about breaking every cardinal rule of the mystery novel." —*Los Angeles Times*

"Grafton's endless resourcefulness in varying her pitches in this landmark series, graced by her trademark self-deprecating humor, is one of the seven wonders of the genre." —*Kirkus Reviews*, starred review

"Sue has over the years created in Kinsey Millhone one of the greatest fictional detectives of all time. Grafton is a writer who gets better and more nuanced with each offering, and I love the fact that the books are all set in the 1980s—I get a kick each time Kinsey frantically searches for a pay phone to make a call."
—David Baldacci, *CBS News*

"Ratcheting up the heat as she heads toward the finish line of her alphabetically-framed series, Grafton has turned in a corker of a novel with *X*, upping her already high-level game." —*The Boston Globe*

TITLES BY SUE GRAFTON

Kinsey Millhone Mysteries

A is for Alibi
B is for Burglar
C is for Corpse
D is for Deadbeat
E is for Evidence
F is for Fugitive
G is for Gumshoe
H is for Homicide
I is for Innocent
J is for Judgment
K is for Killer
L is for Lawless
M is for Malice
N is for Noose
O is for Outlaw
P is for Peril
Q is for Quarry
R is for Ricochet
S is for Silence
T is for Trespass
U is for Undertow
V is for Vengeance
W is for Wasted
X
Y is for Yesterday

And

Kinsey and Me: Stories

IS FOR
YESTERDAY

SUE GRAFTON

G. P. Putnam's Sons
New York

Y

PUTNAM

G. P. PUTNAM'S SONS
Publishers Since 1838
An imprint of Penguin Random House LLC
375 Hudson Street
New York, New York 10014

The Library of Congress has catalogued the G. P. Putnam's Sons hardcover edition as follows:

Names: Grafton, Sue, author.
Title: Y is for yesterday / Sue Grafton.
Description: New York : G. P. Putnam's Sons, 2017. | Series: A Kinsey Millhone novel ; 25 | "Marian Wood Books."
Identifiers: LCCN 2017026401 (print) | LCCN 2017029916 (ebook) | ISBN 9781101614358 (ebook) | ISBN 9780399163852 (hardcover)
Subjects: LCSH: Millhone, Kinsey (Fictitious character)—Fiction. | Women private investigators—California—Fiction. | Extortion—Fiction. | BISAC: FICTION / Mystery & Detective / Women sleuths. | FICTION / Suspense. | GSAFD: Mystery fiction. | Suspense fiction.
Classification: LCC PS3557.R13 (ebook) | LCC PS3557.R13 Y15 2017 (print) | DDC 813/.54—dc23
LC record available at https://lccn.loc.gov/2017026401

First G. P. Putnam's Sons hardcover edition / August 2017
First G. P. Putnam's Sons trade paperback edition / July 2018
First G. P. Putnam's Sons mass market international edition / July 2018
G. P. Putnam's Sons mass market international edition ISBN: 9780525536369

Printed in the United States of America
1 3 5 7 9 10 8 6 4 2

This book is dedicated to those in our small clan who will carry forward into the future:

Addison and Taylor,
Kinsey and Houston,
Erin and Daniel,
and Jacob.

May you live with honesty, integrity, and compassion, offering the occasional heartfelt hurrahs to your ancient Nana, who loves you beyond belief.

ACKNOWLEDGMENTS

The author would like to acknowledge the invaluable assistance of the following people: Steven Humphrey; Judge Brian Hill, Santa Barbara County Superior Court; Sam Eaton, Attorney at Law (retired); the Honorable Joyce Dudley, District Attorney, Santa Barbara County; Paul Ginsberg, Professional Audio Laboratories; Sandy N. Frausto, Senior Deputy, Santa Barbara County Sheriff's Office; Harry Hudley, Bailiff, Santa Barbara County Sheriff's Office; Dan Duncan, Charmagne Horn, and Andrea Veach, Harrods Creek Auto Service, Harrods Creek, Kentucky; Jamie Clark; Florence Michel; Col. Everette L. Pace with thanks for the vintage Lucky Strike cigarette tin that Iris flourishes; Patti Gibson because she asked; and Joey Seay with appreciation for his generous contribution to the Heuser Hearing and Language Institute, Louisville, Kentucky.

Y

IS FOR YESTERDAY

1

THE THEFT

January 1979

Iris stood at the counter in the school office, detention slip in hand, anticipating a hand-smack from Mr. Lucas, the vice principal. She'd already seen him twice since her enrollment at Climping Academy the previous fall. The first time, she'd been turned in for cutting PE. The second time, she'd been reported for smoking outside study hall. She'd been advised there was a smoking area set aside specifically for students, which she argued was on the far side of campus and impossible to get to between classes. That fell on deaf ears. This was now early January and she'd been reported for violating the school's dress code.

She was willing to admit that detention slips were a poor means of establishing her place in a new school. The younger students wore uniforms, but in the upper grades, clothing was at the discretion of the individual student as long as the overall look was considered within bounds. The way Iris read it—no skirts or dresses with hemlines above the knee, no tank tops, no shorts, no T-shirts with slogans, no underwear showing, and no flip-flops or Doc Martens. As far as she was concerned, she was playing by the rules. She'd assumed she could wear anything she pleased, within reason, of course. Climp had a different point of view. In the minds of the school administrators, clothing was meant to show modesty, respect, conservatism, and seriousness of purpose.

Her choice that morning had been an ankle-length claret-colored velvet dress with a ruffled collar, long sleeves, black tights, and high-top red tennis shoes. Her hair was long and thick, a color that fell somewhere between auburn and flame red thanks to a mixture of boxed dyes. Two big silver barrettes held the mass away from her face. On each wrist she wore a wide leather cuff, studded with brass and silver nail heads. As it turned out, all of this was a great big no-no. Well, shit.

The school secretary, Mrs. Malcolm, acknowledged Iris's presence with a nod, but clearly the woman didn't intend to interrupt her work over the antics of a problematic ninth grader. She was busy distributing mail to various teachers' cubbyholes. A student volunteer, Poppy, was stapling together packets of some sort. Iris was a freshman at Climping Academy, the Santa Teresa private school located in Horton Ravine, which was so la-di-da, it totally freaked her out. She was only at Climp because her father had been hired to teach advanced placement math and to coach field hockey. The tuition was twenty thousand dollars a year, which her parents could never have afforded if not for her father's job, which allowed Climp to waive the cost of enrollment.

The last high school she'd attended was in a "mixed" neighborhood in Detroit, which was to say, drugs, thugs, and vandalism, some of which Iris had generated herself when the mood struck her. She'd been uprooted from Michigan and plunked down on the West Coast despite her protests. California was a bust. She expected surfers, dopers, and free spirits, but it was all the same old shit as far as she could tell. Climping Academy was beyond belief. Enrollment from kindergarten to twelfth grade was three hundred students total, with a pupil-to-teacher ratio of nine to one. Expectations were high and most of the students rose to the occasion. And why would they not? These were all rich kids, whose mommies and daddies gave them the best of everything: trips abroad, unlimited clothing budgets, private tennis and fencing lessons, and weekly visits with a shrink—the latter just in case some boob was gifted with a brand-new VW instead of the BMW he had his heart set on. Big boo-fucking-hoo. Her parents often expressed doubts about her private school attendance, citing the pressure to conform and the dangers of materialism. Her parents fancied themselves Bohemians.

One look at her outfit and her homeroom teacher, Mrs. Rubio, had informed her she'd have to go home and change, and when she told Mrs. Rubio she had no transportation, the woman had suggested she take a bus. Like, huh? Iris didn't know anything about bus schedules, so what was she supposed to do? Unlike most of the other students, she didn't live in snooty old Horton Ravine. Moving from Michigan to California had been a shock, the sticker prices for homes being exorbitant. Her parents had purchased a shabby rambling house on the Upper East Side with a mortgage that would keep them enslaved for life. How Bohemian was that? Iris was an only child. Her parents had never wanted children in the first place, a sentiment they were happy to remind her of at the drop of a hat. Her mother, at the age of twenty-five, went in to have her tubes tied against medical advice, and discovered she was pregnant. Husband and wife had agonized over whether to terminate, and in the end they decided it was acceptable to have one child. Often in Iris's hearing, they congratulated themselves on their parenting style, which consisted largely of instilling independence in the girl, meaning an ability to entertain herself and demand precious little.

Her mother had a degree in political science and was currently teaching part time at Santa Teresa City College. She also volunteered two afternoons a week at an abortion clinic, where she felt it was incumbent on her to champion reproductive rights, women's control over their own bodies, and the advisability of women keeping their options open instead of burdening themselves with unwanted offspring.

Meanwhile, having witnessed the sophistication of Horton Ravine, Iris was embarrassed by the way she was forced to live. On the home front, her parents favored clutter and disarray—imagining perhaps that untidiness and intellectual superiority walked hand in hand. Iris couldn't remember the last time the three of them sat down to a meal. Dishes were left in the sink since neither her mother nor father could be bothered with such things. Dusting and vacuuming were too mundane to address. Laundry went undone. If one of them broke down and actually washed and dried a load, it was left in a pile on the living room sofa to be reclaimed as needed. Iris did her own. Her parents believed it was exploitative of the lower classes to hire household help, so those chores were best left a-begging. They were also committed to the notion of equality between the sexes, which spawned an unspoken competition to see who could force the other to knuckle under and pick up the slack. Iris's bedroom was the only orderly room in the house and she spent most of her free time there isolated from the chaos.

Mr. Lucas appeared in the doorway to his office indicating that she should come in. He was a good-looking man, low-key, relaxed, and competent. His hair was the color of California beach sand, his face nicely creased. He was tall and trim, given to cashmere vests and dress shirts with the sleeves rolled up. He tossed a file on his desk and took a seat, lacing his fingers above his head. "Mrs. Rubio has lodged an objection to your outfit," he remarked. "You look like you're on your way to the Renaissance Faire."

"Whatever that is," she said.

"This is the third detention you've been cited for since you arrived. I don't understand this pattern of defiance."

"Why is it a pattern when I've only done two things wrong?"

"Counting today, that makes three. You're here to learn, not to do battle with school authorities. I'm not sure you appreciate the opportunity you've been given."

"I don't give a shit about that," she said. "All my friends are back in Detroit. With all due respect, Mr. Lucas, Climping Academy sucks."

She saw that Mr. Lucas was prepared to ignore her bad language, probably thinking the issue of trash talk was not what was at stake. "I went back and looked at your records. At your last school, you did good work. Here you've set yourself on a collision course. You miss your friends. I get that. I'm also aware California isn't an easy place to live if you're accustomed to the Midwest, but you keep on acting out, you're only hurting yourself. Does that make sense to you?"

"So what's the deal? Three demerits and I'm out?"

He smiled. "We don't give up as easily as that. Like it or not, you're here three more years. We want the time to be pleasant and productive. You think you can handle that?"

"I guess."

She studied the floor. For some reason, she was stung by his tone, which was kind. His concern seemed genuine, which made it all the worse. She didn't want to fit in. She didn't want to adapt. She wanted to go back to Detroit, where she knew she was accepted for who she was. In that moment, Iris realized she had violated her own working strategy in situations like this. The trick was to look abject and give a lengthy explanation for the infraction, which might or might not be true. The point was to fill the air with verbiage, to apologize at least twice, sounding as sincere as possible for someone who didn't give a rat's ass. The secret was to put up no resistance whatever, a technique that had worked well for her in the past. Resistance only fueled the lecture, encouraging the adult-types to pontificate.

She murmured, "What about my clothes? I don't drive, so there's no way I can go home and change."

"Now, that I can help you with. Where do you live?"

"Upper East Side."

"Hang on a minute."

He got up from his desk and crossed to the door to the school office, which he opened, sticking his head out. "Mrs. Malcolm, can you do me a favor and let me borrow Poppy for half an hour? Iris needs a ride home. Upper East Side. There and back, thirty minutes max."

"Of course. If it's all right with her."

"Sure. Happy to."

Iris could feel her heart start to bang in her chest. Poppy was one of the most popular girls at Climp, operating at such an elevation that Iris barely had the nerve to speak to her. She was close to panic at the idea of being in a moving vehicle with her for even ten minutes, let alone thirty.

Once in the parking lot, Poppy turned to her with a grin. "Cool threads, kid. I wish I had your nerve."

The two got into Poppy's Thunderbird. Once Iris slammed the car door, she reached into her bag and pulled out a vintage Lucky Strike cigarette tin, filled with tightly rolled joints, at which Iris was adept. "Care to partake?"

"Oh, shit yes," Poppy said.

That had been January and the two had been inseparable since. To Iris's credit, she was a model of good behavior for the next three months.

Every afternoon, they repaired to Poppy's house, ostensibly to study, but actually to smoke dope and raid Poppy's parents' liquor cabinet. Iris was a genius at concocting mixed drinks, utilizing what was available. Her latest she called a "flame thrower," which entailed Kahlúa, banana-flavored liqueur, crème de menthe, and rum. Poppy's parents didn't drink rum. That bottle was held in reserve should a guest request it. Poppy's father was a thoracic surgeon, her mother a hospital administrator, which meant long hours for both and a preoccupation with medical matters, gossip as much as anything else. Poppy's two older sisters had graduated from college. One was now in medical school and the other was working for a pharmaceutical company. The whole family was high-profile and high-achievement. Poppy was an oopsie baby—a surprise addition to the family, arriving long after Poppy's mother assumed she'd been liberated from diapers, teething, pediatricians, PTA meetings, and soccer practice. Iris and Poppy had that in common, their alien state. It was as though both had been deposited by spacecraft, leaving the mystified earthlings to raise them as best they could.

Most of the time the two girls were on their own, ordering pizza or any other foodstuff that could be charged to a credit card and delivered to Poppy's door. At least she could drive and she often delivered Iris to her house at ten at night. Iris's parents never said a word, probably grateful she had a friend whose company she preferred to theirs.

In April, Iris was dumbfounded when she received yet another summons to the vice principal's office. What'd she do this time? She hadn't been called out on anything and she felt put upon and unappreciated. She'd been doing her best to blend in and behave herself.

Even Mrs. Malcolm seemed surprised. "We haven't seen you for a while. What now?"

"No clue. I'm tooling along minding my own business and I get this note that Mr. Lucas wants to see me. I don't even know what this is about."

"News to me as well."

Iris took a seat on one of the wooden benches provided for the errant and unrepentant. She had her books and her binder in hand so that once she was properly dressed down, she could report to her next class, which in this case was world history. She opened her binder, pretending to check her notes. She was careful to show no interest in the secretary's disbursement of manila envelopes, but she knew what they contained: the Benchmark California Academic Proficiency Tests. These were administered at the beginning and end of junior year, designed to measure each student's mastery of math and English. Poppy had been bitching for weeks about having to perform up to grade level or suffer the indignities of remedial catch-up work. Under certain circumstances, the test results would determine whether a junior was even allowed to advance to senior year. Iris wondered if there was a way to get her hands on a copy. Wouldn't that be a coup? Poppy was her best friend, a diligent student, but not all that bright. Iris could see her limitations, but overlooked her deficits in the interest of her status at Climp. Poppy's boyfriend, Troy Rademaker, was in somewhat the same boat. His grades were excellent, but he didn't dare risk anything less than top marks. He attended Climp on a scholarship it was essential to protect. In addition, he and Austin Brown were among the nominees for the Albert Climping Memorial Award, given annually to an outstanding freshman, sophomore, junior, and senior based on academic distinction, athletic achievement, and service to the community. Austin Brown was the unofficial but equally undisputed kingpin of the junior class, much admired and equally feared for his scathing pronouncements about his classmates.

Poppy wasn't conventionally pretty, but she was stylish and well-liked. Schoolwork was her curse. She was one of those borderline cases where year after year, teachers had talked themselves into passing her along without requiring a command of core subjects. This had always worked to Poppy's advantage, keeping her in lockstep with classmates she'd known since kindergarten. The problem was that grade by grade, she'd been advanced on increasingly shaky grounds, which meant the work only became harder and more opaque. Now Poppy alternated between feelings of frustration and feelings of despair. Iris's role, as she saw it, was to take Poppy's mind off her scholastic woes, thus the dope-smoking and junk food.

Iris couldn't imagine what Mr. Lucas wanted with her. She'd gone for months without a detention slip and she wondered if he understood how much effort and self-discipline that took. She could use a pat on the back, positive reinforcement for what she'd achieved in the way of maturity and self-control. Acting out was easier. She relished the feeling of being unleashed, free to act on impulse, doing whatever occurred to her.

Mr. Lucas entered the office and signaled to Iris, who got up and followed him. Once he settled at his desk, he seemed perplexed. "What can I do for you?"

"I don't know. I got a note saying you wanted to see me."

Mr. Lucas stared at her blankly and then recovered himself. "That's right. Sorry. This isn't actually about you. It's about your friend Poppy."

Iris looked at him with interest. This was a change in the script. "What about her?"

"She has a lot at stake academically and the faculty is concerned about her plummeting grades."

Iris was taken aback. "I don't get it. What's this have to do with me?"

"She's struggling. You probably see that as well as I do. In a curious way she looks up to you as a role model."

"Yeah, curious, no shit. How can I be a role model when I'm fourteen years old?"

"You underestimate yourself. You're a bright girl. You can afford to coast because you manage to keep up without putting in much effort. Poppy has to work much harder than you. She's got the Proficiency Test coming up next week and it's vital that she stay on point. If she doesn't improve her academic standing, she won't get into the college of her choice, which I understand is Vassar."

Iris laughed. "Vassar? No way. She'll be lucky to get into City College for a two-year degree."

"That's not ours to decide. The point is, you could be a big help if you'd encourage her to study instead of goofing off. She needs the support."

Offended, Iris said, "She doesn't need my 'support.' She does fine. I don't understand why you're blaming me if Poppy's bored with school."

"It's more than boredom, isn't it?" He made an O of his thumb and his index finger, putting them to his lips as though he were toking on a joint.

Iris kept her face blank. How the heck could he know

about that? "If you're implying Poppy and I smoke dope, I don't know where you got that idea because you're dead wrong. I might have done that a couple of times back in Michigan, but I've sworn off. Poppy, I don't know about. You'd have to ask her."

With exaggerated patience, Mr. Lucas said, "Look, Iris. I'm not here to argue. I was hoping to enlist your aid."

"In doing what? Dumping my best friend? Because that's what you're suggesting, isn't it?"

"Not dumping her. Cutting back on the time you spend together, just as a temporary measure."

"So now you're telling me who to hang out with?"

"I'm soliciting your help. In terms of schoolwork, Poppy's done okay so far, but she's faltering."

"And that's *my* fault?" Iris found it infuriating that she'd been called into Mr. Lucas's office, not to reward her for good behavior, for which she'd made a special effort, but to heap phony praise on her in hopes she'd give Poppy Earl a boost.

"You're an influence. You have a strong personality. Scholastically, she's not as quick as you are. I'm suggesting it might be in her best interests if you backed off a bit and let her focus on her schoolwork."

Iris started to protest and then she clamped her mouth shut. She could feel the heat rise in her cheeks at the notion that he'd blamed her for Poppy's failing grades. Worse still was the idea that she should sacrifice a friendship for any reason whatsoever. If Poppy's grades needed an assist, there were other ways to go about it than dropping a friend. She said, "I'll think about it."

Mr. Lucas seemed surprised that she'd yielded so easily. "Good. Well, that's great. That's really all we're asking—that you'll give some thought to your effect on her and ease up."

"Right."

He went on for a bit, but Iris had tuned him out. She was livid that the faculty had been discussing Poppy's mediocre grades and pointing the finger at Iris, like it was her responsibility. What the fuck was that about?

She and Mr. Lucas continued to chat, going through a bullshit exchange, while she pretended everything was okay when in fact she was furious.

The meeting ended and the minute Mr. Lucas closed his office door, she scurried into the hall, blind with rage. She halted, feeling the rush of anger narrow to a point. On the wall across the corridor, between the girls' restroom and the janitor's closet, there was a fire alarm box. The process was simple. Break glass, press here. She cast a glance in both directions and saw that the hallway was clear. She used a corner of her history book to break the glass. She pressed the button and an ear-splitting siren sounded. She walked into the girls' bathroom and closed herself into a stall, pulled her feet up, and rested them against the door so if anyone looked under, the stall would appear to be empty. Beyond the quiet of the bathroom, she could hear doors banging open, the high-pitched chatter of students pouring out of the classrooms.

Mr. Dorfman, the principal, was on the intercom, instructing teachers and students to proceed to their stations in an orderly fashion. The drill was one they'd done a hundred times, but the practice was usually announced in advance. She could tell from their shrill response that everyone was uncertain if this was the real deal or not. Something exciting about the idea of a school burning to the ground. Within minutes, the corridors were silent. Iris stood up and left the stall, peering around the door to see if anyone was patrolling for strays. No sign of a soul, so she scooted back across the hall to the office, which was also empty.

She scanned the faculty mailboxes and lifted the first of the manila envelopes she spotted. This was in Mrs. Rose's cubbyhole, the envelope unsealed but secured with a clasp. The copy machine was still humming and it took less than a minute to reproduce the Proficiency Test and the accompanying answer sheet. She put the pages back in the envelope, pressed the clasp flat, and returned it to Mrs. Rose's cubbyhole. Then she went out into the hall and mingled with the students who were returning to the building. She couldn't wait to tell Poppy what she'd done. Thanks to her, Poppy Earl and Troy Rademaker were home free.

Later, Kinsey Millhone would wonder how differently events might have played out if she'd been present in the vice principal's office that day. No one could have predicted the consequences of Iris's impetuous actions in response to Mr. Lucas's summons. In point of fact, Kinsey wouldn't meet up with the principal players for another ten years and by then, the die would be cast. Odd how fate is so often embedded in the aftermath of a simple conversation.

2

Friday, September 15, 1989

Another September had rolled into view and Santa Teresa was in the throes of an artificial autumn generated by the drought, which was in its fourth year. The landscape was scorched and the reservoir that provided water to the city was at an all-time low. In California, a shortage of deciduous trees means that the residents are denied the splendid array of changing colors that heralds the fall in other parts of the country. Here, even the evergreens looked exhausted and the lawns were dead, except for those of the rich who could afford to have water trucked in. In the presence of such severe conditions, a series of wildfires had burned across the state in unprecedented numbers. So much for the weather report. My name is Kinsey Millhone. I'm a female private investigator, aged thirty-nine, living and working in this Southern California town ninety-five miles north of Los Angeles. I'm also single and cranky-minded to hear some people tell it. The small studio I've been renting for the past eight-plus years was once a single-car garage, now expanded, designed, and custom-built by Henry Pitts, my eighty-nine-year-old landlord. Of course, he didn't do the actual labor, but he supervised the construction crew closely, making sure everything was done to his high standards.

In the interest of conservation, Henry had stripped his backyard of grass, which left us with dirt, sand, and stepping-stones. Henry's two Adirondack chairs were arranged in conversational range of each other on the off chance we might want to enjoy a late afternoon cocktail as the sun went down. This was never the case. I didn't want to sit contemplating barren packed earth, which doesn't promote relaxation in my humble opinion. His potting bench and gardening gloves were superfluous and the row of larger tools he'd hung on the side of his garage—shovels, wood-handled garden forks, and pruning shears—had been unused for so long the spiders had spun webs and now lurked in ominous arachnid tunnels in hopes of snagging prey. Henry's cat, Ed, seemed to look on the backyard as one big litter box and he made use of it every chance he could—one more reason to avoid the area.

In terms of my professional life, I'd had a nasty run-in with a man named Ned Lowe the previous March, and he'd nearly succeeded in strangling me to death. I still wasn't entirely certain why I'd been spared, but I felt I should be prepared in case he came flying at me on some future occasion. Most of the time I didn't think about him at all, a defense mechanism, I'm sure. There were moments, though, when I pictured him with an unnerving clarity. Somewhere in the world, he was alive, and while that was the case, I'd be looking over my shoulder, wondering if he'd suddenly reappear. He was a man obsessed and I knew I'd never feel safe until he was dead and buried.

Shortly after the assault, I'd applied for and been granted a permit to carry a concealed weapon. I already owned a Heckler & Koch VP9, which I kept in a locked trunk at the foot of my bed or in a briefcase that I locked in the trunk of my car. I'd paid the processing fee, completed a training course, and passed the NICS, the National Instant Criminal Background Check System, fingerprint and background check. The police department seemed satisfied that I was of "good moral character," and my reasons for applying were apparently persuasive, even if Ned Lowe was nowhere to be found at the time. I worked, preparing myself for another encounter, in which I was determined to prevail. For that, I needed strength, endurance, determination, and skill. A loaded handgun seemed like a good idea as well.

His attack had left me wary of doing my usual three-mile morning jog in the early morning dark, so I'd returned to the gym, mixing weight lifting with stints on the treadmill. This bored the bejesus out of me, but at least I worked out in a room full of fitness nuts, most of them male, with the occasional kick-ass female. I appreciated the bright lights, the noise, the bad music, and the muted television game shows. Most of all the sense of safety. My workouts took place in the middle of the day, and when I emerged from the gym, it was still light outside. Where possible, I took to jogging on the beach path in broad daylight, which I still preferred as long as there was a goodly number of people in evidence.

That Friday afternoon, I was writing a report on the job I'd just completed, working as a temporary front office receptionist/secretary for a general practitioner. The doctor had been subject to thefts of drugs and petty cash and she needed someone to determine who was doing it. She had two partners and twelve on staff and no clue about how to identify the perpetrator. Her office manager was out for three weeks, having surgery for a bad back, and it made sense that the doctor would hire someone to fill the gap. I was sufficiently skilled at typing, filing, and answering the phone that I could pass for an old hand at office work. Anything I didn't know about the medical profession was easy enough to explain, given the fiction that I was from a temp agency.

In the course of the job, I'd found occasion to work

late, which gave me ample opportunity to snoop. Turned out it was the office manager herself who had her hand in the till, supplementing her salary with petty cash and easing her back pain with meds she lifted from the supply cabinet. The detail men dropped off countless samples during their meetings with the doctors in the practice, so she had her choice of the latest remedies. The doctor who hired me was reluctant to pursue a criminal complaint, but my work was done and, more important, I'd been paid.

I'd just removed the last page of the report from my trusty portable Smith Corona and I was neatly separating the carbons from the originals when my phone rang. I picked up the handset and tucked it against my left ear while I stacked the pages and placed them in a file folder. "Millhone Investigations."

"May I speak to Kinsey?"

"This is she."

"Ah. Well, I'm glad I reached you. My name is Lauren McCabe. Lonnie Kingman gave me your name and suggested I get in touch with regard to something that's come up."

Lonnie had been my attorney for the past ten years, so anybody he sent my way was automatically okay in my book, at least until proven otherwise. The name Lauren McCabe set off a distant clanging of bells, but I couldn't place the reference. "Something that's come up" could have meant just about anything.

I said, "I appreciate Lonnie's referring you. What can I help you with?"

"I'd prefer to discuss this in person, if that's all right with you."

"Fine. We can meet at your convenience. What did you have in mind?"

"I'd love to say today, but I play duplicate on Fridays and I'm gone most of the day. I was hoping you could stop by tomorrow afternoon. We're in a condominium downtown and the place isn't hard to find."

"Sounds good. Why don't you give me the address?"

I made a note of the street number on State, three

blocks up from the office I'd occupied when I worked for California Fidelity Insurance. In those days, I investigated arson and wrongful death claims, which didn't often come my way now that I worked independently.

I said, "What time would suit?"

"Let's say four. My husband will be out and we'll have time alone. I know it's a Saturday and I'm sorry if I'm intruding on your weekend plans."

"Don't worry about it. I'll be there."

"Good. I appreciate your flexibility."

As soon as I hung up the handset, the penny dropped and I remembered where I'd come across the name McCabe. There'd been an article on the front page of the local paper at some point in the past two weeks. Unfortunately, the unwieldy accumulation of newspapers was stacked up under my desk at home.

I checked my watch, noting that it was 4:15. The call was excuse enough to close up early and head out. With the job I'd just finished and a new job lined up, I felt I was entitled to the rest of the day off. The drive to my studio apartment took ten minutes, not surprising given the size of the town, which topped out at eighty-five thousand souls. Santa Teresa is wedged between the Pacific Ocean and the Santa Ynez Mountains, one of the few mountain ranges with an east/west orientation. Between the two geological boundaries, we have palm trees, red-tile roofs, bougainvillea, and Spanish architecture interlaced with Victorian. Half the rich folks live in Montebello at one end of town and the other rich folks live in Horton Ravine. The divide is usually characterized as old money versus new, but the separation isn't that distinct.

Once home, I dug my way down through the papers. This felt like an archeological excavation, uncovering in reverse order events that had passed since the article had run. I pulled out the relevant issue and perched on a kitchen stool while I brought myself up to speed. On page one of the first section, there was an article about Lauren McCabe's son's mandatory release from the California Youth Authority on a charge of first-degree murder pursuant to the felony murder rule, that being a killing committed in the course of a kidnapping. Since he'd reached the age of twenty-five, the state was forced to let him go. I noted the journalist was my pal Diana Alvarez, about whom my feelings were mixed. She and I had tangled in the past and there was no love lost between us. Then again, we were both practical enough to know we might help each other on occasion.

The article gave a summary of the events that had taken place ten years before, when Fritz McCabe had been the shooter in the killing of a teenaged girl named Sloan Stevens. Both were enrolled at Climping Academy, the fancy private college-prep high school in Horton Ravine. In a highly publicized cheating scandal, two students were given a stolen copy of the California Academic Proficiency Test and used the answers in hopes of improving their scores. The Stevens girl knew about it and she was alleged to have sent a note to the school administrators naming the two—Troy Rademaker and Poppy Earl—who were subsequently suspended. As a consequence, Sloan Stevens, the purported informant, had been shunned by her fellow students.

Thereafter, a feud developed between the Stevens girl and another classmate named Austin Brown, whom she believed had instigated the social ostracism. At a party to celebrate the end of the school year, tensions had boiled over and Brown was alleged to have ordered her to be forcibly removed to an isolated area where she was subsequently killed. Brown was also identified as the person who had supplied Fritz McCabe with the weapon used in her shooting death. Of the four boys implicated, one testified at the trial in exchange for immunity from prosecution. Fritz McCabe was found guilty of murder one, kidnapping, and tampering with evidence. He was given the maximum sentence, serving his time at CYA until his twenty-fifth birthday, when his release was required by statute. Troy Rademaker had been found guilty of obstruction of justice, tampering with evidence, aiding and abetting, and lying to the police. Austin Brown, who was alleged to have engineered the killing, had fled and was still at large.

Diana had included a couple of quotes from Fritz, who said, "I've paid my debt to society. I made a mistake, but I've put that behind me now so I can move on." When asked about his plans, he said, "I'm looking forward to time with my family and then I hope to find a job and become a worthwhile member of the community."

I took a wild-ass guess that Lauren McCabe's call was related to her son's release from prison. Much to ponder here and I was already curious what sort of task she had in mind.

I went up the spiral stairs to the loft, changed from my work clothes into sweats, and hit the walkway that parallels the beach. The running path is shared by walkers, bikers, and kids with skateboards. It was also sprinkled with city signs advising us to share and play nice. The sky was a wide expanse of unbroken blue with not a cloud in sight and it felt good to be in the open air. I didn't like having to adjust my exercise routine to account for Ned Lowe, but neither did I like the feeling of vulnerability. I would have preferred to run packing my semiautomatic, but that seemed extreme. Last I heard, Ned Lowe had torched his motor home in the desert and was believed to have taken off on foot. In the wake of his disappearance, his photographic darkroom had yielded numerous pictures of the young girls he'd killed.

I finished the jog with a walk to cool down, and then showered when I got home. I spent the next couple of hours reading a mystery novel by Elmore Leonard, marveling as I always did at his ear for low-life dialogue.

At six, I set my book aside and headed for Rosie's, which is the Hungarian dive half a block from my apartment. I'm there three or four nights a week, which is embarrassing to admit, but true nonetheless. I don't cook, so if eating is on my mind, my options are limited.

Walking in, I saw no sign of Henry's brother, William, who'd been felled by a twenty-four-hour stomach flu that had confined him to his bed for the previous five days. He and Rosie had been married for three years and he was usually front and center, tending bar and chatting up the customers while she commandeered the kitchen and bullied diners into ordering what she referred to as the Special du Jour of the Day.

Rosie was at the bar rolling stainless-steel flatware into paper napkins. I spotted my friend Ruthie at a table by herself and she waved, gesturing for me to join her. I held up a finger, indicating a slight delay during which I caught Rosie's eye. "How's William doing?"

"Still chucking up one end and sicking out the other."

I held up a hand, blocking the mental images. William was ninety and I didn't want to hear the details about his bodily woes.

During the late summer months, we'd all been subject to one illness after another: colds, flu, bronchitis, pharyngitis, laryngitis, sinusitis, pleurisy, and otitis media. William, already inclined toward hypochondria, was elated, seeing in our ailments a pointed reminder of our own mortality, which he believed was imminent. The rest of us were not convinced. When our low-grade fevers and hacking coughs went on too long, we cycled through a nearby Doc-in-a-Box and came away with short-term courses of antibiotics, which made us right with the world. Rosie ignored our penchant for pill popping and refused medical intervention altogether. She believed sherry was the cure for just about anything, including galloping pneumonia. Since she alone of the gang had been unaffected, I was inclined to take her word for it. "You like wine?" she asked.

"Why not?" I said. Rosie's wine had all the germ-killing properties of a popular mouthwash.

I joined Ruthie, whose attention was fixed on my cousin Anna, who was sitting with Cheney Phillips, a homicide detective with the STPD. The two had their heads bent together over a crossword puzzle. Anna looked fetching for someone who puts her outfits together with a careless disregard for fashion trends. She wore baggy cargo pants, an oversize bulky-knit gray sweater with a white T-shirt under it, and what looked like combat boots. Her hair was pulled up on top of her head, where she'd secured the bun with a pair of wooden knitting needles. Cheney sat next to her in a chair he'd pulled around parallel to hers. He had his hand on the back of her seat, his legs stretched out in front of him.

"They seem as comfortable together as an old married couple," Ruthie remarked. "Pity you didn't snag him when you had the chance."

Ruthie was the widow of a private detective named Pete Wolinsky, who'd been shot to death a year prior, leaving behind work notes that had led me to Ned Lowe, he of the girl-choking inclinations. She was referring to the fact that I'd had a fling with Cheney two years before, and while nothing had come of it, I'd since experienced a proprietary sense that my cousin was out of line. I'd never confided the particulars of the affair, but Anna should have known enough to keep her hands to herself. I wasn't exactly miffed, since the pairing wasn't a surprise as those things go. Anna was a guy magnet. Who could resist her when she was so pretty and with such a welcoming air about her? Also knockers twice the size of mine. Some would call her "loose," but let's not get into that. Even with my natural bias in place, I could see her appeal. She was open and unpretentious and it was clear she liked guys. No hidden agenda here, more's the pity in my view. I would have preferred her with a load of unassigned rage so that men who fell under her spell would soon realize she left something to be desired. Apparently, not so in Cheney's case.

"She can have him," I said.

"Yeah, right," Ruthie replied with a rolling of her eyes.

"I'm serious."

"I'm not arguing. I'm expressing skepticism."

I was aware that the place was filling up with off-duty police officers. The STPD had settled into Rosie's like a flock of homing pigeons when the Caliente Café, their former roost, had closed following a kitchen fire. Rosie's had previously been the home to a crew of sports rowdies, who jammed the place for the Super Bowl and countless other sporting events. Their softball trophies were still in evidence, along with a jock strap someone had flung over the stuffed marlin Rosie'd hung above the bar. These migratory rowdies had moved on, as though in response to the changing seasons. Off-duty officers were a breath of fresh air by comparison, as their shoptalk centered on crime. This dovetailed with my interests and meant there was always someone willing to kvetch about robbery, murder, assault, and displays of public drunkenness.

Rosie brought Ruthie a martini straight up and brought me a glass of white wine, freshly poured from a one-gallon jug she kept on a shelf out of sight. This was so her patrons couldn't see the label on the cheap brand she bought. One taste was all it took to identify the wine as swill, but none of us had the nerve to bitch. Rosie was a bit of a bully when it came to her place. She told you what to eat, which was inevitably a strange Hungarian dish replete with offal and sour cream. If some bites contained gristle or fat, you quietly spat the offending matter into your paper napkin and discarded it at home. Trust me, she'd catch you if you tried using one of her fake ficus trees as a dumping ground. Mostly you were well advised to keep your complaints to yourself.

"Are you having dinner?" Ruthie asked when Rosie was gone.

"I'd thought so. Has she said anything about tonight's fare?"

"Creamed chicken livers with a side of sauerkraut."

I could feel my mouth purse. "Maybe I can talk her into a bowl of soup."

Ruthie said, "Uh, no. She's made a pot of what's called—I kid you not—Butchering Celebration Soup, along with a roast pork that's baked with the fat from the pig's abdominal cavity."

"I think I'll wait and have a sandwich when I get home."

"I would if I were you. I ate before I came," Ruthie said.

The menu was sufficient to dampen my appetite, but when Jonah Robb appeared, I felt myself brighten, waving him over to the table. He was another Santa Teresa cop with whom I'd had a romance, which might make me sound a little "loose" myself, but that wasn't the case. Yes, there were two of them, but they were the *only* two. Well, okay, Robert Dietz, but he wasn't a local cop. He was a private investigator from Carson City, Nevada, whom I hadn't seen for months.

My dalliance with Jonah occurred during one of his many separations from his wife, Camilla, whose notion of marriage included bouts of sanctioned infidelity—hers, not his. She was back from her latest fling and Jonah had made his peace with the fact, as was usually the case. My relationship with him had never been serious, since I found myself recoiling from his constant marital uproar. Still, he remained a great source of information and I was shameless about tapping his brain trust when the occasion arose. He went to the bar, ordered a beer, and then ambled in our direction.

When he reached the table, I said, "You remember Ruth Wolinsky?"

"I do. Nice seeing you again."

"You, too," she said.

"Mind if I sit?" He placed his beer on the table, pulling out a chair.

"By all means."

"How're you doing?" he asked.

"I'm good," I replied.

He was dark-haired and blue-eyed, trimmer than I'd seen him now that Camilla was home again. Her renewed presence in his life had apparently spoiled his appetite as well as mine. Their two teenaged girls, Courtney and Ashley, were stunning young ladies who'd gravitated to my cousin Anna just as everyone else did. I suspected we'd see the sisters shortly, but for now I had the man's attention.

I said, "I hope you don't mind if I pick your brain."

"Have at it."

"I have an appointment with Lauren McCabe, whose son was just released from CYA."

Ruthie said, "That kid is free? Seems way too soon."

"I'm sure a lot of people feel that way," Jonah said. "What's she want?"

"She said she'd prefer telling me in person, but I figure it has to be related to her son. It's too coincidental, his being released within the past two weeks. She talked to Lonnie Kingman first, which is how she got my name."

"She hired Lonnie to do what?"

"I'm not sure. I haven't talked to him," I said. "I wondered what you could tell me about the Stevens girl. I know she was accused of ratting out two classmates who cheated on a test."

"True. Someone sent an anonymous note to the school, claiming Troy Rademaker and Poppy Earl had access to the test answers. Both were good friends of Sloan's and she swore she hadn't turned them in."

"Who stole the test?"

"A freshman named Iris Lehmann. She was expelled from Climp when the theft came to light and ended up at Santa Teresa High School. The incident must have been a wake-up call because aside from her testimony at the trial, she distanced herself from her pals at Climp and went on her merry way. Eventually, she graduated from S.T. High with honors, so maybe some good came of the incident."

"Doesn't seem like much, given the girl's death," Ruth remarked.

I was still putting the pieces together, trying to get a fix on the story. "You think Sloan was telling the truth?"

"I'd be willing to bet on it. She was a straight arrow. Kids who knew her said she disapproved of the cheating, but wouldn't have betrayed her friends. Whatever the fact of the matter, a kid named Austin Brown took it into his head that she should be punished for the leak. He talked her classmates into shunning her."

"I read about that," I said.

"Well, this is where the story becomes garbled. There was apparently a sex tape made around the same time. The police got wind of it but never laid hands on it. The kids were all very tight-lipped about the contents and we never did get an honest answer about who was involved. Austin Brown for sure. We think Sloan acquired the only copy and threatened Brown with exposure if he didn't put an end to the shunning."

"Ah. Got it. So what happened to the tape?"

"No one seems to know, but the threat must have been effective. The two arrived at a temporary truce and he invited her to a pool party he organized at his parents' cabin off Highway 154. Bad idea. Dope and a keg of beer, plus the tension generated by the clash, which was technically defused but by no means resolved. They'd dated in the past and she didn't seem to see him as a threat. His idea was to scare her into handing over the tape, which she had no intention of doing. There was also talk that she'd insulted him and he'd taken offense. When she wouldn't back down, he and three other guys drove her up to Yellowweed that night—Austin, Troy Rademaker, Fritz McCabe, and another boy named Bayard Montgomery. The ending, you know."

Originally, Yellowweed was the site of a Boy Scout camp that had relocated twenty years before. The grounds had then been converted to a coeducational camp for low-income families, which closed two years later when funds ran short, leaving the area as an attractive spot for impromptu parties and overnights.

"What about the gun?" I asked.

"An Astra Constable registered to Austin's dad. Apparently, Fritz stumbled across the weapon during the party and ended up taking it to the scene. Who knows what was going on in his head? He was brandishing the gun when Sloan made a break for it and headed into the woods. Fritz had no experience with a semiautomatic. He fired and kept firing until it was quiet in the underbrush. Turns out he hit her three times, the final wound being fatal, which he claimed wasn't his intent. Good luck on that score. He was fifteen, tried as a juvenile, and sent to CYA. He was not your model prisoner. He'd been accused of attempted murder; he'd run dope; and he'd made an escape attempt. I don't know what other kind of trouble he got into, but at age twenty-five they had to let him go. The weapon was never found. It was Troy who drove the pickup truck that was used that night."

Ruthie spoke up. "He works as a mechanic at the repair shop where I take my car. He's good at what he does, but it's hard to look him in the eye if you know about his past."

I said, "And Austin Brown disappeared."

"The day he found out Fritz confessed," Jonah said. "Rumor has it, he's left the country, but I'm not sure how he managed it. He was in such a hurry he left his passport behind. A fake would have been easy enough to come by, but it would have cost him plenty."

"He had money?"

"Pocket change. It's possible his parents have been funneling cash in his direction over the years. Not that we have proof. We ran a mail cover for a while, but it netted us zip."

"What do you think happened to the tape?"

"It must have been in Sloan's possession at the time she died, but there's been no sign of it. We got a search warrant and went over her room with a fine-toothed comb, but turned up nothing. Her mother closed and locked the door to her room at that point and she's kept it locked ever since."

The outside door opened again and Camilla Robb came in. She breezed past our table without so much as a nod in my direction and continued to a booth at the rear, where she sat down with her back to the room. Jonah got up automatically and returned his chair to its place at the table. "At any rate, let me know if I can help."

"Ciao," I said, for lack of anything better.

He took his beer with him as he sauntered in Camilla's direction, trying not to look like a dog being called to heel. He slid into the booth across the table from her. All I could see of Camilla was a portion of her left shoulder, her left arm, and her left hand, on which she wore her wedding band, which she was rotating with her thumb.

Ruthie stared after her. "Who the hell was that?"

"Jonah's wife. I'm surprised you haven't run into her before."

"Did she just snub you royally or were my eyes deceiving me?"

"Cut me dead. She's not a fan."

"What'd you do to her?"

"Slept with her husband during one of their many epic separations."

"You naughty girl. Recently?"

"Seven years ago."

"Oooh. The lady knows how to carry a grudge."

"Her best quality," I said.

Ruthie shook her head, but I could have sworn she looked at me with a new respect.

I was home by seven, grateful for the heads-up about the dinner special. I topped off my evening with a hot hard-boiled egg sandwich with way too much mayonnaise and way too much salt. Of special note was the fact that I was able to return to my Elmore Leonard while I ate, which made it a double treat. Though I was unaware of it at the time, this was a lull before the gathering storm, if you fancy such talk.

3

Saturday, September 16, 1989

The McCabes' address on State was marked by a decorative Spanish tile with a stylized number 1319 embedded in a stucco wall of a building adjacent to the Axminster Theater. A wooden door, painted turquoise, opened onto a stairway lined with the same decorative tiles. Halfway up, the stairway was broken by a landing, which eased the climb to the second story. At street level, the row of buildings boasted the local Christian Science Reading Room, a store selling high-end home furnishings, two restaurants, a florist, and a Pendleton's shop.

When I reached the top of the stairs, I knocked at a second, interior door, which was opened moments later by a housekeeper who was on her way out. In her left hand, she carried her purse and a big brown paper bag. In her right, a lightweight vacuum cleaner. I worried she'd make a misstep and take a tumble.

"You need help?"

"No, I'm good. This is lighter than it looks," she said, indicating the vacuum cleaner. She called back over her shoulder, "You have a visitor, Mrs. McCabe."

"Thanks, Valerie. I'll be right there."

"See you Tuesday."

The housekeeper continued down the stairs. Lauren appeared in the doorway wearing embroidered flats, trim slacks in navy blue wool, and a teal silk blouse with long sleeves. She was probably in her early fifties, but she carried the years well, possibly with cosmetic assistance though I saw no overt evidence of surgical tampering.

I'd never seen a woman decked out in so many diamonds: rings, earrings, a necklace, and a jumble of bracelets. Her hair was straight, a shiny unapologetic gray that she wore in a short bob that framed her face. She was blue-eyed, tanned, and attractive without being beautiful. The air around her was scented with lily of the valley cologne, like a faint whiff of spring.

"You must be Kinsey. I'm Lauren McCabe," she said, holding out her hand.

"Nice meeting you," I said. As we shook hands, I registered the strength of the cool, narrow fingers she offered me.

"Please come in."

She stepped aside so I could pass into the apartment ahead of her. A small foyer opened into the living room, where the ceilings were high and light poured in through a series of French doors that opened onto a second-floor loggia. The interior walls were white, the furniture upholstered in neutral tones. In lieu of color, there were textures—wool, velvet, corduroy, cashmere, and silk. A black baby grand piano was dwarfed by the proportions of the room, which was grounded in polished red tiles covered by a muted, palace-sized Oriental rug. Sheers billowed with a passing breeze that made the place seem chilly. She closed two of the French doors, muting the street sounds outside. I felt a moment, not of envy, but appreciation. Living here, you'd be in walking distance of the whole of downtown: retail shopping, hotels, restaurants, movie theaters, even medical and dental offices.

I said, "This place is amazing. Is yours the only unit up here?"

She smiled. "We have it all to ourselves. We had a house in Horton Ravine, but that was sold eight years ago to cover legal bills." Her tone was casual and the reference came with ease. She didn't spell out the circumstances, probably assuming I would know. "I made some coffee if you're interested."

"I'd like that," I said.

She'd already laid out a coffee service: cups, saucers, cream and sugar, cloth napkins, a plate of biscotti, and a large Thermos of hot coffee. It was clear we'd make our way through the niceties before we got to the subject of my visit. I was curious but in no particular hurry to hear what she had to say. I enjoyed the sense of well-being, trying to imagine a life in which this was the norm. After a pleasant interval, she eased into the subject at hand.

"Hollis won't be home until six, which I thought would give us ample time to chat."

"What sort of work does your husband do?"

"He's a tax attorney who manages investments for clients at the bank. Very successful, I might add, if it doesn't sound like bragging. I've never had to work."

"And where's Fritz?"

"He's bunking in with friends for the weekend."

"I read about his release. Must be nice to have him back."

"It is, though it's generated a problem that's caught us off guard."

"Which is why you contacted Lonnie."

"Exactly," she said. "We had hoped he'd help, but he suggested your services instead."

"So this isn't a legal matter?"

"It is and it isn't. It's complicated."

I was wondering why Lonnie Kingman had steered away from the job. In my experience, attorneys relish diving into thorny legal issues, expounding on the depths of your troubles, which they're quick to assure you are worse than you first thought. "Can you tell me what you're dealing with?"

She leaned over and picked up a package that she'd placed on the nearest end table.

"This arrived a week ago," she said. She held out a manila envelope with a bubble-lined interior meant to protect its contents. Originally, the envelope had been stapled shut with an extra width of clear tape added to secure the opening. The package now gaped open and I could feel the contours of a book or a box of some kind.

"May I?" I asked, not wanting to presume.

"Of course. You might need a brief introduction before you understand what you're looking at."

What I removed from the padded mailer was a VHS tape with a label that read "A Day in the Life of . . . 1979." I felt a rush of adrenaline. I held it up, waiting for an explanation though I knew what it was. This had to be the aforementioned sex footage taken ten years before.

"This came in the same envelope," she said. She handed me a computer-generated note; all caps. "TWENTY-FIVE GRAND IN CASH OR THIS GOES TO THE DISTRICT ATTORNEY. NO COPS AND NO FBI. BE READY WITH THE MONEY IN SMALL BILLS. I'LL LEAVE A PHONE MESSAGE WITH INSTRUCTIONS."

"This is the only communication you've received?"

"So far. Hollis went to RadioShack and bought three recording devices to attach to the phones, anticipating a call."

I was on the verge of admitting what little Jonah had told me about the tape, but why interject? I was curious about her version and didn't see a reason to make it easy on her. "Why is this worth anything?"

For the first time, she colored, her cheeks taking on a faint tint of pink. "You know about Sloan Stevens?"

"The girl who was shot to death."

"Tragically, yes. A week or so before, Fritz and Troy and another friend launched a home movie project, absurdly pleased with themselves. I asked about the contents more than once, but they were secretive, all guffaws and self-congratulations. One afternoon, I came across the tape in Fritz's room and I couldn't help myself. Fritz was off at his tennis lesson and it seemed like the perfect opportunity to take a peek. I pictured a melodrama—werewolves or vampires or a shoot-'em-up of some kind.

"When I played the tape, I was horrified. You'll see it for yourself, of course, but I'm warning you. It's despicable. The boys subject some poor drunken girl to sexual abuse. I can't tell you how revolted I was."

"Did you confront him?"

"I didn't have the chance. I left the tape in his machine where I'd found it. I felt it was imperative to talk to Hollis first so we could decide what to do. I thought Fritz should be held accountable, but in what fashion I didn't know. Sloan arrived at the house, asking to speak to him, but I told her it wasn't a good time because something had come up. She didn't argue the point. I told her I was on my way to the club to pick him up. She said she'd talk to him at school. End of the matter as far as I knew. When I pulled out of the garage, she was on the street with her dog, Butch, and I assumed she was walking home since she was headed in that direction. Now I suspect she waited until I turned the corner before she wheeled around and came back."

"She stole it?"

"Let's put it this way. When Fritz and I got home, the tape was gone. He had a fit, convinced I'd taken it. I played dumb and swore up and down I didn't know what he was talking about."

"Isn't it possible someone else took it?"

"I suppose so, but she was the obvious culprit since she showed up just before I left the house."

"Who else was in that group of friends?"

"Poppy Earl, for one. She and Sloan were best friends until Iris Lehmann came along; she's the young girl in the tape being victimized. The truth of the matter is I don't see how anyone but Sloan had time to get in the house and out in the short time I was gone."

"Wasn't the house locked?"

"Locked, but easily entered. We had an open-door

policy with Fritz's friends and all of them knew where the key was kept."

"That was trusting of you."

"We wanted them to feel at home, that this was a refuge where they were free to hang out."

"Where was the key?"

"On a hook in the garage, which I'd left open when I went out."

"What did you tell Hollis?"

"Well, I described what I'd seen, but without the tape, his only option was to take my word for it. He thought I was exaggerating, when if anything, I was toning it down."

"So what was the upshot?"

"Nothing. The tape was gone and that was the last I heard of it until now. Meantime, Sloan was killed and the boys were arrested. Except for Austin, of course, and no one knows where he is."

"He's the kid who came up with the idea of shunning her?"

"That's correct. He was also behind the events that culminated in the shooting. Sloan was apparently using the tape as leverage, forcing him to back off."

I looked at the note again. "Twenty-five thousand seems like an odd demand. You'd think a blackmailer would ask for more."

"Hollis's theory is he didn't want to hit us up for huge sums of money right off the bat. He thinks the twenty-five grand is a down payment, which is one more reason not to shell it out. Anyway, I should probably let you see it before we go on. The video player's in the library."

I got up and followed as she led the way down the hall. We passed a spacious dining room and I caught a glimpse of the state-of-the-art kitchen through an open door on the far wall. The library was on a smaller scale, intimate when compared to the public rooms. The walls were lined with dark walnut and the floor-to-ceiling shelves were filled with a mix of books and art objects, tastefully arranged. There was the requisite antique desk and on one wall an entertainment center, which housed not only the TV but various pieces of electronic equipment, among them a VCR machine. A comfortable array of chairs was oriented toward the television screen. I could picture Lauren and her husband watching the nightly news with their evening cocktails.

Lauren popped the tape in the VCR and picked up the remote control, pressing Play and then Pause in rapid succession. As soon as she determined the tape was ready, she handed me the remote. "You'll think it's going on forever, but it's only four minutes. I'll be in the kitchen when you're done. At the time, Iris was a freshman at Climping Academy and in trouble constantly. You should also be aware that Poppy and Troy were girlfriend-boyfriend until Poppy found out he and Iris had been intimate. The word 'intimate' really shouldn't apply when they behaved badly in front of witnesses while being taped."

"I understand your point."

She hesitated. "To be honest, when I saw the tape ten years ago, I was perfectly willing to let Fritz suffer the consequences. Then Sloan was killed and he went to prison for his part in her death. Now that he's free, my attitude has changed. I'm still angry about what he did, but I'm ambivalent about punishment. He's paid enough and I don't see what good it would do if he were sent back."

As soon as she disappeared down the hall, I pressed Play. Even assuming the tape had serious implications, I was unprepared for the contents, which were alternately vulgar and violent. The opening was benign: two adolescent boys fresh from a swim, drinking beer and smoking dope. The scene appeared to have been filmed in a basement recreation room with a bar, bar stools, and a pool table that came into play partway through the tape. I assumed the younger of the two was Fritz McCabe. The more mature-looking kid, who had a head of dark red hair in a buzz cut, I assumed was Troy Rademaker.

A very young girl appeared, wrapped in a towel and her hair wet, chugging down a beer. Fritz passed her the joint and then poured her a large glass of gin from a bottle on the bar. There was horseplay, and at one point, the scene jumped forward in time. When the tape picked up, the girl was sprawled on the sofa, inebriated and slurring her words. She appealed to "Austin," who was out of camera range, begging him for a kiss. There was a quick cutaway to the infamous Austin Brown, incongruously outfitted in a sport coat and tie. He was seated in an upholstered chair, legs flung over the arm as he leafed through a magazine, apparently indifferent to the scene being played out in front of him. I hit Pause and studied him. He had a face I'd have associated with nobility if I'd known anyone noble: lean and honed and arrogant. I knew I'd been influenced by Jonah's account of him, but I felt myself recoiling all the same. I could easily imagine his lording it over his pals, his detachment marking him as superior.

The girl said, "Pretty please?"

He appeared to be bored. "No way. I'm the director, not a bit player. I'm the guy in charge."

"The auteur," Troy interjected.

"Right. The mastermind," Austin said with a glance at her. "Besides, you look like you're doing well enough on your own."

Her reply came from off camera. "Party pooper. You're no fun."

The view jumped to Fritz and Troy, now naked and aroused, engaged in an ongoing sexual assault on the same girl, who was by then inert and unresponsive, drunk or stoned or both. I couldn't help but notice that the redheaded boy had pubic hair to match. I don't apologize for the observation as I'm trained in such matters; a paid professional. The boys' antics were painful to watch because I could see that it must have seemed like a game to them. They were having a good time being studs, too self-involved to be aware of the significance of their actions, which were clearly criminal. Both would be held accountable by law if the tape reached the DA's office. The extortionist's threat put the McCabes in an untenable position. If they paid the twenty-five-thousand-dollar demand, they risked being on the hook for life. If they went to the police in hopes of bypassing the blackmailer, then Fritz and his friend Troy would end up charged with rape, sexual assault, and god knows what else. As nearly as I remembered, aggravated rape has no statute of limitations.

I was assuming Iris was unaware of what had been done to her or, at any rate, had never filed a complaint. If she'd taken legal action back then, the criminal or civil suit would have been decided and the threat neutralized. I could picture the boys boasting of their sexual conquest, probably blaming Iris for being promiscuous and therefore deserving of their treatment. In their minds, it must have seemed like a prank, something to boost their manly prowess in the eyes of their pals. I'd heard of similar situations, where still photographs of a sexual assault had been circulated among the perpetrators' friends. What possessed anyone to record such vile behavior was beyond me.

I became aware of Lauren, who'd entered the room behind me, watching the last fifteen seconds of the tape. I showed no emotional reaction. As horrific as the tape was, it would be unprofessional to express repulsion or disapproval. Medical personnel follow the same code of conduct, not responding with shrieks of horror and disgust when symptoms of your sexually transmitted disease first surface during your pelvic examination.

I said, "I take it the older boy is Troy Rademaker."

"Yes. He ended up driving the vehicle the night Sloan was killed."

"You have any idea whether he's received a similar demand?"

"I don't think he has money, so there wouldn't be much point."

"What about the camera operator?"

"I believe it was Bayard Montgomery, another friend of Fritz's. Hollis was working for Bayard's father at the time. Tigg Montgomery died a year later."

"When all of this was still going on?"

"During the boys' trial, but before sentencing. He was spared much of it since he was so sick."

"Cancer?"

"Some rare form. I don't know the particulars," she said. "In point of fact, Bayard was never charged. Tigg made a deal with the DA's office—immunity in exchange for his son's testimony, which was damaging."

I folded that information into the mix while she went on. "Hollis and I watched the tape after it showed up in the mail and it was clear the extortionist was counting on our feeling sufficiently protective of Fritz to pay up. Frankly, I have no idea what to do except to see if we can track down the person who sent it to us."

"Any idea who that is?" I asked. "I know the question seems obvious, but I wondered if a possibility crossed your mind when this first came up."

"It had to be someone close to Sloan. She was killed a week or so after the theft, so if she took the tape—and I have little doubt she did—then it was probably in her keeping when she died."

"Do you think her parents could have discovered it while going through her effects?"

"It's possible. What I can't understand is why someone waited this long."

"Maybe the extortionist was going for maximum effect. If the tape surfaced after Fritz was already incarcerated, it would have taken the oomph out of the discovery. Better to wait until he's a free man and then hit him with the threat."

"That hadn't occurred to me, but you're absolutely right."

"You said the girl was Iris Lehmann. Isn't she the one who stole the test?"

Lauren nodded. "She set the cheating scandal in motion, though I'm not sure she's ever acknowledged the part she played. As far as I know, she's never expressed remorse or regret."

"What about Fritz? Does he have any thoughts about who might be behind this?"

"He doesn't know about the tape or the demand for money. Hollis and I felt we should have a plan in place before we brought him into it. There's nothing he can do until we know where we stand."

"What was Sloan's threat? That she'd go to the police?"

"That's my belief. Fritz may be able to shed more light on the subject when he knows what's going on."

"So what now?" I asked.

"Obviously, we can't go to the police without exposing Fritz to charges of rape and sexual assault. Our only hope is to find out who's behind this and put a stop to it."

"I take it you don't intend to pay the money."

"Paying did cross our minds when we realized the bind we were in."

"Bad idea."

"That was Lonnie's advice as well. If it comes right down to it, paying would be preferable to the alternative. Twenty-five thousand is cheap compared to the legal bills we'd pile up if Fritz went to court again."

"Not to be bleak about it, but you're screwed either way. This tape probably isn't the original. The extortionist would be foolish to hand over the sole copy with nothing in return. Which means if this is a copy, I don't see what you'd net if you paid. Copies would still be out there, and as long as that's true, you're in the same jeopardy."

She closed her eyes, as though unable to bear the thought. "The question is, can you help?"

"I'll do my best, but I wouldn't hold out much hope."

"We're in survival mode. We gave up hope a long time ago," she said. "I'm assuming you'll want an advance."

"I'd appreciate that. When I get back to the office, I'll set up a contract and put it in the mail to you."

"How much?"

"Twenty-five hundred for now. For the duration of the job, I'll give you written reports and keep you posted by phone. If I reach a dead end, we'll meet and talk about where to go from there."

I retrieved a business card from my shoulder bag and took a moment to jot down my home number on the back.

Lauren glanced at the card and then placed it on the desk. She opened a drawer and took out an oversize check ledger. She wrote me a check for twenty-five hundred dollars, tore it from the register, and passed it across the desk.

I murmured my thanks, folded the check once, and slid it into my jeans.

She said, "I'll let Hollis know what we've talked about. If he has anything to add, I'll call."

"I'll want to talk to Fritz at some point."

"Of course. Hollis and I will bring him into the loop. I'm not looking forward to the conversation, but I know it has to be done. I have no idea how he'll react."

"Meanwhile, if the blackmailer gets in touch again, let me know."

"Absolutely," she said.

4

As soon as I returned to my car, I sat and made notes on a series of index cards. I'd picked up an assortment of names: Iris Lehmann, Troy Rademaker, Bayard Montgomery, and Poppy Earl. Austin Brown should have appeared at the top of the list, but he'd done a runner and no one seemed to know where he was.

Lauren had entrusted the tape and the packaging to my care and I took a moment to examine the manila envelope. I couldn't see how my having it would help. It was a common bubble-cushioned mailer with no distinguishing characteristics. Not even a brand name that I could spot. Identical items were sold daily at office supply stores, drugstores, and stationery stores across the country. I had no access to sales records even if I wanted them, so tracking down the person who purchased it was out of the question. I was in the same fix when it came to fingerprints, assuming there were some. I had a kit and I could dust, but I couldn't gain entry to a database for purposes of comparison. The same was true with regard to the saliva on the stamp. Chances were the culprit had used common tap water and a sponge. DNA? Forget it. This was the downside of work like mine. I don't have the resources to pursue the fine points. There have been occasions when I've prevailed upon Cheney Phillips or Jonah Robb to run a license plate number, but they aren't supposed to use their computers for outside inquiries and I didn't want to get either one in hot water on my account.

I wondered dimly why I'd agreed to try tracking down the extortionist in the first place. If I managed to pinpoint the individual, what good would it do? If I confronted the perpetrator, he or she wasn't going to admit it. The McCabes couldn't threaten to turn the matter over to the DA because that's what the extortionist was threatening to do to them. This was the equivalent of two cowboys facing off with guns drawn. Neither party could afford to make a move.

As for the tape, I couldn't see how you could ask your local photo shop to make a copy. You'd have the cops on your doorstep within the hour. Then again, the extortionist wouldn't have sent the original, so this had to be a duplicate. I studied the cassette, which was the standard type you could buy countless places.

I took a quick look at my watch. It was 4:45 and I might still be able to hit one of the local camera shops before it closed. I started the car and headed into town. As nearly as I could remember, there was a superstore on Milagro, which was closer to my neck of the woods.

I slid into a parking space and scurried to the door. The hours listed on the sign in the window indicated the place was open until six, which at least alleviated the time constraint. I went in and waited for the nearest clerk to finish his business with another customer, after which he turned his attention to me.

"What can I do for you?"

He was in his midtwenties, tall and thin, with his hair in a ponytail, a scanty goatee, and his left earlobe punctured with a nut and bolt. His complexion was spotty and his bow tie and red suspenders seemed incongruous. What homely truth was he hoping to convey about himself?

I held up the tape. "I'm wondering if you can tell me how to duplicate a video cassette."

"That one?"

"Not this. I'm asking in general."

"When do you need it?"

"The time frame isn't relevant. The question is hypothetical."

"Explain."

"The contents are personal and I wouldn't feel comfortable turning the tape over to a photo shop for reproduction."

"Why not?"

"Uh, let's say, for instance, I recorded nude footage of myself."

"To what end?"

"Maybe I'm an exhibitionist, hoping to titillate my boyfriend."

"You'd be better off showing him the real thing. That's what I'd go for in his shoes," he said.

"The problem is theoretical."

"So you say."

"Actually, the tape shows actions of a questionable sort. The contents drift toward the criminal."

"Why would a nice girl like you get into something like that?"

I ignored the question, which I thought was impertinent. "If a camera store couldn't or wouldn't reproduce the tape, how could I get it done?"

He leaned on the counter, resting his chin on his fist. "I guess you could project the contents on a screen and make a tape of the tape."

I thought about it. "Nice. I like that. You're saying I could make as many tapes as I had blank cassettes."

"True."

He held up an index finger. "Or. Somebody like me might be willing to do the job for you if the payoff was sweet enough."

"Don't think so," I said. "You might feel obliged to contact law enforcement."

"Is this a snuff film? Because I'm willing to contact law enforcement right now, if that's the case."

"No, it's not a snuff tape! What kind of person do you think I am?"

"Someone in possession of a smutty homemade video 'drifting toward the criminal,' to quote you."

I had to exercise patience, the Zen of not gnawing his ear off for being such an ass. "Let's try this. Suppose I want to rent a video camera, can I get one here?"

"Nope. Don't think so. Ordinarily, yes, but given what you've said, I'd be fired."

I returned the tape to my bag, saying, "Thanks, anyway."

"Here to serve," he said.

So much for that idea. At least I had a notion now of how the extortionist managed to duplicate the tape, which I intended to return to Lauren as soon as possible. The damn thing felt like a time bomb. Tick tick tick. I wondered how many copies might be out there and whether anyone else had been slapped with financial demands. I drove home trying to map out an overall strategy, with no particular luck. At that point, I was long on questions and short on replies.

I found an amazing parking spot one door down from my studio apartment, which cheered me no end. I let myself in through the squeaking gate, feeling a rare optimism. I stopped in my tracks. The sidewalk just inside the gate was piled high with junk: a backpack, a sleeping bag, a waterproof ground pad, a duffel, a pup tent, and a portable wheelchair, plus two brown bags stuffed with clothing that smelled sooty even from where I stood. Mystified, I rounded the corner of the building and saw Pearl White on my doorstep, pounding on my door. She was leaning on a pair of crutches that looked like they might buckle under her prodigious weight.

"Pearl?"

"Hey, Kinsey. Long time no see."

"What are you doing here?"

"Looking for Henry. I've been banging and banging and he's not answering."

I'd met Pearl many months before when I was investigating the death of a homeless fellow found on the beach. She was still big; probably size 22 blue jeans and an XXXL sweatshirt that said UCST, like she was a recent college graduate. Not that I have anything against big, but a shower would have helped. The pile of stuff on the sidewalk was doubtless hers, but what was she doing here? She was probably in her forties, though life had treated her so badly, she might be younger. Her wide face was pink, with cheeks tinted with broken capillaries. Her hair was chopped short. Her lower teeth were dark and every other one seemed to be missing.

I asked her the obvious. "What do you want with Henry?"

"Isn't this where he lives?"

I pointed to his back door. "That's his place. This is mine."

"Oh yeah. I remember now. You rent this studio from him. Nice. I don't suppose you're in the market for a roomie? Because I'm looking for a place to stay."

I indicated the crutches, saying, "What happened?"

"I got hit by a car. In the crosswalk and everything. Maybe crossing against the light, but that's not a felony in this state. Broke my hip. I'm gonna sue the bastard if I can find an attorney who'll take my case pro boner. You know someone good?"

"I don't," I said. "You were in rehab?"

"I was, but I'm done with that now. Problem is the doctors wouldn't let me out unless I had a place to go. I remembered Henry because he was so nice when Terrence and Felix died. I had the woman at rehab call and she had a good long chat with him. He said I was welcome here for as long as I wanted."

"Seriously. Henry said that?"

"You don't believe me, ask him," she said.

"What about Harbor House? Why not stay there?"

"A homeless shelter's not equipped. The director said no right off the bat, which was damn rude of him. I'm practically a full-time resident and you'd think he'd have took me in. I threatened to punch his lights out, but he wouldn't relent."

Just then Henry came around the corner in his usual shorts, T-shirt, and flip-flops. He was toting Pearl's backpack in one hand and the two brown paper bags in the other. He seemed to take her presence for granted, which I considered an indication that what she'd told me was correct. He said, "Oh! You're here. I wasn't expecting you until after supper."

"I figured the earlier the better. Give me time to get settled," she said. "I'm hypoglycemic, so I can't go too long between meals or I'll get all shaky and sweaty."

Henry said, "Don't worry about it. I have supper all set up. Kinsey, why don't you grab that wheelchair out front while I let her in?"

I was certain my face reflected my dismay, but Henry seemed oblivious and Pearl certainly wasn't concerned. "Sure thing," I murmured in lieu of breaking my teeth out with a rock.

I returned to the front gate, where I opened the collapsible wheelchair and piled the remaining items in the seat before I rolled it around to the back. Henry's kitchen door was standing open and I could see lights on in the guest room. Pearl of all people. Had the man lost his mind? Maybe he'd been drinking when the call came through. He was a softie by nature, but to have Pearl White in residence beggared belief. Why his act of compassion so annoyed me, I couldn't say. I hate to admit how little sympathy I have for moochers and human parasites. My Aunt Gin had raised me with a strongly worded caution about asking anything of others. Self-sufficiency was her goal. She frowned on the idea of dependency and social indebtedness. Given that she'd raised me from the age of five until her death when I was twenty-three, I was constitutionally unable to argue the point.

I took the liberty of opening the screen door, unloading Pearl's possessions, and placing them just inside. Everything she owned smelled like cigarette smoke. I could hear the murmur of Henry's voice at the far end of the house and I paused for a moment, wondering if I should wait and have a quick chat with him. Nah, probably not. One of us would walk away mad. I went back to my studio and let myself in. It was clear I wasn't going to have supper with Henry at his place or anywhere else. I didn't have the heart to go back to Rosie's, given her enthusiasm for Hungarian dishes made with animal innards.

In desperation, I checked the paper for movies and ended up downtown sitting through *Parenthood*. My dinner was buttered popcorn and Diet Pepsi, which contained none of the major food groups unless corn is considered one. When *Parenthood* ended, it was only eight fifteen, so I treated myself to a double feature, buying a ticket for *Turner & Hooch*.

I got home well after ten. Henry's place was dark, so I assumed he'd gone to bed. One jarring note was the sight of Pearl's pup tent anchored in the middle of the backyard. Maybe clean sheets were too much for her to bear. In my dealings with the homeless, I learned that many prefer the night sky to a nine-foot ceiling, especially those who've been in jail. Ed, the cat, seemed puzzled by the pup tent as well. He sat just outside it, his head tilted as he stared at the zippered flap. I knew what was going on in his tiny mind. Why would anyone elect to sleep in the middle of his litter box?

I managed to avoid both Henry and Pearl for the remainder of the weekend. Really, it was Henry's business if he invited someone to move in. I counseled myself to keep my mouth shut, no small accomplishment for me.

When I left for work Monday morning, the tent was still there and the surrounding dirt smelled like wee wee. I guess Pearl couldn't be bothered to use indoor plumbing in the middle of the night. If Henry ever intended to resurrect his yard, he'd have to have the topsoil replaced before he did anything else. I wondered if human excrement was considered compost. If so, she could probably provide a sufficient quantity to fertilize his roses.

Once in the office, I put in a call to Lonnie Kingman, who was mercifully available. "Hey, Lonnie. Kinsey. I have a question for you."

"And I bet I know what it is. You heard from Lauren McCabe."

"Exactly. I appreciate the referral, but I'm wondering why you declined her business."

"I didn't like the position it put me in. If I agreed to represent the McCabes in the matter of the extortion, I'd have to explain the tape and its contents to the district attorney, which would subject Fritz to possible prosecution. In effect, I'd be saying, 'My clients are being extorted over this tape showing their son involved in a rape.' And then what? I'd end up trying to defend Fritz on that very rape charge? It just wouldn't smell right. Because to do that properly, I'd have to convince the McCabes not to contact the police, which would be inappropriate."

"Got it. I probably should have turned the job down myself, but I feel badly for everyone concerned. Fritz no sooner gets out of prison than he could be facing another criminal charge. The McCabes already paid a fortune for his defense. Who wants to face another round of legal hassles?"

"Amen," he said, as though the two of us had prayed.

After we hung up, I considered the situation. It was, I could see in retrospect, the moment when I could have backed out gracefully, explaining that I'd had second thoughts about how effective I might be. Lauren might have been disappointed or annoyed, but all I had to do was return the retainer and that would have been the end of it.

But I was already hooked. The little terrier in my nature was busy chasing after the problem, throwing dirt up behind me as I dug my little hole. There was a rat down there somewhere and I would have it for my very own.

I typed up the contract detailing the work Lauren McCabe had asked me to do. I wrote her a receipt for the advance, which I'd include with the copy of the agreement. As I filled out the paperwork, it crossed my mind yet again that my mandate was weak. *Find the extortionist and put a stop to the threat.* Oh boy. Best not to think too deeply about what lay ahead.

In addition to her check, I pulled out a couple of other checks I needed to take to the bank and completed a deposit slip. I armed the system, locked up, and hopped in my car. I was gone fifteen minutes and when I pulled into the drive, I was greeted by the sight of a black-and-white patrol car and a uniformed officer, who was coming around the side of the building. He was young, early thirties, slim, and clean-shaven, with an air of competence I appreciated on sight. His name tag said T. SUGARBAKER.

"Is something wrong?" I asked.

"This is your place?"

"My office."

"May I have your name?"

I gave him my name and showed him my driver's license and a business card, watching while he made a note of the information. He kept my business card and handed back my license, which I returned to my shoulder bag. "What's going on?"

"Your alarm went off and the company dispatcher called the number on record. When there was no answer, she contacted STPD. I was sent to check the premises. Kitchen window in the back is broken. It looks like someone took a rock to it."

"Wow. I paid extra for a couple of glass-break sensors, but I thought I was being paranoid. Did the guy actually get in?"

"It doesn't look like it. He was probably scared off by the alarm, but you might want to check."

"Well, you were quick off the mark and I appreciate that."

I unlocked the office and he followed me in. The two of us did a walk-through, he with an eye out for vandalism and me with an eye to theft. I assured him nothing seemed to be missing or out of place.

"I'll turn in an incident report. If you want to file a

formal report, you can stop by the station in the next few days. I can't see asking your insurance company to pay for damages so minor, but it never hurts to have something on record. Sometimes you get a repeat attempt if they think you keep drugs or valuables on hand."

"I don't have either, but I'll be on the alert."

After he left, I sat down at my desk and tried to talk my way through the surge of fear I experienced once I was alone. I thought about Ned Lowe. There are times when I question my reactions, but this wasn't one. There was nothing silly about my suspicions and I didn't chide myself for jumping to conclusions. I had no proof it was Ned unless he'd left fingerprints, which he would have been careful to avoid. I couldn't imagine his purpose, but his thinking was warped in any event and what he considered a legitimate motive would have subjected any other man to a seventy-two-hour psychiatric hold. A 5150, if you want to get technical.

To offset my anxiety, I put a call through to Diana Alvarez on the theory that being annoyed with her would supersede my apprehension. On the desk in front of me, I had the newspaper article she'd written about Fritz McCabe. She answered on the third ring and I identified myself.

"Well, Kinsey. This is an unexpected surprise."

"Like there's any other kind," I said.

"Uh, good point. To what do I owe the pleasure?"

"I'm looking at your article about Fritz McCabe, wondering if you uncovered information you didn't include."

"I expressed my personal opinion, but my editor cut that part."

"What's your personal opinion?"

"I thought Fritz was fortunate he was tried as a juvenile. If he'd been tried as an adult, he might have been eligible for the death penalty or life in prison without the possibility of parole. Instead he served eight years and now he's free."

"Anything else?"

"There's the matter of Austin Brown. I felt he deserved a mention. He's on the FBI's Ten Most Wanted list. You know there's a bounty on his head? Fifty thousand bucks."

"Well, that's generous. The reward's been sitting there all these years?"

"Untouched. Either nobody knows where he is or they're not willing to step up to the plate. I was hoping the story about Fritz McCabe would generate interest in Austin's whereabouts."

"Maybe you could write a separate article."

"Afraid not. My editor says it's old news."

"But Austin Brown is a bad dude. You'd think it would be important to bring him in."

"Not to my editor. If you ask me, this whole story is epic and deserves to be told beginning, middle, and end."

"So far the end is missing."

"Right, but aside from that, it's got all the elements: youth, sex, money, betrayal."

"Death," I added.

"Right. I know it sounds cynical, but Austin Brown is the last dangling thread."

"You have a theory about where he went?" I asked.

"Why? Are you going after him?"

"For fifty grand, I might," I said, though the idea had never occurred to me.

"He's been sighted half a dozen places, but none of those leads were legitimate. People are so eager to help, they hallucinate. Why are you so interested?"

"Strictly curious."

"Fifty thousand dollars' worth at any rate," she remarked.

"Can I tell you my problem?"

"Why not? You've already interrupted my work."

"Sorry about that, but here's the deal. I want to talk to the players in the case, but I have no cover story and no bargaining power. I can hardly pass myself off as a reporter."

"Sure you can," she said. "People are more interested in talking than you'd think. I see it all the time when I'm trolling for interviews. Here's the trick. Imply you have the information and you're looking for confirmation.

Better yet, tell 'em you'd like to hear their version of events before you go to press. Say your editor wants an update and he suggested you talk to them."

"I wouldn't need press credentials?"

"Only if you're crashing a rock concert. People assume you're who you say you are."

"What about Sloan's mother? Do you think she'd agree to meet with me?"

"God, you sound so tentative. I thought you had balls. Trust me, she'll talk. All she does is talk about Sloan's death. People who know her say she's obsessed. For years now, she's left Sloan's room as it was. Closed the door and locked it."

"Someone else mentioned that," I said. "Sounds like she's still sensitive about the loss."

"I'm not sure grief like that ever goes away. In the meantime, she loves going back over the 'facts of the case,' hoping she can make it come out differently. Look her up in the phone book under the last name Seay."

"Spell that."

"S-E-A-Y. Like the word 'sea' with a Y on the end. She's in Horton Ravine."

"Thanks. I'll do that," I said. I glanced at the list of names I'd jotted down after my meeting with Lauren McCabe. "You don't happen to have an address and phone number for Iris Lehmann?"

"The girl who got kicked out of Climp? Why talk to her?"

"I'd like to know what's happened to her since."

"Not much, I'll bet. I have the home number I picked up years ago. Might not be good now, but you're welcome to try. Last I heard, she was working in that vintage clothing shop on State. That might be the best way to contact her, but I can give you the home number if you like."

"That would be great."

"Hang on a sec."

It took her a few minutes to retrieve her address book and flip through the pages. She gave me Iris's home phone number with one condition attached. "You have to swear you'll let me know if anything new develops. That might give me an arguing point for additional coverage of the old case."

"I can do that," I said. "In the meantime, I'd appreciate it if you'd do the same for me."

"Happy to. Of course, then you'd owe me."

"I can handle that."

"Best of luck. I can't wait to see what it feels like to have you in my debt," she said.

After she hung up, I sat and stared at Iris Lehmann's contact information. Hers was the first name on the list of people I wanted to talk to, but I was oddly reluctant to get in touch with her. What if the blackmail demand came from her? I couldn't think why she'd try extorting money on the basis of a sex tape in which she starred front and center. I didn't think her role was a criminal matter, but it certainly would be an embarrassment if it came to light.

5

THE SHUNNING

May 1979

Sloan sat on a bench in the girls' locker room and removed her shin guards and cleats. She pulled her damp jersey over her head and blotted sweat from her neck. She slid out of her shorts, removed her sports bra, and left both in a sodden pile on the floor. She headed for the shower, which was deserted by now. It was Friday afternoon, late May, and no one had spoken to her for weeks. She was the designated social outcast, the assumption being that she had written an anonymous note to the Climping Academy vice principal, naming Troy Rademaker and Poppy Earl as two students who'd been given answers to the California Academic Proficiency Test and had cheated their way to better grades. Word of this betrayal had spread through the school within a day. Sloan had been outspoken in her exhortations to Poppy to abandon the plan to cheat, so when the typewritten note arrived, Austin Brown had persuaded the entire junior class that Sloan was guilty of violating their trust. That Sloan was innocent was beside the point. She was judged to be guilty as charged and her heated denials sounded hollow even to her own ears. Sloan was a jock: tall and sturdy and well-coordinated. She was also smart, studious, and strong-willed. Even so, the isolation was wearing her down.

As she crossed the tile floor, she pulled the rubber band from the tip of the braid that extended halfway down her back. She shook out a cascade of waves, which fell across her shoulders like a cape. If she washed her hair, it would take hours to dry, but that was better than a sweaty scalp. As usual, the shower smelled of bleach, a scent she associated with winning as well as defeat. The hot water was healing and she didn't regret having the space to herself. The effect of the shunning was already deadening and while she feigned indifference, she was acutely aware of the disapproval washing over her. No one addressed a word to her. No one acknowledged her presence. No one made eye contact. If she spoke to a classmate, she received no response. Even a few students in the freshman and sophomore classes had taken up the ban. In the main, the seniors abstained from participation, but she sensed that they viewed her with scorn, thinking she'd brought it on herself.

The cheating scandal was set in motion when Iris Lehmann had pulled the fire alarm bell and then waited until the halls and classrooms had cleared before she scurried into the school office and photocopied the test and answer sheet, which had been distributed to the faculty cubbyholes. The test had been administered on Friday, April 13, and shortly after the grades were posted, some three weeks later, the anonymous note had showed up on the vice principal's desk. Originally, Troy's score wasn't suspect because his grades were usually good. Poppy did better than past performances warranted, so suspicion had already been aroused where she was concerned. In a misguided attempt to disguise their duplicity, Troy and Poppy had answered the same two questions incorrectly. Both were summoned to the vice principal's office, where Mr. Lucas grilled them. Poppy might have talked her way out of it, but Troy had cracked under questioning and he'd implicated her.

Sloan had heard about their intentions in advance and she'd made her disapproval clear. She might not have gotten wind of it if it hadn't been for the cluster of students all a-buzz with the news. Fully half the class knew what was going on and yet she was blamed for the leak. As much as she disliked the idea of cheating, she would never have turned them in. She and Poppy had been best friends since their first day at Climping Academy as kindergarteners. Sloan had always been the better pupil of the two, sailing through classes without effort, while Poppy pulled mediocre grades at best. Sloan couldn't even count the number of times she'd tutored Poppy, working through English and math, quizzing her in history and social studies. The process didn't seem to get easier for Poppy, and Sloan sometimes felt guilty because it all came so easily to her.

Once showered, she dressed, pulled her damp hair into a ponytail, and headed for the parking lot. When she reached her stepfather's snappy red MG, she saw that the word SNITCH had been scratched into the paint on the driver's side. She stared at the damage, realizing she'd be forced to tell Paul what was going on. She'd hoped to endure the ostracism in silence, but the vehicle was his pride and joy and any repairs would have to be billed to his insurance. No point in confiding in her mother, who was generally zonked on booze and the various prescription drugs she took for assorted ills, imaginary and otherwise. Her mother responded to stress by taking to her bed. If she heard about Sloan's excommunication, her impulse would be to phone the school and lodge a long, rambling complaint, which would only make the situation worse.

Sloan and her mother had been close once upon a time, but that had changed abruptly. Sloan had been conceived out of wedlock, a quaint concept that Margaret had confided to her when she was five. Margaret told Sloan she met her birth father in Squaw Valley the winter after she graduated from a small Methodist college in Santa Teresa. She'd been looking for a change of scene and managed to pick up work as a waitress at a first-class resort. Cory Stevens was a ski bum in residence, lean, good-looking, easy-going, adventuresome, and kind. Margaret had assumed he came from money since he lived with no discernible source of income. They'd had a passionate affair, and at Christmas when Margaret learned she was pregnant, she was distraught, thinking Cory was unlikely to settle down. To her surprise, he seemed to take it all in stride. Though he wasn't prepared to marry her, he'd sworn he'd stick with her until the baby was born and provide handsomely for the child. Two weeks later, he'd been killed in an avalanche. Margaret was left with a single photograph of him and promises he couldn't fulfill. She'd moved to Long Beach, had borne her baby girl, and made the best of it.

As a single mother, she'd worked as a secretary for a series of construction companies, making a marginal income. She'd met Paul Seay at a trade show in Las Vegas in 1966. He was a custom builder, owner of Merriweather Homes in Santa Teresa. He was a blue-collar success: stable, down-to-earth, and devoted to her and her little girl. Margaret and Paul had married when Sloan was four and Margaret found herself back in Santa Teresa, where she'd gone to school. Paul had been married before and had two sons, now ages thirteen and fifteen. Justin and Joey lived with their mother during the school year and spent the Christmas holidays and summers in Santa Teresa.

As a child, Sloan had pined for the father she never knew. In the photograph of him, which had been taken at the ski resort, he was dark-eyed and tanned, with a flash of white teeth and ski goggles pushed up in his dark hair. While Sloan was growing up, his image had been the source of fantasies—hopes that he hadn't really perished in the accident. Her mother told her his body had never been recovered and this fact had contributed to her belief that he might still be alive and well. Maybe he'd taken advantage of the avalanche to escape the responsibility of impending parenthood. Sloan wasn't offended to think he'd abandoned her before birth. Instead, she immersed herself in ski lore, thinking that one day she'd go in search of him.

When she was ten and poring over a stack of old ski magazines, she chanced on an article about Karl Schranz, the Austrian skier who'd competed in the 1962 World Ski Championship. He'd won the gold medal in the Downhill, the silver in the Giant Slalom, and a second gold in the Combined. In the photograph that accompanied the text, the face was Cory Stevens's. In point of fact, the photograph was a duplicate of the one she kept on her bed table. Sloan was dumbfounded. Was her father actually this medal-winning Austrian skier?

She had gone straight to her mother. "Is Karl Schranz my real father?"

Margaret's expression was genuinely blank. "I don't know anyone named Karl Schranz, Sloan. Where did you come up with that idea?"

Sloan showed her the two photographs side by side. "This is Karl Schranz and this is my dad. The two are the same and you lied to me! He's not dead. He's been alive all this time."

Margaret had denied this at first, but Sloan had pushed and her mother finally broke down and admitted what she'd done. The story about Cory Stevens and the winter in Squaw Valley was completely fabricated. She'd clipped the photograph of Karl Schranz and framed it so Sloan would have an image to turn to whenever she needed the comfort of a father figure. Sloan's real father, said Margaret, was someone she'd known in the past, but with whom she'd had little contact since. Sloan wasn't sure what to believe. Confused and upset, she'd told Poppy the story in confidence, making her swear she'd keep the secret. Poppy had crossed her heart and hoped to die and two days later the story was all over the school. Poppy had denied telling a soul and Sloan had had no choice but to shrug the matter aside and live with the humiliation.

In point of fact, Margaret's account changed each

time Sloan pressed for information until she understood her mother had no intention of telling her the truth. The only fragment of the original tale that she insisted on throughout was that Sloan's bio-dad was supportive of the pregnancy and promised generous financial support for the child. Beyond that, she refused to budge. Maybe money was meant as the consolation prize, but since it failed to materialize, there wasn't much comfort there. Sloan's fury and disappointment soured the relationship and the bond had never been repaired. Mother and daughter had agreed to an uneasy truce, but Sloan had never really forgiven her. She viewed her mother with disdain, rebuffing even the most well-meaning expressions of love and concern. Paul Seay had stepped into the breech and Sloan had transferred her devotion to him. In another couple of weeks, Paul and Margaret would be driving to Tucson to pick up the boys and bring them back for the summer.

When Sloan got home from school, her dog met her at the door, barking with joy as though he'd never expected to see her again. Butch was a Pyrenees Mountain dog, a hundred and forty pounds of loyalty, patience, and affection. He was two years old—white with a plumed tail and an overcoat of coarse hair that formed a ruffle at his neck. She gave his woolly head a kiss and rubbed his ears. As she hung her jacket on the hall tree, she glanced into the living room, where her mother was stretched out on the couch, a burning cigarette between her fingers. Sloan hated her mother's smoking almost as much as she hated the faulty gait and slurred speech at the end of the day. This was late afternoon and Margaret was asleep, stoned to the gills. Sloan removed the cigarette stub, put it out in the ashtray, and then went upstairs to her room with Butch close behind.

She changed into sweats, retrieved Butch's leash from the mudroom downstairs, and took him out for a walk. This was his favorite time of day and hers as well. Paul had given her the dog for her fourteenth birthday, an oversize bundle of fluff with a big loving heart. At night, he slept in her room at the foot of the bed. By day, he settled in the downstairs hall and waited for her to get home from school. The May sun was lingering a little longer each day and Sloan felt her mood lift as the two followed the road. Half an hour later, when they arrived back at the house, Sloan was startled to see Bayard Montgomery sitting on the front porch in the white wicker rocking chair. He had a big Styrofoam cup in hand, a sixteen-ounce soft drink that he sipped through an oversize straw.

Butch galloped to his side and greeted him with enthusiasm, panting happily while Bayard set his drink aside and gave his big noble head an affectionate shake. "How you doing, boy? Such a fine, great, big old dog!"

Butch was clearly nuts about Bayard, his tail wagging and his mouth open in the equivalent of a doggie smile.

Belatedly, Bayard looked up at her, saying, "Hey. How's by you?"

"I can't believe this. You're actually *speaking* to me?"

Bayard studied her with mischief in his eyes. "I want to work for your dad again. He's letting me run his bulldozer and his excavator, which is really cool. I thought it would be smart to butter you up."

"Are you kidding? I'm a social leper. Austin finds out you've talked to me, he'll consign you to the flames."

"Oh my god!" he shrilled in a falsetto voice. He stuck the fingers of his right hand in his mouth, biting down in mock horror. The gesture was perpetual with him, offered in evidence of his irreverence. His hair was a shaggy mess, tufts sticking up in every direction. Like the finger-biting, his dark unkempt thatch was a signature look along with the devilish glint in his eyes. As was true with Poppy, Sloan had known him since kindergarten.

She could remember him in those early days. Bayard had been withdrawn, a lost little boy who kept his distance from everyone. He was an only child and his parents were in the process of a rancorous divorce. At the age of five, he was torn between the two, victimized by their tug-of-war as they vied for his loyalty. Within a year, his mother had won the point, whisking him off to Santa Fe and a better life, said she. That plan lasted until Bayard reached the age of twelve and began to rebel. Whether it was his conscious intent or not, he so alienated his mother that she deposited him back in her ex-husband's life, surrendering all claim. Tigg Montgomery had re-enrolled Bayard at Climp, where the six-year absence rendered him exotic, a rakish misfit who still kept himself apart from the tight circle of his old friends.

Sloan sat down in the wicker settee, absurdly grateful to be in Bayard's company. The dog settled at her feet. "Let's not talk about Austin or school."

"What do you want to talk about?"

"Anything. I heard your dad was sick."

Bayard made a dismissive gesture and his tone was mild. "He's not long for this world. I'm sure my mother will be thrilled. She's hated his guts for years. Of course, my old man's a shit, so why wouldn't she?"

"I thought you got along with him."

"I'm crazy about the guy and assumed the feeling was mutual. Shows how fucked up I am."

"At least you know who he is, which leaves you better off than me. I'm a quote unquote bastard, which sounds ridiculous in this day and age."

"What's the story?"

"I have no idea. My mother refuses to tell me anything about my bio-dad."

"How come?"

"It's gotta be misguided loyalty or self-protectiveness. She lied to me the whole time I was growing up and when I finally found proof of it, she shut down entirely. Ask her now and she gets all teary and remote and then pours herself another drink."

"Maybe she doesn't know who he is. Maybe there were a lot of guys who could have been your dear old dad."

"Not her. She's not the promiscuous type. She's careful with herself."

"She might have been different back then. A romantic at heart. The guy might have been her one true love."

"It doesn't matter now. My stepfather turns out to be a great guy. Really he's been incredible, especially in the face of her downhill slide."

"When did she start to drink?"

"Who knows? He says she wasn't drinking much when they met. A cocktail now and then, but she wasn't perpetually shit-faced."

Bayard shrugged. "Parents stink, you know that? My dad's a magician. He gives with one hand and takes away with the other. Poof! Now you see it, now you don't. Next thing you know, you're screwed."

"I don't understand."

He waved the question aside. "Not worth going into. Let's just say now that he's fading away, he wants to go back and make amends for stuff he pulled in the past."

"That's not a bad thing, is it?"

"He can do anything he wants as long as he doesn't take it out of my hide."

"Why would his repentance have anything to do with you?"

"It doesn't, to hear him tell it. He and my mother have batted me around for years. It's like being a hot potato tossed from hand to hand. I'm tired of being shortchanged."

"But you've been happy here, haven't you?"

He shot her a cocky smile. "Who knows from happy? You gotta look after yourself. That's all I know. No one else will do it, that's for sure."

He shook the ice in his cup, trying to determine how much of his drink was left. He took a long pull on the straw, draining half the contents. "You want some? Last chance."

"What is it?"

"Bourbon and Coke."

She made a face. "No, thanks."

"Don't blame you. Tastes disgusting, but it warms my heart, or what's left of it at any rate."

"You shouldn't drink."

"I shouldn't do a lot of things, but here I am." He set his cup at his feet, pulled his knees up, and rested his chin on his crossed arms. "Anyway, you're the one who needs help."

"I'll survive. I'm already feeling better now that Austin isn't sucking the life out of me."

"Sorry turn of events, given you dated the guy. Aside from suffocating you, I bet he tried to get in your pants."

She laughed. "How'd you know?"

Bayard's tone was light. "He and I had a 'thing.' "

Sloan said, "What do you mean, 'a thing'?"

"What do you think I mean? Austin goes either way. He doesn't care for the niceties. He likes the chase. He likes seduction. Then he gets bored."

"That's why I wouldn't sleep with him."

"Smart girl. He took up with you when he was done with me."

"I'm sorry, Bayard. I had no idea. That must have been hurtful."

"Hurting people is what he does. Are you wondering if I'm queer?"

"Don't say that. It doesn't matter to me."

"It mattered to my mother. That's why she washed her hands of me and dumped me on Daddy's doorstep."

"Shit. Does *he* know?"

"Oh god, no. That's all I'd need. My dad's a homophobe. He's rabid on the subject. If Austin lets *that* cat out of the bag, I'll be out on the street. Let's not even talk about Dad's money. He'd make sure I never got a dime. Which Austin well knows."

"He's threatened to tell your dad?"

"Sure. He says, 'One phone call, Bayard. One phone call is all it takes.' Then he holds up his finger like this and he doesn't have to say another word. You know what's pathetic? I'm still hung up on him. Just look at Fritz. He's got a crush on the guy as well."

"But if he outed you, wouldn't he be implicating himself?"

"No one would dare say a word. The guy's bulletproof. Kids are scared to death of him."

"Hey, well, me too if you want to know the truth."

"Sloan, I'm telling you, you're stronger than he is. He

hates you because he can't dominate you. But here's the point. He could be bluffing. For all we know, he's a toothless old blowhard. A dickless wonder, so to speak."

"Don't look at me. I'm not going up against him."

"Have you told your parents what's going on?"

"I don't have a choice. Someone scratched the word 'snitch' in the paint on Paul's car. I'll talk to him, but I don't want to be labeled a tattletale as well as a fink. Same thing goes with school. If I tell Mr. Lucas or Mr. Dorfman, it'll look like I expect them to step in. I might as well cut my own throat."

Bayard dropped his gaze. "I can give you a way out."

"How?"

"Ask Austin about the tape."

"What tape?"

Bayard picked up his cup and rattled the ice. "He and Fritz and Troy had a little wingding with Iris, who was drunk and stoned. They screwed her brains out and put it all on tape. She's lolling on the pool table, dead to the world, while Fritz and Troy horse around, sticking a pool cue up her twat. Your pal Austin was there, of course. He didn't participate, but it was his idea. Ever the voyeur."

"When was this?"

"Last weekend."

"Are you serious?"

"Very."

"How did you hear about it?"

"I didn't *hear* about it. I was there. Who do you think did the camerawork?"

"You didn't intervene?"

"I was behaving like a journalist, recording reality without imposing my will or my point of view. I captured the action for posterity. What's wrong with that?"

"Oh, please. You're worse than they are."

"I'm despicable," he said with an impish grin. "Anyway, she did it to herself. She's a needy little girl who'd do anything for attention. Why do you think she stole the test? To curry favor with Poppy. Besides which she has the hots for Troy."

"She does not. Does she?"

"Of course. She's all over him."

"But he and Poppy are going steady. He gave her his class ring."

"There's a lot Poppy doesn't know about the guy. The thing about Iris is she flirts with any guy."

"Oh, Bayard."

"Oh, Bayard, my ass. Take my word for it. The tape is dynamite."

"What would I do with a sex tape? It sounds gross."

"You can use it to make Austin back off. Hard evidence, as it were," he said. "Tell him you'll turn it over to the police."

Her expression was skeptical. "You said he didn't participate."

"He's the one who set the stage, egging the others on, which makes him every bit as guilty, don't you think?"

"He won't see it that way."

"Maybe not, but how can he take the risk? What if his parents find out? That's the crux of it right there."

She shook her head. "Why fan the flames? I defy him and things will only get worse."

"Not so. You need leverage so you can put the squeeze on him. If you have the tape in hand, you can put an end to this."

"Where is it?"

"McCabe's house. He's pondering additional 'edits.' Like it's a major motion picture and he's up for an award."

"Fritz won't just hand it over to me. Why would he do that?"

"Of course not. You'll have to find a way to lift it without his knowing. Shouldn't be hard to do. The kid is clueless."

"It doesn't feel right. I can't afford more trouble than I'm in."

"Wrong attitude. This is just the opposite. This is your 'get out of jail free' card."

"I don't like it."

"You know your problem? You really don't understand what guys are about. You think you can be all nicey-nice and everything will be fine. Austin plays rough. You gotta hit him where it counts. He's a gamesman."

"I don't want to play games."

"Why not? He goes after you, you gotta knock him on his ass. Otherwise you'll never gain his respect. Right now, he's got you where he wants you."

"He can't keep it up forever."

"Are you kidding? He'll escalate. You think you're miserable now. Wait until he ups the ante. Don't you want to beat him at his own game?"

"All I want is to have this bullshit over with."

"Exactly. Go to Fritz's house and get the tape. If he figures it out, all the better. He can carry the tale to Austin. It'll make Austin sweat, which would be good for him. Reveal any weakness and he'll know he's won."

"I feel weak."

"Then get a grip on yourself. You're taking a one-down position, which is all in your head."

Sloan stared at him for a long time and then lowered her gaze. Bayard had a point. Maybe it was time to stop playing victim and take control of the situation. She got up, snapping her fingers at the dog. "I hope this works. If not, I'll have you to blame."

"You surely will," he said.

She clipped the leash on Butch. The dog rose to his feet and trotted dutifully at her side. Bayard watched as she moved down the drive toward the road. Idly, he removed the lid from the cup and finished his drink.

6

Monday, September 18, 1989

I found parking on the nearest side street, locked my car, and walked around the corner to State Street and down half a block. The vintage clothing store was called Yesterday and boasted a window full of garments from eras long past. Judging from the display, Victorian items were in high demand, along with clothing from the 1960s.

When I entered, an old-fashioned bell trilled merrily. The interior smelled of incense, ancient dust, and an amalgam of faded perfumes. The floors were wooden and creaked as I crossed the room. The shelves were stocked with shoes, handbags, and hats. Two racks were filled with cloth coats, fur coats, and fur capes. There were also hanging displays of dresses, skirts, and tops, separated into decades and lined up in the obvious order, from the smaller sizes to the larger ones. In the glass cases that divided the store into aisles, I could see women's dainties: corsets, camisoles, garter belts, hosiery, step-ins, and brassieres that spoke to the changes in women's bodies over the years. There was a time when female amplitude was associated with prosperity. Then there was a period when being thin meant you were disciplined, drove yourself hard, and were careful about what you ate. Now being thin is proof you have enough money to pay for personal trainers, nutritionists, and tummy tucks within a week of giving birth.

I took out a pen and a notebook, hoping to convey my fake professionalism. Iris Lehmann approached from the back of the store, looking much the same as she had in the tape except upright and fully clothed. She wore a long-sleeved lace top faintly yellow with age and a long gray velvet skirt. Peeking from beneath the hem were black leather lace-up shoes with toes so pointed they looked like they would pinch. Her hair was shorter now, auburn highlighted with streaks of red, held in place with an array of combs and barrettes. Her ears were pierced by a series of small gold rings that lined the cartilage at quarter-inch intervals. Those looked painful as well and I wondered if her fashion sense was, in part, a self-inflicted penance.

"May I help you?"

"I'm hoping so. You're Iris Lehmann?"

She smiled, apparently anticipating something nice. Poor thing. "Yes."

"I'm Kinsey Millhone. I'm writing a follow-up story about Fritz McCabe's release from the California Youth Authority. I'd like to ask you a few questions."

Her expression shifted from optimism to wariness. "I don't have anything to say about Fritz McCabe."

"Oh, sorry. I was told you and Fritz and Troy Rademaker were friends in high school."

She hesitated and I watched her debating with herself. It must have been clear I had a few facts on my side, thus tempering any urge of hers to lie. "I knew them. I wouldn't say we were *friends*. We went to Climp together my freshman year. That's all it amounted to."

"I understand you were expelled for stealing a copy of a test."

She stared at me. "Why would you ask about *that*?"

"I did some digging through the old files. I was hoping you could fill in a gap or two."

She squinted. "What's your name again?"

"Kinsey Millhone."

"And this is for the *Santa Teresa Dispatch*?"

"Uh, no. A Los Angeles publication. We picked up the story from the wire services and my editor asked me to pursue the subject."

"I don't have anything to say."

"Nothing?"

"It's ancient history. Nobody cares about that stuff."

"You'd be surprised. Our readers are still very interested in Sloan Stevens's death. You do know Fritz was released from the CYA the week before last?"

"You just said that and I don't give a shit."

I made a point of scribbling a note and then looked up at her. "Any other thoughts you'd like to share?"

"Look, I'm busy here. What happens to Fritz has nothing to do with me."

"I wouldn't be too sure. Someone's unhappy about his being free and wants to get back at him."

That got her attention. "Meaning what?"

"An anonymous party is threatening to turn a certain videotape over to law enforcement. The footage was shot in 1979. You probably know the tape I'm referring to since you appeared in it."

"So what? That tape disappeared ten years ago."

"Well, now it's resurfaced with a note demanding a hefty sum of money or the sender will forward a copy to the DA, who could file criminal charges against the boys who participated."

"That's ridiculous."

"It's not ridiculous to the person demanding the money. Far from it."

"But that's blackmail, isn't it?"

"Not directed at you, but you'd be sucked into the mess."

"I thought the district attorney couldn't do anything without my cooperation."

"Not so. The tape is evidence of a crime. Pursuing the matter doesn't depend on your approval. The DA can file anyway."

"If Fritz is being blackmailed, how much money are you talking about?"

"That's not relevant since the party in question doesn't intend to pay. What we're hoping for is to identify the culprit before the situation gets out of hand."

"Oh, good plan. There's a winner. How will you manage that?"

"By talking to people like you."

"I don't understand why you're involved. You're a journalist, not a police detective."

"Investigative reporter," I said, correcting her. "This is what we do."

"I can't help. I haven't seen any of those guys since the trial."

"You haven't had contact with any of them?" I asked.

"I just told you. I've seen Roland Berg and Steve Ringer, who were both classmates. Everyone calls Steve Ringer 'Stringer' in case no one's mentioned it. I've talked to Bayard a couple of times and that's the extent of it."

"How recently?"

"This is bullshit. Why should I tell you? I'm allowed to talk to anyone I please."

"What about the trial? Did you testify?"

"I had to. They served me with a subpoena."

"Did you think the sentencing was fair?"

"Sloan died. Someone had to pay."

"What about the tape?"

"I never saw it. When I heard it disappeared, I thought that was the end of it."

"How much do you remember about the incident?"

"It wasn't 'an incident,' just a bunch of us messing around."

"You never reported it to the police?"

"Of course not. We were being stupid. It was nothing serious."

"If the tape's put in circulation, you'll be publicly humiliated whether you were serious or not. You were sexually assaulted."

"I was not! Maybe it looks that way, but that wasn't the deal. According to what I've heard, it was a stupid home movie all of four minutes long."

"There's nothing stupid about rape, Iris. I've seen the tape."

"Well, I haven't. You want to know what I hate about reporters?" she said. "You eat this shit up. You act, like, all sympathetic and concerned, but you love every minute of it. Other people's degradation. Other people's shame. If nothing's happening, you generate the trouble yourself, just to see how we react. Write it down. Put it in the paper. You're only doing your job. Right?"

"That's not how I operate."

"Then what are you doing here?"

"I was hoping to be of help."

"Well, go help someone else. I don't need anything from you."

"The others involved might disagree."

"Then talk to them."

"Who would you suggest?"

"You figure it out. This is getting on my nerves."

"What about Poppy? Is she still in town?"

"I have no idea. We're not friends anymore. She and her boyfriend broke up because of that tape."

I had a quick flash of a buck-naked Troy going after Iris as she was lolling about on the pool table. I could well imagine it putting the kibosh on Poppy and Troy's romance. Not many relationships could survive such a graphic betrayal.

I flipped to an empty page in my notebook and jotted down my home phone, which is attached to an answering machine but makes no mention of Millhone Investigations. I tore out the leaf and offered it to her. "This number is local. I work freelance, so I'm easy to reach."

She held up her hands, refusing to take the note.

"You might change your mind," I said.

She snatched the paper without making eye contact.

"Shit. I'm getting married in a month. This is the last thing I need!"

"Let's hope the problem is resolved so you can get on with life."

I spent part of my lunch hour driving to the hardware store, where I picked up window putty and a pane of glass for my broken office window. There wasn't any trick to removing the remaining shards of glass, scraping out the old putty, and applying fresh putty once the new pane was in place, but it took time and I was annoyed at having to do it.

At quarter to four that afternoon, I changed into workout clothes, packed my gym bag, and in a refreshing change of pace, attended the fourth in a ten-week program of women's self-defense classes. I had Ned Lowe to thank for that. Being choked to near unconsciousness had made me wonderfully aware of how fragile life is and how easily I can be subdued. The program was mixed martial arts and all of the lessons were basic and to the point: street-fighting at the level of kicks and punches. We were encouraged to favor strategy over technique. As I'd realized while pinned facedown under Ned's knee, most of what I'd learned about self-defense was bullshit. In the real world, assault is chaotic and we're seldom afforded the opportunity to land a killing chop to the throat or a damage-dealing knee to an assailant's groin.

The odd but unremarkable truth about women is we've had the aggression bred right out of us. Many of us are constitutionally unable to handle any kind of confrontation without bursting into tears. A public encounter with a thug? We're ill-prepared and ill-equipped. There were eight of us in my group and we were warned that one in six of us would be the victim of violent assault at some point. We couldn't help eyeing one another, not wishing others ill, but each of us fervently hoping we wouldn't be the bad guy's statistical choice.

What the class brought foremost to mind was my realization of what poor physical condition I was in. I had assumed that weight lifting and regular cardiovascular exercise was sufficient for self-protection. This was clearly not the case. Within five minutes of hand-to-hand combat, fabricated though it was, I was completely winded and bathed in sweat. I was improving, but the going was slow and I had to counsel myself to be patient and trust in the process. The two women in my group who'd been previously assaulted found the exercises particularly traumatic, as the physical mock battles activated their feelings of vulnerability. I was part of the same spectrum, sensitive to what I considered my own failing to protect myself from Ned Lowe. In every grappling with my well-padded professional opponent, I pictured Ned's sad, puffy face; his pale skin, the bags under his eyes, and his air of weakness, which in truth was completely offset by his ruthlessness. He harbored no empathy for others and was, thus, pitiless in his pursuit of dominance.

At the end of the hour, as I showered and changed clothes, I could scarcely lift my arms. I was home by 5:35, flattened by physical exhaustion. I set my gym bag on the floor near my desk and collapsed on the couch, too wrung out to move. Did I dare brave Rosie's for dinner that night? Occasionally she supplemented her offal cooking with comfort foods and I wondered if I could count on her sense of fair play. Those of us who endured her culinary aberrations deserved the intermittent relief of roast chicken and mashed potatoes.

I was flirting with the idea of a nap when I heard a knock at my door. With various body parts setting up a howl, I staggered to my feet, crossed the room, and checked the porthole. My cousin Anna was standing on my doorstep with the cat in her arms. She caught sight of me and held him up by way of entreaty. I might have waved her away, claiming physical impairment, but who could resist that sweet beast?

Having earlier alluded to the subject of my history with my cousin, it's probably only fair that I pause to fill you in. I had discovered that the two of us were related during the same strange turn of events that resulted in a monetary windfall that put half a million dollars in my retirement fund. Being frugal by nature, I considered the funds inviolate and went on living as I had before, by which I mean cheaply.

When it came to Anna, I'd be hard-pressed to define the family connection, which stretched back a generation to our shared grandmother, Rebecca Dace, who had married my grandfather, Quillen Millhone. My father was *Anna*'s father's favorite uncle, making us (perhaps) second cousins once removed, or something of the sort. It's also possible I was her aunt. Whatever the tie, the relationship had gotten off to a shaky start.

I'd first met her during a two-day jaunt to Bakersfield, California, tracking the family of a homeless man who'd died on our local beach. The trip was only moderately productive, but when I returned to Santa Teresa, she'd followed, thinking a change in scenery might provide exciting new opportunities for her otherwise dead-end life. Next thing I knew, my landlord Henry had offered to let her stay in one of his guest rooms. Given his big heart and her tendency to freeload, she was there for the better part of three months, which annoyed me no end, especially as Henry never uttered a word of protest.

She found a job as a manicurist in a salon within walking distance and Henry made arrangements for her to rent a room from Moza Lowenstein, an elderly neighbor who lived four doors away. Since Anna needed a place to stay and Moza needed the company and the money, it worked out well for everyone. My feelings toward Anna might have been less than charitable, but I kept my mouth shut.

I opened the door and ushered her in, noting that her outfit—a long-sleeved blue T-shirt under denim overalls—rendered her shapeless, which is not easy for someone built as she was. She wore her dark hair pulled up in a bun on the top of her head and not a scrap of makeup. Even so, she looked better than I do on my best day. I know we're not supposed to measure ourselves against others, especially in circumstances where we come up so far short, but faced with a natural beauty like Anna's, it is hard not to despair.

She set Ed on the floor, watching him fondly as he sashayed across the room. "I found him outside and figured he was making a break for it. I thought he was strictly indoors."

"Tell *him* that. He makes a break for it every chance he gets; not from a desire to escape, but to prove to us he can," I said.

I closed the front door, returned to the couch, and lowered myself with caution, muscles protesting the imposition.

"Why are you limping?"

"I just came out of a self-defense class and I hurt everywhere. I take it Henry isn't home."

"Pearl answered the door. I couldn't believe my eyes. What's up with her?"

"She broke her hip. The rehab facility insisted on her finding a suitable place to recuperate before they'd let her out."

"But why Henry? What did he do to deserve that?"

"She remembered how nice he was when Terrence and Felix died."

"Oh, man. There's a lesson in there someplace. Mind if I have a seat?"

"By all means," I said.

She settled in one of the director's chairs, the canvas making a rude noise as it stretched to accommodate her. Ed hopped onto her lap and she kissed him between the ears. Honestly, if she wasn't so crazy about him, I wouldn't be nearly so hospitable.

I said, "You want a glass of wine?"

"No, thanks. I ate dinner last night at Rosie's and my stomach's still upset. Are you having dinner there tonight?"

"I'd thought to. How about you?"

"I don't know," she said uneasily.

"In other words, yes."

"Well, yeah. I don't cook and you can't subsist indefinitely on cheese and crackers because it's bad for your health."

"Not to get personal, but I noticed you and Cheney all cozied up," I said. I was hoping I'd adjusted my tone so as not to sound as grudging as I felt.

"I hope I'm not treading on your turf. He's a nice guy."

"I have no claims on the man."

She set Ed down again. He flopped over where he was and began cleaning himself. "Am I imagining this or did Camilla cut you dead the other night?"

"She's never been fond of me," I said.

"What do you expect? You boffed her husband, from what I hear."

"She was off on a fling, so what was the poor man supposed to do?"

Anna made a face. "I don't get that relationship."

"You haven't heard the story? They met in seventh grade. Thirteen years old and an immutable bond was formed. They call it codependency—a term I picked up from a therapist pal. In Jonah's view, since she's the mother of his children, he's morally obliged to endure."

"I have to admit their two girls turned out fine," she said. "It's that little boy, Banner, who'll pay."

Enough of that, I thought. "How's Cheney's house coming along?"

"Good. Place looks great."

"Glad to hear that. When I was dating him, he never finished anything and it drove me nuts. I have trouble when a cabinet door is open a smidge, let alone when all the hardware is missing."

"People change," she said.

"Not the ones I know."

"I tend to agree, though it's discouraging, isn't it?"

"Very," I replied.

"So how long will Pearl be on the premises?"

"Until Henry kicks her out. You know what a soft touch he is."

"I can't believe she'd move in like that. What a mooch!"

I refrained from pointing out that she'd been guilty of exactly the same behavior the year before. Hers was a classic example of our tendency to project our personal failings onto others and then condemn them for their shortcomings.

"And what's with the pup tent in the middle of the yard?" she went on.

"I'm minding my own business for a change and you'd be well advised to do the same. Put Henry on the defensive and you'll just prolong the siege. With luck, she'll move on and we'll be rid of her."

7

IRIS AND JOEY

Monday, September 18, 1989

Iris left the shop at five o'clock on the dot, making sure she'd locked up properly. They'd never had a burglary at Yesterday, most likely because vintage merchandise had little or no appeal among the criminal element. Why risk jail time for items for which there was no secondary market? They suffered their fair share of shoplifters, the sticky-fingered customers just about equally divided between teenaged girls and middle-aged women, both of whom thought nothing of pocketing lingerie, estate jewelry, beaded handbags, and even the occasional article of clothing as long as it could be easily slipped into a shopping bag or an oversize purse. Iris's boss, Karen, had instructed her to tag the pricier items, which meant the system would beep vigorously if someone left with something concealed on their person or among their packages. More than once, Iris had caught up with a customer just outside the door and had listened to them express surprise and embarrassment that they'd forgotten to pay. So far, they'd all returned sheepishly and made good on the transaction. She gave everyone the benefit of the doubt, though she knew perfectly well who was guilty and who was not.

Today Joey was working late, so she walked the ten blocks to their apartment, which was in a four-plex on the Lower East Side. The area was heavily Hispanic, which is not to say the homes were inexpensive. In Santa Teresa, the term "affordable housing" was a joke. She and Joey rented a tiny one-bedroom apartment with a kitchen that was ten feet by seven, a living room that was ten by ten, and a bedroom that was twelve feet by twelve. The bathroom was sufficient to accommodate a tub/shower, a toilet, and a double vanity with a linen closet on one end and a full-length mirror on the back side of the bathroom door.

Iris had done what she could to introduce a touch of class. The living room and bedroom walls were painted a dark blue, with spanking white trim. A white-painted bookshelf and desk unit took up one wall of the living room and provided a small planning center and an entertainment center, with a four-foot extension on one end that served as a dining room table. The wall opposite had been decorated with mirrored tiles, which created the illusion of more space than was actually there. The living room furniture consisted of a six-foot couch and an ottoman with a seat that would lift to reveal additional storage. There were two small upholstered chairs, an end table, and two floor lamps. Iris had also added some lush-looking fake plants, which made the space seem warmer.

She turned the oven to preheat at 350 degrees, dropped her bag on the small pass-through between the kitchen and living room, and opened the refrigerator door, taking out a package of chicken breasts, a head of romaine lettuce, a small jar of vinaigrette, and a cardboard tube of Parker House rolls. She removed the cellophane from the chicken and rinsed the pieces in a colander under cold running water. She took out a cutting board and neatly whacked the two big breasts into four smaller pieces. The whole time she worked, she was brooding about the journalist who'd come into the store. She wasn't sure what to make of the woman, but she didn't like the questions she'd asked.

She covered two small jelly-roll pans with foil, patted the chicken pieces dry, and placed them in one pan. She took out the Spike, generously seasoned the chicken breasts, and set them in the oven to bake. When the chicken was close to being done, she'd whack the cardboard tube of dinner rolls on the counter, remove the rolls, and place them in the second pan to bake. She took out a packaged mix of fettuccine amandine, filled a saucepan with water, and lit the fire under it. With the romaine, she'd make a freestanding Caesar salad with the lettuce upright in a bowl, glossy with vinaigrette, and sprinkled with Parmesan cheese.

While the chicken baked, she changed out of her work clothes into shorts and a long-sleeved T-shirt. Joey was home by six thirty and the two sat down to eat. By then, the oven had warmed the apartment, which was scented with the crispy-skinned, succulent baked chicken. This was one of Joey's favorite meals. With dinner, they each had an oversize goblet of rosé wine.

She pushed her plate back and lit a cigarette. "You'll never believe what happened at the store today."

Joey was still eating. "What's that?"

"This journalist came in asking what I thought about Fritz McCabe getting out of jail."

"A journalist?"

"From LA. 'Investigative reporter' is how she referred to herself."

As he cut a bite from his chicken breast, he said, "Why would she care what you think about Fritz McCabe?"

"That's what I said. The problem was she knew about a certain tape that was made way back when. She also knew about the note."

He put his fork down. "How?"

"How do you think? She mentioned an 'anonymous party' demanding a large sum of money or the tape would be turned over to the DA. I tried to pin her down. I knew she was talking about the McCabes, but she wouldn't actually come out and say so."

"What'd she say when you asked?"

"Nothing. She sidestepped the question and went on to something else."

"Did you mention that Fritz called all his pals and told 'em about the threat?"

"I thought it was better to play dumb."

"You think his parents went out and hired someone?"

"How else would she know what was going on? We said no cops. Maybe they thought it was okay to phone up the newspapers and get the story plastered all over. I was pissed."

"But why would they do that?" Joey said. "How can they be so dense?"

Iris shrugged. "Strictly speaking, they did as they were told. This is their attempt to do an end run around us. Oh, and catch this. This reporter said 'the people' quote marks had no intention of paying. She seemed pretty sure of herself on that score."

"Well, shit. I don't like this."

"Me, neither. I told her the tape was bullshit, just a bunch of us fooling around, but she was all long-faced and serious. She wanted to know who I'd talked to, but I didn't think it was any of her business."

"What's her name again?"

"Hang on. I have it written down." Iris got up and reached for her purse, where she had the scratch paper where the reporter had written her name and a local phone number. She took out the folded paper and handed it to him.

Joey glanced at it. "I thought she was from LA. This is a local number."

"She says she can be reached up here. I guess just in case I want to unburden myself and confess all, I have a way to get in touch."

"You think she'll pursue it?" Joey asked.

"She's probably being paid to, don't you think? I mean, this wasn't idle curiosity. She was banging away on it. On the other hand, journalists don't accomplish much of anything as far as I can tell, so what harm can she do?"

"I don't know. That's just it." Joey sat for a moment, mulling over the information, his expression dark. "I was going to suggest it was time to follow up, but now I think we should lay low."

"I'm not sure about that. Maybe."

"No maybe to it. Here's the deal. We do nothing. We don't fuel the situation by doing something dumb. We just hang loose until we see how smart she is. Chances are we got nothing to worry about."

"Ha. You hope."

"Don't look at me. It's your game plan," he said.

"*My* game plan? Where were you all this time? Last I heard, you loved the whole idea."

"I wouldn't say I *loved* the idea, but I could see your point. Guy gets out of prison and acts like, ho hum, all done, time to get on with life. Where does he get off?"

"Exactly."

"Other hand, eight years is a chunk of his life any way you look at it. Ask him to cough up a whack of cash on top of that? Might be taking it too far."

"What are you talking about? You're not the one who was sexually abused. Everybody in my support group thinks I should hose the guy but good."

"You discussed this with them? You never told me that. Jesus."

"Not this. I didn't say we were blackmailing the guy. Just that it makes me sick to think he can get away with it."

"What did he get away with? He went to prison."

"He's still guilty of having sex with a minor. Now he's acting like it's no big deal. He should suffer the way I did."

"Would you give it a rest? The first date we ever had, you told me this story. Anytime we meet someone new, you manage to work it into the conversation. Sexually abused by a family friend. Someone you knew."

"Well, it's true. People should be aware."

"You're not making a public service announcement. You get sympathy. That's why you do it."

"You're denigrating my experience. Minimizing the impact. Guys are famous for putting women down. *Why don't you get over it*? *Why can't you let it go?*" she said mockingly. "What you really mean is, 'Why make me eat shit for something that happened to you?' "

"How did this turn into a fight between us? I'm on your side. I've told you that a hundred times. We're talking about Fritz."

"It's all the same thing. You say 'Fritz McCabe,' I hear 'rape.' "

"Let's talk about something else," he said.

"Fine with me. Like what?"

"How about if the money comes through and we use it to take a trip, where would we go?"

8

Tuesday, September 19, 1989

Tuesday afternoon, I closed the office at five. I had toted my portable Smith Corona as far as the door, and I was about to punch in the alarm code when the telephone rang. I was tempted to let the machine pick up, but my conscience got the better of me. I dumped my shoulder bag by the typewriter and went back to my desk, picking up the handset on the third ring.

"Kinsey, it's Lauren. I wasn't sure I'd catch you."

"I was just on my way out."

"Well, I'll try not to keep you long. We have a problem."

"You heard from the extortionist?"

"It's not that. It's Fritz. Last night we told him what was going on and he's not happy with us."

"Unhappy with you? How so?"

"He's angry because we're unwilling to meet the demand. We've gone over our reasoning countless times and we're getting nowhere. We thought he should hear it from you. Is there any way you could pop over here tonight?"

"Of course, though I'm not sure what good it will do. I've never met him and I don't see why my opinion would carry any weight."

"He says he'll take off if we don't come through for him."

"What, like he'll run away from home?"

"He says he can't handle another legal battle."

"You're not fond of the idea yourself."

"I know, but we're not the ones who'll end up in jail. He's come up with a claim about the tape that we think he's fabricated, but there's no arguing the point. Maybe you can talk some sense into him. It's worth a try, isn't it?"

I could feel myself rolling my eyes. I pictured myself in a verbal tussle with the kid, which would be a colossal waste of time. Then again, she'd written me a check for twenty-five hundred bucks, and so far I didn't feel I'd earned my keep. "What time?"

"Seven, if that works for you."

"Sure. I'll return the tape while I'm at it. I'll see you then."

I brooded about the idea during the drive home. To me, it sounded like Fritz was taking control, asserting his point of view over the objections of his parents, who seemed to be throwing up their hands. Did they have no authority? Granted, the kid was twenty-five years old and by rights should have been out on his own, but his years in prison had set him back. With no job and no prospects, he was living with his mommy and daddy again and probably chafing at his dependency.

I found a decent parking space, hauled the typewriter out of the backseat, and took it with me, pausing at the mailbox on my way through the gate. I extracted a fistful of junk mail, bills, and catalogues, separating my mail from Henry's as I rounded the corner to the backyard.

This is the sight that greeted me.

Pearl was barefoot, wearing a bedsheet wrapped around herself toga-style. Her shoulders and arms were exposed, her boobs threatening to flop out if she didn't watch herself. She'd apparently done a load of laundry and she was hanging wet clothes on a makeshift line she'd strung between two of Henry's fruit trees. She navigated a short path back and forth, bending down to retrieve garments from the laundry basket as she swung herself across the dirt on her crutches. Either she was extremely adept at such maneuvering or she wasn't as incapacitated as she implied. Her jeans were the size of denim sails and the bra trailing down from the line was large enough to store watermelons. The two shirts she'd pegged to the clothesline looked too small for her, but I wasn't well acquainted with her wardrobe.

I set the typewriter on my front step, the better to deal with her.

She caught sight of me, but didn't seem to feel her near-nude state required apology or comment. "I don't know why Henry don't plant grass. Look at this dirt ever'where. My feet's a mess."

"He's conserving water. Or trying to," I said.

"He said I could warsh my stuff, so don't look at me like that."

"I was explaining, not criticizing," I said. "Is he home?"

"He went to the store."

At that moment, her pup tent gave a shudder and a fellow crawled out through the flaps. Pearl must have done his laundry along with hers, or that was my guess since he wore jeans and nothing else. With my highly developed detective skills, I deduced the shirts hanging on the line were his. He struggled to his feet in a manner that suggested he'd had a bit to drink.

I looked from him to Pearl. "Who's this?"

"Name's Lucky. He's a good friend of mine."

"What's he doing here?"

"What's it look like? He's hanging out."

I took in the whole of him with a flick of my eyes, not wanting to stare. I placed him in his sixties. He was a scrawny man, but I could see he'd been muscular once upon a time, his frame now diminished by the years. He was so papered over with tattoos it looked like he'd plastered himself with a soggy sheet of Sunday funnies. The tattoos must have been done when he was in his teens because maturity had added a thick mat of chest hair that obscured some of the art. Age had loosened his skin and several sections of his human sketchbook had sagged, spoiling the effect.

He settled into one of Henry's Adirondack chairs and extended his legs and bare feet. Beside him, there was a Styrofoam cooler filled with ice and packed with cans of a generic-brand beer. He removed one, popped the tab, and sucked down the contents. I expected an unceremonious belch, but his dainty manners prevailed.

I turned to Pearl. "Does Henry know about this?"

"What's it to him? This guy's broke and he's got no place to stay, so I made room in my tent. Henry ain't out anything and besides, he hadn't said no."

"Have you asked?"

"I will as soon as he gets home."

"Lucky wasn't here when he left?"

"He was asleep inside and I guess Henry didn't notice him. Anyways, it's none of your business if I entertain my friends. I got rights same as you."

"Now we're talking about *rights*?"

Lucky said, "Now, ladies, there's no need to fuss. I'm only here for the night on account of the fella at Harbor House kicked me out. And before you ask, I'll tell you straight out. I was drunk and unruly and the shelter won't put up with that. Tomorrow, I'll go back."

"Good of you to own up. What makes you think they'll take you?"

"Why wouldn't they? Sober, I'm gentle as a lamb. It's only eight or nine beers makes me surly and cantankerous."

When he grinned, he showed dimples and dark gaps where the better part of his back teeth had been. "I wouldn't have had them beers in the first place except my dog disappeared. He's been with me twelve years and now I don't know where he's at."

"That's too bad," I said. "Have you called Animal Control?"

"No, but that's a fine idea. Do you mind if I use your phone?"

"I do mind."

"Said like someone with a stick up her butt," Pearl remarked.

I took that moment to escape.

I unlocked the studio and let myself in, placing the mail on my desk and the typewriter underneath. The cat streaked out of nowhere and beat me to the finish line. I might have shooed him out again, but he was good company and put me in a better mood. I closed the door and scooped him up, perched myself on a kitchen stool, and settled him in my lap. Ed was a talkative little fellow and he seemed happy for the audience. Having expressed himself in full, he put his chin on his paws and went to sleep. I moved him to my sofa, where he remained.

I changed into my running clothes and headed for the bike path. My three-mile run is a wonderful way to erase stress. I'm not always in the mood, but I push myself anyway for the relief. I finished my cooldown and came back to the studio, where I showered and dressed.

At six forty-five, having savored a peanut butter and pickle sandwich and tossed my paper towel in the trash, I grabbed my shoulder bag and keys and locked the door behind me. I carried Ed back to Henry's place and set him inside the kitchen door. I could hear Pearl and Lucky and Henry chatting in the living room while the evening news blasted from the television set. I smelled beef stew and homemade bread, feeling ever so faintly put-upon at the meal I'd missed. Having been raised as an only child, it's not in my nature to "share."

The days were getting shorter as autumn crept in, but it was still light outside and the air was pleasantly warm. The drive into town was quick and there was ample parking behind the condominium. I cut through the covered vestibule and emerged onto State Street, where a quick left turn put me at the wooden door that opened onto the stairs. I trotted up to the second floor and knocked.

Hollis answered the door. "You must be Kinsey. I'm Hollis McCabe. We appreciate your stopping by."

He extended his hand as he introduced himself. We made the usual polite mouth noises while he ushered me in. He appeared to be older than his wife by a good ten years, his once light-brown hair dusted with gray. He was tall and stoop-shouldered, casually dressed in a brown velour sweat suit. I picked up the scent of the cigar he'd smoked, but the effect wasn't unpleasant.

He led the way into the living room. I took a seat on the couch while he crossed to a wet bar adjacent to the dining room. He poured bourbon over ice. "How about a drink? You'll probably need one."

"Sure. Chardonnay if you have it."

"Of course."

I could see then an open bottle of white wine, sitting in a cooler that was silvered with condensation. Lauren approached from the corridor that led to the library and the bedrooms. She wore a hip-length embroidered tunic over tight jeans and she carried an empty wineglass that Hollis topped off at the same time he poured wine for me. She crossed to the couch and settled at the other end.

"Thanks for making the trip."

"I'm not far. Fifteen minutes max."

I reached in my bag and removed the tape, which I held out to her.

"Thank you. I'm not sure what I'll do with it, but it's probably a good thing to have it in my control." She set it on the end table beside her.

Hollis carried his bourbon to a chair and sat down, placing his drink on the end table next to him. "You want to fill her in before we get Fritz out here?"

"She should hear the story from him. It will save us the repetition."

"Your call," he said.

Lauren set aside her wineglass and walked down the hall. She paused at the first door on the left and knocked. "Fritz? Kinsey's here."

His reply was muffled and the tone was argumentative.

"Five minutes, please. She's doing this as a courtesy," she said.

"I said I'd be out in a bit!"

"I heard you the first time. Quit being a pill."

There was silence. I thought she'd start counting like mothers do with children who misbehave. *"One, two . . . I'm warning you . . . I'm going to swat your behind . . . three, four . . ."* The strategy is weak unless the point is to teach kids to count.

Fritz emerged, banging the door open. "Fine."

I wasn't sure how he managed to cram so much rebellion and ill humor into one word. He was no longer the lean boy I'd seen on the tape. He'd filled out, adding the sort of weight that starchy food produces. This was the first time I'd laid eyes on the kid in person. I associated him with the four minutes of tape, complete with saucy weenie-wagging, an image I struggled to repress.

"Why don't you tell Kinsey what you told us?" she said.

Fritz flung himself into a chair and crossed his arms. "Jeez, Mom. Why don't we jump right in? We haven't even been introduced."

"Kinsey, this is Fritz. Fritz, Kinsey. Now let's not waste any more of her time."

"You're happy enough wasting mine."

Lauren closed her eyes. "Fritz."

"What a bitch! If you don't believe me, why should she?"

Hollis crossed the distance between them in two steps, his fist cocked. "I'll knock the shit out of you if you talk to your mother that way. Use that tone again and you'll be picking your teeth off the floor."

The eruption caught me off guard. I'd assumed Hollis was a mild-mannered middle-aged man who favored the same ineffective parenting techniques his wife employed. Her method entailed wheedling, nagging, coaxing, and expressing her appreciation for any semblance of obedience. I couldn't believe Hollis had threatened to deck his own kid in front of company. The threat made my nerves crackle, and the hair on my arms lifted as though from static electricity. My heart gave an uncharacteristic thump in case I was next.

Fritz was apparently a past recipient of his father's blows because he dropped the attitude. His manner was still sullen, but he wasn't "acting out." I was horrified by the exchange and sat still as stone, waiting for the tension to dissipate. Lauren didn't bat an eye. Meanwhile, Hollis lowered his fist and picked up his drink again as he sat down. Conversation resumed without further reference to parental abuse.

Lauren turned to me. "Fritz tells us it was a lark. He says the tape was made all in good fun."

I said, "I had a conversation with Iris yesterday and she said much the same thing."

"Because it's true! We were just horsing around. We were laughing our asses off. It was Austin's idea and Iris jumped on the plan. She loved the notion of a porno film, which she thought was a hoot. She faked everything, acting like she passed out when she was in on the joke, right?" he said, looking to me for confirmation.

"She didn't actually go that far. She referred to it as 'messing around.'"

"That's what I'm talking about. A put-on."

Hollis said, "Why didn't you say so in the first place?"

"Because I knew you'd do this. I'm telling the truth and you're calling me a liar."

Lauren said, "Your father's asking why you'd offer such an explanation at this late date."

"You only told me about the blackmail yesterday."

"I'm talking about ten years ago when the tape first came to light."

"You said you didn't see it, so how was I supposed to explain? You swore you didn't watch it."

"Because you accused me of taking it," she said. "What could I do except plead ignorance? I certainly wasn't going to offer up the sordid details once this whole business went to trial. I was trying to protect you, not make matters worse."

Hollis said, "Let's back up a bit. We didn't see anything to indicate Iris was 'horsing around,' and what you and Troy did could hardly be classified as high jinks."

"The tape was edited. We stopped five or six times deciding what we'd do next. Those scenes were cut. There wasn't a script. We were making it up as we went along."

Hollis said, "Look, Fritz. We're willing to give you the benefit of the doubt, but just for the sake of argument, where is all of this edited material? Alleged edited material."

"There you go again. '*Alleged edited material*,'" he repeated in a mocking tone, his expression sour.

"Just answer the question."

"How would I know? Bayard worked on the edits and then gave the tape to Austin for his review. When I got it back, the scenes were gone. You can see the jumps on the tape. There must be three or four. Austin must have kept the outtakes."

"Well, now we're getting somewhere. He told you that?"

"Not in so many words. I assumed he had the footage because he was the director and he had the final word. That's how it's done in Hollywood, is what he said."

"Oh, right. A Hollywood production. I can see your point," Hollis said.

"You're doing it again. Being all pissy. Why don't you ask Bayard? He'll tell you the same thing."

"I'm sure he would. Otherwise, what we're looking at is the vicious abuse of a young girl. What is she, fourteen?"

"We didn't *force* ourselves on her. It was consensual and it wasn't even real sex. It was a game and she agreed. She wasn't drunk and she didn't pass out. In between the camera rolling, she was cracking up."

"Son, we'd like nothing better than to take your word for it. But the way things stand, if that tape reaches the DA, you're in very deep shit."

"I know! God. You don't have to repeat yourself. We're in trouble. I get that. What do you want me to do?"

Lauren spoke up, saying, "Providing us with proof would be nice. So far, that seems to be in short supply."

"I don't *have* proof!"

"Which leaves us in a precarious position, wouldn't you agree?"

"Shit, Mom. If you'd just pay the guy, this would all go away, so why don't we talk about that for a change?"

"Your mother told you before. We're not going to pay."

"Why not? Twenty-five grand is nothing to you, so why not do what he says?"

"Because we have no guarantee that would be the end of it. We pay and who's to say the crook won't come back and insist on more? We could live the rest of our lives with the same threat hanging over our heads."

"If Troy and I get nailed on this stuff, we'll be tried as adults. You don't pay, we could spend *years* behind bars. Is that what you want? Because if you ask me, that's really fucked up."

Lauren turned to me. "Why don't we hear what Kinsey has to say?"

"Who cares about her opinion? You're picking up the tab, so she'll say anything you want."

Lauren said, "We'll be picking up the tab regardless. At least give her the courtesy of listening."

"What for? Why not support me for a change? It's my life on the line."

Hollis said, "Fritz—"

I cut in, hoping to head off another verbal slugfest. "I understand your point, Fritz, but there's more to their decision than you may be aware," I said. "The first thing your parents did when this business came up was to consult a criminal attorney. He strongly advised them not to pay for the same reasons they've already given you. You have to draw the line somewhere and this is as good a place as any. The minute they pay, all they've done is open up a can of worms."

"Well, I disagree and I should have a say in this, don't you think?"

"Only if you have twenty-five thousand dollars to spare," Hollis interjected.

"Great. Put it all on me. I've already got my nuts in a vise, so pile it on."

"Darling, since you don't respect our point of view, what do you suggest?"

"Quit farting around. Give the guy what he wants and tell him that's the end of it. Say you won't pay another cent and he can like it or lump it. I don't understand why the idea is so hard to grasp."

Lauren leaned forward. "Do you know how much we've already shelled out for your legal bills? Half a million dollars. We had to sell the house to come up with it."

"You never bitched about the money before."

"Fine. *You* pay if you think it's such a good idea," she said.

"How am I supposed to come up with money like that? News flash. I'm unemployed and I'm an ex-con, so no one's going to hire me no matter what. Even if I had a job, I couldn't earn dough like that in a million years."

Hollis said, "We don't feel it's our responsibility. You put us in this position. Yet again, I might add."

"Fuck you."

Hollis closed his eyes, working to control his temper. "You know, son, it's this attitude that got you in trouble in the first place. You act without any thought to the consequences."

"You've told me that before, *Dad*! And what am I supposed to say? The past is the past. It's over and done. I can't change anything."

Lauren said, "Let's deal with the here and now."

"There isn't any here and now. I'm out," Fritz snapped.

He jumped up and headed for his room, his face suffused with fury. He turned back once, saying, "Do anything you want, but I'll hang myself before I go back to prison, so factor that into the equation." He banged into his room and that was the end of that.

The door slamming was the perfect punctuation mark to a scene that already felt overplayed. One thing about uproar: it's useful in diverting attention from issues you're hoping to avoid.

Hollis caught my eye. "You can see what we're dealing with," he said, sounding strangely satisfied.

9

I left the McCabes and drove home. When I turned onto my street, I realized one of my neighbors was having a party and parking was more problematic than usual. In the middle of the block, I saw a house lighted up and cars lining the driveway, which was only long enough to hold three. Every other space along the curb was filled. I had to circle the block twice and finally had no choice but to wedge my Honda into a semi-legal spot near the corner of Albanil and Cabana Boulevard. As I locked the car, I spotted a sole pedestrian: a man in a black raincoat who turned his face away from me as he crossed the street up ahead. He had his hands jammed in his pockets and the tap-tap of his heels broke the quiet of the night air. Something about his posture and the shape of his head sparked an image of Ned Lowe. I slowed my pace and stared into the shadows, my brain momentarily disconnected from my body. I'd seen Ned on very few occasions—maybe three or four times—which meant my ability to recognize him in the dark was far from certain. Given the weak pool of light cast by the street lamp, the likeness might have been an optical illusion, but the attempted break-in at the office had already generated uneasiness. My mouth filled with saliva like one of Pavlov's dogs conditioned by a bell and I was yanked into the past as though by a shepherd's crook.

I could feel his weight, the pressure of his knee in the middle of my back. Once again, I was facedown on my office carpeting. I couldn't turn. I couldn't move. I had no way to buck his hold. I felt his hand over my mouth, his fingers pinching my nose shut. I was consumed with the need for oxygen, my lungs aflame. I was aware of the scent of his aftershave—musk and patchouli, suggestive of a fortune-teller's waiting room. The scratchy nap of his unshaven cheek, the underlying oil on his skin. I could remember the sound of his breathing as he worked to prevent mine. He was a middle-aged man who looked tired and I remember equating this with ineffectiveness. Big mistake on my part in light of how closely he'd taken me to the brink of death.

I shook my head. The panic faded as rapidly as it had enveloped me and my intellect reasserted control. If Ned was back, why would he risk appearing in my neighborhood unless he was on a scouting mission? And what the hell did he want?

I scurried home. With the dark at my back, I was propelled by fear. As I opened the gate, I saw the glow from the downstairs bathroom light I'd left on for myself, but the coziness wouldn't afford much comfort if Ned had been there, trying to pick his way in. I rounded the corner of the studio. Henry's porch light was off and the backyard was thick with shadows. I stood still while my eyes adjusted to the dark. In the wash of ambient light from the street lamps out front, I could make out the small gray mountain of Pearl's pup tent in the middle of the dirt. Ed, the cat, picked his way daintily across the yard like a wraith and disappeared into the bushes. Henry was going to have to find a way to keep that little guy inside. Pearl and Lucky were sitting in the Adirondack chairs, but all I could see of the pair were ghostly shapes and the tips of their cigarettes like red dots.

"Hey, Lucky. Did you get your dog?"

"Did, but Henry said we ought to take him to the vet in case he has worms. His shots ain't up to date anyway, so the doc said he'd keep him overnight."

"Well, I'm glad you got him back."

"Me, too; man's best friend and all."

Idly, Pearl said, "Speaking of which, you just missed your friend."

"What friend?"

"Some guy was here looking for you. Couldn't have been more than five minutes ago. I'm surprised you didn't bump into him."

"I think I saw him and he's not a friend. He kills women."

She laughed, but when she caught my tone, her grin faded. "He's the asshole who killed those young girls?"

"Ned Lowe," I said.

"What's he want with you?"

"He's hoping to add me to the list."

"Well, sorry, babe. That's for shit. I had no idea. He seemed like a regular dude to me. Not your type, but what do I know? How about you, Lucky? He seem threatening to you?"

"Seemed sneaky. Might've been dark, but I could tell he wasn't a regular sort."

Pearl said, "Really? How'd you come up with that?"

"I could smell it on him."

"I wish you'd spoken up. I'm setting here chatting away with him, friendly as all get-out."

Lucky said, "You're too trusting, Pearl. I told you that before. What if he had went for you?"

"He can't choke me. I got more neck than he can get his hands around. He shows up again, I'll punch his lights out," she said. "Which direction was he headed?"

"Left on Cabana."

"Tell you what. Tomorrow, I'll put the word out among my homies and have 'em keep an eye out. He might've checked into one of the cheap motels near the railroad tracks or be sleeping on the beach. Might even be holed up in that hobo camp the Bogarts was using before they got run off."

The Bogarts were a tight gang of vicious thugs who had staked out the off-ramp for their panhandling.

"This guy is a nasty piece of work," I said. "If you spot him, call the police. Don't take anything on yourself."

"I wouldn't mess with the likes of him. We'll track him down, though. Don't you worry. He's anywhere around here, we'll find him."

I let myself into the studio, where I did a perimeter search to make sure all the locks were secured. I took the stairs two at a time and retrieved my H&K VP9 from the locked trunk at the foot of my bed. While I'd brushed up on my shooting skills, I wasn't convinced I'd have to protect myself, so I'd tucked the gun away for safekeeping. Now I checked the load and took out my holster and my shoulder harness, which I strapped into place, resting my semiautomatic in the shelter of my armpit. I pulled on a windbreaker over my turtleneck and studied myself in the mirror. What was my plan? I pictured spending my days toting an H&K VP9 under my left boob. I could just see myself at the grocery store, reaching for a carton of milk, with the butt of the gun peeking out. If I locked it in the glove compartment of my car, the gun would be just as unavailable as it was locked in the trunk at the foot of my bed. The same was true of my desk at the office. If I wasn't willing to carry it on my person, what good would it do? I grabbed my flashlight, which was sturdy enough to use as a weapon in a pinch, and then I sallied forth and double-timed it up to Rosie's.

Despite happy hour, the tavern was largely empty. On Monday and Tuesday nights, the crowd was usually light. Business picked up toward the middle of the week, Wednesday being hump night. By the weekend, the place would be jammed. Rosie was sitting at the bar, reading the local paper, which we all referred to as the "low-cal" *Dispatch*, for its paucity of coverage, most of it lifted from the wire services. I quizzed her to make sure my "friend" hadn't been in earlier asking about me. She was well acquainted with the details of my encounter with Ned Lowe and assured me she'd be on the alert.

Jonah had just gotten up from a table where Anna Dace was sitting and I watched him shrug into his jacket in preparation for the drive home.

I crossed the room. "Ned Lowe's back," I said without preamble.

He paused as he was turning down his collar. "Since when?"

"I'm not sure. Yesterday afternoon my office alarm went off. Someone broke a kitchen window trying to get in. The alarm company called the cops and the officer who came out found the rock he used. A few minutes ago I saw a man in a raincoat turn the corner from Albanil onto Cabana. I can't swear it was him, but it's a good bet. He'd already stopped by my studio asking for me. Fortunately, Pearl and a pal of hers were there. She's camping in Henry's backyard, and for once I'm happy for the company."

"Let me talk to the watch commander and I'll get back to you. He can step up patrols in the area. Are you okay?"

"I'm fine, but I'm not going to sleep well until you find him."

"Shouldn't be that tough if he's in the area. I'll see that a BOLO goes out and maybe we can sweep him up," he said. "You want me to walk you home?"

"I need to sit and collect myself."

"Understood. You take care. I'll call you the minute I hear anything."

"I'd appreciate that."

"Hey. I almost forgot to ask. How'd your meeting go?"

I blanked on him. "What meeting?"

"With Lauren McCabe."

For a moment, I was stumped. There was no way I could tell him about the tape or the blackmail demand. "Good. It was fine. I met Hollis and Fritz," I said, as though that were relevant.

"She putting you to work?"

"We're still discussing it," I said. If he asked a direct question about what sort of work it was, I'd have to stonewall or lie, which I prefer not to do with friends. He would understand my being protective of a client, but I felt the less said about it the better. "How are Courtney and Ashley? I haven't seen them lately."

"Camilla doesn't want them coming in. She says this is a low-life dive and they have no business being here."

"She makes *herself* right at home, I note."

"She's an adult. They're impressionable girls."

"Come on. An occasional visit doesn't do any harm. You know Rosie keeps an eye on them."

"I told her the same thing. She'll loosen up, I suspect, and in the meantime, they're making themselves scarce, which I should probably do myself," he said. "Good seeing you."

"You, too."

He gave Rosie a wave on his way out. Anna remained where she was, nursing a gin and tonic, her attention focused on a *Cosmopolitan* magazine.

Rosie appeared behind me with a glass of bad white wine without even being asked.

"Bless you," I said.

"I'm keeping baseball bat behind bar. That guy comes in, I make him sorry in the head."

I got up and gave her a hug, which surprised both of us. "Thank you. I mean it. Go for the knees first," I added under my breath.

As Rosie moved away, I turned my attention to Anna. "Mind if I sit down?"

"Help yourself. What was that about?"

I took a seat. "It looks like Ned Lowe is back," I said. I repeated my story about the broken office window and the sighting of the man in a raincoat. I noticed a certain relief in the telling, as though the repetition took the sting out of the two incidents. "Pearl tells me a 'friend' stopped by looking for me shortly before I got home tonight."

"Oh, man. That's not good."

"What about you? How are you doing? You look depressed."

"Who, me? Not a bit. I'm not the one being stalked."

"Jonah said he'd put out the word, but that's not much help." I drained half a glass of wine that went down like water with about the same effect. No wonder people get in trouble with this stuff.

"What will you do?" she asked.

"I wish I knew. I'll step up security measures, but I haven't decided yet if I should carry my gun. I used to park it at the small of my back, but that's Ned's favorite spot. I might buy pepper spray, which is effective as long as you don't shoot your own sorry self in the face."

A shudder went down her frame. "We ought to walk home together."

"Sounds good to me. You ready to go?"

"I am if you are."

I finished the glass of wine and waited while she gathered her sweater and bag.

"You running a tab?" I asked, indicating her drink.

"It's paid for."

We walked the half block to my place following the beam from my flashlight. Once we reached Henry's drive, I watched while she covered the short distance to Moza's. She climbed the porch stairs and after she let herself in, she blinked the outside light twice to let me know she was okay. In the meantime, I was attuned to every shadow and the rattle of leaves in the wind. I moved through the squeaky gate and rounded the corner to my front door. There was no sign of Lucky or Pearl, so I assumed they were safely zipped into her tent. I felt more secure knowing the two were out there like human watch dogs.

I let myself in and locked the door behind me. Before I went up the spiral stairs to the loft, I turned on the outside lights. I hoped the glare wouldn't penetrate the tent and keep the occupants awake, but if so, they'd have to endure. It seemed like a smart move to keep the premises lit up. For the second time in an hour, I checked the locks on all my windows and doors. I still had the door handle alarm unit Robert Dietz had supplied years before when I enjoyed the dubious distinction of being one of five names on Tyrone Patty's hit list. I put the portable alarm on the knob, where it would issue an ear-splitting blare if the door was tampered with. I also did a quick walkabout, making sure Ned Lowe hadn't crept in, flattened himself like a spider, and slithered under my sofa bed. I didn't think four inches was sufficient to conceal him, but I looked anyway.

Once in bed with the light out, I thought about the situation. Ned was the kind of guy who enjoyed the hunt. He'd want to make sure I felt spooked because my discomfort would contribute to his happiness. I was not one of those defiant female types determined not to let a man threaten my peace of mind. What peace of mind? Even the idea of seeing him half a block away was sufficient to keep me awake. To distract myself, I thought back to the encounter with Fritz McCabe. Something in the conversation nagged at me, but I couldn't think what it was. Next thing I knew, I was dead to the world and then my alarm clock buzzed.

I took an alternate route to work. Ned Lowe knew where my office was and he had my home address, but I didn't like the notion of his tailing me. As I pulled into the office driveway, I took a few minutes for a visual survey before I got out of the car, locked it behind me, and crossed the short distance to my door. When I entered the alarm code, the light on the system moved from red to green, which I took as evidence the premises hadn't been breached. I kept the front and back doors locked and the perimeter armed. If Ned Lowe jimmied the lock, hoping to catch me by surprise, I'd have a few seconds of warning.

By the time I sat down at my desk, I realized the question my subconscious had been flirting with, trying to flag my attention. I peeled off my windbreaker, picked up the phone, and put a call through to Lauren McCabe, who picked up after two rings.

"Hey, Lauren. This is Kinsey. You have a minute?"

"Sure. Hollis just left for work and Fritz is sleeping in. What can I do for you?"

"I've been thinking about a couple of things that came up in conversation last night."

"Such as what?"

"I'm wondering why you haven't heard from the extortionist. You'd think he'd have followed up by now. He said he'd leave a message with instructions."

"I've been curious about that myself. Every time the phone rings, I'm prepared for the worst. The same when the mail arrives. I thought maybe he was giving us time to put the cash together."

"Unlikely, but that would be considerate."

"What's your take on it?"

"I think you're dealing with a rank amateur. I'm not even sure this guy has a plan. The longer he waits to act, the more time he's giving you to notify the police or the FBI."

"On the other hand, this is the riskiest moment of any blackmail scheme, isn't it? Once we're told where to drop the money, he has to play his hand. He must be aware we could contact law enforcement and have them lying in wait."

"True, but the whole setup seems odd to me. I mean, so far there's no guarantee there aren't a dozen copies out there. Surely he doesn't expect you to pay until he's addressed that point."

"I can't answer that one. Hollis assumes the terms will be laid out when he gives us instructions about the twenty-five grand."

"Which brings up another point. A couple of times Fritz said twenty-five thousand was nothing to you. I'm not asking about your finances, but I gather you're well-to-do."

"You could say that, I suppose. We're not wealthy, but we're comfortable. More than comfortable," she amended.

"And anyone who knows you is aware of it, yes?"

"No doubt. We're not ostentatious, but we make no secret of the fact that we live well."

"So why didn't the extortionist ask for a hundred thousand dollars or even half a million? You could put that much together, too, couldn't you?"

"Oh, lord. Please don't wish that on us."

"Far from it. I'm wondering about his frame of reference. Maybe to him, twenty-five grand is big."

"Meaning what?"

"Meaning there was a kidnapping case here in town some years ago. I got involved long after the fact, but what struck me was that the ransom demand was low. Turned out later the kidnappers were two teenaged boys who thought fifteen thousand dollars was a lot of money," I said. "The other possibility is that your extortionist has a specific goal in mind and twenty-five is all he needs."

"To do what with?"

"This might be a bid for independence."

There was a moment of dead silence. "You're not suggesting Fritz is behind this."

"It would certainly explain why he's so adamant in his urging you to pay."

"He wouldn't do that to us. The notion's ludicrous."

"You might not like the idea, but it's not ludicrous," I said. "The note and the tape didn't arrive until he got home."

"Coincidence."

"I wouldn't be so sure. I've been assuming his release is what triggered the demand. Isn't that your take on it as well?"

"That doesn't mean the demand *came* from him."

"What if he's had the tape in his possession since he went off to CYA?"

"That couldn't be the case. He was livid when he realized the tape was gone. I'm sure he wasn't faking his dismay. Besides which, we sold the house and moved while he was gone, packing up everything he owned. If he'd had the tape, we'd have found it."

"Unless he left it with a friend. He might have an accomplice who's helping coordinate the deal."

"In that case, why accuse Sloan of stealing it?"

"To take the focus off himself."

I could tell she was getting agitated. "He told us Sloan used that tape to threaten Austin, which means it's much more likely she gave it to someone for safekeeping. I doubt she'd have entrusted it to Iris, but Poppy's a good bet. Actually, it could have been anyone. The point is, I'm not paying you to implicate my son."

"All I'm saying is, I don't think we should rule anything out at this point."

"*I'm* ruling it out, so let's move on to something else."

"What do you suggest?" I asked, trying to keep the frostiness out of my tone.

"The obvious move is to find Troy and Bayard and ask if they'll corroborate Fritz's claim about the missing scenes. If there were cuts and the tape was a hoax, the two aren't in any jeopardy as far as I can see."

"True in theory, but without the original, who's going to believe them?"

"We'll cross that bridge when we come to it," she said irritably. "If Troy confirms what Fritz is telling us, you can move on to the issue of outtakes and tracking those down. Right now, all we have is his word for it. You should also contact Poppy and see if she knows what Sloan did with the tape."

"I can do that," I said. I made a face at the phone to show I wasn't knuckling under without a protest.

Once we hung up, I took out the list of names I'd jotted down after my initial meeting with her. I thought my suspicions about Fritz had merit. Clearly she did not. The fact remained that I was an employee and she had every right to call the shots. At least I'd planted the idea and if Fritz was involved in the scheme, he might tip his hand.

I'd met Iris, but Poppy, Troy, and Bayard were still unknown entities. I should also talk to Sloan's mother to see what she knew. I didn't relish talking to the mother of the dead girl and quickly convinced myself it would be better to cover the easy ones first. I pulled the phone book from the bottom drawer and did a finger search. There was no listing for Poppy, who might have married or left town in the past few years. I did see a Dr. Sherman and Loretta Earl with an address on Eden Way in Horton Ravine. His office address and phone appeared in the listing below and I copied those as well, noting that he was a cardiologist. Bayard Montgomery and Troy Rademaker were both listed and I made a note of their respective addresses and telephone numbers. I put in a quick call to Ruthie and picked up the name of the automobile repair shop where Troy Rademaker was employed. This would give me a running start.

Fortified with the information, I pulled on my windbreaker and grabbed my shoulder bag. I armed the system, locked the office, and then headed for my car. Before I hit the road, I locked my gun in the trunk, not wanting to alarm anyone I chanced to interview. I took my city guide from the glove compartment and spent a couple of minutes looking for Eden Way. Fifteen minutes later, I was swinging through the wrought-iron gate, which stood open at the entrance to the enclave. The cobblestone driveway bordered a sloping front lawn that swept up to the left and terminated in a circular parking area. The house was gray stone, in a mock Tudor style, complete with cross-timbers and mullioned windows. How many of these houses did we have in town? Seemed like every time I turned around, I was looking at a Tudor-style house, expecting Ann Boleyn to emerge. A yardman on a riding mower had created a manicured path across the bright green shaggy grass and I took brief note of his progress.

At the top of the drive, I parked and followed the front walk to the door, where I rang the bell. I turned and looked out, admiring the massive oaks that dotted the grounds. I realized the sound of the mower had ceased and the yardman was coming up the driveway in my direction, wiping his sweaty face with a handkerchief.

"Can I help you?" He wore jeans, a T-shirt, and a baseball cap that he removed, revealing a balding pate with short-cropped gray hair on either side.

"Is this the Earls' address?"

"It is. I'm Dr. Earl." He held out his hand and I shook it.

"It's nice meeting you. I'm Kinsey Millhone. I assumed you worked here and I apologize."

"Not a problem," he said. He was in his late fifties, not heavy-set, but he'd apparently picked up the pounds as the years went by and hadn't yet adjusted the size of his pants. "This is my afternoon off. I mow because it's mindless and allows me time to collect my thoughts. You're the private investigator?"

"That's right. Have we met?"

"I remember reading about you in the paper when Dowan Purcell disappeared."

"That was a bad deal," I said. "Were you a friend of his?"

"We belonged to the same country club, though we didn't socialize. Are you here with regard to him?"

I shook my head. "I'm hoping to locate Poppy. She isn't listed in the phone book, so I thought maybe you could steer me in the right direction."

"My daughter's a popular girl these days. The fellow who just got out of prison was hoping to connect with her as well."

"Fritz McCabe? I wasn't aware of that."

His gaze shifted to a point behind me and I turned to see a black Lincoln Continental easing up the drive with scarcely a sound.

"My wife," he said.

We watched as she pulled into the parking area. The trunk popped open with a muffled thunk. She got out and walked around to the rear, where she pulled out a number of Saks Fifth Avenue shopping bags. She wore a full-length mink coat that seemed excessive in the tangible autumn heat.

When she reached her husband, the two exchanged one of those dutiful kisses that signify marital niceties, but not much else.

"My wife, Loretta," he said. "This is Kinsey Millhone."

We shook hands briefly before he went on. "She's looking for Poppy."

Loretta said, "What's this about, or has Sherman already asked?" Her hair was dark at the roots, the strands highlighted with blond as though the sun had done the job. Her smile carried little warmth and her tone, while polite, had an edge to it.

"I just arrived, so he hasn't had the chance. I'm sorry to stop by unannounced."

"It's a little late to worry about that now, isn't it?" Her smile became more winsome, as though she were being witty instead of rude. Just my luck. Bitchy and brittle as a dry stick.

Dr. Earl put on his cap. "If you ladies don't mind, I'll get back to work."

Loretta moved toward the front door. Over her shoulder, she said, "As long as you're here, you might as well come in."

"If this is inconvenient, I can try you another time."

She didn't deign to reply. She opened the door and paused briefly in the foyer to shed her mink coat, which she tossed across an occasional chair before she continued toward the back of the house.

I followed her, resigned to an excruciating few minutes of conversation, during which she'd spar and parry, doling out information in bits and pieces if she cooperated at all.

But I'd misjudged the woman. As luck would have it, this wasn't Poppy's mother. This was her *stepmother*, steeped in opinions about the girl she couldn't wait to share.

10

THE TAPE

May 1979

Lauren McCabe sat at her desk and wrote a check for twenty-six thousand dollars. It was Friday and the contractor wanted to pay his subs, not to mention himself. She noticed that the builder and his merry band of underlings came to work when it suited them. Some days they came late and some days they didn't show up at all, but when they wanted a check she was expected to pony up right that minute. There was plenty of money in the checking account, but she flinched watching thousands going out the window, week after week. She tore the check from the register and crossed the hall to the front door, which was standing open. The contractor stood on the porch, hands in his pockets, probably hoping to make small talk as he accepted the check. Lauren was having none of it. Her relationship with the man was cordial, but she wasn't in the mood to feign friendliness. "Have a good weekend," she said briskly.

"You, too. And thanks," he said, holding up the check.

She closed the front door without bothering to respond.

The McCabes had owned the house for a year and were in the thick of the remodeling process. She had anticipated the work being finished by now, but there seemed to be no end to it. The contractor was over budget. His bid was supposed to be firm, but he kept running into stumbling blocks. Take the matter of the master bedroom, which had looked fine at first sight. The Pruitts, from whom they bought the house, had added the new master suite, which included his-and-her bathrooms, two spacious walk-in closets, a steam room, and an exercise room. But when the contractor started work on the adjacent wing, where the kitchen walls were coming down, he discovered that the foundation was cracked; probably earthquake damage that had gone undetected until now. He said the Pruitts couldn't have known about it because the cracks wouldn't have come to light at all if the McCabes hadn't tampered with the basic footprint. She and Hollis had discussed it at length and neither could see a way around repairs to the foundation.

The whole of it made her all the more anxious because she and Hollis weren't yet comfortable with extravagance. Early in their married life, they'd been preoccupied with keeping track of pennies so the dollars wouldn't catch them by surprise. It was only after Hollis had gone to work for Tigg Montgomery that the money started rolling in. After years in the banking industry, Hollis had been tapped to oversee the wealth management arm of Tigg's investment firm, a dream job from his perspective. At first Lauren had reveled in the sense of safety after years of feeling financially insecure. In the past two years, his salary had soared and there were generous year-end bonuses as well. They had to do *something* with all the money and at least real estate was tangible. Tigg encouraged them to celebrate their good fortune. He said she and Hollis had limited their options; their horizons had shrunk in exact proportion to their scrimping mentality. He said it was time to "expand and embrace," time to let abundance into their lives and enjoy the many perks of Hollis's success.

To Lauren, having been poor all her life, this newfound wealth still felt impermanent. What came so easily could just as easily be taken away. Gradually, she'd come to believe in their good fortune. Hollis had hitched his wagon to a star. Tigg was a man who seemed to see into the future. He anticipated market trends. He foresaw shifts in the economy that he manipulated to his own gain. The better he did, the more appealing his company became. Friends and acquaintances were so eager to benefit from his financial savvy that Tigg had reached the point where he was turning people away, which only increased the clamor for his investment savvy.

Tigg himself lived modestly and she admired that about him. He was still in the same house in Colgate he'd bought the first year he and Joan were married. True, he had rented a large office complex downtown, but the space wasn't pretentious. He and Joan had divorced. He'd married a second time and when that didn't work out, he'd married again. Lauren had liked the first two wives, but she could barely tolerate the third, despite talk of the third time being the charm. His latest—Maisie—was a raven-haired, blue-eyed twenty-eight-year-old, who'd made a point of involving herself in numerous feel-good causes around town. She was stylish, loved travel, adorned herself in designer clothes and expensive jewelry. She had no children, so she had a gorgeous figure on top of everything else.

Of course, the McCabes and Montgomerys spent inordinate amounts of time in one another's company, even going so far as to vacation together. Tigg was Hollis's boss and it was important to him that the two couples remain close. On the many occasions when Lauren and Maisie entertained back and forth, Maisie always managed to do it better. Lauren had taken note of that. Maisie had a flair for simple but elegant dinner parties, and she harbored perhaps a wee, nearly spiteful sense of competition. Hollis made sure no whisper of distaste ever escaped Lauren's lips. The subject of Maisie and Tigg was sacrosanct and Lauren had learned to keep any negative comments to herself.

At five o'clock, Lauren poured herself a glass of wine and did what she thought of as a "walkabout," her personal tour of the construction to see what had been accomplished, which never looked like much. She and Hollis usually did this together, but he wouldn't be home until seven and Fritz was at a tennis lesson that lasted until six. Given all the noise and the dust, the beeping of the heavy equipment backing up, and countless worker bees trooping in and out, she expected miraculous changes. Occasionally she'd note that a hunk of wall had been torn out or an inexplicable two-by-four had been nailed between two joists. Most of it was the same grim wasteland she'd been looking at for months.

She was relieved when she reached the wing where the guest bedrooms were located. When the time came, they'd freshen up the paint and wallpaper, but for now it was fine. Lauren and Hollis had taken the original master suite and Fritz was in a bedroom in this wing off the den. Fritz had asked them to put in a separate entrance for him, but Lauren had put her foot down. At fifteen, he didn't drive, but he was hard enough to keep track of as it was. Once he had his license, he was going to take off like a shot. She didn't want to give him carte blanche to come and go as he pleased. For now, he was good about showing up for meals, coming in at a decent hour, and helping around the house. In return, she'd instituted an open-door policy with his friends, who were welcome at any time. This measure of hospitality allowed her to keep an eye on the kids Fritz was hanging out with and gave her some assurance that he was behaving himself. She'd had a rough couple of years with him. At ages twelve and thirteen he was argumentative, rude, and uncooperative. She'd put him in counseling and that helped, as did the medication his shrink had prescribed. Now he was back to his old sunny self—the bright, funny boy she'd so adored since birth.

Passing his room, she reached out automatically and

tried the doorknob, pleased to find the room unlocked. During the difficult years, he'd guarded his privacy, protecting his possessions as though he lived among traitors and spies. She knew for a fact that he was smoking dope back then because she smelled it through the heating vents, a phenomenon he was happily unaware of. She liked keeping track of what he did behind her back. It was a form of containment, insurance that his rebellion was well under their control. If he'd strayed too far, she would have stepped in, but he seemed to have gotten what his shrink had referred to as "oppositional defiance" out of his system. Now his vice of choice was an occasional beer, which she decided was harmless in the face of other, far more serious possibilities. His academic record at Climping Academy, the private school in Horton Ravine, had been another indication that he was on track. He wasn't a brilliant student, but the "average" student at Climp was still miles ahead of anyone at the public high schools in the area.

She had named her son Friedrich after her father, but Hollis had started calling him Snickle-Fritz when he was not quite two and Fritz, the shortened version of the name, had stuck. The boy was of medium height, slightly built, which made him appear younger than he was. He wore his brown hair with a side part that was all but obliterated by the natural curl, more pronounced now that he was wearing it longer. His eyes were brown, his complexion clear. He was still baby-faced, though she imagined within a year his features would lengthen and mature. She had seen photographs of Hollis at fifteen and again at seventeen and the transformation had been dramatic.

After years as a loner, Fritz had recently befriended three boys who were also students at Climping Academy. One was a kid named Troy Rademaker, whose father had died the year before when a heart attack took him down. Troy was currently attending Climp on an athletic scholarship, which had been arranged in deference to his reduced financial state. Troy was the youngest of five boys in a family of Irish Catholics. His dad had been a draftsman in an architectural firm when he was stricken.

He'd left enough insurance to pay the house off, but with not a lot left over, which meant that Troy was forced to fend for himself. Lauren thought this was a good example for Fritz, who tended to take his good fortune for granted. There had never been much chemistry between the two, but recently the boys had discovered interests in common, filmmaking being prime.

Troy was stocky, with a buzz cut of red hair and blue eyes. His smile was goofy, showing upper teeth that were crooked and really should have been corrected by now. The second kid was Austin Brown—again, someone Lauren had known for years. Troy and Austin were well regarded, made top grades, and were generally considered all-around good guys.

The third kid in the mix was Tigg's son, Bayard, who was now living with his father and stepmother. He'd been with Joan in Santa Fe for the twelve years since she and Tigg divorced. Tigg didn't get to see him often, but from what she'd heard, the boy was doing well until he reached puberty, when he'd started getting into trouble: truancy, failing grades, acts of vandalism that had cost Tigg plenty in restitution. The previous spring, in desperation, Joan had sent him back to his father with the clear understanding that the arrangement would be permanent. She'd had it with him.

The sudden friendship among the four had taken Lauren by surprise. Fritz was a sophomore, while Austin, Troy, and Bayard were juniors. As a result, when the cheating scandal had come to light, Fritz was mercifully in the clear. Lauren's instinct was to shunt the subject to one side. After all, Fritz hadn't been involved directly, so in some respects he'd been unaffected. The incident involved what was known as the California Academic Proficiency Test, given at the end of eleventh grade to determine eligibility for advancing to their senior year. Austin and Bayard were apparently in no danger of failing, but Troy's grades were critical to his keeping his scholarship. He'd been caught cheating, as had a girl named Poppy Earl, another of the privileged Horton Ravine kids.

She did a quick tour of Fritz's room, gratified to see things reasonably tidy. The bed had been made, and while the covers were lumpy and off-kilter, she appreciated the attempt. She'd learned long ago that if you wanted a job done, you couldn't then turn around and criticize the outcome if it wasn't quite up to your standards. Fritz had picked up his dirty clothes and jammed them in the hamper. The trash hadn't been emptied, but at least all the trash was *in* the can and that was an improvement over the usual chaos. The shades were drawn and the room smelled of adolescent male, a musky unpleasant scent of oil glands and sweat.

She set her half-finished wineglass on the bed table and straightened the spread. The desk was littered with books which she was tempted to reshelve, but she didn't want to tip her hand. Fritz didn't need to know she'd cruised through in his absence. In the VCR, she spotted a video cassette with a hand-lettered label that read "A Day in the Life of . . ." She smiled to herself because she had a fairly good idea what this was. For his birthday in March, she and Hollis had bought him what he called an "awesome" sound system, as well as a television set and a video cassette player, the latter apparently providing the inspiration for the four boys—Fritz, Bayard, Austin, and Troy—to make a documentary. Many meetings ensued and it amused her to listen to the tenor of their negotiations. They had adopted and discarded half a dozen ideas, but they'd finally settled on a topic they were very secretive about. She had been curious, but she'd curbed her natural tendency to probe. She assumed they'd need a script, but one of the other three must have been in charge of the writing. It certainly wasn't Fritz, whose grades in English languished in the C to C+ range. Whatever the subject, they'd taken the project seriously, working into the wee hours the weekend before.

Fritz told her Bayard was editing the footage, using some kind of computer software that allowed him to monkey with the tape. He'd worked on it for two days and finally dropped it off the night before. Troy had come over for supper and afterward, he and Fritz had been closeted in his room with their heads together, laughing away like crazy. She'd tried to jolly them into giving her a preview, but Fritz said the film still needed work.

This, then, was their project in its current state. She checked the cassette window, noting that the tape hadn't been rewound. She'd have given anything to have a peek, but did she dare? She hesitated, glancing at her watch. 5:22. Troy's mother had dropped the boys at their tennis lesson and Lauren had agreed to pick them up at six. The country club was less than ten minutes away so she had a good thirty minutes before she had to leave. The remote control device was on the cart. She picked it up and turned on the set, then pushed the tape all the way into the slot. It took her a minute to figure out how to switch from cable reception to the VCR. She pushed Rewind and waited while the machine whirred and finally clicked to a stop. She knew she was being nosy, but she couldn't help herself.

She pushed Play, keeping half an ear tuned in case Hollis came home early. He disapproved of her prying into Fritz's business, but she didn't like the distance puberty had created between them. She understood that a boychick had to separate from his mother in order to develop into a man. Fritz needed male role models and male bonding. Where she'd been close to her son right up until middle school, Hollis was the one whose company and counsel he now sought. Her instincts and impulses were 180 degrees out of phase and nothing she said seemed to carry any weight. Hollis was, at the same time, the tougher disciplinarian and the more laissez-faire in his concerns. He thought their job was to stand back and let Fritz make his own decisions. Hollis felt the only way Fritz was going to learn anything was to take risks, make mistakes, and suffer the consequences. *She* thought their job was to keep watch over the process and step in if he was headed down the wrong road. If Fritz veered into dangerous territory, it was their responsibility to correct him before the effect of his choices blew back on him. He was a minor. They were liable if his decisions turned out to be poor ones.

Lauren perched on the desk chair, already smiling again in anticipation, wondering what sort of half-baked drama the boys had cooked up. The first images that appeared she recognized as the rec room in the Rademakers' basement. The camera did a slow pan from the stairs, across the pool table, to the wet bar where Troy and Fritz sat in conversation, dressed in bathing trunks. They were drinking beer, or what appeared to be beer, judging from the many bottles lined up to the left and right of them. They'd apparently been in the swimming pool because she could see Fritz's hair was curling with dampness. Troy, a year older than Fritz, was muscular, his chest covered in a fine mat of red hair and freckles where Fritz's chest was hairless and narrow. He and Troy started horsing around in the clumsy way of drunks. Their laughter was shrill and it was clear they were more tickled with themselves than they had any reason to be. The sound quality was poor and there didn't seem to be any coherent dialogue. As she watched, Fritz rolled and lit a joint, taking a deep hit before he passed it over to his friend. Were they seriously smoking dope on film or was the whole scene staged for "documentary" purposes?

The camerawork was shaky. "Handheld" it was called, a technique used to make a film look like authentic found footage. Maybe the boys were making a horror flick. That seemed to be the level of sophistication they were operating from. She half expected a mummy or a zombie to appear, walking stiff-legged into the frame. There was commotion to the right and someone else appeared—a girl wrapped in a bath towel. This wasn't anyone Lauren recognized. If she was a student at Climping Academy, she wasn't a junior or senior because Lauren knew all the kids in both classes. The girl's feet were bare and her wet hair was plastered against her head as though she'd just gotten out of the swimming pool as well. She reached for a beer bottle and chugged it, clutching the towel to her chest. She seemed to be as goofily drunk as the boys, which made Lauren uncomfortable even if the three were mugging for effect. Fritz poured her a tall glass of gin and she chugged half of it down. The two boys began urging her to strip. She did a halfhearted bump-and-grind and when Troy reached for the towel, she backed away from him, holding on for dear life. She was doubled over with laughter, shrieking, "Troy, get away!" As the scene continued, the girl stumbled and nearly fell, but the horseplay was good-natured and she didn't seem upset.

The film stopped abruptly and then took up again. The girl was now on her back, naked and sprawled on the sofa. She lifted herself on her elbows, perhaps intending to speak, but she was apparently not sufficiently coherent. Her movements were clumsy and she seemed to be having trouble focusing her eyes. She was well-developed for someone who looked so young. Her breasts were generous and her pubic hair was a dark bush highlighted vividly against her pale skin. Laughing, she tried again, addressing someone across the room.

"Hey, handsome. Gimme a hand. I need help."

"Who, me?" The voice was one Lauren had heard before but couldn't quite identify.

"Come on and give me a kiss."

The camera made a clumsy rotation turn until Austin Brown was center stage. It never even occurred to Lauren to wonder who was doing the camera work. Austin was sitting sideways in an overstuffed chair, his legs flung over one arm while he leafed through a magazine. He was wearing his usual sport coat, dress shirt, and tie, which seemed incongruous in light of the others in their bathing suits.

"Pretty please?"

He smiled without bothering to look up. "Kiss you, Iris? No way. I'm the director, not a bit player. I'm the guy in charge."

"The auteur," the older of the two boys interjected.

"Right. The mastermind," Austin said with a glance at her. "Besides, you look like you're doing well enough on your own."

Her reply came off camera. "Party pooper. You're no fun."

The time frame shifted, a period of blank tape and then live action again. The camera tracked back to the girl and by the time Fritz reappeared, he'd peeled out of his bathing suit and was swinging it over his head like a stripper. He tossed his Speedo out of frame and she heard Troy guffaw. "Hey, dude. This is awesome. Let's rock and roll."

The camera panned. Lauren caught her breath, her heart suddenly pounding, and her posture stiffened with dismay. "Oh lord no," she said. She put a hand over her mouth, her cheeks burning with shame.

Both boys were naked and fully erect. The girl, Iris, had apparently passed out on the pool table while the boys showed off for each other, egging each other on. Troy was the first to approach the girl, wagging his stiff penis while Fritz sidled up to her and fondled one of her bare breasts. What followed was a full-on sexual assault. They seemed to do anything that occurred to them while the girl lay passive and unresisting. She might have been acting, but Lauren doubted it. The boys flipped her over on her stomach, her bare butt occupying much of the screen. Lauren stared as though hypnotized, grimacing as the tape rolled on. She knew she should shut the machine down, but she still held out the perverse expectation that this was all in good fun. It was tacky and in bad taste, but if the girl was a willing participant, that might make all the difference. From the left of frame, Fritz appeared with an open can of Crisco, which he held aloft, pretending to twist an imaginary mustache like the villain in a melodrama. Fritz held out the can to Troy, who dug his fingers into the white grease. The scene jumped to Troy with his back to the camera as he pumped away at the girl on the pool table.

Lauren covered her mouth as though to repress all sound, shaking her head in horror. Meanwhile, Fritz picked up a pool stick and stuck it in the Crisco, coating the thick wooden handle as he moved toward the girl. Austin Brown's looking on, so cold and unconcerned, made it all the worse. Lauren pressed the Off button. Hands shaking, she pushed the button that ejected the tape. It popped partway out, the title on the label so ironic in retrospect. She turned the VCR off and sat without moving, trying to collect herself. She felt ill.

Disgusting. It was all disgusting, behavior so vile she could hardly take it in. What was she supposed to do? The two had raped and sexually abused the girl. Hollis would die if he knew. This obscene home movie was more than criminal, it was totally depraved. Her first impulse was to demolish the tape—crush or burn or bury it—but she couldn't bring herself to do it. The tape was evidence of a crime and if she destroyed it, then Fritz and Troy could deny everything and what proof would she have?

The doorbell rang, causing Lauren to jump as adrenaline shot through her. Maybe someone else had given him a ride home and he'd found himself without his house key. She couldn't let him know she'd seen the tape until she talked to Hollis.

The doorbell rang a second time.

"Just a minute," she called. Not that anyone on the front porch could hear her.

In a flash, she could see the future stretching out in all its consequences. She and Hollis would have to call the police. Troy's mother would have to be told. They'd have to protect Iris's identity, but Lauren wasn't even sure she'd been aware of what was going on. Had she been drugged? In any case, what would follow? A criminal trial, a civil suit? Fritz in disgrace and themselves mired in ruin? Lauren pictured the repercussions stretching out for years to come.

From the front hall, she heard, "Hello? Mrs. McCabe? It's me, Sloan."

Lauren said, "Shit."

Sloan was one of the many kids who wandered in and out at will. She'd apparently found the front door unlocked, had opened it, and then stuck her head in and called a greeting.

"I'll be right there!" Lauren called.

In a panic, Lauren went through a quick debate. Take the tape or leave it where it was? She didn't dare act on her own. She couldn't make a decision with such profound implications without discussing it with Hollis. They'd always handled the major issues that way. This incident would have to be made public, regardless of the scandal, regardless of penalties that would have to be paid. That she and Hollis would suffer was irrelevant. Fritz could take whatever punishment the law dished out. Neither she nor Hollis would shield him from the outrage and venom he'd have heaped on him when the tape came to light. He deserved every bit of it. And that poor girl? Would she ever be the same?

She left the tape in the machine. There was no time to rewind, but maybe Fritz wouldn't remember that he'd watched a portion the night before. She wanted to smash the plastic housing, rip out the tape, and cut it in tiny pieces, anything to repudiate the contents. She'd do nothing until Hollis got home and they'd had a chance to confer. At the last minute she remembered her wineglass and snatched it off the bed table.

She left Fritz's room, closing the door behind her, and hurried down the hall, setting the wineglass on a console table as she passed.

Sloan was standing in the foyer, well-mannered enough that having entered the house and announced her presence, she was waiting for Lauren to appear. Lauren could see her big white dog peering in the open door from the porch. Butch was a Great Pyrenees, a good hundred and forty pounds of protectiveness that Sloan took with her everywhere. Sloan knew dogs weren't allowed in the McCabe house and the dog apparently knew that too, though his exclusion was cause for an eager whimpering in hopes someone would relent.

Lauren said, "Sloan, sweetie. I'm sorry. I didn't hear you knock. What can I do for you?"

"Is Fritz home?"

"He's not. I was just leaving to pick him up at the club. He and Troy have a tennis lesson."

Lauren was aware she sounded rattled, but Sloan didn't seem to notice.

"Would it be all right if I waited?"

"Not today, hon. This isn't a good time. Ordinarily, it would be fine, but something's come up. I'm sorry."

"Don't worry about it. I can always catch him at school."

"I'll tell him you stopped by."

"No need. It's not important. I'll talk to him on Monday."

Sloan made no move to leave.

"Is there anything else?"

"No, sorry. I'll let you go."

Lauren moved to the door and held it opened, embarrassed to be so pointed in encouraging the girl to go. Sloan gave her a quick smile and retreated to the porch. Lauren closed the door and stood for a moment with her forehead resting against the frame. The nightmare was just beginning and she was already caught in the horror of it.

She grabbed her car keys and proceeded to the garage. She slid into the BMW, turned the key in the ignition, and backed out of the driveway. She did a quick turn onto the street and straightened the steering wheel as she headed toward the club. Half a block down, she passed Sloan, with Butch straining at his leash. Sloan gave her a cheery wave.

Lauren returned the wave halfheartedly in the rearview mirror, as though Sloan might take note of her acknowledgment. Once she'd turned the corner, though Lauren wasn't aware of it, Sloan turned on her heel with a purpose and walked back to the house.

11

Wednesday, September 20, 1989

Poppy's stepmother continued down the hall. "Would you like iced tea?"

"If it's no trouble," I said. With any meeting, the offer of tea or coffee ensures more time together. If you're not offered "refreshments," chances are you'll be in and out the door in ten minutes or less.

When we reached the kitchen, she paused to speak to the woman who was scouring the sink. "Q, sweetie. Could I ask you to fix us a couple of glasses of iced tea?"

"Q sweetie" was a white woman in her sixties, wearing a red bandana tied across her head like Cinderella. She had a prominent nose and a pugnacious lower jaw. "Can do," she said. "Lemon and sugar?"

"That would be nice. We'll be in the family room."

We crossed the hall and she showed me into a spacious glassed-in side porch, comfortably done up with rattan furniture. The sturdy cushions were covered in a geometric pattern of black and red. She settled at one end of the couch and I took a seat in the chair adjacent.

"I'm guessing you're looking for Poppy in relation to Fritz McCabe," she said. "When I read about his release, I wondered if that unfortunate business would open up old wounds."

I could have kissed her for saving me the awkward process of getting down to business. "Apparently so. Somebody seems to have it in for him, and his mother asked me to look into it. Do you know Lauren and Hollis?"

"He handles our investments through the wealth management department at our bank," she replied. "Lauren and I have served together on a number of committees. Both are lovely. What do you mean, someone has it in for Fritz? That sounds ominous."

"The details are complicated and I really can't go into it without Lauren's okay."

"Of course. I wouldn't want you to violate a confidence. How does Poppy fit in?"

"I'm hoping she'll have an insight. Do you know if she's still in touch with kids she went to school with?"

"I'm sure she is, at least with some. Who have you talked to so far?"

"Iris Lehmann, who wasn't exactly forthcoming. In truth, this is a fishing expedition. Poppy happened to be next on my list. I take it she's here in town."

"She's in a cottage near the beach."

As she rattled off the address, I reached in my bag and took out my index cards. She recited the phone number as well. I made a note of the information.

"Will she be home now or does she work?"

"Oh, she'll be home. She's self-employed."

I said, "Ah." Something in the woman's tone suggested self-employment, in Poppy's case, was synonymous with her being a shiftless layabout. "How much do you remember about Sloan Stevens's death?"

"I read about it in the papers like everyone else. Coverage was extensive, especially during the trial. That's all we talked about. We were in a state of shock—the whole community. These were good kids. Or so we thought.

There's not a parent alive who didn't shudder at what happened to that poor girl. My husband was horrified. He'd known her all her life."

"What about you? Did you know her?"

"I knew who she was. I wasn't personally acquainted with the family."

"Did you have children at Climp?"

"My son graduated the year before. I should probably mention Sherman's first wife, Emmie, walked out on him about that time, leaving him to deal with the aftermath on his own."

"That must have been hard on Poppy."

"She shut right down. Refused to talk about any of it. Still won't."

"You're referring to the murder or her mother leaving?"

"I'm not sure she can separate the two. She'd been suspended from school because of a cheating incident and that was upheaval enough. Sloan's death was devastating; a blight on so many lives. Of the young people involved, none of them have turned out well. One way or another, they've all been marked by the tragedy."

"I wasn't aware of that," I said. "I understand Austin Brown is still at large."

"It's hard to imagine him as a fugitive. I won't say I'm sympathetic, but he thought he was going to be a prominent attorney like everyone else in his family and where is he today?" Her question was meant to be rhetorical, but she paused before she went on. "Fritz, as you know, spent the last eight years in prison, getting into trouble and suffering the consequences. Bayard Montgomery doesn't work. In fact, he doesn't do much of anything. His father left him a fortune, which has insulated him from the necessity for a job. When you're not obliged to support yourself, you're essentially rudderless. Then there's Iris, who hasn't amounted to a hill of beans. I don't know about Troy."

"He's an auto mechanic."

"Supporting my point," she said. "My former husband was an estate attorney and when Troy's father died, he did what he could to salvage the situation. The

Rademakers were good Catholics and of the five boys, Troy was the last one at home. His father was a draftsman with an architectural firm. He died of a sudden heart attack, fifty-two years old, with mortgage insurance, but not much else. Mary Frances was able to pay off the house and she did what she could. Troy's brothers had all finished college by then and Troy understood he was on his own. I think that's why he was tempted to cheat, to make sure he could keep his grades up, protecting his scholarship. When the scandal erupted at Climp, that was the end of that. Without financial aid, he had no chance for a decent education. Of course, the years in prison didn't help his cause. A good mechanic is a treasure, but I'm sure Troy had a different vision of his future."

"What about Poppy?"

Loretta waved a hand. "She's a mess. It might sound harsh, but it's the truth. Both of her sisters are high-achievement types. Adrienne's a pediatrician and Cary does R and D for Pfizer pharmaceuticals. That's research and development."

"Got it," I said.

"They both knew from an early age what they wanted to do in life and they went after their goals with a vengeance. Poppy was Emmie's midlife surprise. Sherman would be the first to tell you they hadn't planned on a third child. As a result, Poppy had it tougher than the other two. The way he tells it, the older girls were self-motivated and they competed to see which one of them could outshine the other. Poppy came along eight years later and got the short end of the stick. I guess there was only so much brainpower to go around. He and Emmie watched her struggle through elementary school and junior high. It was painful, but there wasn't much they could do to help. Tutors, of course, and summer school was inevitable since she usually fell short in at least one class during the academic year. She may have a learning disability that was never diagnosed."

"Her sisters went to Climp?"

"Oh, yes. No question about that. Sherman and Emmie argued about sending Poppy, but she always felt she was being slighted, so they didn't dare break the tradition when it came to her. She should have done well at Climp. Small class sizes, a teaching staff that was top drawer. It's not like she didn't try. She just couldn't keep up. In my opinion, though no one ever asks, of course, Poppy's a spoiled brat. She's terribly defensive and she's so *glum*."

I laughed at the unexpected term. "Glum?"

"Always down at the mouth. Nothing goes right for her. She has the same competitive streak as her older sisters, but while they're striving to get ahead, using their energy to accomplish something in the world, Poppy's focus is on them. Whatever they have, she feels she should have the same thing, earned or otherwise."

"Do you get along with her?"

"Not at all. I'm surprised you'd ask. If I liked the girl, I wouldn't be saying half the things I've said. She takes shameless advantage of her father, which means that he and I do battle every time something comes up. Not that I have much say in the matter. In some ways, I have her best interests at heart; more so than he does, at any rate. He doesn't see it that way. He's busy trying to assuage his guilt because she's had such a hard time in life. In my view, she brings her problems on herself, but she's convinced it's all a conspiracy. Half the time she persuades him it's his fault."

"Do you know Sloan's mother? I'm wondering how she fared in all of this."

"I know her, but not well. She had a drinking problem in those days, but after Sloan was killed, she never touched another drop. That's the only good that's ever come out of it."

"I've been thinking I should talk to her, but I don't want to intrude."

"No worries on that score. Margaret isn't shy when it comes to Sloan. Her daughter is all she talks about."

"Are there other children?"

"Two boys from Paul Seay's first marriage. Both are still around as far as I know. A year after Sloan died,

Margaret and Paul divorced. The boys were of an age where they needed their father's influence, so they elected to live with him. I don't know what his first wife thought about it, but apparently, there was no bad blood. The older one in particular adored Sloan. I understand he looks after Margaret, who really doesn't have any other friends.

"Tell her you're writing an article. She's always phoning journalists, trying to keep the story in the public eye. She's convinced that one of these days someone will read about Sloan's death and blow the whistle on Austin Brown, wherever he might be."

I pumped her for information for as long as I dared and then returned to my car with Poppy's address in hand. I took the back way out of Horton Ravine, using the road that ran along the bluff and then exited through the rear gates. From there, I followed the road down the hill and on to Ludlow Beach. Santa Teresa City College was planted on the hillside opposite, with imposing views of the Pacific Ocean. I drove another block and a half, made a left turn, and then a right onto her street.

Poppy lived in a small board-and-batten cottage, one of eight forming a U-shape that enclosed a gracious swath of lawn. There were a number of these small rental properties in Santa Teresa—mini-communities that shared common ground. Though small, each of the structures boasted two bedrooms, a living room with a working fireplace, a kitchen, and one bathroom. The floors were hardwood and there were shutters at the windows, which also sported flower boxes planted with an array of marigolds. I knew all of this because one of the units was available to rent and the sign posted out front detailed the amenities.

Poppy's cottage was one of three to the right of the grass courtyard. I knocked at her door.

A neighbor peered out of her window, which looked out onto Poppy's porch. "She's not here," the woman yelled through the glass.

"Do you know when she'll be back?"

The woman shook her index finger to indicate no

without further explanation. I stood there for a moment, debating my options. If I thought Poppy was returning soon, I'd wait for her, but it was coming up on noon and I wanted to feel I'd been productive. I decided against leaving her a note. There was no way to spell out my questions without meeting her face-to-face, and as was usually the case, I didn't want her forewarned. Nothing worse than giving people time enough to organize their stories. Meanwhile, the auto repair shop where Troy was employed was only seven blocks away, so I returned to my car and headed in that direction.

Better Brand Auto Repair was located in a narrow building that had enjoyed a former life as a service station. Out in front, where the gasoline pumps had been planted, there was a covered parking pad that once sheltered patrons who'd pulled in to fill the tanks on their Model As. The current business specialized in luxury imports: Mercedes-Benz, BMW, Nissan, Volvo. KEEP THE HORSES RUNNING UNDER YOUR HOOD said a separate sign board. I opened the door and went in.

Two adjoining offices occupied the rooms to my left, with space enough for a narrow counter that separated the reception area from the two-person bay that housed two desks, two rolling chairs, phones, a printer, an adding machine, files, and bookcases lined with manuals. On the near side of the counter, there were two chairs, a coffee machine, and a water dispenser with paper cups. The one woman working was middle-aged, businesslike, and brisk without being unfriendly. Her hair was a complicated arrangement of braids and curls, held in place with little metal clips shaped like butterflies. On one wrist, she wore a collection of stray rubber bands.

I said, "Hi. I'm looking for Troy."

"He took an early lunch."

"Do you know when he'll be back?"

"Oh, he's here. You'll find him at a picnic table in the side yard."

I retraced my steps, going out the office door and around to the left as specified by the thumb she'd hooked over her shoulder. Against the side of the building there was a large metal trash bin and a rolling cart filled with tires. Four vehicles parked along the fence were covered with canvas car cozies. I crossed the cracked asphalt driveway to a grassy patch where a wooden picnic table had been planted with a bench attached on either side.

Troy had his metal lunchbox set out on a square of waxed paper that he was using as a place mat. He'd placed his sandwich, a cluster of green grapes, a Baggie full of carrot sticks, and an oatmeal cookie in a semicircle along the edge, the whole of it anchored by a small milk carton of the sort you get in elementary school. The exterior of the lunchbox featured characters from *Sesame Street*: Ernie, Oscar the Grouch, Big Bird, and the Cookie Monster.

He pushed the last of the sandwich into his mouth and took a swallow of milk while he watched me approach. His coppery red hair contrasted nicely with his navy blue coveralls. He wiped his hands on a paper napkin, saying, "Help you?"

"Kinsey Millhone. You're Troy."

"That's right." His chin and jaw were well defined and his blue eyes were small, sheltered under pale brows. His hands were oil-stained, his fingernails edged in black. His smile revealed endearingly crooked teeth. Even from across the table, I could smell peanut butter on his breath.

"Sorry to interrupt your lunch."

"I'll keep on eating, if it's all the same to you."

"Please do," I said. I sat down at the table and turned sideways so I could lift my feet over the bench, which was permanently affixed.

He tossed a grape in the air, moving his head so he could catch it in his mouth. He missed and the grape bounced off the table and out of sight. He smiled sheepishly and held out the grape cluster. I took three.

He popped a grape in his mouth and looked at me with interest. "I'm guessing social worker, parole officer, or US Marshal. Which?"

I looked down at myself. "In this outfit? None of the above."

"Private eye."

"Right."

"Then you must be here about Fritz."

I pointed at him by way of reply. "Have you seen him since he came home?"

"Nope. Even as a free man, I stick to parole conditions. No alcohol, no firearms, and no contact with convicted felons."

"I'm impressed."

"No need. I told a fib. We did talk. He called yesterday and told me about the tape. He said his parents hired a detective. Putz that I am, I was picturing a guy."

"Happens that way sometimes. I'm used to it," I said.

"How'd you end up working for the McCabes?"

"I was recommended by an attorney who's a friend of mine."

He broke his cookie in half and took a bite. "That's tough—the demand for hush money. You have any idea what they'll do?"

"They don't want to pay, that's for sure. I take it you weren't slapped with a similar demand?"

"No point. I'm broke. You think I should hire an attorney?"

"I don't know what an attorney could do for you until we see where this goes."

He smiled ruefully. "I can't afford one anyway, so scratch that idea."

"Who represented you at the trial?"

"A public defender, but she's moved on to private practice. She did a shit job anyway, at least from my perspective," he said.

"People who go to jail often say the same thing."

"I'm ignoring that remark," he said. "So what's the plan? Sit around waiting for the other shoe to drop?"

"There's a chance I'll catch up with the blackmailer first and that might change the game."

"Scale of one to ten. How likely is that? Ten being guaranteed."

"I'd give it a three."

He laughed.

"You have family?" I asked.

"Mom and four brothers. She's still in town, though I don't see much of her. Couple of times a year at best. Brothers are spread all over and I don't see much of them, either. I'm the son who disappointed everyone. They keep telling me I let the family down, like I'm not aware of it."

"I'm sure you learned something."

"No doubt, but I'm not sure what. I take that back. I learned how easy it is to do nothing. We all knew Austin was a creep."

"What kind of creep?"

"A dangerous one. What you have to understand about the guy is that he liked to ferret out our secrets and use them to lord it over us. He had this thing he used to do with Bayard. He'd raise his index finger and say, 'One call, dude. One call.' "

"Meaning it would only take one call to blow the whistle on him?"

"Pretty much," he said. "And no, I don't know what Bayard's secret was."

"Did he have something on you?"

"Well, yeah, but I'd just as soon not get into it."

"Come on. This is just between us. I won't tell anyone."

He thought for a moment and then said, with some reluctance, "Okay. Here it is. I stole five hundred bucks."

"When was this?"

"After my dad died, my mom was strapped for cash. He'd left enough insurance to pay off the house but she needed a short-term loan to cover the house payment until the money came in. I was soliciting donations for our church to provide Thanksgiving dinner to needy families. The treasurer assumed we'd be honest about how much we'd collected. I shorted her by five bills, which I always intended to pay back. Guess I better get on it now I brought it up. The point is, I was ashamed of myself. Mortified that I'd done it."

"Did Austin use that against you?"

"Once. That's how I ended up driving my truck that night."

"He sounds like a bully."

"That was our fault in part. We just didn't have the guts to stand up to him. How can I atone for that? I keep saying I'm sorry, for all the good it does. The dead don't come back. Done is done and what I did was bad."

"Sounds like you've taken responsibility."

"Which doesn't erase regret. I don't know what else to do but get on with life and be the best person I know how."

"Are you married?"

"Wife and two little boys. The older is two and the little guy is three months. He has some medical issues that are costing us an arm and a leg, but what can you do? Half the couples we know are up to their eyeballs in debt. My wife's great. Kerry's one of a kind. She knows I went to prison for what I did. We dated before I went in and then kept in touch. I couldn't have made it without her."

"Where did you do your time?"

"I lucked out. I was assigned to Mountain Home, which was the first mobile Conservation Camp. Inmates take a two-week training course the same as civilians and then they put us on a crew working the fire lines, mostly in Tulare and Kern counties. Santa Ana winds were bad back then. Bad every year since, now that I think about it. We chopped brush sometimes eight hours at a stretch. Forty-five pounds of gear you're carrying and you're up against flames forty and fifty feet high. Hard work. Exhausting. On the plus side, you're housed in semi-trailer rigs. No locked doors and no barbed wire. Good food. Spare time, you play pool or go out and shoot hoops. Sometimes you forget you're in prison."

"How long were you incarcerated?"

"I was sentenced to five years, but ended up serving less. This place belongs to my brother-in-law, Jim. Otherwise I'd be unemployed. His last name is Brand, which is how he came up with Better Brand Auto Repair. How'd you know where to find me?"

"My friend Ruth Wolinsky has her car serviced here."

"She's nice."

"Yes, she is," I said. "What did they charge you with?"

"Accessory after the fact, obstruction of justice, kidnapping, lying to the police, plus anything else they could throw into the mix. Oh, aiding and abetting, which they take very seriously."

"I'm surprised they didn't hit you with felony murder. I thought if you participated in a kidnapping that resulted in death, you were on the hook the same way Fritz was."

"Technically, yes. But the DA seemed more interested in Fritz than the rest of us. He was the one who pulled the gun and forced her into the truck. There was definitely some wheeling-dealing going on in the background and I confess I didn't inquire too closely, not wanting to look a gift horse in the mouth and all that stuff. I was willing to cop to most of it anyway. I mean, we all lied to the police. We alibied each other and destroyed evidence. But here's the truth. I never thought she'd die. Farthest thing from my mind. Austin was an asshole, but I didn't think he'd go that far."

"What happened that night?"

"Oh, man. Most of the time, I block it. It's been ten years and I still carry images I don't like. You want to ask questions, I'll tell you what I can."

"I understand there was a party. Where did that take place?"

"Austin's parents had a cabin off the pass. Originally, we went up there to celebrate the end of the school year. Good fun that turned ugly in the end, but that's what alcohol and dope will do. Austin and Sloan started butting heads. He said she insulted him and she owed him an apology."

"What did she say that set him off?"

"You know about the cheating scandal?"

"Sure. You and Poppy acquired a copy of an academic proficiency test and Sloan was accused of sending an anonymous note to the school administrators, telling what you'd done. Austin accused her of snitching and persuaded her classmates to shun her."

"It got worse. The night she died, she accused *him* of

writing the note, which made total sense once she said it. Of course, Austin went ballistic on her and demanded a retraction. He thought all he had to do was apply the screws and she'd cave. He took her up the mountain so she'd know he meant business."

"So this was after the party?"

"Right. When most of the kids were gone."

"How many of you were left?"

"The four of us and her."

"Meaning you, Fritz, Austin, and Bayard Montgomery."

He nodded. "Bayard was supposed to give her a ride home, but then the situation got complicated. Austin was ordering everyone around. We were giving him static, but not doing much else. At one point, she took off and Austin sent me and Bayard and Fritz after her.

"Thing was, she was still in her bathing suit with a shirt over it. She'd borrowed shoes from Austin's dad and she was clumping down the road. She was pissed off by then and she wanted to get the hell out of there. We thought she'd gone to get dressed and didn't even realize she'd disappeared until Bayard went looking for her. Anyway, she left her clothes and her purse at the cabin when she took off. We forgot all about that until later when we realized we better get rid of her stuff."

"Because by then you'd decided to claim you'd dropped her off on State Street alive when you knew she was dead."

"More or less."

"Not 'more or less.' You knew she was dead and you were covering your butts. I'm not trying to be nasty. I'm stating the obvious."

"Okay, sure. I admit it. Fritz made a bad mistake, but it was really all on Austin. This was damage control. We had to protect ourselves."

He was showing the first hint of defensiveness. I'd assumed he was being straight, reporting as truthfully as he could, but I realized he was editing as he went along.

I shook my head. "Sorry. I interrupted you. Once she took off, how'd you manage to get her back to the cabin?"

"We went after her in the truck. There was only the one road to the highway and she'd made pretty good progress. She was a jock and she was in great shape."

"She returned voluntarily?"

"Not really. I was driving, so Bayard was the one who got out to talk to her. He tried to be reasonable, but she wasn't buying it. We knew Austin was furious and things would only get worse if we showed up without her."

"What was Fritz doing all this time?"

"We made him ride in the truck bed, so he was following the conversation. He could see Bayard wasn't having any luck. Meanwhile, he had a gun that belonged to Austin's dad, so he hopped down and started yelling. He pointed it right at her and told her to get in, which she did."

"That was gutsy of him."

"That's where the kidnapping charge originated. He scared the shit out of me. Fritz was a twerp and for him to step in like that was out of character. Anyway, she did what he told her. He put her in the front seat between him and me. This time Bayard rode in the truck bed and we took off."

"Did she put up a fight?"

"Not with the gun in her ribs."

"So you guys take her back to the cabin and then what?"

"It was clear she wasn't going to back down, so that's when we took her up to Yellowweed."

"That's on Figueroa Mountain, as I remember it," I said.

Troy nodded. "Fritz and Bayard and Austin walked her up this steep trail to the campsite. Austin started hammering away at her, trying to make her say she was wrong and she was sorry. Later, Bayard said what he felt so bad about was not coming to her defense. We could have made a difference if we'd tried."

"Where were you all this time?"

"Down at the road in my pickup truck. By then, I was so freaked out my hands were shaking. I figured Austin would hassle her. You know, make her eat crow and apologize, but I thought then he'd be satisfied and we'd be heading down the mountain back to town. I waited and they were gone so long I decided I better go up and see what was happening. If Austin was still pissed, I'd do what I could to defuse the situation. I started up the path in the pitch dark. I was at the halfway point when I heard someone shout and then *pop, pop, pop, pop, pop*. Six or eight shots. Could have been fired in the air is what I hoped. Fritz whooping like a maniac. By this time I was close enough to take a look and I busted out in tears. Bayard was really shaken. He looked like he'd been hit by a truck. Fritz was all hyped up. Said he'd never killed anyone and he was totally stoked. He was jumping around like a wild man.

"Austin made me go back to the truck and get a shovel so we could bury her. By then, he'd taken the gun off Fritz and he's standing there reloading it, calm as can be, like he didn't have a care in the world. I was crying so hard I couldn't see what I was doing. Fritz sobered up, seeing me bawl like that. He'd turned white by then. All the blood drained away from his face. I thought he'd pass out. Next thing you know, he was blubbering the same as me."

"And Bayard?"

"He sat on the ground and rocked back and forth, kind of moaning to himself. We were all sick about it. Austin told us to shut the fuck up or we'd get the same as she did."

"Why move the body?"

"We didn't move her far. He said it would mess up whatever forensic evidence we might've left."

"And now you have the tape to deal with."

"Out of the frying pan," he said.

"So what's the story on that?"

He hung his head, shaking it with embarrassment. "Sounds stupid now, but it started out as a joke. Make a pseudo-porn film and then shop it around. We probably could have made some money if we'd pulled it off. It was supposed to be a satire. A mockumentary."

"Whose idea was it?"

"Austin's. He didn't want to dirty his hands, but he was happy telling us what to do."

"And Iris?"

"Oh, she was in on it."

"Really. She looked drunk to me."

He shrugged. "I was the one drunk. No doubt about that. Smoking dope and downing too much beer and gin. The movie was in bad taste, which is no excuse. We were dumb fucks. That's about all I can say. A few weeks ago, I went back to Iris and I made my peace with her. I figure she was entitled to a formal apology."

"Peace is good. At the same time, four minutes isn't much of a movie whatever your intentions."

"It was all we could manage before we ran out of steam. The point is, none of us took it seriously. It was a lark, you know? We were all laughing our asses off."

"I guess Austin had the last laugh."

"I'm sure he's still yukking it up, wherever he may be," Troy said. "I suppose you've considered the idea that he might be the one behind this blackmail scheme."

"I hadn't thought of that," I said, "but I'm sure he could use twenty-five grand about now. What's your hit on it?"

"I don't think he'd have the balls to come back. He'd never risk it."

"What if he had someone else collect for him?"

"Still risky. Coconspirator gets picked up, how long you think it'd take the cops to sweat it out of him? Why put your ass on the line for a fellow like him?"

"You have any idea who might have sent the tape?" I asked.

"If I did, believe me, I'd say so. I'm not a fan of Fritz's, but the threat of going back to prison is a nightmare."

"Cruel and unusual punishment," I said.

"You got that right." He stirred restlessly. "I ought to get back to work. Don't want to take advantage. Jim is a good guy."

He stood up and crumpled the waxed paper into a

wad and tossed it along with his empty milk carton into the trash.

I held out my hand and we shook. "I appreciate your honesty. Reliving this stuff can't be easy."

"No complaints. It's what I deserve," he said.

12

IRIS AND JOEY

Late morning, Wednesday, September 20, 1989

Joey sat on the edge of the swimming pool and applied sunblock to Iris's shoulders and back. They were at Bayard's house drinking beer, wine, and Bloody Marys with Bayard, Poppy, and Fritz. Fritz had brought along a water toy shaped like a long blue Styrofoam noodle and he was currently floating in circles with the noodle tucked under his arms. Bayard was stretched out on one of the two matching chaises longues. He was deeply tanned and his skin glistened with suntan oil. Poppy lay facedown on the matching chaise in a white bikini. She'd applied a sunblock that left a white residue on her shoulders and arms, rendering her skin so pale she looked anemic.

Lazily, Bayard said, "How's the construction trade these days? Must be doing well or you wouldn't have a day off."

"Booming. We're doing good," Joey said. He lit a cigarette, drew on it deeply, and then handed it to Iris.

Iris said, "Thanks, babe."

She turned to Bayard. "Fritz tell you about the PI his mom hired?"

Bayard said, "First I've heard of it. What's the deal?"

Fritz waved off the notion. "She won't last long. My dad doesn't care for her."

Bayard laughed. "A girl detective? You gotta be kidding me."

"Why is that so funny?" Iris asked.

"Don't go all righteous on me, Iris."

"I'd just appreciate it if you'd get up to speed. This is the twentieth century . . ."

Bayard ignored her, homing in on the subject. "What's his objection?"

"He just has no use for her and he's made that clear."

"How come she's still on the job if she's so useless?" Bayard asked.

"He's pissed off because Mom's been running the show and he doesn't like the way she's doing it."

"How come this female wonder hasn't talked to me?" Bayard said.

"Or me?" Poppy said, chiming in on his complaint.

"I'm sure she'll get around to it."

Poppy said, "Has anyone talked to Troy?"

Iris raised a hand. "I called, but his wife said he's at work. She couldn't get off the phone fast enough."

Bayard said, "Come on, gang. He's a family man. What's he want with us? I ran into him last week and he barely made eye contact. There's a chill in the air now that this has come up again. He's keeping his distance."

Iris made a face. "So what else is new? He's been doing that for years."

"None of us are feeling exactly chummy," Poppy remarked.

Fritz said, "I am."

"You would," Poppy said.

Fritz wasn't so easily put off. "I mean it. I love being with you guys."

"We think you're a peach as well," Bayard said.

"Right."

Poppy sat up and put her feet flat on the patio. Despite the sunblock, she was already looking burned, her skin a hot pink. "You know what I think? The blackmailer can't be someone who knew about the tape way back when."

Bayard looked at her with interest. "How so?"

"Because he assumes the action is real. He's taking it as gospel when you guys were just joking around. Otherwise, why would he think the tape was worth anything?"

Bayard said, "That's your view? It was all a big joke?"

"That's what you told me. Isn't that correct?"

She looked from Bayard to Joey, who said, "Don't look at me. I'm new on the scene."

Joey turned his attention to Fritz. "So what's the story on the money? Any chance your parents will change their minds?"

"About what?" Poppy asked.

"God, Poppy! Try to keep up. I get tired of having to stop and explain," Bayard said. "His parents don't want to pay. They've left him hanging out to dry."

Fritz said, "For the time being it's a non-issue, since we haven't heard a peep from the guy."

Bayard frowned. "He's not pressing you to pay? Sounds like he's not all that serious."

Fritz said, "The guy's a sadist. He wants us to sweat."

Poppy said, "Do your parents know you've told us all this stuff?"

"Are you kidding? No way. They're acting like this is all hush-hush. They don't want word to get out."

"I can understand their concern," Bayard said. "Information's dangerous."

Iris scoffed. "Information isn't dangerous."

"It is in Austin's hands."

"He's right about that," Poppy said. "He's always airing other people's dirty laundry. Anything to embarrass and humiliate us. If he hadn't hit the road when he did, there's no telling what kind of havoc he could have wreaked."

Bayard's tone was mild. "What'd he have on you, Poppy?"

Her smile faded. "None of your business."

Iris lowered herself into the pool and began to breaststroke to the far side, her hair trailing in the water.

Bayard turned to Fritz. "You still hogging the couch at Berg and Stringer's place?"

"I'm not hogging. They invited me."

Bayard said, "I can assure you I'm not as generous, so if you're looking for another host organism, don't come to me."

"What a shit. I haven't asked you for anything," Fritz said.

"Let's keep it that way."

Fritz pinched his nose and ducked under the water, coming up with a splash. He draped his arms over the flotation device and flipped the hair out of his face. "Oh hey, guys. I almost forgot. I got a good one for you. This will really crack you up. Remember I told you about Blake Edelston and Betsy Coe?"

Iris had reached the far side and she was dog-paddling back. "We know. They've been dating for months."

"That's not what I'm talking about."

"What *are* you talking about?" Bayard asked.

"I'll tell you if you'll shut the fuck up."

Bayard widened his eyes and bit his fingers as though chastened.

Fritz was so intent on his story, he didn't catch the mockery. "What happened was Blake went off to this sales convention in Las Vegas? While he's there, he meets this redheaded hottie and the two screw like bunny rabbits for two days. He thinks he can get away with it. Just keep his trap shut and who's the wiser. Turns out he picked up HPV from this chick and now he's passed it on to Bets."

Poppy said, "What's HPV?"

"Where have you been? It's a virus . . ."

"A virus, Iris," Bayard interjected, feeling clever at the wordplay.

Fritz picked up as though Bayard hadn't interrupted. "A sexually transmitted disease, dummy. Betsy's on the warpath. Now she's got these genital warts and she knows *she* didn't do anything." Fritz started cackling, the same braying laugh that got on everyone's nerves.

Poppy said, "That's gross, Fritz. I can't believe you're telling us."

Fritz was still so caught up in his enjoyment that he didn't pick up on the general chill. "No, no. That's not the point. Blake's always acting like he's so pure and above it all. He screwed around a hundred times and never got caught. You should have heard her on the phone. She tracked him down to Stringer's place and I picked up every word she said. I was all the way in the other *room*."

Joey said, "You know what, Fritz? You're out of line."

"What'd I do? I didn't do anything."

"Yes, you did," Iris said. "Blake's sex life is none of our business and it's sure as hell not our business who has an STD. You know what your problem is?"

"Aside from the fact that he's stupid?" Bayard put in.

Iris went right on. "You have no filter. Whatever crosses your mind, comes straight out of your mouth."

"Name one time."

"How about this blackmail attempt? Tape shows up and you're on the phone five minutes later, blabbing away. You're a tattletale."

"I'm not. I was scared. You're my friends. I was warning you in case the guy came after you."

Poppy said, "You also blabbed about how much he was asking for, what your parents said, what you said, how pissed off you were—"

"Because you *asked*."

"Nobody asked you if Betsy had a venereal disease," Poppy said.

Iris laughed. "Yeah, loose lips sink ships. Haven't you ever heard that one?"

"I know things I haven't told anyone," Fritz said indignantly.

Poppy said, "Such as what?"

"I don't know. Such as my theory about Austin."

Bayard thumped himself in the forehead. "Jesus, Fritz. You're about to blab something else."

Iris said, "What's your theory? Out with it. This is good. We can keep a secret even if you can't."

"This is not a secret. It's just this idea I had. People keep wondering if he's dead or alive? I think he's dead."

Poppy said, "Well, that's interesting. Based on what?"

"None of us have heard from him. If he were alive, he'd have been in touch."

Bayard said, "Why would he communicate with us?"

"We're his friends."

"No, we're not. Austin never had friends. We all hated him."

"I didn't," Fritz said.

Bayard looked at him in disbelief. "Are you shitting me? He treated you like dirt. Insulted, berated. I don't think I ever heard him say a nice word to you. And there you were, falling all over yourself promising to love, honor, and obey."

"He's a lot smarter than we are and I admired that. Shit. If I knew half of what he knew, I'd trade my silence for money anytime."

Bayard said, "You'd do that? After what this blackmailer has done to you? Nice attitude, Fritz. Really admirable."

Fritz shrugged. "What can I tell you? I learned it from him."

"Then you better unlearn it fast. Austin's an asshole. You don't want to follow in his footsteps."

Iris said, "Hold on. Forget that and back up. If he's dead, what happened to him?"

Fritz said, "I don't know. He was under pressure. He's one of those guys who'd rather die than go to jail. If he thought the cops were onto him, he might have killed himself."

"The cops *were* onto him. Thanks to you," Bayard said.

Poppy said, "Austin wouldn't kill himself. He's too self-centered."

"Maybe someone else did the job for him," Fritz said.

"Who'd kill Austin?" she asked.

Bayard said, "Who wouldn't?"

Poppy's attention was fixed on Fritz. "Answer the question. I'm really curious."

"Why would anyone kill him? To keep him quiet," Fritz said.

"About what?"

"That's just it. If he had something on you, killing him would be the only way you'd ever be safe."

Iris said, "What do you mean, 'if he had something on you'? What kind of something?"

Fritz said, "Like, suppose you were into kiddy porn and he found out. Maybe you're up for a great job that requires a background check. Austin would expose you just for the hell of it. He had something on just about everyone."

Poppy said, "We all have secrets. So what else is new?"

Fritz piped up. "I know what he had on Bayard."

Bayard snorted. "Me? Great. Now you're going to tell my secrets?"

"Give me a dollar and I won't," Fritz said, and then he pointed at Bayard and cackled. "You ought to see the look on your face!" His laughter was forced, as though he recognized his humor had bombed again. The general tenor of the gathering had soured.

Bayard shook his head. "You just can't give it up, can you?"

"Your problem is you can't take a joke."

"You're the one with problems," Poppy said, "not the rest of us."

Bayard said, "Good point. How do you know Austin's not the one who sent that anonymous note to your parents? If anyone knew how dangerous the tape was, he did."

Poppy's tone was skeptical. "What are you saying? He goes around *blackmailing* people? That's far-fetched."

"I can see his point," Joey said, coming to Bayard's defense. "What's he living on? He's gotta have money. Dude can't hold down a job. He's on the run, always looking over his shoulder in case someone's spotted him and knows who he is."

"Oh, please. You think he's blackmailing the McCabes? Even Austin isn't that devious," Iris said.

"Yes he is," Bayard said.

"Or *was*, if I'm right about him being . . ." Fritz ran a finger across his throat.

Poppy raised a hand. "You are so full of shit. If someone killed him, where's the body?"

Iris said, "That's easy. Dump him in the ocean. Biggest graveyard in the world."

"Good idea. Feed him to the sharks," Bayard remarked. "That would eliminate any telltale evidence."

Fritz said, "I know the perfect place."

"Where's that?" Bayard asked.

"I'll show you sometime," he said. "Anyway, I didn't claim it happened here in town. It could have been anywhere. I mean, how long has he been gone?"

Bayard said, "Not long enough. If we're lucky, he ran into someone who wouldn't put up with his arrogance."

Poppy said, "Nope. Don't buy it."

Fritz said, "I'm not trying to talk you into anything. I'm just giving you my opinion."

Bayard said, "You better hope he's dead, Fritzer-boy. You're the one who snitched. If he comes back, he'll be out for blood. Namely yours."

"What about you? You testified against him in court."

"He doesn't know that. He'd flown the coop by then."

"He might still have friends here. Suppose somebody leaked information?"

"Now you're talking like he's alive. So which is it?"

Fritz said, "How come you're on my case all the time?"

"Because you're a pain in the ass."

Iris got to her feet and pulled on the short cotton robe she was using as a coverall. "Well, folks. Fun as it is to sit and listen to you bicker, I'm out of here." She gathered up their towels and swim paraphernalia.

Joey stood as well and slipped his feet back into his flip-flops.

Poppy put a towel over her shoulders and found her

sunglasses. "I better get back myself. I have things to do, but thanks, Bayard. This was fun."

"Hey, come on," Bayard said. "Don't everybody leave at once."

"Thanks, man," Joey said. "Appreciate the invitation." He and Bayard shook hands.

As the three of them gathered their belongings, Bayard looked down at Fritz, who was still treading water. "Aren't you wanted somewhere else?"

"Not me. I'm free as a bird."

"Well, I'm not," Bayard said.

"There you go again . . ."

Bayard closed his eyes briefly, adjusting his attitude. "You're right. I'm a dick. Hell, you might as well stay for lunch. Ellis can rustle us up some sandwiches."

"How am I supposed to get home?" Fritz asked.

"I'll drop you off at your place. I have errands to run anyway."

Fritz brightened. "Seriously?"

"Yes, seriously," Bayard said. He turned back to the others. "Come on. I'll walk you guys out."

The four of them—Bayard, Poppy, Joey, and Iris—straggled through the patio doors and then crossed the living room. Fritz dog-paddled over to the side and lifted himself onto the edge of the pool.

In the car on the way down the drive, Joey said, "What did you think of that discussion about Austin?"

"Being dead or alive? I don't know how you could prove it one way or the other. What's your take on it?"

"Beats me. I never even knew the guy. Here's what occurred to me. If we were clever, we'd create a diversion."

Iris looked over at him. "Like what?"

"We need a shadow suspect. A stand-in for the blackmailer. Someone other than us."

"Nobody thinks it's us."

"I'm saying we conjure a boogeyman. That way, our fearless girl detective can forget everything else and chase after him."

"Who'd you have in mind?"

"Who's the obvious candidate?"

She looked at him for a moment. "Austin."

"There you go," he said.

"Why do anything?"

"Because Fritz has gotten complacent."

"No he hasn't. He's scared shitless, crying in his beer because his mommy and daddy won't pay up."

"Yeah, but what's he doing about it? Fuck all. We need to remind him how much trouble he's in."

"Ha. Like he doesn't know that already."

"I'm saying reinforce the threat. Put the squeeze on him. I've been thinking about it and I have it all worked out. We call and leave Fritz a message on the answering machine—"

Iris interrupted. "How do you know he won't pick up? Or his parents?"

"If they do, I hang up and try again another time. When I get the machine, I can make it sound like it's Austin. 'This is a voice from your past. I'm tired of screwing around. You either get the money or else.' Something to that effect. Fritz just said if Austin were alive, he'd be in touch. He hears that message and he'll assume it's him. Those recordings distort voices anyway, so that will work to our advantage. I'll give him instructions for where to deliver the money and then we'll get this show on the road."

Iris said, "There's no point telling him where to deliver the money when he doesn't have it."

"This is to light a fire under his butt. Get him motivated. Otherwise, what's his incentive for doing anything?"

"Come on, Joey. What's he supposed to do? It's obvious his opinion carries no weight with his mom and dad."

"Not our problem. That's his to work out and he better hop to," Joey said. "It's time to remind Fritz how much he stands to lose."

"So what are these instructions of yours? I'm dying to hear."

"He needs a deadline. Something concrete so this doesn't drag on and on. I'll say someone's going to pick him up somewhere downtown. Give him a day and time. Then we can drive by the location and check to see if he's cooperating."

"And if he's not?"

Joey shrugged. "We try something else."

"You know what? So far, this feels like we're just making shit up as we go along."

"It's called being flexible. If he comes up with the dough, we'll come up with a plan."

"You better think about it in the meantime."

"Baby, that's all I do." He looked over at her. "It'd be funny if this worked, wouldn't it?"

She smiled. "I don't know about funny, but it would be a hoot."

13

Wednesday afternoon, September 20, 1989

I ate lunch at my desk, trying Poppy's phone number at intervals to no avail. In the afternoon, to fill my time, I took the index cards out of my bag and typed up my notes, making a display of productivity to soothe my conscience. I was no closer to finding the McCabes' extortionist than I'd been at the outset, and the lack of progress undercut my confidence. I was entertaining a teeny tiny wee regret that I'd agreed to the job in the first place. Whatever the problem, a desire to be helpful is a risky proposition, a lesson I never seem to learn.

At five, I closed up the office and headed home. Traffic was light through the downtown streets and I was on Albanil, searching for a parking place, when a little red Mercedes-Benz convertible whizzed by. I turned my head in time to spot Cheney in the driver's seat and I felt a small jolt of happiness. Then I saw his passenger, the way-too-pretty Anna Dace. As I watched, he slowed and turned onto the parking apron in front of Moza Lowenstein's garage.

He killed the engine, got out, and walked briskly to the passenger side, where he held the door for Anna as she emerged in a long white sweater and a skirt so short, it scarcely covered her underpants. His expression was grim. She kept her head down, dashing tears from her cheeks as the two proceeded to Moza's front door. Neither seemed aware that I was in range, which suited me just fine. Anna took out her house keys and let herself in. She and Cheney chatted briefly through the open door and then he returned to his car and drove away. I hoped the poor dears hadn't had a lovers' tiff.

I changed clothes and went for my run, reflecting on life and love while my thigh muscles protested, my chest heaved, and sweat collected at the small of my back. As is true of so much in life, it was none of my business if the two of them had embarked on a relationship. Furthermore, if they quarreled, that wasn't any of my business, either. I hadn't planned to go to Rosie's that night anyway and I certainly wouldn't do so now. What if I were there and the two came in for dinner? Was I going to sit pretending not to notice while they kissed and made up or stared soulfully into one another's eyes over plates of Rosie's peculiar food? No, I was not.

I finished my three-mile stint and then used the three-block walk home to cool down. I passed through the gate and proceeded to the backyard. No sign of Lucky or Pearl, so I headed for Henry's back door, which was open to the late afternoon air. I knocked on the frame, tilting my head to the screen. "Hey, Henry? You there?"

I heard "Yo!" but the voice wasn't Henry's. It was Pearl's.

She came thumping into the kitchen from the hall, swinging her bulk between her crutches. She'd wrapped herself in an enormous apron. I watched her hump herself over to the back door and unlatch the screen. I stepped into the kitchen, noting the big pile of dirty dishes and utensils on the counter. Flour dusted the floor like a light snowfall. Henry's proofing bowl had been placed on the back of the stove with a towel over it.

"I take it Henry's not here."

"Lucky asked to borry his car so he could reclaim his dog from the veterinarian. He'd just sucked down a six-pack of beer, so Henry decided it'd be smarter if he drove."

"So now we've got a dog living here, too?"

"We gotta keep him *somewheres*. Animal Control was this close to putting him down, so Lucky had to fetch him or the poor thing would be dead."

"Didn't he have to license the dog?"

"So?"

"So that cost money. I thought he was broke."

"Henry lent him the money," she said. "What's that sour look?"

"You don't want to know."

"I do, too. That's why I asked."

"I'll tell you what bothers me. Having you camp in Henry's backyard like it's a national park. The rehab facility wants you indoors with access to a toilet. Not hobbling around in the dirt on crutches, peeing on the few plants Henry has left."

"Who put a bug up *your* heinie bumper?"

"It pisses me off that you take advantage of him. When are you going to pay your own way? You have no ambition, no self-discipline, and no skills."

"That ain't my fault," she said indignantly. "I've applied for jobs all over the place and no one'll hire me. It's discrimination and you know why? I'm a woman past forty and I'm mortally obese. Hey, I'm white and that's a plus, but otherwise I'm screwed, which the government knows or they wouldn't be sending me disability checks."

"What disability?" I asked, exasperated.

"My hip is broke. Where the hell have you been?"

I closed my eyes, practicing self-restraint. "Once your hip is healed, what's your disability?"

"I don't know. Mental?"

"You're not mental. Get serious. You're healthy,

you're smart, and you have energy to spare. It's time to pitch in your fair share."

"My share of what? This ain't even my house. I bet it was paid off years ago, so what am I pitching in for? Air and sunshine?"

"Food. Utilities. Washer and dryer. Hot showers . . ."

"I can get all of that for free at Harbor House."

"Then what are you doing here?"

"Well, I'll tell you what I'm doing here, Miss Smarty-Pants. I was saving this for a surprise, but I can see I'll have to let you in on a little secret. Henry's teaching me to bake. That way I'll have a skill and I can hire on as a baker's apprentice."

"You don't have the patience."

"I most certainly do! I'm putting up with you and that big mouth of yours, ain't I? Anyway, I watched him put a batch of dough together and it's no big deal. Just yeast, water, and flour. Mix her up, knead her until she's smooth, and that's it."

I moved over to Henry's bread proofing bowl and picked up the towel. In the bottom was a dispirited wad of ragged flour. "Is this 'her'?"

"Yep! You set her in a warm place and Nature does the rest."

I picked up the empty yeast packet lying on the counter. "I've got news for you. 'Her' is dead. You know the expiration date on this packet of yeast? June of 1984."

"Well, no wonder! I had to hunt all over and finally found that at the back of the pantry." She humped her way over to the counter and peered into the bowl. "That don't look good at all. Guess I better start me another batch."

"Why don't you wait until Henry gets home and have him demonstrate?"

"Why can't you do that?"

"I don't know how to make bread."

"Well, I'll be darned. That's the best incentive I ever heard. Conquer this and I'll have me a way to lord it over you instead of the other way around."

* * *

I let myself into the studio, took a shower, and then dressed. When I came down the spiral stairs, I sat down at my desk and tried Poppy's number again. I really didn't expect her to pick up, so when she answered after four rings, my instinct was to hang up. I didn't want to put her on notice that I wanted to talk to her and I didn't want to go through the awkward process of explaining my purpose on the phone. I depressed the plunger while she was still saying, "Hello? Hello?"

I got in my car and went around the block, coming out at Cabana Boulevard, where I took a right. She was only four blocks away, which I could have walked in the time it took. The eight cottages that formed her courtyard showed various degrees of domestication—potted plants on one porch, wicker furniture on another. One patch of yard sported a birdbath and another had a weed whacker lying on its side. I imagined a small insular group of folks who minded each other's pets when someone went out of town.

I knocked and when she came to the door, I said, "Poppy?"

"Yes?"

Her response was so guarded, I thought she was lying through her teeth. She didn't look much older than twelve, with pale blue eyes, lank blond hair, and pale cheeks overlaid with sunburn. She was so thin the knobs of her elbows stuck out like the wooden couplers in a set of Tinker Toys. The blue cotton dress she wore had cap sleeves and a sash that appeared to tie in back like garments I'd worn in fifth grade. It wasn't even stylish at the time.

"If you're selling something, I don't buy from you door-to-door types," she said.

"Sorry." I reached in my shoulder bag and took out a business card that I handed to her. I don't think I look anything like a door-to-door salesperson, but what do I know? "I chatted with Troy Rademaker and he suggested I talk to you. That's me," I said, pointing to my name like she couldn't read it for herself. "Your stepmother was kind enough to give me your address."

"A private investigator? What did I do? I didn't do anything."

"I'd like to talk about Sloan. I understand you were best friends."

"Troy told you that?"

"A couple of other classmates as well. Do you mind if I come in?"

"Not until you tell me what this is about."

"Fritz McCabe was recently released from CYA. You probably read about it in the paper."

"I don't read the paper. It's depressing."

"Has he been in touch?"

"What business is that of yours?"

This was going to be my punishment for the ease with which I'd extracted her stepmother's poor opinion of her. I said, "He served his time and now he's home again. A question's come up about a videotape he was in."

She narrowed her eyes. "Did he hire you to come around here asking about that?"

"Not Fritz. I work for someone else."

"What's this have to do with me?"

"I was told the tape was in Sloan's possession shortly before she died. I guess there's still a chance it's hidden in her room. The other thought was she entrusted it to you."

As I said this, it dawned on me (belatedly, I grant you) that it didn't matter who'd been entrusted with the tape. Maybe Sloan had given it to someone or maybe it was still in her room when her mother closed and locked the door. The tape's whereabouts for the past ten years wasn't the point. The point was, who had reason to do Fritz McCabe harm? Who wished him ill and who wanted to turn his newfound freedom into misery?

"Sorry, but she didn't 'entrust' anything to me. I knew she had the tape and I told her I wanted to see it, but she said she'd left it somewhere. She was supposed to let me know when she got it back. She never got a chance. Anyway, right now I'm in the middle of something and I don't want to take a break."

Out of the corner of my eye, I picked up movement

in her next-door neighbor's window and I caught sight of the woman I'd encountered briefly on my initial visit. I realized Poppy had offered a response and I hadn't heard a word.

I said, "I'd rather not go into it standing on your front porch. Your neighbor's been listening to every word we've said."

She glanced at her neighbor's window. She and the woman exchanged a look that Poppy held, unblinking, until the woman withdrew.

She stepped back then, allowing me to enter her living room.

She'd filled her small house with an odd assortment of 1940s furniture: heavy blond pieces inlaid with dark laminate. The wooden arms of the chairs had rounded edges and the upholstery was dark plush. The fabric reminded me of the seats in movie theaters when I was a child: short, scratchy nap of some indeterminate color. Usually there were old boogers plastered on the undersides. The area rug was green, tone-on-tone, with a pattern of overlapping leaves.

She went into her small kitchen to the breakfast nook, and I followed like Mary's little lamb. On the kitchen table, she'd set up a cutting mat, an X-acto knife, a pile of postcards, and a container of a milky substance I assumed was glue.

She'd dissected six or eight postcards, creating strands of color that she affixed to heavy-duty poster board. The design seemed to be abstract except for the occasional reference to one of the fifty states. It was interesting how decorative the word "Ohio" became when it was intermingled with "Wyoming." Nearby, she had a photograph of Sloan propped up against a cereal box.

I picked up the photo of Sloan and studied it briefly.

"How much have you heard about the tape?" she asked.

"Just Fritz's claim Sloan stole it from him. I'm wondering where it ended up."

"Why don't you ask Bayard Montgomery? They were

big old buddies back then. I was just at a pool party at his house."

She seemed to be loosening up and I wondered if I could press her for more. She was preoccupied with her project and it seemed to temper her initial hostility.

I said, "I'm not clear about the sequence of events. I remember reading about it in the paper, but that was ten years ago. As I recall, Austin Brown invited her to a pool party at his parents' cabin up on the pass and things got out of hand. Were you there?"

"Sure, but I left before any trouble set in. Really, everything was fine at first. School was over and everyone was in a good mood. The cabin had a swimming pool and we were in and out of it, playing music and cooking hamburgers and doing stuff like that."

She used the X-acto knife to tease an area of dark blue from the postcard from Arizona. I could see that she was re-creating the photograph of Sloan in pixels of color, but the image wasn't clear at such close range.

"Why didn't you party at Austin's house? Didn't he live in Horton Ravine?"

"He wanted privacy. He'd bought a keg of beer and a lid of dope and he didn't want his parents to know."

"Who invited Sloan?"

"He did. The way I heard it, she was jogging that morning in her neighborhood. He was with Troy in Troy's pickup and asked if she wanted to join them. She said she had to take care of her dog and get cleaned up from the run, so Troy said he'd swing by later. Iris and I got there before they did, which was one forty-five or so."

"I thought Sloan was being shunned," I remarked, nudging the conversation back to the point.

"She was, but Austin agreed to call it off."

"Where were her parents all this time?"

"They drove to Arizona to pick up her stepbrothers. The two of them spent summers here with their dad."

"When you saw Sloan, did she seem frightened?"

"Not at all. It was a party. I didn't think she was in danger and neither did anyone else."

"Who was there?"

"Bayard and Troy and a few other guys."

"Any other girls besides you?"

"Maybe four or five. Iris for sure because I gave her a ride up."

"You're talking about Iris Lehmann?"

"Right. She was my best friend at the time."

"But not now?"

"I see her now and then," she said cautiously.

"What about Fritz?"

"He was a show-off. He got everything he deserved."

All-righty then, I thought. "So it wasn't a big party; just a dozen or so."

She shrugged, but offered nothing more. She'd reverted to her former caution and I wondered if something had happened that day that she didn't want to talk about. I'd have to coax her back into the conversation before she shut down altogether. In the adjacent dining room, I noticed an old-fashioned Underwood typewriter with a rolling desk chair pulled up to it. The surrounding tabletop was covered with books, files, and typing paper, some of it wadded up and cast aside—the universal symbol of writerly angst.

I indicated the poster board. "Is this what you do for a living? I should have asked you earlier."

Her eyes strayed to the typewriter. "I'm working on a screenplay."

"You're a writer?"

"Well, no. Not really. This is a movie about the murder."

Her cheeks had acquired a pink tint and her expression was earnest. "People are always telling me I should put it down on paper since I was there and saw it firsthand. I don't mean when she was killed."

"Are you writing a fictionalized account?"

"Well, it's not a documentary, so I guess you could call it true fiction or something along those lines. People swear a movie like this could be a box office smash, especially if I include a starring role for a big-name actor, which I intend to do."

"Whose part do you see as the starring role?"

That was a stumper. She shrugged. "Austin's, I guess."

"Really."

"He's, you know, the antagonist and now that he's a fugitive from justice, it makes him kind of an outlaw. Like an antihero."

"In other words, someone the audience admires," I said.

"Uh-huh."

"You have a literary agent?"

"I don't need one. A couple of months ago, I met someone who works for a Hollywood production company and she promised to show the script to her boss as soon as I finish it. That way I don't have to pay the agent's ten percent off the top. She says in the film business, it's all about who you know."

"So I've heard. How far along are you?"

"Page twenty-six. It's harder than I thought. You have to know all these technical terms."

"What, like fade out, fade in?"

"Exactly."

Talk about no hope. Her stepmother had loved telling me what a poor student she'd been, so the notion of her writing anything worth money seemed far-fetched. "What are you calling the screenplay?"

"I was thinking about *Yellowweed*," she replied. She paused long enough to study me. "Do you have siblings?"

"I don't. I'm an only child," I said, wondering where she was going with this.

"You're lucky. You have no idea what it's like growing up in a house where your sibs think they're so smart. All my family ever cared about was money and prestige."

"I understand your mother walked out about the time Sloan was killed."

Her expression darkened. "Right. Thanks a lot, Mom. Way to go. My sisters were out of the house by then. They acted all hurt and upset, but what was it to them? They had their own lives. I was the one stuck at home. My family's never had a clue who I am or what I care about. Forget creativity or the arts or anything original. They're all science types."

"You seem to be doing okay. This place is great."

"My dad pays the rent, which irritates the shit out of Loretta because it's money she could be spending on herself. She doesn't say so, but I know she sees me as a big old loser. When my screenplay sells, I'll at least have enough money to get the hell out of Dodge."

"I think it's nice that they're willing to pitch in financially," I said, trying to inject an optimistic note. Meanwhile, I was thinking that her denying Sloan had given her the tape might be a big old lie. What if she'd had it in her possession all these years? If the tape had triggered the end of her relationship with Troy, wouldn't she take pleasure in getting back at him? He hadn't been approached for money, but if the tape became public knowledge, he and Fritz would be tarred with the same brush. Nice belated revenge for his betrayal of her. I pictured what she might do with twenty-five thousand bucks. Thumb her nose at Loretta, at the very least.

Miss Mopey was saying, "All they care about is getting me out of their hair. Emotional support would be nice, but I guess that's too much to ask."

I didn't want to foster additional lamentations, so I shifted the subject. "Have you had a chance to talk to Fritz since he got out?"

"He's stopped by a couple of times, which I try not to encourage. He acts all goofy, like he has a crush on me. Wouldn't you know it? Cute guys won't give me the time of day. Doofus like him is all over me."

"Do you mind if I ask a few more questions about Sloan? It might be helpful going back over events. Since you're hard at work on the script, this might stimulate your memory."

Mollified, she said, "Like what?"

"It must have been a shock when you heard she was dead."

"A big shock. Horrible. I didn't believe it at first. Iris found out before me and she called, crying so hard I couldn't understand a word she said. Then when I got the point, I thought she was making it up."

"When was this?"

"When we heard what happened? Three days after the party, I think. Something like that."

"Where did you think Sloan was all that time?"

"I had no idea. We weren't hanging out that much, so it's not like we were in constant touch. Austin said after they closed up the cabin and came down the pass, they dropped her off downtown and then went straight to his house."

"To do what?"

"They goofed around, playing Ping-Pong and Foosball. I know they watched TV because I remember him describing a couple of the shows."

"Would have been mostly reruns, wouldn't it?"

"What's that supposed to mean?"

"Meaning he mentioned the shows to lend credence to his story. If he'd already seen episodes, he could rattle off enough details to be convincing."

"Oh."

"Did it occur to you they might have done something to harm her?"

"Not really. I was kind of bothered about the dog. She must not have thought she'd be gone long because she left Butch in the backyard. When it got dark, the next-door neighbor heard him howling and she took him in. She's the one who called the police. Sloan never would have left him like that. She'd have come back for him no matter what."

"So you did or didn't believe Austin's account?"

"I didn't have any reason not to. He was as worried as the rest of us when it turned out she was missing."

"What made them decide to kill her?"

"I don't know. I'd already left by then. Anyway, I don't think they *decided* to do anything. It just happened."

"You're saying four guys in the woods at night with a loaded handgun, and the girl who accompanies them just 'happens' to die?"

"But that's how it was. It all came out at the trial. It wasn't premeditated or anything like that—except for the hole Austin dug, and he only did that so she'd take him seriously."

I could feel myself squinting in disbelief. "Austin dug a grave before he took her up there that night?"

"I wouldn't call it a *grave*. It was a hole he dug at the campsite where she was shot."

"If it was the hole they buried her in, wouldn't you call it a grave?"

"Sure, if you put it like *that*."

"Who found the body?"

"Hikers."

"As I understand it, the murder weapon was never recovered."

"It wasn't, but everybody knew the gun was Austin's because he had it at the cabin, waving it around."

"I'm assuming the police questioned all of you when the body came to light. Austin, in particular."

"Sure, but they didn't have enough to charge him. He told the cops the same thing he told us. He said they dropped her off on State Street and that's the last they saw of her. I guess he was pretty torn up by then since he'd dated her."

"I'm sure he put on a good show," I said. "And then what?"

"The two detectives just kept after them and after them."

"This was at the police station?"

"Some of the time and partly at Austin's house. This was two or three days running, but they hadn't been booked or anything like that. I know they separated the guys and talked to them individually, but they all said the same thing."

"I'll bet, alibis being what they are," I said. "Did the police read them their Miranda rights?"

"They weren't under arrest."

"Didn't anyone ask for an attorney?"

"Austin said they didn't need attorneys since she was fine when they dropped her off."

"And his *parents* didn't object? I thought he came from a family of hot-shot lawyers."

"He did, but he said if they hired one, it would look like he needed one."

"He *did* need one. He still does. You're talking about homicide."

"I think it was more like an unfortunate accident. Fritz didn't know anything about guns. Austin had to show him how to take the safety off."

"Were you aware that Austin intended to leave town?"

She shook her head. "I think he acted on impulse the minute he got word Fritz had told on him."

"'*Told on him*'? Like they were little kids?" I knew I sounded outraged, judgmental, and condemnatory, but I couldn't help myself. I watched her and wondered why she wouldn't meet my eyes. Probably because I was talking to her like the idiot she was. I took what I hoped was a deep, calming breath. "Is there anything else you want to tell me?"

"Not really. Except Iris and I were scared to death."

"The two of you were scared? How so?"

"Well, what if Austin showed up again? What if he'd come after us? We were there at the cabin the day she was killed. We were, like, witnesses."

"To what?"

She closed her mouth. She waved a hand in front of her face as though a gnat had singled her out for pestering. "Nothing. I hope we're done here because I have work to do."

I knew I'd pressed her to the point of defensiveness, which is seldom productive. "I guess this covers it for the time being. If any other questions come up, can I come back and talk to you?"

"I think I've said enough."

"Not quite, but I'm sure I'll find a way to fill in the blanks."

She murmured something.

I said, "Sorry, I missed that."

"I said your information's out of date. Sloan's mother decided it was time to empty her room and pack up her stuff, which she did a couple of weeks ago."

"How did you hear about Sloan's room being emptied?"

"I didn't hear about it. I helped."

14

Wednesday evening, September 20, 1989

I was home later than usual and after the usual hassle found a semi-decent parking spot at the end of the block. When I reached the gate, I pulled the mail from the box, surprised that Henry hadn't yet collected it. It wasn't until I rounded the studio to the backyard that I realized something was wrong. Henry, in a T-shirt, shorts, and flip-flops, stood on his back porch as still as stone. Pearl, suspended between her crutches near the clothesline, appeared to be anchored to the spot. In the kitchen window, Ed the cat was puffed up, his white fur looking like dandelion fuzz, every hair standing on end.

The pup tent was in its usual place, the opening flap zipped shut. In front of the tent flap, a massive black dog chewed on a rubber baby doll. His coat was short-haired except for his shaggy buff-colored tail and an incongruous golden ruff at his throat. He had a huge head and a dark, deeply wrinkled face with a small gold dot over each eye. His brown eyes were focused intently on his toy, which he gnawed on vigorously without doing serious harm. The minute he caught sight of me, he rose silently to his feet, his head low, his ears back. His tail was tucked in close to his body and oddly kinked. A growl rumbled through his chest like an engine turning over. He fixed me with a look, snarled once, and then barked. While my body froze, my heart was doing double time.

"Well, he's a charmer," I remarked.

Pearl said, "I wouldn't make a move if I was you."

"Not to worry. How long has this little standoff been going on?"

"I'd say twenty minutes. Does that sound about right to you, Henry?"

"Close enough. I heard her shriek and came running out to see what was wrong. The dog refused to let her move. I thought to intervene, but he didn't seem to care for it. He rushed me and barked so close to my shin, his hot breath felt like ankle wind."

"This is the mutt you rescued?"

Pearl said, "That's him."

"Where's Lucky?"

"In the tent sleeping off a drunk. Him and Henry went and fetched the dog from the vet. Lucky said it stressed him out and he ain't over it yet. All them poor sick pussycats and puppy dogs. One of 'em had got hit by a car and the doc had to amputate his hind leg. Lucky said it was the awfulest thing he ever seen. Nothing but a stump was left. He got home and had to knock back four beers just to settle his nerves. Minute he went in the tent, the dog put hisself in charge and put us on notice. Nobody better move or he'll bite the shit out of you."

As though to demonstrate the point, the dog barked so savagely his chest quivered and his front feet came off the ground. All three of us jumped as though jolted by a cattle prod.

"What kind of dog *is* that?" I said, trying not to move my lips.

"Part mastiff and part Rottweiler. He's got some golden retriever in the mix as well. The mastiff and Rottie parts are all loyal guard dog. The retriever part loves to fetch. I throwed him his baby and he brought her right back to me, but after Lucky went in the tent he didn't want to play no more."

"He have a name?"

"Killer."

"Very nice," I said. "How're you doing, Henry? Everything okay?"

"More or less. Pearl says you were here earlier looking for me."

"I thought we should talk about putting in a home alarm to cover your place and mine. Ned's on the loose. He stopped by yesterday."

"Pearl mentioned that. Nothing wrong with home security."

"I'll be happy to split the cost."

"No need. My treat. What company?"

"Security Operating Systems. They installed the alarm at my office."

"S.O.S. Clever. I'll give them a call."

"Actually, with Killer on the premises, burglars wouldn't have a chance," I said. I turned to Pearl. "Any news on Ned's whereabouts?"

Pearl said, "My homies ain't seen him, though a pitcher of him might be nice. You talk about a middle-aged white guy and it don't exactly set off alarms."

"I'll see what I can do," I said.

Henry said, "Oh. Before I forget, I wanted to remind you of Rosie's birthday. We're having a little party for her Friday night."

"Glad you mentioned it. I'd blanked on that."

Pearl said, "Lucky and me are invited too, so don't give us no guff."

"We'll do it after supper and I'll be baking the cake."

Pearl said, "He was going to make an angel food cake, which is a type of sponge cake. Stiff-beaten egg whites is used as leavening instead of baking soda or baking powder, but I suggested a sheet cake, which will feed more."

Henry said, "Very good, Pearl. I'm impressed."

Pearl shrugged modestly.

"Friday's the twenty-second?" I asked.

"Indeed."

"Gifts?"

"I leave that up to you."

I glanced at Pearl. "How long is Lucky apt to sleep?"

"I hope it ain't long. I gotta pee."

"Me, too," Henry said weakly.

The dog lifted his head and bared his teeth. The hair on his back rose magically in a stiff line from his shoulder blades to his tail, making him look like a hound from hell. I wasn't sure about Henry or Pearl, but I was ready to repent.

"Might be some Rhodesian ridgeback in him, too," Pearl said.

"Anybody have a plan?" I asked.

"Fresh out," she said.

"Henry?"

"He can't be as suspicious of you as he is of Pearl and me. I think he associates us with Lucky's disappearance. I don't think he's made up his mind about you."

"He seems pretty opinionated from where I stand," I said. "Have you tried calling Lucky's name to see if you can rouse him?"

"We gave up. That guy passes out and he's down for the count," Pearl said. "See if you can get him to play."

"Lucky?"

"The fucking dog," she said, exasperated. "Pardon my potty mouth, Henry. I know you don't hold with talk like that."

Henry accepted her apology philosophically, by now accustomed to my occasional salty outbursts.

"When you say *play*, what are you picturing?" I asked Pearl.

"You know. Frolicking about and dancing on his hind legs."

"Frolicking?"

"Okay, so skip the frolicking. That's asking too much. Tell him what a good boy he is. Praise his baby. The dog's fierce, but he's not all that smart."

"Oh, come on. He's not going to fall for that."

"You got a better idea?"

"Not really."

I stood and regarded the dog, thinking of the many accounts I'd read of humans savaged by their faithful four-legged friends. I'd just met the dog and he'd already taken a dislike to me. I watched him settle on the ground and go back to slobbering on his toy, apparently content. He gnawed on his dolly's arm, then proceeded to lick her tiny rubber feet. From the kitchen window, Ed the cat had relaxed his vigilance, but looked on with concern.

"Well, get on with it," she said.

"I *am*! Don't nag."

Slowly, I lowered myself into a squatting position, knees popping, uncertain if I'd ever be able to stand up again. I said, "Killer, what a nice doggie you are. Good boy! Is that your baby doll?"

The dog grumbled to himself as he drooled on his toy, uncertain what to make of my behavior.

"Is that your baby doll? What a nice baby! I love that baby. Can you bring her over here?"

Killer paused in his attentions to his baby doll, perhaps willing to share if given the proper incentive. He cast a wary eye in my direction.

"Bring her over here, Killer. Come on. Come on, boy!"

I slapped my knees and repeated my appeal. I was making myself sick with all this goofy talk, but the dog didn't seem to mind. I could see him weigh my request. His tail thumped twice and the ridge of hair settled. He knew his baby was deserving of praise and applause and he couldn't help but take pride.

"Bring her over here. Bring your baby."

Bashfully, he lumbered to his feet as if the idea had just occurred to him. He gave his baby a playful toss, checking out of the corner of his eye to see what I thought.

I said, "Good boy! What a good boy!"

He picked her up tenderly and brought her half the distance. I warbled out more encouragement. I realized later I was activating the golden retriever in his nature. Finally, he carried the baby close and laid her at my feet. I waited until he barked expectantly, stepped back, and wiggled, front legs on the ground and his butt in the air, his gaze fixed on his toy.

"Thank you. What a good boy! I'm going to pick her up now. Is that okay?"

Nothing hostile in his response.

Gingerly, I reached for the baby, moving slowly in case he changed his mind. I picked her up and tossed her across the yard. He bounded over the dirt, grabbed her in his mouth, tossed her, caught her again, and then returned and placed her at my feet.

Henry said, "Keep at it. I'll be right back." He made a beeline for the back door and slipped into the house.

"Right behind you," Pearl said and followed him in.

Killer and I played fetch for the next twenty-five minutes. No sign of Henry. No sign of Pearl. If my attention flagged at all, the dog got all broody and caused me to fret about dog bites. Ed observed from his window perch, amused but mystified, probably thinking only a dog could comport himself so foolishly. I wondered if I'd be driven insane before the day was done. As it happened, Killer's baby was all tuckered out and he had to lie down with her between his front paws so she could have a little rest. I staggered to my feet and made a slow backward walk to my front door, where I took out my keys and let myself in, keeping him firmly in my sights.

Among the mail that had come in, there was a plain brown 8-by-11-inch mailer. My name penned across the face. No sender's name, no postage, and no return address. I studied it briefly and then opened it with caution. I'd once had someone gift me with a couple of tarantulas in a similar envelope.

The sheets I pulled out were copies of Ned Lowe's mug shot and a brief account of the warrants out on him. The black-and-white photograph didn't do him any favors. It must have been taken years earlier because he looked younger but just as tired. He'd sported a stingy mustache in those days, and the bags under his eyes hadn't yet puffed up to their full proportions. He was a homely man, which was not so much a matter of his features as the beaten look in his eyes. It may have been that quality that led me to assume he was harmless. Perhaps he'd adapted the expression as the perfect camouflage.

Arizona and Nevada State Police detectives are looking for Ned Benjamin Lowe, 53, a suspect in the disappearance of Susan Telford, a 14-year-old white female, last seen on the morning of March 28, 1987, on Paseo Verde Parkway in Henderson, NV. Additionally, he is a person of interest in the 1986 disappearance of Janet Macy from her home in Tucson, Arizona. In both cases, the victims were approached by a man claiming to be a photographer scouting for modeling talent in the fashion industry.

Police say Ned Lowe is wanted on active and extraditable felony arrest warrants. Anyone with information about his whereabouts is asked to contact state police.

The phone numbers for both agencies were listed, along with the advisory note that all calls would be kept confidential. The number for an anonymous tip line was also given.

I picked up the handset and put a call through to Jonah at home.

"Hello?" Camilla.

"May I speak to Detective Robb?" I said. Ho ho. Clever me, asking for him by rank and last name so she wouldn't realize who was calling.

There was a stutter of silence before she slammed the phone down in my ear. Guess she's smarter than I thought.

Three minutes later the phone rang.

I answered warily, thinking she was calling back to scream at me.

"Hey, Kinsey. Jonah."

I pulled the handset away from my ear and squinted. "How'd you know to call me?"

"She slammed the phone down in someone's ear. I figured it was you."

"Is she there now?"

"She went out and banged the door shut. I'll pay for this later, but what the hell. You called about the bulletin."

"I did, and thanks for dropping it off. I take it your officers haven't picked up any sign of him."

"No, but it's early yet. The subject came up at the squad meeting and everybody's on board. We'll cover the beach-area motels and spread out from there."

"That sounds great. I've got a couple of homeless pals checking the Rescue Mission and Harbor House. They're also scouting freeway underpasses and the old hobo camp. I was thinking about canvassing motels in Winterset and Cottonwood."

"Have at it."

The line went dead, so Camilla must have doubled back, hoping to catch him in the act.

With Killer still parked in the backyard, I decided I really had no compelling reason to leave the house. My cupboard was bare, but I could probably make it until Lucky woke up. I decided to use the time to type up my notes, so I hauled out my portable Smith Corona and removed the lid. I took out my index cards and sorted through the information I'd assembled. As I converted my handwritten notes to a proper report, I let the facts flow over me, making no effort to channel the stream. Coming to any conclusion at this stage of my investigation would serve to filter out competing possibilities. The only notion I tagged for further consideration was that the blackmail scheme was the brainstorm of a newcomer to the scene. Those who'd participated in the taping ten years before—Fritz, Troy, Iris, Austin, and Bayard—saw it as a spoof. The extortionist apparently had no idea the taping was a pseudo-pornographic prank and therefore worthless for ransom purposes.

I sensed the contours of a story behind the story I'd

been hearing, but I wasn't sure what it was. I'd picked up fragments, but I was missing a cohesive narrative. Troy had accepted responsibility for his part in Sloan's death and I felt his remorse was sincere. Fritz was still busy pointing a finger at someone else—anyone else—hoping to shift the blame. Austin, of course, had simply absented himself and therefore, as far as anyone knew, had escaped the consequences. What I found myself thinking about were the players peripheral to Sloan's shooting death. Poppy and Iris being a case in point. I wondered how many moments had come and gone when one of them could have stepped up to the plate—made a phone call to the police, mentioned the situation to a parent or someone in a position of authority. By doing nothing, Sloan's so-called friends had sealed her fate as surely as Fritz had with his gun. In hindsight, did any of them recognize the price she had paid for their passivity? Their failure to act was all the more damning for the ease with which they rationalized their behavior afterward.

I looked at the two names that remained on my list. Given the cleaning out of Sloan's room, her mother should be next, but I felt myself resisting. I don't know how you talk to a woman who's lost her only child. True, I could pose as a reporter interested in the case, but lying to a woman who'd suffered such a loss taxed even my highly developed skills at bending the truth. I can fib with the best of them, but I couldn't give this woman the impression that I was promoting justice for Sloan when I was being paid for something else altogether and not doing too well with that.

Then there was Bayard Montgomery. So far, no one had much to say about him. I knew he was the unseen camera operator when the sex tape was made and I couldn't help but wonder if this was his mode of operation, being at the same time the recorder of events and the man fading into the background for reasons of his own. I moved his name to the top of the list and I went to bed feeling cowardly, but relieved.

15

THE THREAT

May 1979

Sloan had dated Austin for an intense five months early in her junior year at Climping Academy. Initially her sense of self-worth was bolstered by his attention. He was a jock and a straight-A student. He'd spent two years at a prep school back East and part of his personal style was the dress shirt, tie, and sport coat he wore every day. He held himself aloof, which lent him an irresistible air of command. His classmates looked up to him and he used that to his advantage. He seemed to observe them from a distance, awarding praise if others pleased him, expressing his disdain if they fell short. He used sarcasm and disparagement as whips, operating with such authority that kids couldn't help but play up to him, seeking his approval, hoping to avoid reproach.

Sloan had kept her distance from him, knowing she was vulnerable to attack. She was nearly six feet tall and self-conscious about her height. She'd towered over her classmates since the sixth grade, which is when the girls seemed to mature as if by magic, leaving boys behind. Sloan was also exposed because of her questionable parentage. Not only was her mother an alcoholic, but her birth father's identity was a blur. In a community like Horton Ravine, despite liberal sentiment, she felt like marked goods. That she was statuesque only made her more conspicuous. Her friend Poppy was a people pleaser, petite, blond, and soft-spoken, traits Sloan admired but couldn't emulate. She was boisterous, acting out her social discomfort with a braying laugh. She wore no makeup and had no gift for fashion. She liked sweats and running shoes. Most Sundays, she went to church, and for the past two summers, she'd worked as a counselor at the church-run camp for grades six through nine. She was aware that behind her back, some referred to her as Miss Goody-Two-Shoes.

One Friday in October, at the end of the school day, Sloan stood at her locker loading the books she'd need for the weekend. She looked up and caught sight of Austin leaning against the wall with his gaze fixed on her.

"You need help?" he asked.

"I'm fine. What about you?"

He smiled. "I'm fine, too. Thanks for asking."

His eyes were an odd green and he wore a dress shirt the same shade, his tie a tone darker. Even ten feet away, she was aware of his aftershave, which had a fresh, clean scent. She couldn't imagine why he'd initiated conversation with her.

"Did you want something?" she asked.

"You interest me."

"*I* do?"

"You don't think you're interesting?"

She laughed uncomfortably. "No."

"What's been happening between you and Poppy? I thought you were best friends."

Sloan wasn't sure what to make of the shift in subject matter. She didn't want to think about Poppy, whose company she'd missed the last few weekends while she was studying. "We're still friends."

"But not best friends. Not if you're hanging out on your own all the time."

"What business is that of yours? I've been trying to keep my grades up. Poppy and I are allowed to do whatever we want."

"Sure, but it's weird. You'd think she'd prefer to study with you than just go out with Troy all the time."

"What's your point?"

"As it turns out, I like you better without her," he replied.

"Lucky me."

"Don't be flip. I'm trying to say something here if you'd give me a chance."

She shut her locker door and snapped the combination lock. "You know what? I don't care. You're a shit. You're mean and you're arrogant and you put people down. I don't like that."

"Fair enough. How about I'll be nice?"

"Oh, right. For how long?"

"As long as you're nice to me. Does that sound like a deal?"

"But I'm not nice to you. Calling you a shit was rude."

"But honest."

"Austin, this conversation is bugging me. What are you up to?"

"Let's go out. On a date. Just the two of us. We'll talk."

She gave him a jaded look. "You know, I've seen you in action. This is just your way of setting me up."

"I'm not setting you up. Why would you say that?"

"You did the same thing to Michelle, and Heather before her."

"Ohhh, I get it. You've been watching me. Keeping tabs. I like that."

Sloan shook her head in disgust. "You are such an egotist."

"My best quality," he said. "Turns out Heather isn't that bright. Michelle said I insulted her, so she broke up with me."

"She did not."

"Yes, she did. You can ask her yourself."

"Maybe I will."

"Good. I'll call you tomorrow after you've talked to her. I can tell you what she'll say. I didn't call her often enough. We didn't go anywhere fun. She kept asking if I thought her boobs were too small, which I denied. She couldn't leave the subject alone, so I finally told her she was right, her tits were minuscule, and she got all pushed out of shape, so to speak."

"Her boobs aren't too small. That's ridiculous."

"Then *you* deliver the news. I got bored repeating myself."

Sloan laughed.

The final bell rang and she and Austin parted company. Later when she asked Michelle about him, Michelle said he didn't call often enough and all he wanted to do was study when she wanted to go out. She didn't mention her boobs.

Austin phoned the next day and asked if she wanted to see a movie, which she agreed to do.

As the weeks passed, she realized how different he was one-on-one: soft and warmhearted. He said he liked spending time with her because she was serious. She didn't put on airs and she didn't flirt with other guys. Sloan responded with a warmth of her own, amazed by his openness. With everyone else, he was much the same: brittle, standoffish, and harsh. She could see friends eyeing her, wondering why she put up with him. There was also an unspoken curiosity about what he found appealing in her when so many girls had set their caps for him and failed.

At one point, she asked him point-blank, "What's this about? I don't get it."

He smiled. "Are you asking me why I like you?"

"I am. And no bullshit."

"Let's see. I'd have to say it's because you're unaffected and you're smart and you're an all-around good person. And you don't even realize how beautiful you are."

She was braced for his usual snide comment, the zinger that undercut any kind word he said. Instead, he took her hand and laid it against his lips.

What was she to do with him if not believe?

Both Sloan and Austin came from families with money, but the fact that Sloan's stepfather was in the construction trade placed him in a lower order than Austin's dad, who was a high-priced attorney. Austin's mother was also an attorney, as were his two brothers, all of them sharp-witted and blunt. She and Austin hadn't dated that long and he was already eager for her to get to know his family. On the occasions when she had dinner at his house, she was intimidated by the lot of them. In their company, she receded, not wanting to draw attention to herself, anxious to avoid their intrusive curiosity and quickness to judge. They didn't have conversations. They had disputes and skirmishes, intellectual warfare, wherein each of them tried to outdo the others. Any tactic was acceptable in these verbal jousts. The point was to be fast, to unseat your opponent at the first opportunity. The point was to be right, and if not right, then to win by fair means or foul. Austin put up a good fight, but he couldn't prevail. His parents and his brothers were merciless, cutting him no slack. Sloan couldn't bear watching him shrink as the battles went on. The others seemed challenged and invigorated where Austin's wounds went unnoticed or, if noticed, were subject to scorn.

Over the next two months, the relationship proceeded full steam ahead. What she hadn't anticipated was Austin's hunger to be close. They talked on the phone for hours, studied together, played tennis, hiked, and watched television. He looked for her before and after school. At first, she reveled in his devotion and then gradually felt herself longing for air. She'd never had a boyfriend and therefore had no sense of what was "normal" and what was not. She was used to spending time on her own, doing as she pleased. Now she was attuned to him, protective of his self-esteem, which she realized was fragile. Given his family dynamic, it didn't surprise her that much of the time he was guarded, quick to find fault with others before anyone found fault with him.

He craved physical contact. He liked keeping an arm slung across her shoulders. The gesture was possessive and Sloan liked the public demonstration of his claim on her. He was forever kissing and nibbling her, smelling her hair, murmuring in her ear. As their romance progressed, so did his demands, which were always couched in coaxing and adoration. There were only so many ways she could evade the force of his neediness, which became suffocating as the relationship went on.

Her stepfather was the one who finally took her aside and spelled out his concern. "Look, Sloan, I don't mean to butt in. I can see Austin's crazy about you, but there's something about the kid that seems off to me."

"Off?"

"He's too intense. He's all over you, everywhere."

Sloan laughed. "Well, he is. Sort of."

"Is that what you want?"

"Not really. I mean, not all the time, but I can't tell him that because I don't want to hurt his feelings."

"His feelings aren't your responsibility. I'm not saying you should end the relationship, but you might want to slow down. Take a break now and then; have some time apart. Otherwise, you're going to paint yourself into a corner you can't get out of."

"What am I supposed to say to him? You have no idea how sensitive he is. I don't want him to think I'm rejecting him."

"Sensitive? Are you kidding? I've heard how he treats his so-called friends."

"Who told you that?"

"You did before you first started dating him. He's vicious and snide. He's a bully. You said so yourself."

"Well, he's not. That's a show he puts on in public. With me, he couldn't be sweeter."

"Because he's getting what he wants. Just wait until you raise your hand and decline and you'll see what he's really like."

"You think so?"

"If I didn't, we wouldn't be having this talk. Ask me,

I'd say he's an emotional cripple looking to you to hold him up."

"You don't know what you're talking about."

"Sorry. That last bit was out of line. Anyway, it's your call. I just want you to know you have my support. Taking care of yourself doesn't mean you don't care for him."

He gave her a hug and that was the end of the discussion as far as she was concerned. It was odd, though, afterward, how his observations affected her. At the time, she dismissed his comments. He didn't know Austin. He didn't understand that under that tough exterior, he was insecure. She could see how the relationship must look to Paul, but it wasn't like that. She didn't disagree entirely. She just wasn't sure what to do. Austin behaved like he was starved for love. Given the way he was treated at home, who wouldn't be? She didn't see how she could keep him at bay without injuring him. She adored him. She really did, and she didn't want him to feel slighted. She was new at this and there wasn't anyone she could talk to about how to handle the situation. There was a time she would have confided in Poppy, but those days were gone. Poppy was all about Iris now and Sloan was on her own.

In some ways, she saw herself as stronger than Austin, so maybe it was up to her to set aside her feelings in deference to his. His own mother was hard as nails and she'd seen the way the woman treated him. In an argument—and every conversation in that family was an argument—she rode roughshod over him, belittled him, and scoffed. Sloan had to be careful that nothing she said could be misconstrued.

The problem was his persistence, his pushing, his tendency to prevail in any contest of wills. She didn't even like to think of it that way, but sometimes she felt any conflict between them acted on him like a stimulant. If they disagreed, he'd mount a campaign to prove his point of view was better, that his desires should take precedence. This was behavior he'd learned at home and he had no control over the impulses that drove him to be victorious. Over time, she could feel herself losing ground. Her natural ebullience had been tempered by his needs. In her desire to please him, she'd surrendered most of her preferences, acceding to his own.

One afternoon, she was lying on her bed, propped against the pillows, putting pink polish on her toenails. The bed was unmade and the floor was littered with clothes. Sloan's desk was barely visible under a layer of books, papers, and sports paraphernalia she'd tossed on top. The closet door stood open and the rod was jammed with hangers. Folded sweaters had toppled together in a pile, hanging over the edges of the shelves.

Austin was circling the room, examining the various knickknacks she had on display. He picked up a small ceramic angel. "What's this?"

"An angel. What's it look like? Poppy gave me that when we were in second grade."

"And this?" He was holding up a photograph.

"My fake dad. I told you about him," she said.

"Tell me again."

"My mom cooked up this whole story about him. She claimed she met him at a fancy ski resort and they had a passionate affair. When she found out she was pregnant, he stood by her. He wouldn't go so far as proposing marriage, but he promised financial support. Then he died in an avalanche and she ended up raising me on her own. All I ever had of him was a photograph and that was a laugh. Turned out to be some famous European skier she'd never even met. She cut the picture out of a magazine and put it in a frame. When I was ten, I came across the exact same photo in a ski magazine and I couldn't believe my eyes. I thought he was still alive. No such luck. She'd lied about everything."

"So who was your birth father?"

"No clue. She told me later it was a one-night stand, but that's probably a lie as well. I finally gave up. I mean, what difference does it make when my stepdad is such a good guy?"

"You're not tempted to investigate?"

"Based on what? Whoever he is, he's probably a jerk. Otherwise, he'd have taken responsibility."

"If he's alive, you might have grounds for a lawsuit. Assuming he promised financial support."

"Good luck with that idea," she said. "Oh. Quick request while I'm thinking about it."

Smiling, he said, "What?"

"I need a day to myself. My room's a mess and my mom's on my case."

He surveyed his surroundings. "Doesn't look bad to me."

"Are you kidding? Place is a pigsty."

"So it's a pigsty. I can help."

"Don't think so, but thanks. It's a one-person job. Usually I turn up the sound on my stereo, so conversation's impossible anyway. She'll want me to do a closet purge and take stuff to Goodwill."

"Fine. We'll connect when you're done and take Butch for a walk."

"Don't you have things to do on your own?"

"Nope. My time belongs to you."

"Sweet," she said. "I, on the other hand, could use some breathing room. I have chores piled up you wouldn't believe."

"Chores? You don't do chores. Name one."

"That's not the point."

"What is the point?"

She should have picked up the warning in his tone, but she was intent on painting her toenails. "Shit." She reached down and deftly swiped a spot of polish from one toe. "Mostly what I need is downtime. Not a lot, but a little bit. This much." She held her thumb and index finger a quarter of an inch apart.

Austin's tone had chilled. "Maybe I misunderstood. Are you telling me you need *space*?"

"No, I don't need *space*. All I'm talking about is one day."

"Are you tired of me?"

"That's not it at all. Don't turn this into a federal case."

"You don't have to be huffy. It's a simple question."

"Which I answered."

"Because if you're bored or irritated by my company, I can take a hike. No problem. In fact, I can make it permanent. Give you all the time alone you want."

"I'm not irritated or bored."

"Well, that's not what I'm hearing. You talk like you can't wait to get away."

"Forget it. I'm sorry I mentioned it."

"No, no. Don't be sorry. Say anything you like."

"You'll just take it wrong."

"No, I won't."

"Austin, you're turning this into World War Three when all I wanted was an afternoon to myself."

"Oh, I see. First it was a day and now you're saying you want an 'afternoon,' so which is it?"

"Get off it. You're being a butt."

"So now suddenly it's my fault? Something I'm doing to *you*?"

Sloan murmured something darkly to herself, not looking at him.

Exasperated, he said, "You know, I've heard this crap before and it's just an excuse. I'd prefer it if you'd come right out and tell me the truth. Is there someone else?"

"How could there be someone else when we spend every fucking minute together?"

He seemed to stiffen before her eyes. "I didn't realize my company was so offensive. I beg a thousand pardons for the imposition. I wish you'd spoken up sooner so I could have relieved you of the burden before it became so onerous."

When she looked up, she realized he'd left the room.

She made a face to herself. Horse's ass. What was *that* about?

She was on the verge of jumping up and following him downstairs, but she heard the front door slam and decided she'd better give him time to cool off. She wasn't sure where this little fit had come from, but it was clear he wasn't in the mood to listen to reason.

On Monday when she saw him at school, he cut her

dead and he hadn't spoken to her since. When the shunning came up, it was simply an extension of the big freeze. Until now.

Sloan locked herself in her room and watched the tape she'd stolen from Fritz. She wasn't sure what to expect, but it wasn't this. She was acutely embarrassed at what she saw. All she could think about was Poppy, who was so crazy about Troy. She'd die if she saw this. There was Iris, stark naked and behaving like a slut; Fritz acting like a fool; Troy with a hard-on, greasing his dick with Crisco so he could stick it in her friend. Sloan looked on with disbelief, mortified by the sexual shenanigans unfolding before her eyes. It wasn't until the cut-away to Austin that Sloan felt her attention shift. Austin was the *director*? *The man in charge?* What kind of scumbag was he? There was something so *pathetic* about Iris asking him for a kiss when he'd engineered this entire assault. Of course, Iris was an exhibitionist who'd do anything for attention. But there sat Austin, superior and above it all, smirking at the "boys," who were practically wetting themselves with excitement while Iris was completely out of it. Sloan watched the tape a second time, rage sparking to life.

Oh yes, the shunning would stop. The shunning would now most definitely come to a screeching halt.

She intercepted Austin at his car in the Climp parking lot the following Monday afternoon. Students streamed out of the building, moving toward their vehicles. Some turned to look at the pair with curiosity, knowing the shunning was Austin's doing, wondering if the encounter between the two was the prelude to a showdown. Sloan wasn't sure Austin would even speak to her, but since in his view she'd rejected him, she reasoned that he'd be avid to hear what she had to say. He'd expect an apology. He'd imagine her groveling, hoping to get back in his good graces.

"We need to talk," she said.

"By all means. Be my guest. I've been looking forward to this."

"It's about the shunning."

"What about it?"

"I didn't write that note. I didn't contact the school. I didn't tell anyone what Troy and Poppy did. I'd never do such a thing and you know it."

Austin studied her with mock concern. "That's not the word on the street."

"What 'word on the street'? You did this. You instigated the whole deal. Nobody talks to me. No one looks me in the eye."

"You credit me with too much power. I'm flattered, but I can't force your friends to snub you. How would I do that?"

"I don't know how, but you did."

"I'm willing to believe you're innocent, but how are you going to persuade everyone else?"

"Austin, don't."

"Don't what?"

"Don't do this to me. I know you're mad. I know you're hurt, but that wasn't my intention. All I wanted was a little time for myself."

"And your wish was my command."

"I'm sorry. I really am. I mean that."

"Nothing to be sorry for. Hope you've enjoyed yourself."

Sloan stared at him. "I can see this is not going to get us anyplace."

"Afraid not."

"Then why don't we talk about the tape? And please, don't play dumb. You know what I'm referring to." She could tell she'd caught him by surprise.

"What is it you want to know?" A note of caution had crept into his voice.

"Whose idea was it to make that *movie*, if that's what you want to call it?"

"You saw it?"

"Of course I saw it."

"How'd you manage that? I gave it to Bayard for editing and he passed it on to Troy so he could have a look and then it went back to Fritz, who swore he wouldn't let it out of his sight."

"Fritz is a moron. You trust him, you're dumber than I thought."

"The point is, why come to me? You should be interrogating him."

"How so?"

"The equipment is his. His parents gave it to him for his birthday."

"Why is that relevant?"

"How do you know he didn't come up with the idea himself?"

"Yeah, right."

"Better yet, ask Iris. She said she's always wanted to be a porno star. Well, I guess she got her wish."

"She was drunk."

"She was *pretending* to be drunk. It was a stunt. Iris was in on it from the get-go. No one ever laid a hand on her."

"Really? That isn't what I saw. I saw Fritz and Troy shove foreign objects up her ass while she was sprawled on a pool table completely out of it."

"She was sober. Take my word for it."

"Bullshit. Early on, Fritz pours her a glass full of gin and she belts it down. Next thing you know, she's slurring her words, begging you for a kiss."

"I thought I just told you, I never laid a hand on her."

"You said *no one* ever laid a hand on her."

"I didn't touch her. Not once. I can't answer for anyone else."

"But there you sat in a sport coat and tie, idly looking on while those guys assaulted her. Fritz got out a fucking can of Crisco for god's sake, and there's Troy, dick in hand, ready to grease it up so he can stick it to her. Iris is fourteen and you were egging them on. You were the director, *the man in charge*. Isn't that what you said? Do you know the penalty for sexual abuse of a minor?"

"What sexual abuse? You've got no proof."

"Oh, but I do. The tape *is* the proof."

Austin fixed his attention on her. "That's bullshit."

"Uh, no. Not so. I have the tape and I stashed it somewhere safe. If the shunning doesn't stop, I'll take it to the police. And by the way, there goes law school for you. How do you think your family will feel about that?"

"You're nuts. I had nothing to do with it."

"Fine. Explain to the cops just how blameless you are."

"The tape is fake."

"Doesn't look like that. Now do you want to call off the shunning or not?"

"This is laughable. You think you can push me around?"

"To this extent, yes."

"Sorry to disabuse you of the notion, but no deal. The shunning goes on for as long as I say."

"Last chance," she sang.

"Last chance, my ass. Treat me like shit and that's what you get back."

"No, Austin. That's what *you'll* get."

16

Thursday, September 21, 1989

Thursday morning, I stopped by the office to pick up messages and mail and found nothing of note. I set the alarm system, locked up, and then drove to the Horton Ravine address I'd found for Bayard Montgomery in the telephone book. Most of the ravine was swathed in coastal fog, but on the elevated acreage where Bayard lived, there was full sun. His house was built along contemporary lines, sleek and low, the exterior sheathed in broad expanses of glass and vertical redwood beams weathered to a silvery hue. The lawn had been replaced with a drought-tolerant ground cover and looked more like Arizona than the typical California landscape of palms and bougainvillea. The climate in this part of the state is considered Mediterranean, but the coastal lowlands are actually semi-arid, and when water is scarce, the region reverts to desert conditions.

While the sex tape had provided graphic images of

Fritz and Troy without their underpanties, I'd never seen a photograph of Bayard, so I was unprepared for the guy who answered the door. I figured Bayard, like his classmates, was in his mid- to late twenties, but he looked closer to forty, dark-haired, unshaven, and barefoot, wearing jeans and a form-fitting white T-shirt with the word "factotum" in lower-case black letters across the front. I assumed "factotum" was just another crappy rock band I'd never heard of.

I handed him a business card and said, "Kinsey Millhone. I'm a local private investigator. I apologize for showing up without calling first, but I'm hoping for a few minutes of your time."

"Bayard's the one you want. He's been expecting you."

"He has?"

"Isn't this about the tape?"

"How did you know?"

"Let's just say a little birdie told me. He and Maisie are out by the pool. If you'll follow me."

"Sure."

"I'm Ellis, by the way."

"Nice meeting you," I said. Here I'd tried to be so dainty, conducting my business without revealing who I was working for and why, while everyone involved seemed to know. I tried to picture all the phone calls that had been flying around since I'd begun my inquiry. These "kids" may not have been on speaking terms for the past ten years, but they were certainly communicating now. Fritz to Troy to Bayard. I wasn't sure if Iris and Poppy had been included in the telephone round-robin, but chances were good.

I tagged along behind Ellis, parsing what he'd said. Fritz had apparently alerted Bayard that his parents had engaged my services. If he'd called before Saturday simply to alert him to the blackmail scheme, my name wouldn't have come into it. It did save me an awkward introduction, but the advance notice had given Bayard time to consider exactly what and how much he'd tell me. Given my natural skepticism, I distrusted others' ability to tell the truth. Heaven knows I have a problem with it myself.

Meanwhile, I was busy taking in the details of the interior of the house, at least the portion I managed to spy with my little eye. The floors were highly polished concrete. The furnishings were modern, which is to say reduced to basic geometric shapes. All of the upholstery fabrics appeared to be selected for people wearing wet bathing suits. The space was airy: high ceilings, white walls flooded with natural light. In the middle of one conversational grouping in the great room, there was a sixty-inch-square coffee table made of driftwood. The surfaces were stripped down to the occasional artful object—a pedestal bowl planted with succulents, a perfect orange placed beside an 8-by-8-inch oil painting of a perfect orange. This was clearly the work of a precious interior designer working with unlimited funds. I knew it was unreasonably expensive because the results were so understated. I wanted to dislike the effect, but the truth was, I loved the look.

We crossed the room and passed through the floor-to-ceiling glass folding doors that opened directly onto the patio. The pool looked like a gaudy cocktail ring, a giant oblong of turquoise sunk in a setting of stone. Bayard and Maisie were nut-brown, newly basted with oil, and stretched out on two oversize wooden recliners upholstered in white. Neither seemed to be worried about getting oil stains on the fabric. On the built-in table between them, there were two Bloody Marys topped with small red and green peppers on stainless-steel skewers. Maisie was in a royal blue bikini and a broad-brimmed hat, with a band of blue-and-white-checked ribbon around the crown. Bayard wore sunglasses and a skimpy black Speedo, the bulge in front suggesting this was where he carried his leather sap.

Ellis said, "This is Kinsey Millhone, the PI."

Bayard swung his feet to the side and sat up, then removed his sunglasses, which he placed on top of his head. He laid a small white towel across the back of his neck and used the ends to mop the sheen of sweat from his face. His hair was dark and thick, sticking out in sections like an unruly pile of twigs. His eyes were chocolate brown and carried a touch of merriment, as though he were on the verge of laughing aloud.

"Nice meeting you," he said, offering a handshake. He was lean and muscular, but there was a puffy quality to his features that suggested a lifestyle of waste and excess. Maisie stayed where she was, her face largely concealed by her hat brim.

Ellis stood at the ready in case something else was required of him.

Bayard said, "You're here to talk about the tape."

"That and Sloan Stevens. Would you prefer discussing this in private?"

"That's a fine idea. Why don't we step into my office?"

I expected to move into the house, but Bayard picked up his Bloody Mary and crossed to a glass-topped table with an oversize tan umbrella that shaded the area. He gestured at a chair and I took a seat, keenly aware that Maisie and Ellis were both in hearing range. I had to guess there'd been a briefing prior to my arrival as all three seemed aware of my purpose in visiting.

He sat down across from me. "Would you like a drink? Ellis makes an evil Bloody Mary that will put you right with the world."

It was nine thirty in the morning.

"I'm fine for now," I said, as though in mere moments I might need to belt down a shot of something eighty-six proof.

Ellis excused himself and disappeared into the house.

"I mistook him for you," I said sheepishly. "He's a friend of yours?"

"An employee. He's worked for me the past five years. Butler, valet, personal trainer, accomplished chef, and chauffeur."

"That's fancy. I don't think I know anyone else with a chauffeur."

"It's a matter of practicality since neither one of us drives. I lost my license after three DUIs and she let hers expire. As much as we drink, we're doing the public a service by putting him behind the wheel. Not that we're alcoholics by any stretch. You know how I know? Alcoholics go to all those meetings," he said.

He shoved four fingers in his mouth and pretended to bite down. The gesture had a comic quality though I'd already heard the joke.

"This is Maisie. Rude of me not to introduce you before now. Take your hat off, sweetheart, and show Ms. Millhone what a pretty face you have."

She lifted her hat and set it to one side, gracing me with a languid stare. She made no move to greet me, which left me free to study her without appearing to be too interested. She had long, glossy, jet-black hair and clear blue eyes, her black lashes long and thick. She was beautifully made up, her foundation a perfect blend with her skin tone, eyes subtly shaded to enhance her coloring. Given her flawless complexion, the impact was electric. She was slender and her stomach was so flat, it was nearly concave. I judged her impressive cleavage to be original equipment without surgical enhancement. Some women have all the luck. She appeared older than he was, but the difference in years wasn't sufficient to cast her as his mother. A girlfriend, perhaps? Her placid manner suggested she was living on the premises and hadn't simply stopped by for a drink and an early morning swim. She put her hat across her face again and returned to the serious work of maintaining her tan.

Bayard leaned close and whispered theatrically, "She's my wicked stepmother—Tigg's widow. He didn't leave her much when he died, so I'm making it up to her. She's never had a job in her life. She has style, but that's a hard sell these days."

The scent of yesterday's bourbon wafted from his skin like aftershave.

I said, "What about you? Do you work?" I knew the answer, but I was curious how he'd respond.

He smiled. "You think I could afford all this if I had a *job*? What kind of work would I do? I don't even have a college degree. Turns out I pay Ellis more than the average attorney makes. You like the place?"

"It's incredible."

"I designed it myself. It took three years to build and we've been in it for five. Tigg had this dump of a house in Colgate, a 1950s ranch style in a subdivision with third-of-an-acre lots. He was busy demonstrating how humble and down to earth he was by continuing to live in the first home he'd ever bought. I had that pigsty sold within a month."

"What sort of work did he do?"

"Investments. He was a wizard with money and made a number of folks in this town very, very rich."

Maisie spoke up. "It's fortunate he died when he did. He was actually a flimflam man who narrowly escaped jail."

"Not quite the case, but I did have to make good on a few promises," Bayard remarked.

"Someone told me he died during the trial."

"True, but not before he brokered a deal in the matter of Sloan's untimely demise. I was granted immunity in exchange for my testimony. I answered every question asked of me as truthfully as I knew how. Poor Fritz."

"Why 'poor Fritz'?"

"Because he was smitten with Austin and Austin's the one who set him up. That night at the cabin . . . I'm assuming you know the basics of what went on . . ."

"More or less," I said.

"Austin suggested we draw straws to determine who would carry the gun. Troy went first, then me, and both of us drew long straws. Fritz pulled the short straw, so the honor was his. Austin didn't show us the last remaining straw, which fell to him, of course. I suspect the last two straws were both short, so he'd already made up his mind Fritz was 'it.' "

"Really."

"Look at the situation. Fritz was fifteen at the time of the shooting, so Austin assumed he'd be tried as a juvenile, which he was. His record was clean and this was a first offense. Not that killing is a minor matter, by any stretch, but Austin thought he'd skate out from under the worst of it. He could have done that, too, if he'd behaved himself."

"You're saying he knew in advance Fritz would shoot her?"

"I'm saying Austin knew if anybody used that gun, Fritz was the least experienced and the most likely to fire wild," Bayard said. "Either way, better Fritz than him. Once Fritz broke down and confessed, Austin took off. By the end of it all . . . irony of ironies . . . Troy was tried as an adult and sentenced to five years, of which he served half. Fritz ended up at California Youth Authority until his twenty-fifth birthday, essentially eight years. Imagine his dismay."

Irritably, Maisie said, "Bayard, she's here to talk about Sloan. You're obfuscating."

"Oooh. Catch you using such a big word," he said with mock admiration.

"You want me to define it? Darken, confuse, evade. You do it all the time. Someone poses a question you don't like and you start beating around the bush."

"Thank you, Maisie, but nobody asked you to butt in," he said mildly.

"Sorry, sir."

Personally, I appreciated her intervention, which allowed me to pick up the thread. "I understand you and Sloan were good friends."

"I was the only one who stood up for her when she was shunned." He finished the last of his Bloody Mary and set the glass aside with a smart tap of glass on glass.

"I'm told the shunning was Austin's idea. Why'd you put up with him? You must have known what kind of person he was."

Bayard's smile was pained. "Thing is, all of us were a little bit in love with him. He was mean. He was unpredictable. We were all insecure and none of us knew how to handle him. If he smiled on you, you felt special and life was good. As long as you were in favor, you felt important. If he turned on you, you'd be stricken and you'd do anything to get back in his good graces. I can see it now, but I couldn't see it back then."

"Was it general knowledge that Fritz had a crush on him?"

"Sure. That's why he worked so hard to impress Austin. That gun business was a case in point. Fritz pulls it out of the drawer and he's waving it around. Scared the shit out of us because he'd been drinking and who knew what he'd do? Stringer and Patti and Betsy took off about then. The situation was volatile. So Austin's putting Fritz down, insulting the shit out of him, which he'd been doing all day. Fritz was practically wetting his pants trying to show Austin what a cool guy he was. Later, Austin hands him the gun and makes a point of showing him how to take the safety off. Fritz is walking around, acting all goofy because he's suddenly the apple of Austin's eye. Austin set him up. He knew exactly what was going down. Have you seen a photograph of him?"

"There's a cut-away to him on the tape."

"I'm not sure you were treated to the full effect. There's something intimidating about him—an inbred contempt. He's handsome and haughty and very sure of himself. He behaved like an aristocrat and we paid tribute. He and Sloan had a brief romance. Austin broke it off."

Maisie stirred on her chaise and sat up. She picked up her drink, slipped her feet into her sandals, and crossed the patio without a word, leather soles clacking on the pavement. There was something frigid in her body language.

"Is she upset?"

"Don't worry about it. She's a temperamental girl."

I found myself following her progress into the house, where she disappeared from view. Subterranean frictions set my teeth on edge. This was a pair who fought in front of others without raising their voices or modifying their smiles: verbal abuse framed as jest, with words flying back and forth as softly as cotton balls. I returned my attention to Bayard.

"Why was Sloan the one made to suffer? If Austin rejected her, wasn't that sufficient punishment?"

"Not the way he saw it. He's sensitive about his public persona and careful nothing will tarnish his façade. He was also highly competitive. No one got in his way."

"I notice you switch between present and past tense. Do you think he's dead or alive?"

"Alive. I mean, he must still be out there—unless you've heard something to the contrary. Death is the great unmasker, don't you think? Alive, he could be anyone, anywhere. Dead, he'd be identified as soon as his prints were run."

"He's in the system?"

"I assume so. If he applied for a driver's license, they'd have his thumbprint, wouldn't they?"

"Why was Sloan such a threat to him?"

"If he ever shows up again, I'll ask."

"I'm puzzled by the underlying dynamic between them. Did you understand what was happening?"

"I knew about the falling-out. I didn't know his intention, if he had one."

Ellis appeared with another Bloody Mary. Bayard thanked him briefly and Ellis withdrew, padding silently into the house.

"You never guessed?" I asked. "No inkling at all about how the rift would play out?"

He did a one-shoulder shrug. "He'd called off the shunning. To all appearances, that was that. If he had any lingering animosity, he didn't let it show. He made a point of inviting her to the party. If he was angry, why would he do that?"

"Maybe his plan was to lure her up there so he could kill her," I said.

"Why would he want to kill her?"

"That's what I'm asking you."

Bayard gave that some thought. "I'm guessing his plan, if he had one, was impromptu. I don't think he wanted her dead. He wanted her submissive. She stood up to him. He thought scaring her would make her back down."

"Which explains the grave he dug earlier?"

He focused on me fully. "I'd forgotten about that."

"The grave site didn't come to light until the body was found," I said. "That's where he buried her. I should say 'you' since you all participated."

"Right. Until then, as nearly as I could tell, there was nothing sinister going on. It was summer. The end of school. We were partying. Any intuitions I might have had were blunted by dope and alcohol."

"At least you don't pretty up your part in it," I said.

"I wish I could claim credit for candor, but I'm not nearly so innocent."

"Tell me about the tape. What was that about?"

"Essentially a practical joke. It was a lark, you know? We were laughing our asses off. Given the extortionist's demands, I guess you could say it backfired, which is too bad for Fritz."

"Fritz says you did the editing. What happened to the outtakes?"

"No idea. I've always thought Austin took them when he left."

"Someone told me your father left you very well-off."

"Extremely well-off. Embarrassingly rich."

"I'm wondering why the extortionist didn't come after you with a similar demand."

"There'd be no point. I never appeared on camera, so if the poor fool came after me, he'd find out I'm untouchable."

"How did Sloan know about the tape if she wasn't in it?"

"I told her."

"*You* did."

"Sure. I suggested she steal it and use it as leverage."

I said, "Really." I was having trouble folding his revelations into the mix. He seemed both unsparing of himself and completely matter-of-fact, which left me wondering about his motivation. I couldn't tell if he was operating out of guilt, rationalization, or some other sentiment.

"She didn't like the idea, but I talked her into it," he said.

"How do you deal with that in retrospect?"

"You're asking if I'm ashamed of the part I played? Of course, but it's something I have to live with. I wish it had turned out differently, but it didn't."

I waited, giving him no prompt. I decided I might learn more if I let him decide where to go next. He was quiet for a moment.

"Here's something I never told anyone. After Sloan died, I asked if I could have her dog. He's an absolutely incredible animal and I'd have taken comfort in caring for him, but her mother turned me down. I guess we're all still looking for ways to hang on to Sloan. Poppy's writing about the murder. Troy's atoning with good deeds."

"What good deeds?"

"When he got out of prison, he raised the money to establish a scholarship in her name."

"A worthy cause."

"Typical of Troy. Hiding his light under a bushel," Bayard said, "which is actually a corruption of the biblical quote. 'Neither do men light a candle, and put it under a bushel, but on a candlestick; and it giveth light unto all that are in the house.' These days we're admonished to be modest about our accomplishments, which spoils all the fun."

"Impressive that you can recite that," I said.

"Humility annoys me. I keep the quote handy in case someone pulls that horseshit around me."

"What about Iris? How has she managed to hang on?"

"Easy. She's engaged to Joey Seay."

"Sloan's *stepbrother*?"

"Oh my, yes. Am I the first to mention it?"

"She said she was getting married. She didn't tell me who."

Bayard regarded me with a sparkle in his eye and it was clear he was having a high old time at her expense. "I wonder what kind of game she's playing," he said. "If you think about it, she's responsible for everything that went down back then. Because she stole the test, Troy and Poppy cheated. Because they cheated, someone turned them in. Because Austin blamed Sloan for it, she was shunned and ended up using the tape to threaten him. Because Austin retaliated, she died. Cause and effect; like the fruit of the poisonous tree."

"Put it like that and Sloan's mother couldn't be happy about having Iris in the family."

"You'd have to ask her. Maybe she hasn't put it together in quite the same way. I guess we all see what we want to see."

"But how did they connect? Iris and Joey. It seems so convoluted."

"Not at all. They met at Santa Teresa High School, which is where Iris was sent when she was kicked out of Climp. After Sloan's death, the two boys decided to move in with their dad. Joey was in the same graduating class she was. His brother, Justin, was two years behind."

Bayard's eyes shifted to the door, where Ellis stood.

"Phone for you," he said.

Bayard pushed his chair back and got up. "Sorry. You're welcome to stay if you like."

"This is fine. I appreciate your time. I may pick this conversation up again once I've had a chance to digest the information."

"Anytime."

Ellis accompanied me to the front door and I returned to my car.

I opened the door on the driver's side and slid under the wheel. I sat for a few minutes jotting down notes on my index cards. When I glanced back at the house, I saw Maisie standing at a window, her blue eyes fixed on mine. I held the look, perplexed, and she finally broke off eye contact. What was *that* about? I tucked the index cards in my bag, turned the key in the ignition, and put the car in reverse. When I checked the window again, she was gone.

17

I spent the bulk of Thursday afternoon canvassing motels in Winterset and Cottonwood. Canvassing, like surveillance, is an unrelenting bore. So often, the results bear no relationship to the energy you expend. I've sat for hours in a parked car, hoping to catch sight of my subject to no avail. On other occasions, I pick up the trail almost by accident. Patience is the key. There's no point in getting surly about the chore, because it comes with the turf. In this case, it was such a relief to get away from Bayard and Maisie, I couldn't complain. It says something about the state of relationships these days when hunting for a stone-cold killer is more restful than being witness to a romance.

Winterset is located five miles south of Santa Teresa and covers approximately 1.5 square miles, rising to an elevation of one hundred and twenty feet above sea level. The population, at the last census, showed fewer than twelve hundred souls. The Cape Cod–style bungalows perched along the hillside, which now sell for more than a million bucks apiece, were once summer homes for white middle-class migrants coming up from Los Angeles.

Cottonwood, seven miles further south along the 101, is known for the tar springs a Spanish expedition spotted on the beach in 1769. Petroleum-derived pitch is black in color, thus giving rise to the phrase "pitch-black." The native Indian tribes used this foul-smelling substance to caulk their canoes. Petroleum seeps are still visible in the area, which is also home to a number of scenic offshore drilling platforms. A small cottage industry has sprung up creating products that remove pitch from the bottoms of your feet after a day at the Cottonwood beach.

"Naturally occurring asphalt or bitumen, a type of pitch, is a viscoelastic polymer." I know this because I looked it up in the encyclopedia set my Aunt Gin was conned into buying from a door-to-door salesman. In the fourth grade, I wrote a report on the subject, which I knew was accurate because I copied it word for word. "Even though this polymer seems to be solid at room temperature and can be shattered on impact," I wrote, "it is actually fluid and flows over time, but extremely slowly. The 'pitch drop' experiment taking place at the University of Queensland demonstrates the movement of a pitch sample over many years. For the experiment, pitch was put in a glass funnel and allowed to drip out. Since the pitch experiment began in 1930, only eight drops have fallen. It was recently calculated that the pitch in the experiment has a viscosity that's approximately two hundred and thirty billion times that of water."

I got an F on the report and a testy lecture on plagiarism, which was news to me. I went back and added quote marks, but Miss Manning wouldn't raise my grade. Shit. What did she expect? I was nine years old.

The combined townships of Winterset and Cottonwood boast one hotel, twelve motels, and three inns, the latter being a fancy designation for an overpriced B&B.

These establishments are located just far enough away from each other that I was forced to drive from point to point. I also stopped in at chain restaurants, diners, and service stations, doling out Ned's mug shot, the brief note about his criminal history, and my business card. Fourteen of the businesses I approached had nothing to report, though the employees expressed suitable alarm at the notion of offering courtesies to a homicidal maniac.

The clerk in the second-to-last motel was a fellow named Bradley Benoit: white, in his seventies, with gray bushy eyebrows and a bald, freckled pate. When I slid the bulletin across the reception desk to him, he politely slid it back.

He said, "Let me tell you something, young lady. The law in California requires hotel and motel operators to collect and record data about their guests in either paper or electronic form. The register must contain the guest's name and address; the number of people in the guest's party; the make, model, and license plate number of the guest's vehicle if the vehicle will be parked on hotel property; the guest's date and time of arrival and scheduled date of departure; the room number assigned to the guest; the rate charged and the amount collected for the room; and the method of payment."

I was about to cut into the conversation, but he was just warming up.

"In addition, we're required to turn such records over to law enforcement upon request. I don't see any reason to comply since this compels business owners to collect personal data on our customers and turn it over without proper warrants or consent. As citizens, we have privacy rights which we shouldn't be expected to waive simply because we're traveling. You know what this violates?"

"No clue."

"The Fourth Amendment of the United States Constitution."

I tapped a finger on the police bulletin. "Do you see this gentleman? He's wanted in connection with the kidnapping, assault, rape, and murder of a number of teenaged girls, so while I applaud and support your point, I'm really not concerned about his constitutional rights. All I want to know is whether you've seen him. A simple 'yes' or 'no' will suffice."

"I have not."

I handed him a business card. "Thank you for your time."

"You needn't be impertinent," he said.

At the last motel, the Sand Bar, I had better luck.

A registration clerk named Sebastian Palfrey recognized Ned, but said he'd checked out three days earlier. As was true of the previous clerk, Sebastian was white and in his seventies. Perhaps this was a new employment trend among retirees. He wore wire-rimmed spectacles and his long gray hair was pulled back in a ponytail. The second and third fingers on his right hand had turned golden from cigarette smoke.

"Is Ned Lowe the name he used?"

"I don't believe so, but I can check."

"Thanks."

He pulled up a stack of registration cards. "This may take a minute. These are in date order and I'm behind on my filing." He went through the cards, reading each in turn. "Here we go. Hoover. J. E. Hoover."

"J. Edgar Hoover. Very cute," I said. "Can I see the address?"

He turned the card so I could read it and then handed me a piece of scratch paper. "Probably bogus," he remarked.

"You never know. As long as he's being cocky, he might have thrown in a truth or two just to amuse himself." I made a note of the address, which was in Louisville. "Did he show you a photo ID?"

"A Kentucky driver's license, which looked all right, but might have been counterfeit. I've never seen a real one, so there was no way I could challenge him even if it had occurred to me."

"Any idea why he chose this motel?"

"Rooms are forty-nine dollars a night, which is cheaper than most. He paid cash, stayed for three nights, and checked out on Monday."

"What about his mode of transportation?"

He angled the registration card. "You can see here, we have a box for vehicle make and model. He left it blank."

"You didn't see a car parked outside his room?"

"I never thought to look. We don't charge for parking, so it's all the same to me. He had a backpack, now that I think about it. Lightweight aluminum frame with a red nylon sleeping bag secured across the top."

"If he was traveling on foot, it seems like he'd have been conspicuous in an area like this."

Palfrey offered an apologetic shrug. "He said he was passing through. Given his boots and camping gear, I assumed he'd been hiking. He might have been headed to a trailhead."

"Don't think so. He showed up in Santa Teresa midday on Monday," I said. "Did he mention his destination?"

"Not a word. He's a quiet fellow. I like to chat with guests because it establishes a friendlier atmosphere for folks away from home. Small talk didn't interest him. He was polite, I was polite, and we let it go at that."

"If you think of anything else, could you let me know?"

"I'll be happy to. Wish I had more to offer."

"You've been a big help."

I was uneasy on the drive back to Santa Teresa. The attempted break-in at my office on Monday was consistent with Ned's checking out of the Sand Bar Motel and traveling north. I'd spotted him in my neighborhood on Tuesday night, which placed him squarely in Santa Teresa. So far, the STPD and Pearl's homeless pals hadn't turned up any sign of him. Ned was like a poisonous snake—better to keep in sight than to wonder where he might strike next. There had to be a way to find him.

It occurred to me that I ought to have a conversation with Ned's second wife, Phyllis Joplin, who was living in Perdido the last I'd heard. I'd learned about her when the now-deceased detective Pete Wolinsky had picked up an early whiff of Ned's pathology. Pete had put together a list of the women who'd been closely associated with him and suffered in consequence. I'd known Pete early in my career and I'd thought little of him until I understood how astute he'd been at ferreting out Ned's history. First on the list was the high school girlfriend Ned had been obsessed with who'd since moved out of state. Next was the name of the girl he married shortly afterward, who'd died under cloudy circumstances. His second wife, Phyllis, had had the strength and the good sense to divorce him. A psychologist named Taryn Sizemore, who dated Ned for two years, also managed to disentangle herself.

Over the span of some twenty-five years or so, he'd used his hobby, photography, to present himself as a scout from the New York fashion industry, crisscrossing the Southwest in search of fresh talent. The last two names on Pete's list had turned out to be two of the young girls he'd murdered. As good as his word, he did indeed take their pictures, along with their lives. The police had discovered hundreds of additional photographs in the darkroom he abandoned in the dead of night. Not all of his photographic subjects had been killed and there was no apparent pattern to those who survived. He was by then married to his third wife, Celeste, who'd been rescued by friends shortly after his crimes came to light. From that point on, he had the full fury of law enforcement breathing down his neck. So far, he'd managed to evade capture.

I'd never met Phyllis face-to-face. I pictured her big and blond, but I was probably way off. After Pete's death, I'd spoken to her by phone. She told me Ned specialized in wooing vulnerable women, who were easy to dominate. When she met him, she was newly divorced, unemployed, overweight, and had developed a nervous condition that made her hair fall out in clumps. Early in the romance he made a point of turning on the charm, which morphed into neediness, and shortly thereafter turned murderous. He introduced her to asphyxiophilia, the happy practice of choking your bed partner to the point of losing consciousness as a means of increasing sexual arousal. She was embarrassed to admit the hold he had on her because by then, she found him repulsive in every other aspect of their lives together.

I took out my address book and looked up her number. I dialed and she picked up on the first ring, rattling off the name of her business, which I didn't catch. I knew she was a certified public accountant, but that was the extent of it. "Phyllis. This is Kinsey Millhone up in Santa Teresa. We spoke six months ago."

"You're the private detective. I remember you," she said. "I hope you're calling to say Ned Lowe is dead."

"No such luck. He's been spotted in the area and I thought you should know."

"Well, I appreciate the warning. I heard he's wanted in five states, so I've been rooting for someone to shoot him down in cold blood."

"We all have our hopes and dreams," I replied.

"I'd have said 'shoot him down like a dog' but I don't want to denigrate our four-footed friends."

"What about Celeste? I'd like to warn her that he could show up on her doorstep. Any idea how I can get hold of her?"

"Good question. How'd you find out he was back?"

I noticed she'd bypassed my question about Celeste, but I let that slide for the moment. "He tried to break into my office. I had an alarm system installed six months ago, so he wasn't able to accomplish much except to break a window with a rock. That was Monday of this week. Tuesday night while I was out, he stopped by my studio asking friends about me."

"This is making me sick. I thought we'd seen the last of him, but clearly not. I trust the police are on it."

"They're doing what they can. They've stepped up patrols and they've circulated his mug shot to the motels and hotels in the beach area here. They've also notified law enforcement in Perdido and Olvidado. A couple of my homeless pals have alerted the local shelters. I just got back from a run to Winterset and Cottonwood, distributing fliers with his photograph and a thumbnail account of what he's wanted for. The manager of the Sand Bar Motel recognized him. He told me he'd stayed there for three nights and checked out Monday morning."

"How'd they get a mug shot? I didn't know he had a record."

"He assaulted a young girl in Burning Oaks. This was maybe six years ago. He was arrested, booked, photographed, and fingerprinted. He posted bail and he was released OR. The girl disappeared shortly after that and they dropped the case. As far as I know, that's his one and only police contact."

"He's a cunning son of a bitch. Any idea what he's up to?"

"That's what I've been asking myself."

"I'll tell you my guess. The man wants his trinkets."

"Ah. From the young girls he killed," I said. "I remember Celeste telling me about his so-called souvenirs. She found the key to a locked file drawer and removed them while he was off on a business trip."

"I don't think she understood the significance," Phyllis said. "All she knew was how furious he became when he found out what she'd done."

"I take it she didn't leave anything with you."

"Oh, hell no. Are you kidding me? That's evidence. If she'd given me that stuff, I'd have handed it over to the police. She must have held on to it herself."

"Well, I know she didn't pass it on to Pete Wolinsky before he died. Ned went to great trouble searching his widow's house and never found a thing. What puzzles me is how abruptly he's managed to drop out of sight. It's like a disappearing act. Now you see him, now you don't. He has to be around here someplace."

"You might try RV and mobile home parks. He likes taking his housing with him. He's like a hermit crab in that respect."

"Good suggestion. Thanks. What about the house he and Celeste owned in Cottonwood? What's happened to that?"

"Still sitting there as far as I know. If the bank foreclosed, I'd have seen the notice in the paper."

"You think it's possible he's taken up residence there?"

"Possible," she said without conviction. "Utilities have been cut, so he'd have a roof over his head but not much else."

"What about his friends?"

"Ned doesn't have friends."

"What about acquaintances? He must know someone in the area."

"I doubt it. No one who'd put him up, at any rate. There's nothing warm and fuzzy about our Ned. He's a robot who's learned to mimic human behavior with no emotional underpinnings. That's what makes him so good at manipulation. He has an uncanny radar for your innermost needs and he feeds you malarkey so good you're convinced you've found your soul mate. I fell for it myself and I always thought I was one smart cookie."

"You know where Celeste is these days?"

"You already asked me that."

"I'm keenly aware of it, Phyllis, which is why I asked you again."

"Look, she changed her name and relocated. Even with an alias, her number's unlisted. She's not taking any chances."

"She must have been in touch or you wouldn't know that much."

"She called once to let me know she was okay. I have the name and address around here someplace. I made a note on a piece of paper I stuck in a box. I moved six weeks ago and I still have unopened U-Haul cartons stacked up in the back bedroom."

"When you find it, why don't you call her and let her know what's going on? That way you won't betray a confidence."

I heard a phone ringing on her end. "You want to get that?"

"The machine will pick up," she said. "I got an idea. Why don't you come down for a glass of wine and a bite of supper? We can talk about Ned and maybe brainstorm ideas."

"I'd love that. When?"

"I'm tied up tonight. What about tomorrow night?"

"No good. I'm going to a birthday party in the neighborhood."

"How about Saturday?"

"Sounds good. I can bring the wine if you like."

"Don't worry about it. I've got plenty. I just bought a condominium in a gated community. I'll leave your name with the security guard and he'll direct you from there. The units look like row houses. You'll think they're all connected, but they're set up in pairs, so there are actually two of us, A and B, at this street number. Once you get to my building, you'll enter the vestibule and press the call button under my name. That will ring me upstairs and I'll send the elevator down for you. Or, if the elevator's down, you can press the call button just inside the door, identify yourself, and I'll bring you up. Come around five and we can sit out on the balcony and watch the sun set. I'll do us up a little something. I'm not much of a cook, so don't get your hopes up."

"I don't cook at all, so anything you do will be a treat."

"Let me give you my new address."

I made a note of it and told her I'd be there at five on Saturday.

We hung up and I continued to sit, contemplating the question of Ned's whereabouts. I was already having doubts about Phyllis's suggestion regarding mobile home and RV parks. A quick check of the phone book showed ten mobile home parks in the area: two close to downtown and the remaining eight in Colgate. While it had sounded like a dandy suggestion, I couldn't picture him buying or renting a mobile home. In truth, mobile homes aren't mobile at all. A mobile home functions as a fixed base of operations in a park with permanent water and electric hookups, a street address, and monthly rent due on the lot where it's moored. Ned was the last person in the world who'd settle down in a community where he was wanted for murder.

As for RV parks, there were two: one fifteen miles north of the city and the other one forty miles north. I ruled those out on the premise that Ned wouldn't want to place himself at such a geographical remove. To all appearances, he'd been on foot when he checked out of the Sand Bar, and he was certainly on foot when I caught sight of him on Albanil Tuesday night. With a backpack and sleeping bag, he was most likely camping somewhere close by. I couldn't rule out the possibility that he had a car at his disposal (owned, rented, or stolen) but it would put him at risk for parking tickets, moving violations, and equipment infractions that might expose him to notice by traffic enforcement officers.

I armed and locked the office and went home. Ed, the cat, was sitting on the sidewalk, just outside the gate.

"What are you doing out here?"

Ed wasn't feeling chatty, so I reached down, picked him up, and carried him around to the backyard. I deposited him inside Henry's kitchen door and returned to my place. I changed into my sweats and running shoes and used the run as a moving meditation on Ned Lowe. What was his thinking process? He had to have shelter; at the very least, a place where he could hole up out of the public eye. He'd have to eat, which meant fast-food places, coffee shops, bars, or restaurants; more likely a local market where he could stockpile supplies. He needed access to a toilet, which suggested service stations, the public bathrooms at the marina, or the use of the men's room in a city park, which might also provide cover. Wherever he was, I needed to run him to ground soon, for my safety as well as the safety of others. Though I didn't know it at the time, this was a thought that would come back to haunt me later.

18

IRIS AND JOEY

Thursday, September 21, 1989

Iris and Joey parked in the public lot behind the Clockworks and walked through the passageway to State Street where the front door was located. For years, the place had been a teen hangout, the bulk of the business devoted to soft drinks and cheap snacks, creating the illusion of a bar without the alcohol. They did sell two off-brands of beer and generic red and white wines if you could provide tangible proof you were of age. Most of the patrons in those days were the under-eighteen crowd feigning maturity with none of the responsibilities.

Joey opened the door and held it for Iris. The two paused in the entrance, scanning the crowd for some sign of Fritz. The place was smoky and dark, the walls painted charcoal gray, with lighting that consisted primarily of green and purple neon tubing. Suspended from the high ceiling were oversize black gears, abstract suggestions of the interior of a clock: the anchor, the escapement wheel, with oscillating wheels and springs. Two years before, the owners had upgraded the establishment, which was now a full bar. They'd bought the storefront next door and had broken through the connecting wall. The expansion allowed them to double their space, which now included a second room with a jukebox, six pool tables, and six pinball machines. It was Thursday night and the place was jammed. The crowd was restless and noisy, which created an odd intimacy. Iris spotted Fritz sitting alone in a booth to their left.

"There."

"Got him," Joey murmured.

Fritz spotted them and smiled, vigorously waving his hand like they might not otherwise notice him.

Iris kept her eyes pinned on Fritz, her smile in place. Under her breath she said, "I hate that guy. Look at the stupid smirk on his face. Bet he's still proud of himself for what he did to me."

Joey put a hand in the middle of her back, gently steering her toward Fritz's table. "Don't go down that road, Iris. This is all sweetness and light. As far as he's concerned, we're best buds. Happy to have him back in our midst."

"Don't you dare leave me alone with him."

"Not to worry. Be cool."

Fritz half rose from his seat, slightly off balance until he steadied himself. Joey reached out and shook his hand and Iris made a halfhearted gesture toward a kiss on the cheek. Fritz was smoking a cigarette. Nearby there was a half-filled ashtray and a nearly empty highball glass. He'd missed the ashtray with one butt and had put it out on the tabletop. He sat down again, perhaps a bit more abruptly than he intended. "Hey, guys. I didn't expect to see you."

Joey said, "Iris got restless, so here we are. What's your drink of choice? I'm buying this round."

"Seagram's Seven and 7."

Joey turned to Iris. "What about you, babe?"

"Beer's fine with me. I'll go. You can sit here and talk to Fritz."

"You sure?"

"Not a problem. I'll be right back."

Joey handed her a twenty-dollar bill and she moved away from the table and crossed to the bar, pushing her way past singles who were lined up five deep.

Joey slid into the bench opposite Fritz. "How long have you been here?"

Fritz smashed his cigarette out, grinding it in the ashtray. "'Bout an hour. I can't stand being home. My folks are always on my case. Yammer, yammer, yammer." He raised his hand and made a puppet mouth with his thumb and fingers, saying, "Blah blah blah. Know what I mean?"

"Iris and I are lucky. We don't have to put up with that shit."

"I'm gone every chance I get. Hanging with Stringer and Berg out at their place, which is way cool. Me and the guys are like this." Fritz held up his crossed fingers.

"What's the latest on that business about the tape?"

Fritz made a face. "Not good. They won't pay."

Joey leaned forward. "You're kidding me! They won't pay? They actually said that?"

"Oh sure. They claim if they pay now, the guy will just come back for more. Some horseshit like that."

"Are you serious? He said if he didn't get his money, he'd turn the tape over to the DA."

"What's it to them, you know? They're not going to jail. Me and Troy are the ones who'll pay. I don't know how many times I have to say this."

Iris appeared with two bottles of beer and Fritz's Seagram's Seven and 7Up, which she passed across the table to him.

Fritz said, "Thanks, Iris."

She scooted in beside Joey. "So what did I miss?"

"Parents still won't pay," Fritz said morosely. "Hired a detective."

"A detective?" Iris said.

"Some woman," Joey replied. "Remember? He was telling us about her up at Bayard's."

Iris made a face. "That's dumb. What's this detective supposed to do?"

"How the hell do I know? I guess run around and ask questions."

"Wait a minute. I know the one," Iris said. "This woman comes into the store telling me she's a newspaper reporter, claiming the public is still interested in Sloan's death. She's asking all this shit, including wasn't I the one who stole the test. Then she starts talking about the tape. I was floored."

"When was this?"

"Monday, I think. She's standing there telling me it's sexual abuse. She referred to it as rape and she's asking if I reported the incident to the police. I said it wasn't an 'incident,' it was a joke."

Fritz frowned. "I said the same thing. You know, like the tape was just us goofing off. Troy said he'd back us up." Fritz struggled to fire up another cigarette and Joey tactfully took the lighter and gave him an assist.

"What about Bayard?" Joey asked.

Fritz tried unsuccessfully to blow a smoke ring. "Sure. I mean, it's not his butt on the line, but he'll support what we say. We all tell the same story. It's a joke. Anyway, point is my parents are willing to pay big bucks to find out who's shaking us down, but won't pay a cent to get me off the hook. Troy's just riding on my coattails. He doesn't have money, so it's not his lookout."

"Good deal for him," Joey said.

"Very good," Fritz said.

Iris raised a hand. "I don't get it. On one hand, you're saying the tape is harmless because we weren't really doing anything."

Fritz gestured. "Right. I told 'em we were horsing around. In between takes, we're cracking up and like that. You know, like improvising."

"Okay, but then you turn around and tell them to pay so you won't have to go to jail, so which is it? How can you go to jail if it's a joke?"

"Good point, Iris," Joey said.

Fritz waved him off. "Because they say, where's the proof? I'm supposed to produce the outtakes and I'm telling them no way. Austin took 'em when he left, is what I said."

"That's good. I like that," Iris said.

Joey rested his arms on the table. "Is that why they hired a detective? To track down the outtakes?"

"No clue. Anyway, don't worry about her. My dad has no use for her. Waste of time, he says. Bet he fires her. He likes to fire people. I ever tell you that? Power tripping."

"So can you talk them into paying?" Joey asked.

"I better. Either that or find a way to get my hands on some cash. Ha. My parents are hanging me out to dry. I find twenty-five thousand, you can kiss my ass good-bye."

"Jesus, that must be driving you nuts," Iris said.

"It is. I'm so jumpy, I can't sleep. I lie there and just go over it and over it. You know, like I'm obsessing about where I'm getting twenty-five thousand bucks to save my own skin."

Joey snorted at the very idea. "How are you going to come up with money like that? It's not going to happen."

"Maybe I'll rob a bank. Otherwise I'm living with this blackmail guy breathing down my neck. Things don't go his way, I got the cops at my door."

Joey shook his head. "Shit, I don't know what to tell you, man. The whole deal sucks."

Iris said, "They have to *pay,* don't you think? You know they have it."

"No question," Fritz said. "They, like, majorly have the money."

Joey said, "I'd keep on 'em if I were you."

"I'm doing my best. Have to or I'm screwed."

Iris said, "Well, anything we can do to help . . ."

Impulsively, Fritz reached out and covered her hand with his. "Hey, guys. I just want you to know how much this means to me. Having you on my team." His voice trembled. "You're the only ones I can talk to about this . . . you know . . . crap going down in my life. It's the pits. I'm serious. I don't know what I'd do without you."

Iris eased her hand out from under Fritz's.

Joey reached over and patted Fritz's hand and then held it between his own. "Take it easy, dude. We're here for you. I mean that. Like, anytime."

"Thanks." Fritz turned his head, dashing at his eyes with his sleeve.

19

Friday, September 22, 1989

Friday morning, I bypassed the office and drove to Horton Ravine. I'd called Margaret Seay the night before and our phone conversation had been brief. To my relief, talking to the mother of the dead girl was easier than I'd thought possible. I'd introduced myself and then asked if we might meet so I could talk to her about something that had come up related to her daughter's death.

"Related in what way?"

"This is about a videotape."

She was momentarily silent and then said, "I'm free at eight tomorrow morning if that's not too early for you."

"That will be fine," I said, after which I confirmed the address and rang off.

* * *

Margaret Seay still lived in the house she'd shared with her then-husband, Paul, ten years before. The residence fit my notion of the Midwest: a two-story frame house, painted a cheerful yellow with white shutters and white trim. The roof was metal with a standing seam construction that must have provided a lovely sound during a rain, on the off chance we're ever treated to inclement weather again. There was a wide porch along the front, with a white wooden swing, white wicker furniture, and red geraniums in wooden planters painted white.

I parked in the driveway and made my way up the walk. I rang the bell and waited. The door was answered by a woman in her early fifties. She held the door open without a word and I stepped into the foyer, saying, "Thanks for seeing me. I appreciate it."

"It's been a while since anyone asked about Sloan," she said. "This is my stepson Joey."

The young man she introduced looked like he might be in high school, in jeans, running shoes, and a letter jacket. His hair was damp and earnestly combed, with a few strands breaking free at the crown. His ears protruded and his forehead was creased with a look of worry that seemed odd for someone as young as he was. This was Sloan's stepbrother, now engaged to the infamous Iris Lehmann.

I held out my hand. "Nice meeting you," I said. "I'm Kinsey Millhone. I hope I'm not interrupting."

Margaret said, "Not at all. This is fine. He stops by most mornings on his way to work." She put a hand against his cheek. "Why don't we chat later?"

"I'll call. Good meeting you, too," he said with a small wave to me as he let himself out.

"What sort of work does he do?"

"He's a project manager for his dad, whose company is Merriweather Homes. He's due on the job site at eight thirty, which gives us time to have coffee before."

I followed her into the living room. The floor plan was one I'd seen dozens of times. Living room to the right, dining room to the left, and a stairway that went up from the entrance hall to the second floor above. I pictured a kitchen off the dining room, and beyond that, a combination laundry room and mudroom leading from the kitchen to the back porch, which probably extended along the width of the house. A study or sunroom, corresponding to the size of the dining room, would adjoin the living room. The symmetry was pleasing. The walls were painted a soft white and the furniture was a tasteful mix of traditional and antique, with jewel-toned floral upholstery fabrics on the couch and solid-colored coordinating fabrics—teal and amethyst—on the sofa pillows and occasional chairs. The whole of it was immaculate.

Margaret Seay was probably my height, five foot six, built along sturdier lines than I. She wore her black hair short in a pixie cut that might have seemed inappropriate for a woman her age if it hadn't so perfectly suited her. She wore glasses with dark frames and a slight tint to the lenses. She had dark eyes and a clear complexion, with little or no makeup and no jewelry. She wore a blue silk knee-length dress with a darker blue silk jacket. Her low-heeled navy shoes had probably been selected with comfort in mind. She seemed solemn and attentive, someone not given to smiles or animation.

"Please sit down," she said. She took a seat in a small chair with a padded seat and an oval upholstered back done in a ruby velvet. She kept her feet flat on the floor and put her hands in her lap, one cupped loosely in the other as though she were posing for a formal portrait.

I sat in a matching chair. Only then did I notice the dog lying nearby. This had to be Sloan's dog, Butch. I'd never seen a Pyrenees Mountain dog, but this guy was big, with a white coat, a plumed tail, and coarse hair that formed a shaggy ruff at his neck. His snout was gray and the hair around his eyes had turned milky white with age. He roused himself and stood politely, then approached in a halting gait that suggested arthritic pain. He crossed the distance between us and placed his chin on my knee. My guess was that his sight might be failing, limited to light and dark. I felt the tears well up unbidden. I let him sniff my fingertips, though I wondered if his olfactory sense had faded as well. I rubbed his silky ears and smiled, watching as he closed his eyes. "This is Butch?"

"Yes."

"What a sweet guy. How old is he?"

"Thirteen, which is old for a big dog like him, but he's in good health. He's a sweet-natured fellow and I don't know what I'd do without him."

"I'm not a dog person myself, but he's a dear."

This was apparently sufficient small talk for her purposes.

She said, "You came to ask about the tape Sloan was rumored to have had in her possession when she died."

"How much do you know about it?"

"Just that it was thought to be the motivation for the shooting. I should tell you, however, that when the police searched her room, there was no sign of it. Why is it so important after all these years?"

"You know Fritz is out of prison."

"I read about that in the paper. I hope you're not going to tell me he's a good friend."

"Not at all," I said.

"Then what's this have to do with me?"

I was quiet for a moment, trying to figure out how much I was at liberty to tell her. "Ordinarily I wouldn't discuss a job without my client's express permission, but I don't see how I can ask you to trust me if I don't trust you."

"Fair enough. I do know how to keep matters to myself."

"I hope so because I'm counting on your discretion. Fritz McCabe's parents hired me because someone threatened to send a copy of that video to the district attorney's office if the McCabes don't hand over twenty-five thousand dollars. Again, this is confidential. I'm telling you because I hope you can help."

"I don't see how," she said, perplexed.

"I talked to Poppy Earl and she told me you decided

to open Sloan's room a couple of weeks ago and dispose of her effects. The time frame coincides with Fritz McCabe's release."

"You think the two are connected?"

"It's a possibility worth pursuing. I think his release generated the blackmail scheme. What I don't know is whether someone's been holding the tape all these years or whether the tape came to light when Sloan's room was emptied."

"I can assure you the police turned her room upside down at the time and found nothing. I locked the door the minute they were gone. Have you watched the tape?" she asked.

"Yes."

"Are you going to tell me why it would be so damaging if it were sent to the authorities?"

"Essentially, what was recorded was a sexual assault on a minor. This was a case of aggravated rape and it's possible the participants would be held accountable even at this late date. I was told it was meant to be a joke, a pornographic spoof, but the scenes that would support that claim have been excised."

"I take it Fritz McCabe is one of the accomplices."

"That's correct," I said. "I know Poppy helped clear Sloan's room. I'm wondering if anyone else was involved?"

"Sloan's two stepbrothers, Justin—and Joey, whom you just met. Joey was the one who talked me into it. He's Paul's older boy. He said keeping her room intact would never bring her back. Others have told me the same thing, but the finality of it didn't sink in until I heard it from him. He adored her and if he was letting go, I knew I should do the same. I couldn't handle the job myself, so I asked some of her friends to pitch in. Four of them agreed."

"What did you do with her belongings?"

"I asked those same friends if they'd like to choose something of hers as a keepsake. Three chose an item. After that, Joey and his fiancée had a yard sale that netted them a couple of hundred dollars. Anything that didn't sell, we donated to the Goodwill."

"Do you remember who took you up on your offer of a keepsake?"

"Poppy Earl was one."

"Really. She didn't mention it."

"She and Sloan were very close for years. She was upset when she saw the room again. I'm sure it brought back memories."

"May I ask about the other three?"

"Of course. Patti Gibson, Steve Ringer, and Roland Berg. It was a very emotional experience for them."

"What about you? How have you fared over the years? I don't have children, so I can't even imagine what you've been through."

"It's kind of you to say so. Paul and I divorced a year after my daughter died. He said he couldn't go on living with me. Some thought he was callous, but I couldn't fault him. I was impossible in those days. I drank heavily throughout Sloan's adolescence. Once she was gone, I realized what that must have cost her, but I had no way to atone. I couldn't even ask her to forgive me. I stopped drinking the day of the funeral, which took every ounce of strength I possessed. Beyond that, I had nothing left to give. My two stepsons moved in with us that first year, and when Paul left, they elected to go with him, of course. When Sloan died, they were thirteen and fifteen and their presence only caused me pain."

"Grief's a tricky proposition," I said. "When my Aunt Gin died of cancer, I was relieved. She was a difficult woman and raised me according to her own strange views of femininity. The relief didn't last long and what arrived in its place was pain, but at least I knew her death was coming. Violent death is something else altogether. I don't know how you make your peace with it."

"I will never make my peace with it. Sloan was my only child and she's dead. I say that because it's the central fact of my life. She's been dead for ten years and she'll be dead for the rest of time. She died when she was seventeen and that's all the life she gets. In the paper, Fritz claims he's paid his debt to society, but he hasn't paid his debt to me. He calls what he did a 'mistake' that he's now putting behind him so he can move on with his life. A neat dodge on his part, but he's not off the hook. Why should he enjoy happiness when mine was taken away?"

I knew she didn't expect a response, but I was chilled nonetheless.

She continued in a tone of voice that was deceptively mild given the content. "I've given this a great deal of thought and what I've realized is that revenge doesn't have to be an eye for an eye. Retaliation can take any number of forms. It doesn't need to be crude or obvious. The point is, the pain should be equivalent; not tit for tat but something comparable."

"I'm not quite following."

"It's simple. When Fritz killed Sloan, he robbed me of what I loved most in the world. You'd think in order to even the score, I'd have to kill the person he loves most, but there are other ways to ruin someone's life. I think about what I'd do to him if I could. I want my pound of flesh."

"Even after ten years?"

"The passage of time isn't relevant. What I care about is right now, finding a way to make him suffer as I do. Not the same loss, but one that would carry an equal weight. I plan how I'd cover my tracks, what I'd say if the police showed up at my door."

I said, "You'd find that tougher than you think. Guilt makes your hands shake. It makes the blood drain out of your head. Suddenly, you're not as cool and composed as you thought you'd be. I've been on both sides of the law and you don't want to go down that road."

"So I've been told. My friends keep urging me to forgive, but that's ridiculous. Sloan's gone and she's never coming back, so if I weave my bloody little fantasies, what difference does it make?"

"None, as long as you don't act them out," I said.

Even as the words came out of my mouth, I could see the application here. She was not an entirely unlikely candidate for devising an extortion scheme. Not an eye for an eye, but misery for misery.

"My dear, acting out is not the point because then the game would end. If I gave up the hope of reprisal, I'd forfeit the anger, which is better than pain."

"Let me ask you this. If you'd found the tape, what would you have done?"

"I'd have walked it straight to the district attorney's office."

"You wouldn't have considered trading your silence for twenty-five thousand dollars?"

"I already have all the money I need. What I don't have is satisfaction. That, apparently, will have to wait."

"Until what?"

"Until the final piece falls into place, whatever that may be. In the meantime, I find ways to keep busy. I call newspaper editors. I talk to journalists. I send out copies of the articles about the crime."

"I hope you don't mind my asking, but why would you do that? There's no mystery about 'whodunit.' "

"I'll admit, as time passes it's becoming harder to generate interest in the story. Sometimes I go back and read the transcript of the trial, just to remind myself what went on. It's old news, but what other choice do I have? I'll keep pushing as long as Austin Brown's still out there. If I can keep the story alive, there's a chance someone will spot him and turn him in. At any rate, you didn't come here to listen to my sad song. Is there anything else I can help you with? I'm afraid I have nothing to say about where the tape has been."

I could feel myself shaking my head. "I think the point is that whoever had the tape saw Fritz's release from prison as a way of making him sweat," I said. "I would like to have Joey and Justin's contact information."

"I hope you don't think either one of them is behind the threat to the McCabes."

"Not at all. I'm just hoping one or the other has something useful to contribute. I'd also like to talk to Patti, Steve Ringer, and Roland if you'll put me in touch with them."

"Of course."

I gave her my business card, and in exchange, she gave me the requisite names, addresses, and phone numbers. Having just added five players to the list, I couldn't claim I was narrowing the field, but the focus was getting sharper.

20

THE POOL PARTY

June 1979

Sloan ran the usual circuit of roads in Horton Ravine with Butch prancing along at her side. She kept him on a lead though it wasn't necessary. He was accustomed to her rhythm and her pace and he enjoyed the morning air as much as she did. She preferred making the run early, six o'clock at the latest, but that morning she'd slept in, a rare luxury for her. The school year was over, and in another two weeks, she would take on her responsibilities as a junior counselor at the church camp, which was located twenty-five miles north in the Santa Ynez Valley. The meadows at the campsite would be sunny and hot, smelling of sage and bay laurel. It would be cooler in the shadow of the mountains, though the creek beds would be dry and any remaining grass would be parched to a yellow haze.

At eight that morning, her parents had left for Tucson to pick up Justin and Joey, Paul's sons from his first marriage. The boys were thirteen and fifteen and they would be attending the first two-week session of church camp, which they'd done the previous three summers. In the meantime, the plan was for the four of them—Margaret, Paul, and the two boys—to head north from Tucson to the Grand Canyon, where they'd spend a few days exploring before they returned to Santa Teresa. Sloan was happy to be on her own. She had a summer reading list and looked forward to spending her days in the hammock on the back patio with Butch asleep in the shadow of the netting. She and Bayard had mapped out a bike trip, but the departure date was a week away.

She'd reached Randall Road, which went uphill in a long, slow arc that would put her back in range of the house. She was panting from the climb, sweat trickling down the side of her face and accumulating at the small of her back. She heard a vehicle coming up behind her, Jackson Browne's "Running on Empty" blaring at top volume. She veered to the right and glanced back as Troy's pickup truck came into view. Austin's head and right shoulder extended from the passenger-side window as he beat time on the truck side with the flat of his hand. Troy slowed and then kept pace with her, peering at her across the front seat while Austin smiled at her lazily as she jogged.

He said, "Pool party. End of school. My parents offered the use of the cabin, so we came to ask if you're free."

"Today?"

"You're entirely correct."

She came to a halt, breathing heavily, leaning over with her hands on her knees. She shook her head. "I can't believe you're inviting me. Last time we spoke, we were at each other's throats."

"My fault entirely. Far as I'm concerned we have a truce. I called off the shunning, so that's a done deal. Hand over the tape and we're square. Everything turns out to the good."

"What brought this on?"

"This is me behaving like a grown-up. You can do the

same. You already have a head start on me. So what do you say?"

"I'll think about it."

"Come on, kiddo. No hard feelings, okay?"

"We just forgive and forget?"

"Why not? It's summer. Life's too short to hassle. You have something else on your busy social calendar?"

"Nope. My folks are gone. I'd have to feed the dog and take a shower."

"No problem. We're making a grocery run and then we'll pick up a keg. I'm taking Mom's station wagon. Troy can swing by to pick you up in an hour. Bring your bathing suit."

"Where's the cabin?"

"Up the pass on the 154. Horizon Road goes off to the left shortly before the summit. The cabin's another two miles down."

"Give me the address and I'll meet you there. I'd rather take my own wheels."

"Won't work. Parking's limited. We're keeping the number of cars to a minimum so the neighbors won't raise a stink. Stringer's bringing a crew in his van. Maybe a dozen of us altogether, so it should be fun. We can party into the wee hours if we so desire."

She wasn't really in the mood, but it seemed churlish to decline when he was offering peace. It wasn't as though her time was spoken for. "Okay, but I can't stay long. Couple of hours."

"No biggie. Poppy has a family thing, so she's leaving at four. I'm sure she'd be willing to give you a ride."

"That should work. Can I bring anything?"

Austin shook his head. "Thanks, but we're covered. Ciao!"

The two sped off and Sloan stared after them with Butch looking up at her in happy anticipation. Whatever she did, he was up for it, ready, willing, and able. She met his eyes with a smile. "Come on, baby. Let's get you home."

The two jogged slowly the remaining distance to the house.

She took him to the backyard, where she freshened his water, filled his bowl with kibble, and left him munching noisily as she secured the gate. He'd be fine in the backyard for a couple of hours. His dog house was close by and he could take shelter from the sun if he needed to.

She went into the house through the back door and took the stairs two at a time, peeling off her T-shirt. She considered taking the tape to the party, but decided to leave it where it was until she was sure Austin was sincere. He was capable of manipulating anyone, but if he meant what he said, she was willing to make the deal. He was right about life being too short. Fighting took energy and she had better things to do.

Once showered and dressed, Sloan was about to dry her hair when she heard the doorbell ring. Shit. Troy was early. She set aside the hair dryer and secured her mane of damp hair on the top of her head with a big plastic clip. She anticipated an afternoon swim, so there was no point in worrying about it. She tucked her hairbrush in the gym bag with her bathing suit and carried it with her as she trotted down the stairs. When she opened the front door, instead of Troy, she found Poppy standing on the porch. She seemed thinner, her T-shirt and shorts hanging loosely on her delicate frame. Her pale hair was parted in the middle, the long strands wispy and thin. She had her car keys in hand and her 1955 pale green Ford Thunderbird parked in the drive. Her parents had given her the two-seater the September when she turned sixteen. She'd twice flunked the written portion of her driver's test and therefore didn't have her learner's permit, so Sloan ended up driving the car before she did. That was a lifetime ago, when everything between them was fine.

She and Poppy were still technically friends, but the distance between them was palpable. She put on a bright smile. "Hey. This is a surprise. How are you?"

"I'm good. I hope it's okay to drop by without calling first."

"Not a problem," she said. "Troy's picking me up shortly.

You're going to Austin's party, aren't you? They said you'd be there."

Poppy nodded. "I'm giving Iris a lift. I'm on my way over to her house now and then we'll head up the pass. She's supposed to be at my house, so her parents better not find out or my ass is grass."

"Austin told me you have a family obligation at four and I was hoping I could bum a ride back with you."

"Sure." Poppy shifted her gaze to the side yard and then to Sloan's face. "Mind if I come in?"

"Oh, of course. Sorry." Sloan held the door open and Poppy stepped into the entryway.

"Where's Butch?" she asked.

"In the backyard, probably snoozing. I didn't want to leave him cooped up inside while I was gone."

Sloan crossed the foyer to the living room with Poppy on her heels. The room was cool and orderly, done in neutral tones. Sloan took a seat in her mother's rocking chair and Poppy settled on the couch. The two had barely spoken for months and she was praying Poppy wouldn't quiz her about the tape. As far as she knew, very few people had seen it, but word was out and there was already sly speculation about the contents. "You want a Coke?"

"No, thanks. I can't stay. I just wanted to say hi. Are you doing camp again?"

"Starting week after next. What about you? Are you working?"

"Maybe part time at McDonald's. I'm still waiting to hear."

Sloan removed the clip from her hair and gathered up a few damp strays before securing it again. "I should finish drying my hair before it frizzes up on me."

"I need to ask you something," Poppy said. Her pale cheeks were tinted with pink. Sloan was already feeling cornered and she dreaded what was coming next. "I heard Kenny Ballard and some guys smirking about a video the guys made. Someone said you had a copy."

Sloan blurted out the first thing that occurred to her. "I haven't seen it. I don't even know how I ended up with it." Her tone was casual, but the statement sounded so lame, she expected Poppy to call her on it.

"Really? You haven't seen any of it?"

"I caught maybe fifteen seconds. Fritz is smoking a joint and acting like a nerd. It seemed stupid, so I shut it off."

"Maybe after the party, can I come over and watch with you? We could leave closer to three, which would give us plenty of time."

Sloan couldn't believe Poppy would push the point. She'd never seen her so anxious or insecure. Sloan was the self-conscious one, but now their places were reversed. She didn't like lying, but what choice did she have? It would serve no purpose if she told Poppy the truth. Sloan responded in what she hoped was an offhand manner, though she couldn't look her in the eye. "It's not here. Someone else has it and I probably won't get it back for a couple of days."

"Someone else? Like it's already in circulation?"

"No, no. I left it somewhere by mistake, which is why I haven't had a chance to watch the rest of it. The guys are just goofing off. It's supposed to be a parody."

"Are you sure?"

"No, I don't know for sure. That's just what I heard."

Poppy frowned. "Someone told me Troy's getting it on with Iris."

"Really? Well, that's weird. Who told you that?"

"I don't know. Someone mentioned it in passing. I was, like, totally freaking out, but when I asked Troy, he acted like it was no big deal. I don't know who to believe."

"You know what? I don't like all this gossipy stuff. It's not a good idea. That's how rumors get started and look what happened to me."

"It isn't gossip, Sloan. I'm asking for information."

"Why don't you ask Iris? She's the one you should be talking to."

"I did, but she says she was drunk and doesn't remember."

"Why worry about it? You know Troy isn't interested

in her. The tape's just some dumb thing they did. Like a prank or a joke."

"But why would someone claim he was screwing her if he wasn't? I heard Fritz was in on it, too, which is really pathetic if you ask me."

"I agree, but just because people say something doesn't make it true. Anyway, why come to me? I'm in the same boat you're in."

"I don't know who else to ask." Poppy's gaze was intense and pleading. "When you get the tape back, will you let me know? I can come over anytime."

"Poppy, just drop it, okay? You know how those guys are."

"You think if I asked Bayard, he'd tell me? He was the cameraman, wasn't he?"

"Well, yeah, but still . . ."

"I'll feel like such a fool if I walk into this party with everybody knowing something I don't. Like I'm the butt of the joke. Swear you're telling me the truth?"

"Promise," Sloan said. She glanced at her watch.

Poppy took the hint and stood up, saying, "I better let you go. Thanks for clearing the air. Let me know when you get the tape back."

She leaned over impulsively and gave Sloan one of those awkward hugs where one party is seated and the other bending down to the embrace. Sloan patted her back, feeling acutely uncomfortable. She pulled herself out of the rocker and walked Poppy through the foyer to the front door. She made a show of waving as Poppy slid into her car and took off. When she finally closed the door, she leaned on it briefly, feeling thoroughly undone.

Troy pulled into the driveway at one o'clock and gave a brief toot on his horn. She flipped the thumb lock on the front door and pulled it shut behind her, her gym bag in hand. When she reached the truck, Troy leaned over and opened the passenger-side door. She hopped in and slammed the door.

Sloan said, "You'll never believe what just happened.

Poppy showed up and she's grilling me about the tape. I didn't know what to tell her."

"Shit." Troy groaned and pretended to bang his head on the steering wheel. "She's been on my case for days and what am I supposed to say? I can't remember the half of it except it wasn't good." He indicated the gym bag. "You have the tape?"

"Not *with* me. I'm not an idiot. What if Austin grabbed it and went right back to treating me like shit? Let's see if he keeps his word."

"I wouldn't worry if I were you. It's summer. You can't shun someone you're not going to see for three months. Everybody's bored with it anyway."

"Good to know," she said. "Not that it's a comfort at this late date."

Troy put the truck in gear and took off. As he drove through the front gates of the Ravine, he said, "You've got balls threatening Austin. He's a crazy son of a bitch."

"How else could I get him off my back? It's the only leverage I had."

"He must have loved that."

"Well, it worked, didn't it? What I don't get is why you guys made it in the first place. Talk about gross!"

"It wasn't meant to be serious. We were just horsing around."

"It doesn't look like 'horsing around.' You and Fritz are buck naked and Iris is stoned or drunk. It looks like full-on sexual assault."

"Austin said it was supposed to be a spoof. I couldn't see the harm." When he reached upper State Street, he slowed for a light.

She looked at him in disbelief. "Honestly? You screw the poor girl when she's completely out of it and you can't see the harm?"

The light turned green and he proceeded through the intersection, heading for the 154. "I guess it got out of hand. Anyway, she wasn't *that* far out of it."

"Yeah, right. I could tell."

"It's true. What you saw was edited, all the bloopers taken out. We were cracking up the whole time, laughing our asses off. None of us could keep it together. Like in one take, Fritz dropped the joint in his lap and about set fire to his pubic hair. Then Iris fell on her ass trying to do a striptease. I was laughing so hard I had beer spewing out my nose. We thought it was hilarious."

"Oh sure. Hardy-har-har. What happened to the cuts? Because none of that shows up in the copy I have."

"Bayard worked on edits. He must have taken out the hokey stuff."

"Oh, come on. That's bullshit. What I saw was horrible. Troy, if the cops get hold of that tape, you and Fritz will end up in jail. Austin doesn't come off that well, either. He's sitting by idly in a coat and tie, lording it over you, like he's too good to participate. But then you hear him refer to himself as an 'auteur.' "

"Jesus. Why don't you do us all a favor and destroy the damn thing?"

"Good plan. I will. Better for everyone, including me."

"Just don't tell Poppy."

"What if someone else spills the beans?"

"Then I'm fucked."

"Could I say something on another subject? You know I had nothing to do with that anonymous note, don't you? I'd never do such a thing to you."

"Of course not. I never believed Austin's claim. I forget now how he ended up pointing a finger at you, but once the idea was out there everyone seemed to fall in line. Not that it matters now, but it did take me out of the running for the Climping Memorial Award."

Sloan said, "Oh, me too if the faculty suspects I'm guilty. I might be innocent as all get-out, but I've been tainted by the accusation. Everybody hates a snitch. Faculty opinion is bound to be affected, proof or no proof."

The minute the words came out of her mouth, Sloan felt a tiny exclamation point light up in her brain. It hadn't occurred to her to explore the issue of why the anonymous note was sent to the school in the first place. She'd been so caught up in defending herself that she hadn't considered the motive or what was at stake. It suddenly dawned on her that Austin was the obvious beneficiary. Five juniors had been nominated for the Albert Climping Memorial Award, Austin among them. Patti Gibson and Betsy Coe weren't strong contenders. Sloan could hold her own, but Troy was the impressive candidate in light of his community service. He did school-based mentoring of underprivileged boys. He volunteered time at the homeless shelter and he assisted in a program to provide holiday meals to families in need. In exposing Troy and then pointing an accusing finger at her, Austin had effectively knocked both of them out of the running.

She was tempted to run the idea by Troy to see what he thought of it, but decided to keep the notion to herself, in part because she wasn't sure there was a way to confirm her hunch. The charge was serious and she needed to consider the implications. She wasn't sure what action she might take even if she was right, but it made sense to explore the notion before she did anything else.

She stared at the road ahead and something heavy settled in her chest.

21

Friday, September 22, 1989

On my way through town after I left Margaret Seay, I stopped off at a bookstore, thinking a book was the perfect gift for Rosie, whose birthday celebration was coming up that night. A book has no unwanted calories and you don't have to worry about sizes as long as the subject matter appeals to the recipient. Rosie's life was about cooking. Also, bossing people around, but I didn't think a book on bullies would be appropriate. I spotted a cookbook devoted to Hungarian cuisine and a quick riffling through the pages revealed recipes every bit as repulsive as the dishes she favored. I pulled out my credit card and gladly paid two dollars extra for the gift wrapping.

After that, I drove to the office, where I let myself in, locked the door, and armed the periphery. As was so often the case, my sense of progress was ever so faintly undermined by murmurings of another sort. At some point during the past couple of days, something had come into my consciousness that I hadn't properly registered. I couldn't for the life of me recall where I was at the time. I remembered a dim sensation of recognition, but my attention had been fixed elsewhere and I hadn't grasped the significance. I knew the revelation wasn't connected to Margaret Seay or to Sloan. An echo had reverberated in my brain without my catching the implications. I sat down at my desk, swiveling in my swivel chair, which made wonderful squeaking sounds. I closed my eyes, hoping to quiet the chatter in my head. It's difficult to tune into that sixth sense with all that babbling that goes on.

What had I heard that I hadn't taken in at the time?

In moments of doubt, my strategy is to go back and review my notes, which is what I did now. Information is odd. Facts can look different according to how you line them up. Sometimes I shuffle my index cards and then place them in a random sequence, unrelated to the order in which I've collected them. Sometimes I lay them out like a hand of solitaire or pretend I'm telling my own fortune with a Tarot deck. This time, I reorganized the cards according to subject matter, making one pile for the notes I'd taken about the tape, another pile for my notes about the cheating scandal, and a third pile about the shooting.

I picked up the stack of cards that pertained to the tape, which was the crux of my investigation. Then I sorted them according to the principal players: Iris Lehmann, Fritz McCabe, Troy Rademaker, and Bayard Montgomery. I turned them over one by one, letting my eyes drift down through the material I'd recorded in my self-generated shorthand after each of the conversations.

I sat up, embarrassed by my belated appreciation of what should have been obvious at the time. In describing the motivation for the tape, they'd all used the same words and phrases. *It was a lark. We were laughing our asses off.* Who the hell uses the word "lark" unless the discussion is about birds? I didn't think any of the four realized they were echoing each other's comments or they'd have paid greater heed to their accounts.

I checked my watch, wondering where the day had gone. It was close to five and I'd hoped to grab a bite to eat, shower, and change clothes before the birthday party. I gathered up my cards and rubber-banded them together. I grabbed my shoulder bag and shoved the cards into the depths while I searched for my keys. I went through the ritual of arming the system and locking the door, and then I headed for my car, thinking what a pain in the ass my security measures had become.

I could have initiated the upcoming conversation with any of the four, but Troy had been the most amenable. Besides which, he and Kerry were not far away, a stone's throw from Sea Shore Park, which sits on a bluff overlooking the Pacific. The proximity to the ocean should have made the location desirable, but the houses were built in the 1950s and mirrored one another with a depressing similarity. Exteriors were stucco, painted Easter egg colors that had long since grown dingy. The roofs were shake and the trim was plain, peeling paint in most cases. Aluminum window and sliding glass door frames were pitted by the salt-laden sea air, which also wreaked havoc on the condenser coils in ancient air-conditioning units I could hear from two doors away. The front yards were small and flat. In most cases, the drought had left them bald, with sparse tufts of grass here and there.

It crossed my mind that Camilla and Jonah lived in the same area, but I let that slide.

I parked my car and as I approached the Rademakers' front door, I picked up the cooking scents of half a dozen dinners wafting from nearby houses. I stood on the porch and knocked. There was a brief wait and then Troy answered the door. He'd showered and changed from his navy work coveralls into a T-shirt and shorts. He was barefoot.

His look was blank, not exactly welcoming. "Oh. You."

"Sorry. I know it's not an ideal time to stop by, but I have a question that will only take a minute."

He stepped out on the porch and pulled the door shut behind him. "What's this about?"

"The tape."

He said, "Shit."

Bored or annoyed, I couldn't tell which.

"Mind if we sit?"

He didn't seem happy about it, but he gestured to two white molded plastic chairs of the sort I'd seen sold in drugstores.

Once settled, I reached into my bag and pulled out my cards. "I've been going over my notes and came up with something that struck me as odd."

"You couldn't have *called* to tell me about this—whatever the fuck it is?"

"I thought talking face-to-face was a better idea," I said, inwardly wincing at his use of the F-word. Ordinarily, I don't object to it, but this was jarring, given his former friendliness. I couldn't understand what had changed. This was not the same Troy I'd spoken with two days before. That guy seemed open, honest, and decent. Obviously, I was treading on dangerous ground, but now that I was here, I didn't have much choice but to plunge ahead. I turned over the first card.

"At the McCabes' Tuesday night when Fritz talked about the tape, he referred to it as a hoot and a game. To quote him, you guys were just 'horsing around.' Interview with Iris, you guys were just messing around. Wednesday when you and I talked, you called it a hoax, a spoof, and a mockumentary."

Troy glanced at his watch.

"When I talked to Bayard, he said the tape was essentially a practical joke."

"Okay."

I held up the cards. "Three of you used identical phrases. You said 'it was a lark.' And, 'we were laughing our asses off.' "

He stared at me. "So what?"

I studied him as I spoke. "It was a cover story, wasn't it?"

I waited and when he said nothing, I went on. "I don't know which of you came up with the idea, but it's clear you coached each other so if a question was ever raised, you could all claim you were goofing around. I think you talked Iris into the idea as well. Back then, she was drunk, stoned, or both, but now—by some miracle—she's singing the same tune you are."

He was silent, staring at the porch paint. I waited, thinking he was wrestling with his conscience. He finally raised his eyes to mine. "You know what? I'm done talking to you."

"Why is this suddenly a problem? If I'm wrong, just tell me I'm wrong."

"We will not have this conversation. I told Kerry you'd stopped by the shop and she didn't like it. At all. She says you don't have any right to question me about this stuff."

"I'm sorry she feels that way. Lauren McCabe thought you might be helpful."

"Helpful to Fritz maybe, but she doesn't give a shit about me. She'd throw me to the wolves if she thought it would prove useful to that sniveling son of hers. You can tell her to shove 'help' up her ass. In the meantime, I'd like you to get the hell off my property."

His tone was dead and the look in his eyes was cold. I was paralyzed by embarrassment. The last thing in the world I'd expected him to do was give me the boot. Clearly, it was naïve of me to think he'd confirm my theory and confess everything with relief.

I don't remember how I managed my exit, but my departure wasn't graceful. Troy stood on the porch, staring pointedly, until I started my car and pulled away from the curb. The shirt at the small of my back was damp with flop sweat as I drove off.

Thus far my day had been a strange mix of enlightenment and mortification and I looked forward to Rosie's birthday party for the comic relief. I reached home with just enough time to shower and change clothes. As I came out of my studio, wearing a turtleneck, tights, and a skirt, I was surprised to find Lucky standing at my door. He'd cleaned himself up, taking advantage of Henry's largess. He stood freshly showered, shaved, and radiating the scent of Henry's aftershave. In front of him, Pearl sat in her wheelchair in jeans and a peasant shirt I'd never seen before. Killer sat near the tent flap, his gaze fixed on me.

"You two look festive."

Pearl said, "Thanks. I think we can tart ourself up pretty good."

Lucky seemed self-conscious, shifting from one foot to the other. "Honor of Rosie's birthday, I been sober six hours."

"Good for you," I said. "I hope you can keep it up."

"Trouble is I keep thinking I should have a drink to celebrate."

Time to stop talking about alcohol, I thought. "Where's Henry?"

"He went to the party early to help set up," Pearl said. "We decided to wait for you."

"I appreciate that."

"Look what I done," she said. In her lap she held a loaf of homemade bread that peeked out of an aluminum foil wrap. The crust was a golden brown and the top listed only slightly to one side. It smelled heavenly, as though she'd pulled it from the oven just a short time before.

I realized then that Lucky held a parcel in one hand. "Made Rosie a present as well," he said shyly.

"I didn't realize you were friends."

"Oh sure. Pearl and me stop over there every couple of days. She's always good to us, even if we've had a nip. Yesterday she give us each a bowl of this new recipe she found for Veseporkolt. Pork kidney stew over dumplings."

"Delish," Pearl said enthusiastically. "Lot of chewy bits."

I looked at Lucky. "What'd you make?"

"It's kind of a secret."

"Well, I can hardly wait. What about Killer? Is he going?"

Lucky shook his head. "Health Department don't allow it. I took him over a couple of times, but Rosie said she'd get in big trouble if she let him stay. He'll be fine where he is. We'll put him to bed early; zip him in the tent with his dolly and one of Henry's soup bones."

I waited until Lucky herded Killer into the tent, which took some pushing from behind, and then the three of us covered the half block to Rosie's, a small mismatched processional, bearing our gifts.

When we arrived, the preliminaries were already underway. William was back on his feet after his bout of what he swore was bacterial dysentery. "Not the tropical sort," he was quick to point out.

For the celebration, he'd suggested posting a sign on the door saying "Closed for a private party," but Rosie wouldn't hear of it. Opinion was divided on whether she was intent on encouraging business or eager to have an enthusiastic assembly on hand to generate good cheer on her behalf. Since the party didn't start until after dinner, she'd been relieved of the need to cook for the celebrants, which gave us all cause to rejoice.

Henry's Michigan siblings had decided not to make the trip, as it would have been both arduous and expensive. His sister, Nell, was still convalescing from her hip replacement surgery, and her brothers, Charlie and Lewis, wouldn't travel without her. Everyone else was there: Anna Dace and Cheney Phillips, Moza Lowenstein, Jonah Robb and his two teenaged daughters, Courtney and Ashley. Camilla wasn't in evidence, which I thought was cause for celebration in itself. Neighbors and day-drinkers had mobbed the place on the assumption the champagne would flow freely, which it did. A number of police department personnel were also on hand, some in uniform and some in civilian clothes. Rosie was wearing a new muumuu, a solid lavender shade that for some reason softened her face.

Henry had made two gallons of vanilla ice cream, along with a sheet cake large enough to feed the multitudes. Everyone had piled their wrapped gifts on the bar, and after the cake and ice cream disappeared, William had Rosie perch on her usual stool so she could open them. In addition to the Hungarian cookbook I gave her, she received a dark red cashmere shawl, a paperweight with a daffodil embedded in its center, and a lily-of-the-valley cologne and talcum powder set. William bought her a pale blue nightgown and matching robe, which elicited whistles and applause. He'd also purchased a gift certificate for a dinner for two at the Edgewater Hotel, complete with limousine transportation to and from. In a show of optimism, Henry gave her a rain gauge, a rain hat, and a matching umbrella. Ed, the cat, contributed a pair of oversize plush slippers shaped like calico cats. We were seldom treated to Rosie's playful side, but she basked in the attention, blushing like a maiden, which undermined her usual drill sergeant air. She opened Lucky's gift last, and I found myself on tiptoe trying to see what he'd done. She held up a necklace of cloth strands, beautiful soft shades of rust, navy, and lavender intermixed with white.

She turned to him with surprise. "You make?"

Pearl interceded, saying, "He's a regular artist. Harbor House has this bin where they collect old T-shirts for anybody that needs a little wardrobe pick-me-up."

"I warsh 'em first," Lucky hastened to add. "Then I work my special magic. Every necklace is one of a kind. What I do is cut acrost the T-shirt bottoms and stretch the loops until the sides curl up like that. Those are colors I seen you wear and I thought they'd go good with your hair."

He settled the necklace over her head with such pride that Rosie was forced to fling a napkin over her face and use the edges to mop her eyes.

This, then, was the tender scene into which Camilla Robb appeared like the evil fairy at Sleeping Beauty's christening. I was vaguely aware that the outside door had opened and closed behind me, letting in a gust of chilly air. I assumed it was a late guest, so I didn't even turn to look. Henry was facing me and it was his quizzical reaction that suggested something was amiss. Anger is like a sneeze. If you sense someone's on the verge of letting loose and you're standing within a six-foot radius, you better make a move to protect yourself. I was blissfully unaware, not realizing a threat was imminent.

When Camilla materialized on my right, I was surprised, but not alarmed. I remember noting how much shorter she was than I'd realized. Also noted was the fact that her shapeless peach wool coat added a good twenty pounds to her frame. She had her three-year-old son affixed to one hip. She'd hooked her purse over the shoulder opposite, but the strap was too short and the bag slid off when she least expected it. Banner was too big to be carried and his legs dangled almost to her knees. Between supporting his weight and hitching up the errant pocketbook, she was distracted, but not sufficiently so to mitigate her wrath.

Here's how dumb I was on this occasion. Even when she planted herself directly in front of me, it didn't occur to me a confrontation was in the wind. At first, it didn't seem to occur to anyone else, either. Henry was alert—I could see his brow furrowing—but with Rosie at stage center, the good-natured banter among party guests continued without pause. When Camilla finally launched her shriek-fest, her voice was so laden with fury her speech was barely audible. As the volume and timbre rose, the general hubbub diminished to a hush. The effect was the same as the house lights in a theater dimming before the curtains open for act one.

She wielded a crumpled piece of paper that she shook in my face. "You did this on purpose, you *bitch*! Don't think you're going to get away with it . . ."

I shot a glance over my shoulder, wondering who she was screeching at. Everyone else was looking right at me.

Her voice dropped. "I know your type. Pretending to be so *innocent*. Well, guess again, sweetheart, because you don't fool me. I *knew* you were still screwing him. I KNEW it."

I tuned her out. I couldn't help myself. It was like a clear glass window sliding up between us. I watched her lips move. I absorbed her verbal assault without comprehension. I felt heat wash up along my spine and settle at the base of my neck. I was rooted in place and the net effect was to sharpen my perception.

I'd never seen Camilla at close range. On the few occasions when our paths had crossed, she was always at some remove, usually in the company of Jonah and the kids. Given her emotional chokehold on him, I'd assumed she was a beauty, imbued with an irresistible combination of charisma and sex appeal. This was not the case. Her body was thick, a residual effect of her last pregnancy. Beyond that (except for the slightly bulging blue eyes) she was plain. Dissatisfaction had sketched lines between her eyes and created a bracket on either side of her mouth. I could tell she'd once been pretty—seventh grade perhaps, when she and Jonah met and bonded like termites. It's a little-known fact that in a termite colony, several species form lifelong attachments, the female "queen" and a single male "king" giving birth to an entire kingdom.

Oddly, the moment between us felt intimate. Every other conversation had fallen away as though a spell had been cast. Camilla and I might as well have been alone. I focused on the crumpled fistful of paper, which appeared to be a bill. This was an instance where my ability to read upside down was far better than being clairvoyant. The letterhead was that of the Santa Teresa Women's Health Collective, whose many practicing physicians specialized in gynecology and obstetrics. I blinked as sound returned.

She was saying, ". . . oldest trick in the book and shame on you. Jonah's a married man, in case you hadn't *heard.* He has a family of his own that he adores, so you will never compete with *this*. Never." Her last reference was to Banner. I was certainly willing to agree with her on that. We were all aware of the cherished place Jonah's youngest child held in his heart.

Hold on a minute. *Obstetrics?*

"You think I'm *pregnant*?" I yelped.

If she'd had a hand free, she'd have slapped my face. As luck would have it, in order for her to land a blow, she'd have had to park her purse or drop the child, and either action would have spoiled the effect.

My consternation, while sincere, seemed to shift her into high gear. The hot pink in her cheeks made the color of her coat seem more flattering.

"Don't play dumb with me, missy," she said. "The minute I saw this, I called the clinic and told the woman the bill wasn't mine. I said I wasn't a patient and I'd never been in the damn place. She swore I was there on the tenth of August and again Wednesday *of this week*! I said I certainly was not and what the hell was she talking about? She got all snippy about it and guess what? Pregnancy test, office consultation, prenatal vitamins. That's when she caught the mistake. Oops. They weren't supposed to send a bill because the visit had been paid for at the time services were rendered . . ."

I couldn't think of a thing to say to her. I wasn't *pregnant*. The charge was preposterous, but I couldn't refute the accusation without offering the following lame-ass excuse: I hadn't been sexually active for more than a year! Ha ha ha! That irrefutable fact wasn't any of her business and I didn't feel I should announce the news to all and sundry by way of a defense.

Banner had had as much of his mother's hysteria as he could take. His face crumpled and then he opened his mouth and wailed, his sobs accompanied by big theatrical tears. Courtney pushed through the crowd and took him from her mother's arms. She patted him briskly, set the child on his feet, and walked him to the far end of the bar, where one of the three television sets was tuned to a football game. She picked up the remote and began to cycle through stations, finally settling on an ancient episode of *I Love Lucy*. Banner was instantly more interested in Lucy's antics than he was in the drama playing out nearby. His sister lifted him onto a stool and then perched on the bar stool next to his. She placed a basket of popcorn in front of him and his cares were erased.

Meanwhile, Camilla, gearing up for another round, had lost track of her point. What could she do with a four-word response from me? Not much, which meant she was forced to repeat herself. Clearly, the weeping child had broken her verbal stride. It's difficult to sustain an outburst when your timing's off.

Jonah said, "Camilla, that's enough."

I turned with a flash of gratitude, thinking it was about time someone came to my defense.

He moved to her side, took her by the elbow, and propelled her toward the door. She jerked her arm from his grasp as the two stepped outside, but he was clearly the one in charge. I thought she might resume screaming once they reached the street, but the minute the door closed behind them all was quiet.

Inside, the moment of stunned silence stretched to the breaking point. Moza Lowenstein was deaf and had no idea what was going on. Bewildered, she looked from face to face, hoping someone would explain. Ruthie stared at me in disbelief. She was a *registered nurse*. If I'd told her I had a medical condition, she'd have offered her professional advice. Henry refused to meet my gaze, perhaps imagining a scarlet A now emblazoned on my chest. He and William were raised in an era where adultery wasn't spoken of in polite society and a verbal rampage like Camilla's would have been considered low class. Even the mention of pregnancy was too personal for mixed company. We all stood there awkwardly, wondering what came next.

Given the brevity of our collective attention span, the revelers sparked to life again a scant fifteen seconds later. We were there to eat cake and ice cream, drink, and celebrate. No one gave a rip about Camilla's sordid complaints, especially since I was the designated slut. Every crowd has a mind of its own. Someone could have choked on a shrimp, necessitating an ineffectual Heimlich maneuver, followed by an impromptu tracheotomy achieved by means of a ballpoint pen, and the reaction would have been the same. Once the patient was taken away in the ambulance, there would have been the same silence and the same collective shrug. Then the party would have picked up right where it was before the unpleasantness erupted.

Camilla's diatribe had been cut short and she was now off the scene. Jonah's stepping into the fray must have been as surprising to her as it was to me. I hadn't given him credit for sufficient backbone to stand up to her. In the time I'd known him, he'd endured so much humiliation, it was a wonder he'd survived. Evidently, the man had untapped reserves of strength and I was filled with admiration. Seconds later, I was pulled up short.

Wait a minute!

If I wasn't pregnant, who was?

My first thought was of Jonah's voluptuous daughters. Both were gorgeous, boy-crazy, and no doubt the subject of the crotch-pinching fantasies of their horny high school classmates. At the ages of fifteen and seventeen, they were prime candidates for unwanted pregnancies, STDs, and other unsavory consequences of libidos in overdrive. I stole a quick look at Courtney and then Ashley in turn, but neither seemed stricken with shame or embarrassment. Courtney was preoccupied with Banner and Ashley had decided her ponytail would look better in a French braid, which she was plaiting with her head bent and her arms raised above her head.

I caught sight of Cheney and my focus jumped from his troubled expression to Anna's. Now *she* looked like someone stricken with shame and embarrassment, which made perfect sense. She and Cheney had been an item for months. I wasn't sure how long, but apparently long enough. She had followed me to Santa Teresa from Bakersfield the year before. A short time later the cops had migrated from the Caliente Café to Rosie's place and that's where their paths had crossed. Anna's recent emotional upheaval suddenly made sense. It also explained why Cheney was hovering. I rearranged my mindset. Anna's baggy sweater wasn't a fashion statement; she was disguising her baby bump. Jonah must have taken her to the clinic. Maybe Cheney was tied up and Jonah had stepped in as a personal favor. What I couldn't fathom was Jonah's doing something as idiotic as listing his home address on Anna's paperwork. Why put himself in the line of fire when Cheney was rolling in dough and could have taken her anywhere?

I thought, *Oh my*, and the truth opened up before me like a miry pit.

Anna and Cheney weren't having an affair; Anna and *Jonah* were. Cheney was the "beard," running cover for the two. The three of them had created an optical illusion and I'd bought into it. How had I missed the obvious? Naturally, Jonah was drawn to her. I'd never seen a man who wasn't. Even Henry and William became a bit giddy in her presence. Poor Jonah was starved for affection and desperate for companionship.

At the time Anna entered our lives, Camilla (the skank) was still off somewhere, taking advantage of the "open marriage" she'd thought was such a keen idea, as long as it applied solely to her. Jonah wasn't actually allowed to participate. His brief fling with me had come to nothing except to fill him with guilt. Then along came Anna, who had no interest whatever in a relationship. What could be more perfect? She didn't intend to marry and she abhorred the idea of having kids. I remembered quite clearly how she'd likened the prospect of motherhood to Virginia Woolf's suicide, which she'd accomplished by filling her pockets with heavy stones and wading into a river. Essentially, Anna had proclaimed she'd rather drown herself than give birth. I had no doubt she'd made clear to Jonah that her desire for freedom was paramount. She wanted to travel. She yearned for a life of adventure. She was saving her money so she could move to New York City, where she hoped to launch a career in modeling or acting, assuming she ever learned to act. What now?

I couldn't imagine how she'd slipped up, but I was certain I'd hear about it. The larger question, of course, was how she intended to remedy the situation.

More to the point, had she already done so?

22

There was no indication the party would ever break up. I waited a decent interval and then eased out the door without saying my good-byes. Henry was gone by then. I'd been trying to catch his eye, but he was studiously avoiding me. Rosie, usually abrupt, judgmental, and quick to censure, sent me any number of sympathetic looks. I raised an index finger and signaled in the negative, wagging it back and forth like a metronome, hoping she'd pick up the message about the misunderstanding. Her response was to pat her own heart to show how moved she was. There was too much noise for conversation and the one time she was close enough to talk, she'd taken my hand and held it between her own, shaping it like a biscuit.

William looked mournful at the sight of me, probably calculating the odds of my dying of childbed fever. As far as these people were concerned—absent my standing on a tabletop, calling for tampons—I was "with child." It was all too tedious for words. Eventually, I'd get it straightened out, but good news doesn't travel fast. That's because good news is usually too boring to repeat. The cold hard truth will fall on stony ground, whereas your all-around trashy rumor will flourish like a weed.

I walked the half block home, let myself through the squeaky gate, and rounded the side of the studio. Henry's house was entirely dark. I knew he was there, but the only evidence of life was Ed, whose pale shape seemed to glow in the darkened kitchen window. He looked out at me with his small, hopeful face. How could he break my heart without making a sound? Pearl and Lucky had stayed on at the party, where they'd drink free booze until they both toppled sideways. Killer was nowhere in sight and I imagined him still zipped in the tent and having a fine snooze, his dolly between his paws.

I let myself into my studio and locked the door behind me. Camilla's harangue had left me exhausted. I wasn't accustomed to verbal abuse in my personal life. In my professional life, okay, fine. My sideline, process serving, brings out the worst in human nature. An eviction notice, a summons, an order to appear—these are life's little ways of informing you that you've blundered badly and payment is now due. Camilla's hostility was another matter altogether and I'd done a piss-poor job of protecting myself.

I flung myself down on the couch, too done in to stagger up the spiral stairs.

There was a tap on the door. I closed my eyes briefly and prayed it was Henry. I pictured him too worried to sleep, finally braving the darkness to assure himself that I was doing okay. I was desperate to clear up the confusion about my nonexistent pregnancy so I could be redeemed in his eyes. I crossed to the porthole and flipped on the outside light. Anna was standing on the porch, her hands shoved in the pockets of her navy pea coat. She was clearly in a black mood. I slid back the chain and opened the door.

As I ushered her in, she pointed a finger at my face. "Not one word of blame or criticism."

"Far be it from me," I said. "My only question is how you managed to screw up so badly."

"I don't want to talk about it."

"Shit, who would?" I said. I closed the door and indicated one of my kitchen stools. "Why don't you have a seat?"

She peeled off her pea coat and took a quick look around, uncertain where to put it. I took it and draped it over a captain's chair. Even with the stress of her condition, she was beautiful, blue-eyed, dark-haired, skin like cream. She and Jonah shared the same striking coloring. I felt a seismic shift in my attitude. Whatever her failings, she'd managed to bring Camilla Robb to her knees. Score one for the home team. We were, after all, blood kin.

She perched on a kitchen stool, leaned forward, stretched her arms across the counter, and placed her cheek against the cool surface. "Can I talk you into pouring me a glass of wine?"

"Absolutely not."

"I'm open to anything. Drano?"

"I'll heat water for a cup of tea."

"Decaffeinated, if you have it. I'm trying to be good about this until I decide what to do."

"I thought maybe you'd already done it."

"I'm keeping my options open."

"Hey, wait a minute. Didn't I see you nursing a gin and tonic Tuesday night?"

"That was soda with lime. Jonah paid for it."

"Well, that's better."

I took my teakettle from the stovetop and filled it with tap water, then set it on a burner that I turned to high. I took out the box of tea bags and the sugar bowl, along with two mugs. My carton of milk was only two weeks old and it still smelled okay. "What's Jonah's attitude?" I asked.

"Keep it, of course. So far nobody knows but him and Cheney and now you."

"What about the crowd at Rosie's?"

"People at the party think it's you."

"Camilla doesn't. Surely Jonah's corrected her by now."

"I haven't talked to him. He's off driving the family home. Well, not her. She brought her own car."

I couldn't see the relevance of the transportation arrangements, but in moments of crisis, we tend to focus on the mundane or the irrelevant.

She lifted her head and propped her chin in her palm. "I hope I can count on you to keep the news to yourself."

"Don't be ridiculous. I'm telling Henry the first chance I get."

"Crap. He'll tell William and then Rosie will find out."

"What difference does it make? You're pregnant regardless. That's the issue you have to address."

"I *am* addressing it. Sort of."

We listened to the churning gravel sound of water coming to a boil.

"How far along are you?"

"Fifteen weeks."

"So that's what, three months?"

"Coming up on four."

"If you're thinking to terminate, that's pushing it."

"Big time," she said.

"Well, I sympathize."

"You do?"

"Not a bit. I thought it sounded good."

I put a tea bag in each mug. "What went wrong? You're too smart to get caught out like this."

"It's not my fault. Remember over the summer when we were all sick as dogs? I had that bout of bronchitis I couldn't shake. I went through two different courses of antibiotics, which nobody mentioned could offset the effectiveness of birth control pills."

"News to me. I'll keep that in mind."

"Turns out it's not true. I asked the doctor and she says it's nothing but an old wives' tale."

"So this was just your dumb luck? You're on the pill and get pregnant anyway?"

She made a face. "Uh, not quite. I was taking Saint-

John's-wort. It's an herbal remedy that's sold as a supplement."

"Remedy for what?"

"Depression."

"I didn't know you were depressed."

"Well, I am *now*."

"Why would a doctor prescribe Saint-John's-wort? That seems weird."

"Not a doctor. The woman working at the health food store."

"Oh, good for you. A specialist."

"Well, she *acted* like she knew what she was talking about. I told her I was anxious and tired and had no appetite. I wasn't sleeping well, either. Maybe two or three hours a night. She said it sounded like depression and I should pick up a bottle of Saint-John's-wort. Now I find out if you're taking it, you're supposed to use backup birth control . . . you know, like a condom or something, just to be safe."

"It didn't occur to you a supplement might have negative side effects?"

"Kinsey, it's *organic*. It's not like a drug company manufactures it. The plant grows in meadows and on roadsides. It's completely natural."

"So are death cap mushrooms and oleander leaves."

"You said you wouldn't criticize."

"I never said that. You did."

I poured the sputtering hot water into each mug. We dunked our tea bags up and down.

She said, "So what should I do?"

"That's up to you."

"Don't be a butt about it."

"I'm not going to tell you what to do!"

"All right, fine. Be that way. What would you do in my place?"

"How do I know? There are choices you make in theory, based on principle, but when it comes right down to it, who knows what any of us would do? I'll tell you one thing: whatever decision you make, you're going to have to live with it every day for the rest of your life."

"Shit, I'm sorry I asked."

Having exhausted the topic, we finished our tea and then I walked her the three houses down to Moza's and bid her good-night. I returned to my studio, enacted my nightly ritual of security measures, and went to bed shortly thereafter. I didn't expect to sleep. There was too much emotional turmoil in the air.

I was wakened by the telephone ringing. My first reaction was irritation, thinking I'd just that moment dozed off. I glanced at the clock, which read 7:22. I realized it was Saturday morning and the call was cutting short my opportunity to hibernate until noon.

I picked up the handset and managed a croaky hello while trying to sound like I was wide awake. I don't know why we're all in denial about being hauled abruptly out of a sound sleep when it's the other person's fault.

"Kinsey, this is Lauren."

I rubbed a hand across my eyes. "Oh, hi. What's up?"

I really wasn't all that happy to hear from her and if I'd known what was coming, I'd have felt even worse.

"We got a call last night from Troy Rademaker," she said, as though our lives were peopled with countless other Troys. "He says you showed up at his door yesterday accusing him—along with Bayard and Fritz, I might add—of lying when they claimed the sex tape was just a hoax."

"That's pretty much the case."

"I don't think so, dear," she said in a withering tone. "Pretty much the case is you're fired."

She slammed down the handset.

I hung up and put a pillow over my face, though I knew there wasn't any point. I was awake and I might as well get up and shower so I could get on with my day. So what if it was a weekend and I was unemployed? Worse things had happened. Not that I could think of one offhand.

By the time I brushed my teeth, showered, shaved my legs, shampooed my hair, dressed, descended the spiral staircase, and consumed my bowl of Cheerios, I could see the bright side of what might have seemed insulting at first blush. Lauren McCabe had turned out to be a pain in the ass. I was glad to be shed of her, and Hollis as well. Fritz was a first-class jerk and whatever became of him henceforth was no concern of mine.

I washed my bowl and spoon and left them in the rack. Then I snagged my car keys and my shoulder bag and drove to the office, coolheaded enough to exercise all the proper security precautions, making sure Ned Lowe wasn't lurking in the bushes when I unlocked my door and disarmed the system. The whole rigmarole felt silly, but I resisted the urge to relax my vigilance. I locked the door again, armed the perimeter, crossed to my desk, and pulled out my portable Smith Corona. I removed the hard cover and set it aside. I found a sheet of letterhead stationery, a carbon, and a second sheet and made a neat paper sandwich that I rolled into my machine. By way of formalizing the change in our relationship, I typed the following:

> Attention: Mr. and Mrs. Hollis McCabe
>
> As per our telephone conversation this morning, I am writing to confirm that our professional relationship has been severed. Enclosed is a check in the amount of twenty-five hundred dollars, which represents your advance payment to me for services, which you have deemed unsatisfactory. As of this date, September 23, 1989, the business arrangement between us has been terminated.
>
> Respectfully submitted,

I signed my name with a flourish, folded the letter, and found an envelope on which I typed the names and the address. I pulled out my checkbook and wrote a check for the twenty-five hundred dollars. I slid the letter and the check into the envelope and licked the flap. I affixed a stamp and hopped in my car and drove to the main post office, a few blocks away. When the doors opened at ten, I was the first one in line. I sent the letter by certified mail, signature required and return receipt requested.

That done, I went home and did a massive fall cleaning. I must have been more upset about being fired than I thought, because my Cinderella complex had been kicked into high gear. I moved furniture away from the walls and dusted baseboards. I vacuumed. I scrubbed tubs, sinks, and toilets, mopped floors. I dusted the shutters. I took a toothbrush and cleaned the grout between tiles. When the studio was properly spit-shined, I changed into my sweats, jogged for three miles, and then went to the gym, where I lifted weights for an hour. After that, I took a nap, which had all the benefits of a coma without my being close to death.

At 3:45, I crawled out of bed, brushed my teeth, and took another shower, then put on the same tights, skirt, and turtleneck I'd worn the night before. Between the wardrobe shortcut and the absence of makeup, my so-called beauty regimen took thirteen minutes. Coming out of the studio, I spotted Pearl in her wheelchair, her feet propped up on one of the Adirondack chairs. She was sunning herself, eyes closed, but she turned her face idly in my general direction when she heard me shut and lock the door.

"Henry says keep an eye out for Ed. Cat's been gone since last night."

"Really. Well, that's worrisome."

"You know him. Henry's been out walking the neighborhood, calling him, but so far, no luck."

"Well, if he doesn't show up soon, let me know and I'll pitch in."

"He'll probably wander home, but keep an eye out just in case."

"Will do," I said.

The drive to Perdido, which should have taken twenty-five minutes, took fifty. Late-day traffic on the 101 is sluggish even on the weekends and I knew enough to allow way more time than I'd ordinarily need. With the ocean to my right and the autumn sun beginning to fade, I felt myself relax for the first time that day. The drought had turned the chaparral a ghostly gray, patches of vegetation so dry that they formed a silvery haze that hovered over the hillside as it undulated along the coast. The rugged hills that rise straight up from the highway are considered young, a geological casserole of sandstone and shale, with occasional outcroppings of limestone appearing in the western portion of the range. Five million years ago these mountains were lifted along the San Andreas Fault, which tracks like the ragged spine of some prehistoric beast some eight hundred miles through California. The Santa Teresa coastal plain is so riddled with cracks that it's a wonder we don't have daily temblors sufficient to rattle our china off the tabletops.

I had checked my *Thomas Guide* for the address Phyllis had given me and I took the Sea Side Boulevard off-ramp and followed the road toward the harbor, where a small community of restaurants and beach shops was flourishing. Her condominium development, the Haven, was located two blocks from the water, a complex of twenty-two buildings that more nearly resembled the architecture of New England than the usual California style. These structures were symmetrical, with double-hung sash windows, balustrades, and dormers. The frame siding was painted gray with white trim. The rooflines were just irregular enough to be interesting. The buildings were three stories high and stood shoulder to shoulder, with the outdoor living spaces cleverly arranged so that they were not directly visible from one to the next. Privacy was probably an illusion, as I was guessing the construction allowed sound to carry, sometimes amplified, from one condominium to the next.

I'd been told the community was gated and when I pulled up, I waited while the security guard checked to make sure my name was on the list. He gave me directions that I followed carefully, counting my left and right turns since the structures were identical. I found the correct street and the number address she'd given me. What struck me as odd, even on the most superficial observation, was that the electronic gates seemed to be window dressing. The grounds weren't fenced, and while automobiles were only admitted after proper scrutiny, anyone could walk in from neighboring streets. I caught sight of an unmanned rear gate that was activated by cars leaving the property, but the lag time on the closing mechanism was sufficient to allow an incoming vehicle to drive through unimpeded and unchecked.

While the apartments appeared to be connected, much in the way of row houses, the three-story units were actually linked by twos, with garages at street level and two slots each for guest parking. A covered walkway led from the parking area to an enclosed garden entry, with a door that opened into a vestibule, which in turn opened into a small lobby. The interior walls were mirrored to suggest more space than had been allotted. There were fake plants and a few pieces of faux-Colonial furniture. There were two built-in mailboxes with spaces below where packages could be left. The elevator doors stood open. Inside the car, a panel had two call buttons, one for each owner. An intercom made it possible for the visitor and the resident to communicate before access was granted.

P. Joplin was listed on the left and an *E. Price* on the right. There was an Up button, but when I pressed it, nothing happened. I was guessing the residents operated the elevator with a key. If company arrived or if a repairman needed to be admitted, the resident sent the car from the second floor down. The doors were otherwise left in the open position, with the Up button inoperable. As was true of the exterior measures, interior security was more of an illusion than a reality. I saw no evidence of a camera in the lobby or the elevator car, which meant that the occupants of the two units above had voice contact when someone called up, but no visual verification process. The company that owned the complex had gone to great lengths to create a sense of safety while neglecting to build in true safeguards. It made me uneasy to think Phyllis was unaware of the shortcomings in the system, since for her the idea of a gated community was what had made her feel secure.

I rang her call button and waited. When there was no response, I checked my watch. It was 5:10. I rang a second time with still no answer. I pushed out the door into the garden courtyard and looked up to my left. There were lights visible on the second and third floors of her apartment. I wasn't certain how the rooms were laid out, but it made sense to imagine public spaces—living room, dining room, kitchen, and balcony—on the second floor, with the third floor reserved for the master suite, guest bedrooms, and perhaps an office or study. A quick visual survey of neighboring units showed exterior balconies on both the second and third floors, which supported my supposition.

I returned to the elevator and pressed her call button again. It was possible she'd forgotten our date or perhaps something had come up and she'd tried telephoning after I'd already left my studio for the drive down. Or she could be picking up last-minute items at the grocery store. Or she could be "away from her desk," which is to say, in the bathroom. Or what? There must have been half a dozen other reasons she might not be picking up the call. Even so, I didn't like it.

I rang the button for E. Price. After a brief pause, a man said, "Yes?"

"Hi. My name is Kinsey Millhone. I was supposed to meet Phyllis here for drinks at five, but she doesn't seem to be answering."

"Her guest is already here."

"I'm her guest."

"Then who buzzed me half an hour ago?"

"Not me," I said.

"Oh. Well, that's odd because I ran into her as she was getting back from the grocery store and she told me she was expecting company."

"What made you think I was already here?"

"My mistake. I assumed Kinsey was a man's name so when you, or I should say, when a guy rang a while ago, I thought her guest was early so I buzzed him on up."

"How do you know it was a guy?"

"Because I talked to him. I asked what he wanted

and he said something about her call bell being on the fritz, which is why I sent the elevator."

I could feel the cold, like Freon, seep from the core of me through my rib cage. "What did he look like?"

"I don't know. I was in the middle of a phone call so I just left the handset on the kitchen counter while I sent the car down. I knew Phyllis was home so I figured she'd answer her door when the guy got up here."

"What's your first name?"

"What?"

"What does the E stand for, Mr. Price?"

"Erroll."

"Well, Erroll, I think you should activate the elevator and let me up there. Either that or go knock on Phyllis's door yourself and see if she's okay."

"You think we have a problem?"

"I think we have a big problem."

An instant later the elevator doors slid shut and the elevator moved up.

23

Saturday, September 23, 1989

Erroll Price was waiting for me as I emerged from the elevator. The foyer on the second floor was a duplicate of the lobby below. Strong lighting, mirrored walls, fake plants, and the few pieces of furniture were meant to divert attention from the fact that there were no exterior doors or windows. This rendered the space claustrophobic, all the more so because Erroll was such a commanding presence. He was oversize: tall, big-boned, heavy set, and muscular, in a pair of faded red sweatpants and a white T-shirt. He was barefoot. His skin was the color of fudge frosting and his black hair was a glistening halo of ringlets.

"I brought a key to her place," he said. "The deal is if she's out of town, I take care of her plants, bring in the mail, and stuff like that. She does the same for me. I already knocked and rang her doorbell while you were on your way up."

"Let's try one more time."

The door was splintered. Nonetheless, I knocked and rang the doorbell simultaneously, which netted us no response. I stepped back as Erroll pushed open the door, calling, "Phyllis? You home?"

He peered in and then held out an arm instinctively to block my forward motion. I peered past him and saw Phyllis lying facedown on the carpeting in the living room.

"Oh no," I said.

I crossed the room and knelt beside her, wincing at the sight of her external injuries. Her left eye was blackened and swollen shut; probably her right eye as well though it was hidden by her position on the floor. Her nose was broken, her left cheek battered and puffy, and her jaw was askew. Blood oozed from her nose and mouth and saturated the carpeting under her. Her left arm was caught beneath her torso and might have been broken, judging from the oddity of the angle.

Erroll leaned down and pressed two fingers against her neck, checking for a pulse. "Phyllis, can you hear me? This is Erroll. The guy's gone. You're safe. We'll take care of you."

He rose to his feet and went into the kitchen to the phone mounted on the wall.

He dialed 9-1-1. I could hear him talk to the dispatcher, telling her the situation, the address, and the nature of the injuries.

I remained kneeling beside her. I leaned close and listened to her stertorous breathing. She made a sound in her throat, a cross between a moan and a mewing. I patted her free hand, murmuring nonsense I hoped she would hear and find comforting. I would have turned her over on her back, but I was afraid of moving her.

I picked up the scent of something scorched and I looked up. Smoke poured from the wall oven, threatening to trigger the smoke alarm. I moved swiftly into the kitchen, turned off the oven, and activated the vent fan above the stovetop. A half-sheet pan in the lighted interior bore blackened canapés that were impossible to identify. I found a hot pad and removed the sheet pan to the granite counter. Then I unlocked and opened the glass-paned door to the balcony to let in fresh air. On the counter, there was a cutting board with radishes, carrots, baby turnips, and celery hearts ready to be trimmed. A bottle of Chardonnay sat in a wine cooler. She'd taken out wineglasses that she'd washed and left upside down in the dish drainer. There was something painful about the sight of these homey activities undertaken with such innocence.

Erroll finished his conversation with the 9-1-1 dispatcher and returned to my side.

"I don't know what she was baking, but it's a charred mess now," I said.

"Cheddar cheese crackers. She makes them all the time for company. The guy must have rung the bell shortly after she put 'em in the oven. Usually takes twenty minutes."

"Which means he barely made it out of here before we showed up. How did he get away?"

"He must have gone down the back stairs."

"Which go where?"

"Two-car garage. He could have let himself out and headed for a side street."

I let my gaze travel up the stairs to the second floor. "What if he's still on the premises?"

"Wait here."

He approached the stairs in giant strides and took the steps two at a time. At the third-floor landing, he looked in both directions and then moved to his left. To me, the place had an empty feel, but I didn't think we should make assumptions. I followed Erroll's progress by way of the series of thumps on the ceiling as he moved from room to room, opening and closing doors. When he finally came downstairs again, he carried a quilt. "He trashed the place, but otherwise no sign of him."

He shook out the quilt and laid it over Phyllis, saying, "Hold on, baby. We're going to get you some help here real quick."

Erroll appeared at my side. "I alerted the gate guard and he'll direct the cops and the ambulance, but I should be out front to flag them down. You okay here alone?"

"I'm fine."

He squeezed my shoulder and departed, leaving the apartment door open. I heard the elevator doors close and then it was quiet. I picked up the sound of a grandfather clock. I looked behind me and spotted it on the far wall. The wood was a beautifully burnished mahogany. The round clock face was topped by a moon dial, both trimmed in brass and chrome. There were three cylindrical brass weights and a flat brass pendulum as big around as a dinner plate. There was something comforting in the hollow click of the mechanism as the pendulum swung back and forth.

I focused on surroundings I'd expected to see under far different circumstances. The living room was a big open space, with a formal dining room off to the left. A white marble-topped counter separated the living room from the kitchen, which had a row of windows along the back wall. On the balcony, I saw patio furniture that had been arranged with a view to the ocean, currently beyond my visual range. She'd chosen atypical wall colors, a mauve and eucalyptus green, with slate-blue drapes and wall-to-wall carpeting. In theory, this was more interesting than the usual white walls, but the dark-toned carpeting and heavy drapes had affected the nature of the light coming in. Instead of eye-pleasing, the hues came across as gloomy. She'd introduced a number of oversize palms with wide, thick leaves that dominated the space. Floor-length cloths on the tables made the room feel stuffy. She didn't seem to favor empty wall space or bare surfaces. Two mirrored walls, instead of creating an illusion of more space, simply doubled, in reflection, the already crowded feel of the rooms.

I looked down at her. She'd mentioned being overweight when she'd met Ned, so her petite size was unexpected, as was the dark auburn hair she wore in a French twist that had come undone in the battle she'd waged. I was convinced he'd done this, though I had no proof. I'd have been willing to bet he'd timed his attack with an eye to my arrival, but how he'd managed to track her down and how he could have known the day and time of our get-together was a mystery. I don't believe in coincidence. Somehow my phone conversation with her had resulted in an information leak. I'd spoken to her two days earlier, which was when we'd agreed to meet. Since then, I hadn't discussed the drinks date with anyone, so I assumed she'd mentioned it.

Her theory was that Ned was on the hunt for the treasure trove of souvenirs he'd removed from his young female victims. If he harbored the notion that she had the trinkets in her possession, he might have tried reaching her at her old address and discovered that she'd moved. He could have traced her to her current location through utility connections in her name or by way of a former neighbor, who might have passed along her new address with the best of intentions. Erroll had made the final hurdle easy for him by sending the elevator down when he should have checked with Phyllis first.

The burglar chain had been snapped off the front door, suggesting Ned had caught her off guard, kicking hard enough to splinter the hollow-core wood door. On the wall to the left of the door, a table had been toppled and an ornamental plate had bounced on the thick carpet, where it lay still intact. It looked like she'd made it as far as the stairs before he'd grabbed her from behind and hauled her backward. I could see the tracks her heels had left where he'd dragged her across the floor. At some point, he'd dealt her a blow severe enough to drop her, but there was no sign of a weapon. Had to be a blunt object of some kind. The soundproofing in the units must have been far more effective than I imagined because if Erroll had heard them, he'd have come across the hall to find out what was going on.

In the dining room, I spotted an elegant leather handbag that had been emptied on the floor: her wallet, a makeup pouch, a pill bottle, hairbrush. Ned was probably looking for her house keys, which would have included the key to the elevator. My arrival must have cut short the rampage, forcing him to flee down the back stairs. Who knew how long he'd been gone before I rang her call bell that first time? Or maybe it was my buzzing that told him it was time to leave.

I could hear the high, thin wail of two sirens, which diminished and finally shut down abruptly as the vehicles pulled up outside. Moments later, I heard the low wind of the ascending elevator and then the doors opened. Erroll led the way into the apartment, followed by a uniformed officer and three paramedics bearing a collapsible gurney. They needed space to work effectively, so I held out a hand to Erroll, who pulled me to my feet. The medics were already checking her vital signs, assessing her injuries in preparation for moving her.

I turned aside, unable to watch as one of them started an IV line.

"I want to take a look at the third floor," I said and headed for the stairs. I thought Erroll might follow, but his attention was fixed on Phyllis. The paramedics conducted a murmured conversation as they applied first aid measures.

When I reached the top of the stairs, I turned to the right. I looked into the master bedroom and bath, both of which were untouched. Retracing my steps, I peered into one of the guest rooms, where she'd stacked the moving cartons she hadn't yet unpacked. Ned had done the job for her, slashing at the packing tape, then dumping out the contents, which he'd flung in all directions. He'd managed to rip open ten of thirteen cardboard U-Haul boxes, tossing books, files, and office supplies. The scene looked chaotic, but I could see a certain systematic order to the disarray. He'd dispatched her first, knocking her out cold so that he could proceed without interruption. Three boxes remained sealed, which meant he'd been forced to abandon the task. He'd made two attempts to search my premises for his trinkets: first at my office, where he'd failed to gain entry, and the second time when he'd come to my studio and found Pearl and Lucky on hand. He must have changed the focus of his hunt from me to Phyllis. I crossed the hall and did a quick eyeball search of the second guest room, which she'd set up as her in-home office. Ned hadn't gotten this far because the room was untouched.

When I returned to the second floor, Erroll was in conversation with the uniformed patrol officer who'd responded to the 9-1-1 call. The officer was taking notes, but paused while the paramedics lifted Phyllis onto the gurney and immobilized her with straps. Erroll accompanied them as they maneuvered the gurney into the hall. A third paramedic, this one female, carried the IV bag, keeping pace as they eased into the elevator. The officer and I remained in the living room while Erroll stepped into the elevator and keyed in its downward journey.

The officer introduced himself as Pat Espinoza. He was in his thirties, clean-cut, physically fit, and he carried himself with confidence. They should have posted his photograph on a billboard promoting employment with the Perdido Police Department because he was just exactly the sort you'd want showing up at a crime scene while you were still trying to get your head together.

Erroll had filled him in on the basics while I supplied the back story. He told me a detective was on his way and asked if I'd stand by, which I was happy to do. What seemed odd to me later was that I couldn't reconstruct the sequence of events and conversations with any continuity. I remembered most of it, but there were gaps that I had to write off as having been gobbled up piecemeal by emotions I was trying to repress.

I realized Erroll had returned but I wasn't sure how long he'd been back. He stood rigid against the wall, his head back, eyes closed. I heard voices in the foyer and then a tap at the door, which stood open. He roused himself as a plainclothes detective appeared. He was in his sixties, with fly-away gray hair, rimless bifocals, unruly eyebrows, and a salt-and-pepper mustache.

Erroll moved away from the wall. "Erroll Price," he said.

"Detective Crawford Altman. Perdido Police Department."

The two shook hands as Erroll said, "That's my place

across the hall. This is Kinsey Millhone, a friend of Phyllis's. She's a private investigator from Santa Teresa."

The detective turned his attention to me and we shook hands. At close range, I could see all the lines in his face, including a six-inch silver scar that distorted the lid on his left eye. He looked more like a mad scientist than any detective I'd ever seen.

"Why don't you have a seat? We'll chat as soon as I've talked to Mr. Price."

"Sure thing," I said.

I wandered into the kitchen, too restless and hyped up to sit down. Through the bank of kitchen windows, I could see the waterfront a block away. The sun wouldn't actually set for another hour and the cloudless blue sky was a contradiction to the events that had transpired. The one-story houses on the block between the condominium complex and the waterfront did nothing to obscure the view. The masts from the boats moored in the harbor swayed and tilted gently as a motorboat putted along behind them. Since this was a Saturday, there were tourists on the boardwalk and I counted the businesses that filled the wedge I could see: a fish-and-chips place, a T-shirt shop, a small art gallery that probably sold nautical scenes by local painters.

I turned around and looked past the counter that divided the kitchen from the living room. Erroll and Detective Altman were still talking. I'd done a quick survey of the third floor, but I hadn't seen the back stairs. There were two doors to my left. The first opened into a spacious combination pantry and laundry room. I moved to the second door and used my shirt hem to open it, thinking Ned might have laid a hand on the knob. I found myself looking at the interior stairway that led down to the ground floor. I followed the stairs down, keeping my hands to myself. If Ned had left prints anywhere, I didn't want to smudge them and I certainly didn't want to add mine to the mix. At the bottom, there was a door with an automatic lock, which had been wedged open with a car jack. On the floor, miscellaneous pieces of sterling-silver flatware and been dropped and abandoned. The two-car garage was empty. The car jack was a nice touch, implying a burglary in progress with the intruder making sure he could load the car and then get back into the apartment for whatever additional items he might steal. This was Ned being subtle.

I felt anxiety stir and I recognized the sensation—old-fashioned guilt. I kept thinking that Ned was only able to trace Phyllis because I'd made a date with her. I couldn't imagine how he'd done it, but the assault wasn't a random act of violence by an unknown assailant. This was Ned's doing, and when it was my turn to discuss the situation with Detective Altman, I'd have to tell him the whole long tale. Had I messed up? I must have, because what other explanation was there for the timing? Ned had arrived at the condominium shortly before I had. I hadn't said a word to anyone about seeing Phyllis. I hadn't even mentioned my destination when I left for Perdido. It *had* to be Phyllis who'd inadvertently leaked the particulars.

Detective Altman materialized at my side. "Sorry for the delay," he said.

"Hang on a second," I said and caught Erroll's attention. "Phyllis has a car, doesn't she?"

He seemed surprised that I'd ask. "A 1988 Olds Cutlass Supreme. Custom paint job. It's bright red. Car's her pride and joy."

"Well, it's not in the garage, so Ned must have stolen it as his way out of here."

Altman said, "Who's Ned?"

I removed the police bulletin about Ned Lowe from my shoulder bag and passed it to him. "This is probably the man you're looking for. He's her ex-husband."

"This was circulated in the department earlier in the week," he said. "Let me get Pat on it. You know the plate number by chance?"

Erroll said, "LADY CPA."

Altman left long enough to pass the information along to Officer Espinoza.

When he returned, Erroll said, "Any objection if I go back to my place? I have work to catch up on."

"Fine," Altman said. He handed Erroll his card. "Give me a call if you think of anything else."

Once Erroll left, Detective Altman turned his attention to the bulletin. "Does she have a restraining order out on him?"

"I doubt it. They've been divorced for years, but he may be operating under the belief that she has something he wants. He took mementos from the young girls he killed, mostly cheap costume jewelry from what I heard. He must have thought I had the items, but he was unsuccessful in his attempt to get into my office and studio. I guess he gave up on that plan and decided to try her instead."

I filled him in on my initial dealings with Ned and developments to this point, keeping details to a minimum on the assumption he'd stop and quiz me if he needed clarification. "The thing is, we talked about all of this on the phone two days ago, which is when she invited me for drinks. We'd had phone conversations in the past, but we'd never actually met face-to-face and she suggested I drive down."

"Did anybody else know you were coming?"

"Not that I'm aware. I'm sure I never mentioned it to anyone and if Phyllis did, that still doesn't explain how Ned got the information."

"Good you arrived when you did. Any later, he'd have finished the job."

"If he meant to kill her, he'd have strangled or smothered her once he'd knocked her out. He wanted me to find her. That's how his mind works. That way he has the pleasure of beating the shit out of her and putting me on notice at the same time. The bad news is Phyllis never had his trinkets, so he was wasting his time."

"I've got a couple of crime scene techs on the way. They'll dust for prints and maybe pick up latents that will tie him to the assault."

24

I spent much of Saturday night sitting in the ER waiting room at Perdido Memorial Hospital, hoping for word about Phyllis's condition before I made the twenty-five-mile drive back up the coast to Santa Teresa. Phyllis had been taken into surgery without regaining consciousness. She'd been a patient at Perdido Memorial on a prior occasion and the surgical team had no choice but to proceed on the assumption that her medical history was up to date. In the morning, someone would put a call through to her insurance company to determine if her policy was still in effect.

I wasn't a family member and therefore I was technically not entitled to access, but the floor nurse, Malcolm Denning, was willing to bend the rules. Once Phyllis was out of the recovery room and transferred to ICU, he allowed me to look in on her briefly. She was heavily sedated. Her left arm was in a cast and her jaw had been wired shut. The bruised left cheek and blackened, swollen eyes looked worse, which wasn't surprising. X rays had revealed a comminuted skull fracture, meaning it was broken in three or more sections and therefore brain swelling was a very real danger.

At my side, Malcolm said, "Someone contacted a neurosurgeon from UCLA and he's on his way. I don't know who's been pulling the strings, but this doc is the best. She'll be in good hands."

"That's good news."

I gave him my business card with my office number on the front. I jotted my home number on the back. "Can you keep me informed?"

"Can't go that far, I'm afraid. I'm not authorized to release medical information, but you can check with the desk in the morning if you want an update. You won't learn much, but it's better than nothing."

"Thanks."

As I turned to go, I saw Erroll standing at the nurses' station. I thought I might be hallucinating, but his physical characteristics were so distinct that I knew it couldn't be anyone else. He was wearing a dark three-piece suit, a white dress shirt, and a pair of black loafers that must have cost more than the money I'd refunded the McCabes.

I said, "Erroll?"

He caught sight of me and raised a hand in greeting. He finished his conversation, excused himself, and walked down the hall in my direction. "I was hoping I'd find you here. Can you spare a few minutes?"

"Sure."

He took me by the elbow and steered me back to the empty waiting room, where we sat down in adjacent chairs. "I'd have been here sooner, but I had some business to take care of."

"What sort of work do you *do*? When I met you this afternoon, you were in sweatpants and barefoot. Now you look like a foreign dignitary."

He looked down at himself with a wry smile. "I'm an attorney. I have a sports management firm that represents professional athletes. Our job is to negotiate contracts and make sure they're smart about their money so they don't end up broke. On my way over, I stopped by the office and called a good friend of mine whose company handles personal security. He's sending a gal who'll park herself outside ICU and make sure Ned can't do any more harm."

"That's great. I hadn't even thought of that," I said. "Someone told me a neurosurgeon from UCLA was on his way."

"He's a good friend as well. He should be here shortly, but I wouldn't advise you to hang around. It will take him a while to do a workup."

"You arranged all of this in the hours since I saw you?"

"I owe her. She wouldn't be where she is if it weren't for me. I don't know what I was thinking when I let the guy in, but it's a mistake I won't repeat."

"Security in that complex is for shit anyway. Why isn't there a camera in the elevator?"

"The guy selling these units touted the call buttons and the resident-operated elevator key to control access. Heavy emphasis on the security guard at the gate; no mention of CCTV," he said. "I use the place when I have business in the area, so it's not an issue I think about."

"She said she just moved in."

"That's right. Five or six weeks ago. I met her that first day and the two of us hit it off," he said. "How do you know her? I didn't have a chance to ask you earlier."

I gave him a brief rundown of my dealings with Phyllis and my bitter acquaintance with her ex. "Now Ned has transportation, so who knows where he's gone?"

"Her car is too conspicuous to drive more than a day. He'll dump it first chance he gets. Altman said he'd make sure the information is in the pipeline. And not just Perdido PD. County sheriff's office and California Highway Patrol."

"Ned's slippery. I don't know where he's holing up, but he's managed to make himself scarce. We canvassed motels down here and picked up a lead from the manager of a place he stayed over last weekend. He was spotted twice in Santa Teresa after that, but he dropped out of sight until this. We even have the homeless population on red alert, checking the beaches and other sites used by transients. So far, all we have is the wreckage he's left in his wake."

"How are you holding up?"

"I've lost touch with how tired I am, but I know it's time to hit the sack. I was just heading for my car when I saw you."

"Come on. I'll walk you to the parking lot, just in case he's out there hoping to catch you by surprise."

By the time I started for home, it was close to three a.m. The road was sparsely trafficked and I rolled down my driver's-side window, letting cold air stream in as a means of keeping myself alert. There was nothing I could do for Phyllis and nothing I could do about Ned, whose shadow cast a pall I couldn't seem to shake. My prime concern was whether I was in any way responsible for his finding her. I knew I hadn't said a word to anyone, but somehow Ned had gotten wind of her address and he'd gone after her with a vengeance. There had to be a leak somewhere. Phyllis wasn't careless with personal information, but others might not have exercised the same caution.

In addition to my worries about Phyllis, I was still brooding about being fired, though it was my own damn fault. Lauren McCabe had told me point-blank her son wasn't to be considered as a person of interest when it came to the extortion threat. Despite the McCabes' initial skepticism, they'd apparently accepted his claim that the tape was a hoax. Then I'd gone to Troy and voiced my suspicion that the hoax business was no more than a cover story. Wrong move on my part. He must have headed straight for the phone to alert Fritz that I was questioning the assertion. Of course, the minute Troy stonewalled me, I knew I was right. Not that it made any difference. Since I had been shit-canned, the identity of the extortionist wasn't my problem now. The question weighed on me nonetheless. I wouldn't pursue it. I wasn't even tempted to do so, but it was unfinished business and that didn't sit well with me.

I slept late on Sunday morning and finally dragged myself out of bed close to noon. I brushed my teeth and then pulled on my sweats and my running shoes. I found an old fanny pack, where I put my house keys and a folded twenty-dollar bill. Henry's back door was open and I could smell bacon and eggs. Killer was sleeping on the welcome mat on Henry's back porch, and since there was no sign of Lucky or Pearl, I assumed he'd invited them for brunch. I can be churlish about such things. At the moment, however, I was still feeling raw from the lack of sleep and I didn't much care.

I crossed the yard to his back door, stepped over the snoring, slobbering pooch, and knocked on the screen. From what I could see, the three of them were just finishing their meal. Henry set his napkin down and got up to let me in.

"Kinsey. Good to see you. I knocked on your door earlier, but got no response. Why don't you come in and join us?"

I waved off the invitation, saying, "Thanks. I'm on my way out, but I wanted to check on Ed. Is he back?"

"No sign of him. As soon as we clean up here, we'll do another run through the neighborhood. He's done this before so I'm not worried. Yet. Moza tells me there are half a dozen houses he visits, begging for treats." Henry's tone was polite throughout, but he wasn't making eye contact. No big surprise, since he was still laboring under the notion that I was knocked up.

"You think he was picked up by Animal Control?"

"I doubt it. Just to be on the safe side, I called and left a message. I haven't heard back, but I'm sure he'll turn up."

"Well, I have to go out for a couple of hours. If he doesn't show up in the meantime, leave a note on my door, and I'll help with the search. We need to talk anyway."

"I should think so," he said.

I was too tired to get into it right then and it wasn't a discussion I wanted to embark on if Pearl and Lucky were listening. I said, "See you later."

He said, "Take care."

I stepped over the dog again, pausing to watch him whimper and twitch in the throes of some doggie dream. I hoped he caught whatever he was chasing. I walked around to the front, let myself out through the squeaky gate, and headed for the beach path. I didn't have the energy to jog, so instead I walked. I followed Cabana Boulevard three blocks to State Street and then eight blocks up State past my old office at California Fidelity Insurance. The walk was good for me, allowing me to take in changes in the downtown businesses I wouldn't have noticed by car. Some shops had closed down, some had moved, and one was trumpeting yet another in a series of liquidation sales.

Eight blocks later, I reached a hole-in-the-wall Mexican diner where I sat at the counter and loaded up on carbs: huevos rancheros, *sopes*, beans and rice, two cheese enchiladas, a chicken taco, and three cups of coffee. Then I walked the sixteen blocks back to my place. There was no note on my door, which I hoped meant Ed was home safe and sound. Pearl, Lucky, and the dog were gone and Henry's place was buttoned up tight. I let myself into the studio, locked the door behind me, and went back to bed. It was 1:35 by then and I slept through the rest of the day and through the night. I'm too old to be pulling an all-nighter. Witness the toll it took out of my poor beleaguered hide.

By Monday morning, I was feeling restored to my usual optimism. I did make one adjustment in the aftermath of Ned's attack. I hauled my H&K and holster out of the trunk at the foot of my bed. If Ned was declaring war, I'd be carrying. I pulled my navy blue windbreaker over my rig and checked the effect. Not bad. I'd half expected a note from Henry slipped under my door, confirming that Ed was safely in hand, but there was no word.

By the time I emerged from my studio at eight thirty, Cullen, the technician from the S.O.S. Alarm Company, was coming out of Henry's back door, already at work on the installation that would provide security for both his residence and mine.

I said, "Hey, Cullen. Is Henry here?"

"No ma'am. He just left. He showed me where he wanted the control panels and then he and the lady in the wheelchair went over to Kinko's to have fliers made up about the cat. One of the neighbors said she thought she saw him over on Bay, so that scruffy guy with the big dog is checking that out. Henry says they have it under control and he'll call you if he needs help."

"Good. Tell him I'll touch base with him in a little bit."

"You want to show me where you'd like your alarm panel?"

"Just inside the front door is fine. Henry has a key to my place."

"Thanks. Have a good one."

"You, too."

Once at the office, I let myself in with my usual OCD routine: unlocking the door, using my code to disarm the system, arming the periphery, and relocking the door. If I'd had dead bolts and burglar chains, I'd have mobilized those as well. I didn't want to live like this, concealed carry included, but I had to be sensible, even if my caution bordered on the paranoid. In the meantime, I scooped up the mail that had been shoved through the slot Saturday afternoon and proceeded into my office proper, where I sat down at my desk.

This is how the subconscious works, mine at any rate. I'd been fretting about Phyllis and Ned off and on in the upper regions of my brain. While I was chewing on the issue of how Ned had picked up her address, the speculation had sifted down into my Dark Side like lightly falling rain. Answers—those little kernels of truth—had stirred to life much in the way seeds germinate when conditions are right. By this point, my conscious mind was bored with the subject, since I'd been running the same questions relentlessly with no tangible relief. I was restless, ready to move on to a problem more easily solved, so I really wasn't thinking about anything at all. And that's when the following notion popped into my head: I'd been assuming that the puzzle of Ned's whereabouts and the mystery of how Phyllis's address had been leaked were two separate issues.

But what if they were one and the same?

I rejected the idea at first because it seemed so unlikely. There was only one set of circumstances I could think of that would net one answer for those two questions. Then again, if I was right, it would make sense of Ned's disappearance and what passed for his clairvoyance. I reached for my shoulder bag and searched the depths until I found the Leatherman tool set Henry had given me for my birthday. I slipped the minitools in my windbreaker pocket, opened my bottom drawer, and took out the heavy-duty flashlight that was a mate to the one I had at home. As I rose from my swivel chair, I touched the holstered gun under my left arm like a talisman.

I left my inner office and walked down the hall to the back door, where six months earlier Cullen had placed a second alarm panel, identical to the one he'd installed at my front door. I disarmed the periphery, unlocked the back door, and went out. I took a left and moved along the walkway that runs between my bungalow and the look-alike bungalow next door. My telephone junction box is mounted to the side of the office and when I reached it, I stopped.

The box is a bland gray, some kind of heavy-duty plastic, maybe three inches thick, six inches wide, and seven inches high. The General Telephone logo was embossed on the front. There was a bracket that read CUSTOMER ACCESS, with an arrow pointing to a metal snap, labeled SNAP, and an arrow pointing to a screw, labeled SCREW. Those guys really had it down. Running from the bottom of the box there was a fat round black wire, a bright blue wire, and a gray conduit an inch in diameter that contained the cable connecting my box to the wires mounted on the telephone pole at the street. The black wire and the bright blue wire trailed down from the box and disappeared into the crawl space through one of the vents that allows fresh air to circulate under my office.

Now a third wire had been added, this one white. I opened my Leatherman and removed the minitools. I had a choice of nineteen, all neatly folded together like a pocketknife with assorted blades. I selected a pair of needle-nose pliers that I used to loosen the snap. Then I used the Phillips-head screwdriver to remove the screw. The telephone company probably had special tools that performed the same job in half the time, but I had to make do.

I stuck the Leatherman back in my windbreaker pocket and then opened the junction box. I have two lines into my office, one for the telephone and a second for my combination printer and fax machine. My phone number was neatly written in black marker pen beside one set of wires and my fax number was inked beside the second set. Alligator clips had been clamped to the two contacts that served my phone line. Attached to the alligator clips was the white wire, which extended from the bottom of the box and disappeared into the crawl space along with the other two wires.

All three bungalows are built over a three-foot concrete footer. A sizeable vent opening had been cut into the stucco just above the footer to provide air flow to the area under each bungalow. The vent cover is a flimsy wooden trellis, easily removed to allow access to the crawl space. I squatted, lifted off the vent cover, turned on my flashlight, and peered into the space. The dirt floor was approximately five feet below the subfloor and flooring joists, running flat for a distance of fifteen feet and then slanting down and away toward the far corner of the bungalow. The soil was dry, but I suspected a good rain (if we ever had one) would result in puddles that would feed the mold spores that had been proliferating there for years. Construction debris was still in evidence: broken bricks and wood scraps dating back the seventy years since my landlord and his father had built the cottages.

There were 3-foot-by-3-foot cinder block piers at intervals. One section of the dirt had been covered with widths of plastic sheeting and there were rolls of pink fiberglass insulation like hay bales left out in a farmer's field. I couldn't believe my landlord had been too cheap to have the insulation properly tacked into place. I'd have to have a little chat with him. I didn't like to think about the shoddy workmanship for which I paid rent. Okay, it wasn't *much* rent, but cheap is cheap.

The beam of my flashlight picked out the three phone wires, which meandered from the vent opening across the dirt to one of those telephone company handsets used to determine if there's a dial tone. I was curious about that myself. I inched my way across the hard-packed soil, using my elbows for leverage. Just as I extended a hand to pick up the phone company handset, there was the shrilling of a telephone above me. I jumped, banging the back of my head on a joist. Without even thinking about it, I pressed Talk and said, "Hello?"

"Kinsey, this is Ruthie. Did I catch you at a bad time?"

"It's not the best. Is it all right if I call you back?"

"Sure. It's nothing urgent. I just wanted to know how you were feeling."

"About what?"

"The bun you have in your oven."

"I don't have a bun in my . . . oh, the bun in my oven. You mean the bun Camilla mentioned Friday night at Rosie's?"

"What other bun is there?" she asked.

"Forget it. We'll talk later."

I pressed the button disconnecting her, and then stared down at the instrument I was holding. I pressed the button that said Talk and listened to the dial tone, which was actually emanating from the telephone sitting on the office desk right above me. This was how Ned Lowe had managed to tap into my phone line without ever entering my well-fortified work space.

25

Monday, September 25, 1989

What I realized then, which was just as appalling in my opinion, was that in addition to his tapping into my phone line, he'd dragged in his aluminum-frame backpack and red sleeping bag. The man had been bivouacking under my office floor for nearly a week. I swept the beam of my flashlight across the area, focusing on a portable radio, a homely supply of canned goods, a can opener, and a small Coleman stove complete with wind baffles in case a hurricane blew through. All of this was neatly arranged on a wooden produce crate he'd toted in from outside. He'd set his hiking boots to one side of the crate and he was collecting his trash in a plastic grocery bag. How thoughtful of him. In addition, he had a small bottle of Tennessee whiskey and a Thermos with a twist-off lid he was using as a cup. I pictured him at the cocktail hour, propped on one elbow, surveying his dirt kingdom while he sipped his sour mash and reviewed his day.

When had he come up with this idea? It occurred to me that the day he'd broken my kitchen window, he might have been conducting an experimental mission to test the feasibility of the plan. The bungalows on either side of mine were unoccupied and the downtown neighborhood is scarcely populated at night. Once he moved in, all he had to do was wait until dark and he could come and go as he pleased. In the interim, he could nest under my office during daylight hours, safe from prying eyes. Except for his bathroom needs (which I was hoping he tended to elsewhere), he had a cozy little habitat with all the comforts of home.

I crouched and stuck my head in the vent opening.

To the left, there was a gasoline can that seemed odd unless he was using unleaded fuel in his little cook stove. There was another possibility, of course. The last time he was on the run, he'd set his recreational vehicle on fire and escaped on foot. I hadn't seen any trace of the bright red Oldsmobile he'd stolen, but Erroll was right about its being too conspicuous to drive for long. Ned would torch the car. He'd probably ditched it somewhere and hoofed it here on foot. Burning the car seemed extreme when all he had to do was wipe down his fingerprints and abandon it. It might take a week, but someone would steal it, strip it, or a nearby resident would become suspicious and have the car towed off to the impound lot.

I checked the area to the right, where I spotted a Havahart trap suitable for groundhogs, raccoons, and other medium-sized beasts. The spring-loaded door had snapped shut and the trap was empty. Maybe he baited it at night in case a skunk decided to take refuge in the base camp he'd established for himself. I picked up a faint noise. I cocked my head and squinted. The sound came again; a metallic jingle that sounded like the rattling of a length of chain. It crossed my mind that it might be Ned, but I didn't think so. There was no indication I'd interrupted him unless he'd heard me out on the sidewalk and had slipped into the shadows out of sight.

I pulled my head out of the opening and paused to

study my surroundings. Had the noise come from outside the crawl space or from within? It was shady between the two buildings, almost to the point of being chilly. I let my gaze linger at the section of street I could see in the gap between the two bungalows. The neighborhood was quiet, which is why I like it. Ned must have liked it for much the same reason. So little traffic. So few pedestrians. He couldn't have anticipated my being onto him, since I'd just figured it out myself. This put me one step ahead of him for once.

Now that I knew where he was holing up, all I had to do was call Cheney Phillips and have him stake out the location until Ned showed up again. Cheney, Jonah, or someone in law enforcement would rally the troops, set up the snare, and catch Ned Lowe in the loop. In the meantime, I intended to leave no sign that I'd been there. Let Ned proceed on the assumption that his lair was undiscovered. As long as he didn't show up in the next ten minutes, I was fine. I had no fantasies about nailing him on my own. Forget a citizen's arrest. I know when I need help and this was clearly a situation that called for the big guns. I thought about dialing 9-1-1 on the spot, but a police response with sirens wailing would tip him off if he were anywhere in the area. This had to be played with subtlety, without alerting him that I had discovered what he'd been up to.

My legs were beginning to ache from my crouching position: knees bent, buttocks resting on my heels. I eased my head and shoulders into the vent and let my gaze travel across the barren landscape. Beyond Ned's diminutive settlement, the crawl space was enveloped in gloom, though the dark wasn't absolute. Three other vent openings, one on each exterior wall, admitted a faint illumination, but no discernible air flow. The dirt sloped to the left, creating more headroom toward the center of the space.

I was still staring into the shadowy depths when a squealing ruckus erupted. I was so startled, I jumped, banging the back of my head forcefully on the wood-framed opening. Shit! For a moment, I thought I'd pass out. My heart thumped hard from the shock and I struggled to catch my breath. The throbbing was intense and I felt darkness close in on me and then retreat, leaving me cross-eyed with pain. I put a hand against the back of my head, where a knot was already rising in response to the self-inflicted blow. I pulled my hand away and checked my fingers, hoping I wasn't bleeding, which I was not.

What the hell *was* that?

There was a strangled wailing sound that made me jump a second time. Obviously, it was some kind of animal. I couldn't see what it was because a cinder block pier cut short my line of sight. A nest of rats? A raccoon? Maybe the beast was caught in a second Havahart trap, though I had no idea why Ned would need two. There was a moment of quiet and then the frenzied scuffling started up again. The animal had to be staked to something because its panic was palpable. There was a sudden piercing smell of urine and feces where the creature had lost control of its bowels trying to free itself. Even a sleepy-eyed opossum could turn vicious if cornered. I didn't want to get anywhere near wildlife that frantic, but I needed to understand what was going on. As far as I knew, there were no beasties living under my office, so whatever it was, Ned had brought it in with him. But why?

Ned was a man who liked to do things for effect. Witness his savage beating of Phyllis Joplin in a time frame that guaranteed my finding her. He'd camped under my office for the shock value. He must have enjoyed thinking about my reaction when I realized where he'd been this past week. He might even have intended to alert me to the fact that he was five feet below me every time I sat down at my desk. No point in being clever without an audience.

So what was his intention? Having set the stage, what additional form of savagery did he have in mind? The low howl started up again. The animal was clearly agitated. I hesitated. Really, it wasn't my problem. My job was to get to a clean phone line and notify law enforcement. What bothered me was the idea of leaving any creature at the mercy of such a man.

Was I going to have to go in there and have a look?

I didn't see a way around it. I considered circling the bungalow and trying the vent opening on the far side of the building, which would have given me a clear line of sight, but I knew the remaining vent covers were nailed shut. The last thing I wanted to do was set up a banging, hammering announcement that I was on Ned's case.

I shrugged out of my jacket and laid it down on the dirt just inside the hole. I took off my holster, removed the H&K, and tucked it in the waistband of my jeans at the small of my back. Awkwardly, I eased in through the vent opening, first extending my left leg, and then the rest of me, bent double, and hoping like hell I wouldn't knock myself in the head again. Once in, I hunkered in a space that was barely sufficient to allow me to duck-waddle my way toward the cinder block pier that blocked the animal from view. I told myself all I had to do was get close enough to see what I was dealing with. If I couldn't free the creature myself, I'd call Animal Control and have them send someone over to save the poor thing. I hated the idea of tipping my hand, but in the greater scheme of things, it was better to keep Ned's sick nature in mind and do what I could to prevent any further brutality.

I decided I could make better progress if I lowered myself to my hands and knees and either crawled or hunched my way across the dirt, using my elbows and toes to propel myself. The soil smelled metallic. I didn't dare look up at the subfloor just above me because it might have been a hotbed of spiders and centipedes, either of which would have had me levitating. At the very notion, my heart gave one big thump and then a series of little ones, like an internal jolt with aftershocks following. I put my head down, trying to still my panic. Was the goal worth the risk? I was assuming Ned arrived and departed after dark. But what if he showed up now? I wasn't certain what frightened me more—coming face-to-face with a frantic animal or finding myself fifteen feet from freedom with Ned Lowe putting in an unexpected appearance and blocking my escape.

It didn't bear thinking about. It did occur to me that once I exited the crawl space and returned to my office, I'd have to make sure Ned hadn't let himself into the bungalow while I was under it. I didn't want a replay of the choking incident and I wasn't quite ready to test my martial arts skills, as I was only coming up on week five. I crawled forward a few feet and looked back at the vent opening, which seemed smaller. The distance between me and the outside world was lengthening and I still couldn't identify the animal except for the occasional gyration as the creature flung itself this way and that in its attempt to flee whatever restraints were binding it. I would have abandoned the attempt altogether but I knew how Ned's mind worked. The thing about psychopaths is that from the time they're little children, they're incredibly cruel. Even before their pathology is fully developed, they are cold and clinical, completely without empathy.

I groped my way by inches, reassured by the bulky gun I'd shoved into my waistband at the small of my back. I had my flashlight at the ready and three more feet to go. No point in worrying about the risk since I'd committed myself. It might be folly, but I'd gone so far now that it was easier to proceed than to retreat. I dragged myself another foot and a half, bracing myself on my elbows while I pushed down on the toes of my shoes for thrust. I leaned forward and peered into the dark. I turned on the flashlight again and swept the beam into the area behind the cinder block pier.

When I understood what I was looking at, I uttered a low cry of surprise and disbelief. It was Ed; limp with exhaustion, eyes closed, fur matted. Ned had buckled him into a body harness that hung from one of the floor joists. I'd seen similar harnesses at pet stores: a lightweight nylon vest for use if you thought your cat would enjoy being walked like a dog. Most cats don't care for this idea at all. The vest wasn't causing Ed any pain. The problem was that the O-ring in the back center of the harness was attached to a metal eye Ned had screwed into one of the joists. He'd made sure the chain connected to the harness was so short, the cat's feet barely touched the ground. How long had the cat been dangling like that? Ed's struggle must have been amusing to Ned because there was no possibility of escape.

I gathered Ed in my arms like a baby, supporting him with a hand under his belly in hopes he'd feel secure. He fought me at first, already conditioned to do battle. Sweet Ed, with his one green eye and one blue, with his little stub of a tail. His heart was rat-a-tat-tatting hard and I knew the fight or flight reaction had thrown his whole system into hyperdrive. I sat down, hunched over, my head canted to one side to avoid contact with the floor joists. I kept my left arm lifted sufficiently to keep him level instead of sagging under his own weight. He was shivering with tension, but I would have been willing to swear he knew who I was.

My initial impulse was to unbuckle the harness, but I realized if I freed him, he'd be out of there like a shot. If he made a beeline for the vent opening and escaped, he'd be vulnerable to Ned's recapturing him, which was unthinkable. I waited and when he was calmer, I leaned back and straightened my body so I could reach into my jeans pocket where I'd stashed the Leatherman. Oops. Not there. I remembered then that I'd slipped it into the pocket of my windbreaker, which was a good twenty feet away. I reached up and felt for the eye screw, which I was able to turn, but only with great effort. I was using my thumb and index finger, which gave me very little purchase. I'd been weight lifting in the months since Ned half choked me to death, so at least I had strength in my arms. Even so, it was a strain holding the cat in my left while I was forced to work with my right arm lifted above shoulder height. I found sweat trickling down my face and twice had to stop to mop the side of my face on my sleeve.

I renewed my effort, knowing the sooner I got out of there, the better. This was slow going and once I succeeded in unscrewing the piece, I'd still have the cat to contend with as I hunched and dragged myself back over to the vent. I heard a car door slam out on the street. My heart did a quick two-step. I paused. As though sensing my worry, the cat contorted himself, arching his back in a bid for freedom. He was agile and quick and though I managed to subdue him temporarily, I wasn't sure how much longer I'd be able to maintain control of him. There had to be a better way to go about this.

My gaze fell on the telephone company handset that had allowed Ned to eavesdrop on every phone call I made. I couldn't believe it hadn't occurred to me before. All I had to do was call for help, which was a more sensible solution to the problem than wrestling with a cat and unscrewing a metal eye at the same time. I picked up the sound of footsteps scratching on the walk between bungalows. I snatched the handset in my right hand and punched in Henry's number with my thumb, trying to keep the cat calm at the same time.

One ring.

Under my breath, I was saying, "Come on, come on! Pick up."

I leaned sideways and looked toward the vent hole, which was now eclipsed by someone standing there, the light dimmed by half.

Two rings.

Henry and Pearl and Lucky must still be out hunting for the cat.

Three rings. Four.

The answering machine picked up and I had to wait while Henry went through his cheery greeting. At the beep, I whispered, "Henry, this is me. Listen I've got a situation here. I've got Ed and I'm un—"

The line went dead.

I closed my eyes. I'd left the junction box open and the trellis leaning against the side of the bungalow. Now my navy windbreaker was clearly visible inside the opening. I knew who was out there. My old friend Ned had come back from a trip into the world at large and he wasn't going to appreciate finding me in his personal space. I looked down at the cat in my arms. He'd be better off fending for himself. Carefully, I steadied him with one hand while I unbuckled the harness. In the blink of an eye, he raced into the darkness in the far corner of the crawl space and disappeared.

I reached around behind me and carefully extracted the H&K from my waistband. I pivoted and pulled myself out of sight. For a moment, I sheltered in the lee of the pier, leaning against the cinder block while I gathered my wits about me. I leaned forward and checked the vent. Ned had moved away from the opening, but I was sure he hadn't gone far. I pushed away from the pier and rolled forward until I was stretched out on my stomach with my arms extended in front of me. I gripped the gun with my right thumb wrapped around and touching the middle finger on the grip. I wrapped my left hand around my right with my left thumb lapped over my right thumb. The butt of the H&K rested on the dirt, which meant I could maintain a steady grip on it without tiring. I kept my right arm stiff, with my left hand pulling back slightly. This served to steady my hands and wrists.

The Heckler & Koch VP9 is manufactured from a stamped steel main frame with a polymer trigger guard. The high-profile fixed sights are fitted with two red rectangles on the rear sight and a white stripe on the drift-adjustable front blade sight. There is a lever on the left side of the pistol grip to both decock a cocked hammer or manually re-cock it for a single-action first shot. A manual firing-pin safety is located at the left rear of the slide. Putting it in the down position locks the firing pin, and flipping it up to the level position unlocks it. I flipped up the safety and pulled the slide back.

So far, the two of us hadn't exchanged a word. He knew I was under the bungalow, but he couldn't be sure where. I knew he was out there between the two bungalows, but I had no visual verification of his location. There's something about human nature that inclines us to make eye contact when we're having a conversation. I didn't want Ned to stick his head in the opening because if I was forced to shoot, my target would be the top of his skull, a fatal injury in most cases. Let's not even talk about the mess.

I was hyped. I focused on my breathing, clearing my mind of everything but the task at hand. My brain, for reasons of its own, suddenly replayed my phone conversation with Phyllis, almost word for word. We'd talked about Ned wanting his trinkets from the young girls he killed. I'd asked her if Celeste had given them to her, and she said if she'd had them, she'd have turned them over to the police as evidence. The implication was that the items were still in Celeste's possession. I'd asked her twice if she knew where Celeste was. The first time, she blew me off, breezing right over the question to something else. The second time I asked, she told me Celeste had changed her name and location and, even then, had an unlisted phone number. She'd said she'd written it on a scrap of paper that she tossed in a U-Haul box six weeks before. At the time, she hadn't unpacked everything so she couldn't lay hands on it. I'd told her to keep the information to herself. All I wanted was to have Celeste informed that Ned was back. Shortly after that, Phyllis had invited me for drinks and that's when she'd given me her new address. Ned, in the crawl space where I was now, had probably been scribbling down the information at the same time I was.

He'd beaten Phyllis senseless on the assumption that she'd found the scrap of paper with Celeste's new name and location. He must have thought she was holding out on him. His subsequent tearing into her moving cartons suggested that he hadn't gotten the answer he wanted and was forced to search. He must have been frantically hunting for the information when I rang her bell.

From outside, he said, "You know what I've got out here?"

I kept my mouth shut, sighting down the barrel.

"Can of gasoline. I was going to use it to set the Olds on fire, but I can use it just as easily to burn this place down."

"My landlord has insurance so I don't give a shit."

"I think you will. Because even if the flames don't get you, the smoke inhalation will."

"Well, Ned, dear, I'm looking at a can of gasoline so unless you went out and bought a second one, you're lying through your teeth."

"If you think I'm lying, why don't you put me to the test?"

"Because right now it's your turn to guess what *I've* got."

He sounded amused. "I know what you have. A fucking cat that scratched the hell out of me."

"Aside from the cat."

"Okay, what?"

"A gun."

"Not relevant. Because you know what this is?"

I heard liquid splashing, the sound swiftly followed by the harsh scent of gasoline. I made sure the two red rectangles bracketed the white line on the barrel. "I don't want to have to shoot you, Ned."

I made a face at myself. What the hell was I talking about? This man was about to turn Ed and me into charcoal briquettes. Under the circumstances, shooting his ass was the only appropriate course of action. The first trick was to guess whether he was standing to the left of the vent opening or to the right. The second trick was to catch him before he got out his handy-dandy lighter.

I had to do my calculations in an instant. I figured that since I was prone and aiming for the vent opening, I'd be shooting at an angle that placed the bullet's trajectory somewhere between his left hip and his thigh. The bullet would also have to tear through the bungalow's wood frame, moisture barrier, plaster, and exterior stucco. My magazine carried nine rounds of 9x19 mm Parabellum that I thought would do the job. I shifted my sights to the left of the opening and squeezed the trigger. The barrel bucked neatly, the brass leaped up, and the bang was so loud, I knew my ears would ring for a week. There was a certain jaunty aspect to the hot dancing brass, at least from my perspective. I brought the sights back to the right side of the opening, breathed in, breathed out, and fired again.

Ned shrieked like a girl. He must have been thumbing the striker on his pocket lighter, which he dropped when he was hit. I heard it clatter to the walk with a sharp metallic note. Through the opening, I caught a glimpse of him clutching his right thigh, which must have felt like it was on fire.

I squeezed the trigger and fired again. This time, I had no intention of hitting him. I just wanted him to know I was sincere. I was also hoping someone in the neighborhood would call the police with a report of shots fired. I heard Ned stumble down the walk between the two bungalows. His breathing sounded ragged and I could tell he was working hard to suppress his sobs. From his gait, it was clear he was limping badly, dragging one foot, and probably bleeding through his trouser leg. Moments later, I heard the distinct sound of a car starting up and peeling out with a chirp.

Meanwhile, the flame from the lighter must have made contact with the puddled gasoline because I heard the liquid catch fire with the dull sound of a stove burner as it whumped to life. A cloud of black smoke appeared and with it, the wavering aura created by flames.

Gun in hand, I made a mad scramble toward the vent on the opposite wall. I turned over on my back and shattered the trellis with two savage kicks. Then I pushed my way through the opening into fresh air. Ed materialized from the dark and, in his infinite feline wisdom, streaked out right behind me.

26

IRIS AND JOEY

Wednesday, September 27, 1989

On Wednesday evening Iris and Joey settled down on their tiny patio, which was just big enough for two wicker chairs with a small table between. Because their apartment building was set back from the street, traffic noise didn't bother them. The lighted businesses stretching off from the intersection made the scene as changeable and engaging as a wood blaze crackling in a fireplace. They never tired of watching the passing cars, the pedestrians, neighbors walking their dogs. Joey topped up her wineglass and paused to light a cigarette for himself and then one for her.

When the phone rang, he leaned back and snagged the handset from the planning center. The cord had been stretched so often, the coil had flattened in places. "Hello?"

He sat up. "Oh hey, how're you?" he said.

As Joey listened, he got up and walked around his

chair to the patio door. He carried the long phone cord with him so it wouldn't get hung up on anything. He made a point of maintaining eye contact with Iris, who was trying to gauge the caller's identity from Joey's responses. He put his hand over the mouthpiece and pantomimed "Fritz" so she'd know who he was talking to.

Iris could hear Fritz's miniature voice, like an agitated buzzing sound, but not what he was saying.

Joey's focus sharpened. "Really?"

It was clear Fritz was excited. She could tell by the pitch of his voice and the rapidity with which he was speaking. She heard him crow once, completely smitten with himself.

Joey said, "I don't believe it. You've got to be kidding. Tell me again and slow down, for god's sake."

Joey was doing the big rolling-arm gesture, urging her to join him. Iris stubbed out her cigarette, jumped up, and eased into the living room, where she crossed to Joey's side. Apparently, Fritz was repeating the news, whatever it was. Iris tilted her ear toward the receiver just as Joey said, "How'd you get your hands on twenty-five thousand bucks?"

"I didn't say I had the money. I have a plan for getting it," Fritz said. "It's foolproof. Well, almost."

"Oh, shit. What plan?"

"Don't worry about it. Not an issue. I got it wired."

"Is this legal or illegal?"

"Let's say it's semi-legal. Close enough at any rate," Fritz said. "No concealed weapons are involved." He laughed at himself, enjoying the momentary superiority of knowing more than Joey did.

Joey put a hand over the mouthpiece and he and Iris exchanged a look of disbelief. Iris rolled her eyes and opened her hands as if to say, *What now?* Joey turned his attention back to Fritz. "What happens when your parents find out?"

"They won't until it's too late. Once the money's paid, that's the end of it, right? So how can they complain?"

Joey ran a hand across the top of his head. "Dude, you're scaring me."

"Don't worry about it."

"I'm just looking after you, Fritz, so hear me out. Let's say you have the cash in hand, now what?"

"That's why I'm calling. He left a message on the answering machine. He's picking me up at the corner of State and Aguilar. Noon on Friday. I should be set by then."

"I can't believe you'd agree to get in a car with some faceless unidentified stranger."

"I didn't *agree* to anything," Fritz said. "I didn't even talk to him. Those were the instructions he left."

Joey gave Iris the thumbs-up, both of them amazed that the plan was working so well. "What if he turns around and holds you for ransom or something like that? You could be in way over your head."

"Don't be such a dick. If he looks like a badass, I'll toss the money in the front seat and take off on foot. What's he going to do, run me down?"

"But once you've seen him, doesn't that make you a liability? He can't afford to have you on the loose. You talk to the cops, look at mug shots . . ."

Hesitantly, Fritz said, "I'm thinking this could be Austin."

"Really. Well, that's a changeup. What brings you to that conclusion?"

"He said, 'This is a voice from your past . . .' Almost has to be him, don't you think?"

"I thought you were convinced he was dead."

"I said if he was alive, he'd be in touch. Didn't I say that? Well, now he's been in touch."

"You're saying Austin's behind this whole blackmail scheme," Joey said, stating it as a fact instead of a question, curious to see if Fritz would confirm.

"Okay, yeah. I guess I am saying that."

"I hate to remind you of this, but Austin swore he'd come back and kill anyone who blabbed about Sloan. That's you, isn't it?"

There was a moment of silence.

"Why would he come back to collect twenty-five grand and then kill me?"

"Why wouldn't he? That gives him the best of both deals. You deliver the money and he takes you down. Mission accomplished."

"Actually, that did cross my mind and it's one of the reasons I called. I want you to come with me so the guy doesn't get any ideas."

"Me?"

"Like an insurance policy. It would keep things on the up-and-up."

Iris got Joey's attention and waved an index finger back and forth vigorously.

Joey said, "I'm not sure about this. It sounds risky."

Fritz's voice jumped half an octave. "What do you mean, you're not sure? You said anything you could do to help. This is 'help.' This is what I need."

"Why don't you ask Bayard?"

"I guess I'll have to call him if you won't help. I was hoping you'd say yes."

Joey said, "Let me see what Iris says. She's out right now but I'll talk to her as soon as she gets back. You're at home?"

"Right. Call me as soon as possible. I'm counting on you, buddy."

"Fine. In the meantime, see if you can talk Bayard into it."

"Thanks a fuckin' bunch. I should probably mention that Bayard doesn't believe it's Austin's voice on the machine. He thinks it's yours."

"Well, that's stupid on the face of it," Joey said. "Where'd he get that idea?"

"I let him listen to the message."

"Dude, you're nuts. Why would I do that to you?"

"I don't know, Joey. Why would you?"

"Yeah, right. Up yours. I'm done with this conversation."

Once Joey hung up, he and Iris stared at each other, trying to absorb this unexpected turn of events.

Iris said, "So what's this big hot scheme of his?"

"You heard the same thing I did. This is Fritz being coy for once. What a dork."

Iris shook her head. "That message was a mistake," she said. "You shouldn't have set it up that way because now we're stuck."

"Wait a minute. So far we've threatened Fritz, but we haven't done anything. Once we take the money, we're guilty of grand theft or theft by deception or some damn thing."

"That's the point. The money is the point," she said. "It's like when a jury awards you . . . what's it called? Damages. I'm entitled to compensation for the pain and suffering I've been through."

"Forget pain and suffering. You were stoned. You don't have a clue what went on."

"Not so. You're wrong. The tape brought it all back. What they did was humiliating."

"Get off of that for a minute. Let's stay in the here and now."

"Would you shut up? You sound like a therapist. You forget we're not 'taking' the money. He's giving it to us."

"But under duress. Extortion's a crime."

"Joey, we knew that from the get-go. Why worry about it now?"

"Okay. So we didn't think it through."

"Not 'we,' Joey. *You* didn't think it through because you didn't believe we'd succeed."

"Hey, you didn't either, so don't put it all on me."

"I don't understand what you're so worried about. We come up with a plan and it works. Why is that so hard to accept?"

"Because until now, we've always had an out. Just drop the whole thing and take a walk. No harm, no foul. This is the point of no return. If we pick him up on that corner, then he'll know it's us."

"So what? Good news for him. He's dealing with his pals instead of some tattoo-covered loser."

"It doesn't work that way. We've been lying through our teeth, pretending to be his friends while for all practical purposes, we're robbing him at gunpoint. We can't do this."

Exasperated, Iris said, "Okay. Shit. We don't pick him up and he never knows it's us. What does that buy us?"

"He can give the money back. He can tell his parents it was all a big mistake."

"And he corrected this big mistake by doing what?"

"I don't know. He got the money. He went to the place where the guy said he'd pick him up and the guy's a no-show. So Fritz brings the money back, every dollar accounted for, they put it back where it was, and that's the last they hear of it. Extortionist never contacts them again. Problem solved."

Iris blinked. Reluctantly, she said, "That's actually not a bad idea."

"It gives us an out and no one's the wiser."

"What about all the time and energy we put into this?"

"A pipe dream. Who cares? We had fun. Fantasy revenge without any consequences."

She thought about it, tilting her head this way and that.

Joey said, "Please. Do this for me. We're not crooks. We're just a couple of lunkheads, harassing some twerp who did you wrong ten years ago. Now we lay it by and it's done."

Iris said, "Shit. I was ready to rock and roll."

"We do this and we'll be caught. I can feel it in my bones."

She sighed. "All right. Crap. I agree. You were brilliant to come up with the idea of creating a phantom suspect. We'll be out of it and that private investigator will be chasing her own tail. Good luck with that."

"Fine, but you're the one who has to call Fritz and tell him we can't help."

"Why me?"

"Because I told him you'd have the final word."

"What am I supposed to say?"

"Shit, Iris. Be inventive. You're a genius when it comes to ad-libbing."

Grudgingly she picked up the handset. "You're just saying that because you want to get laid."

"Pretty much," he said.

27

Monday, October 2, 1989

The week following the fire was a quiet one and I assumed life had returned to normal. Since Lauren McCabe had fired me, I no longer had to worry about Fritz and the extortion threat. I should have known it was simply the lull before the storm. In that lovely interval, I found myself reviewing the sequence of events—my discovery that Ned was camping under my office, my confrontation with him, and the shots I'd fired while he was splashing gasoline against the bungalow with an eye to seeing the structure engulfed in flames. Henry had picked up my aborted message mere moments after the line went dead. He'd put in an immediate call to the fire and police departments. I hadn't had time to tell him where I was, but he claimed if I wasn't home, I was always at the office, so that's where he sent the cavalry, riding to my rescue. By the time the Mounties arrived, I had put the fire out myself, using the fire extinguisher I retrieved from under the sink in my kitchenette. I'd had it for years and it was gratifying to have the chance to test its efficiency. Worked like a charm. A cursory inspection of the framing on the bungalow suggested that good-sized splinters had been torn off when the three bullets ripped into the wood and I was hoping they were currently embedded in the flesh of Ned Lowe's thigh. With luck, there was more injury to him than there was to me. The gasoline hadn't had a chance to saturate the stucco siding and Ned hadn't spilled enough of it to do much more than superficial damage. Nonetheless, I spent the following four days dealing with my landlord's insurance company. The claims adjustor was having trouble understanding how this series of mishaps had come to pass.

The crime scene techs had been alerted and they got busy collecting evidence: Ned's hiking boots, sleeping bag, and backpack frame, which would doubtless be impregnated with his DNA. Now, not only were there outstanding warrants for multiple murder charges, he was wanted for grand theft auto, arson, trespassing, criminal mischief, and animal cruelty. Ed wasn't hurt, but he was traumatized by the experience and didn't leave Henry's house again for a week.

While the fire hadn't spread, my office smelled like smoke, charred wood, and the heavy dousing of water the fire department had lavished on the bungalow to knock down any smoldering remains of the original blaze.

At that point, my paranoia had leapt into the red zone. I spent twenty minutes daily on my hands and knees crawling around on my office floor, looking for listening devices. Since the alarm system prevented Ned's getting in, he'd have been limited to spike mikes and voice-activated tape recorders. I did a cursory search for eavesdropping equipment above waist level, but found none. True to form, I typed up a report of the incident on the theory that the necessity might arise for further review. I calmed myself with the knowledge that no real harm had been generated. Ed was safe. I was safe and for once being unemployed, instead of being worrisome, was a profound relief. I sat down in my swivel chair and entertained happy thoughts. When I heard the knock on my office door, I was tempted to ignore it. A quick look at my appointment calendar showed that it was Monday, October 2, and I wasn't expecting anyone. I would have ignored my visitor, pretending I wasn't in, but anyone standing at the office door had a clear view through the window to the desk where I was sitting.

Lauren McCabe.

I went to the door, disarmed the periphery, unlocked the door, and let her in. If she noticed the lingering odor of burnt bungalow, she made no mention of it. It was then that I realized how totally self-absorbed she was. Why this came as a surprise I do not know. I assumed she'd come to argue about the money I'd refunded and I was prepared, in the spirit of forgiveness, to put the twenty-five hundred dollars back in my own account. I returned to my swivel chair. She sat down in one of the two guest chairs across the desk. She placed her leather handbag on the chair next to her.

She didn't look good. Technically, she was properly put together as befitted someone of her means. She wore a white tunic with a heavy silver belt, gray wool slacks, and black patent-leather flats that made her feet look huge. Maybe tall women are better served by high heels. Her complexion was blotchy and her lipstick was eaten away in the middle, leaving a strange outline of stark red around her mouth. Her gray hair, while still neatly framing her face, had lost its luster.

"I'm assuming you received my note," I said. I felt it was a generous move on my part to introduce the subject of her having fired me, thus saving her the awkwardness of raising the issue herself.

Her look was blank. "What note?"

"The note I sent you, along with a check reimbursing you for the twenty-five-hundred-dollar advance you paid me."

"I haven't checked the mail in days. I've been too upset about Fritz."

I said, "Ah."

That felt like a setback. In truth, once I'd recovered from the insult, I was glad to be shed of the job, which had felt iffy from the outset. The only reason I hadn't been dismayed at the sight of her standing at my office door was that I knew she had no further power over me.

Meanwhile, she frowned in bafflement, saying, "Why would you return the advance?"

"Because you fired me. In my note, I confirmed the severing of our professional relationship as of September twenty-third."

Her now-blotchy complexion was suffused with pink and while her tone was calm, there was a stubborn undercurrent. "I think you misunderstood my intent. I may have disagreed with some of the steps you took, but there's no need to return the advance when the job is ongoing."

"Uh, not ongoing. That's the point. In effect, I fired you back."

"That was precipitous and completely unnecessary. I think you could at least have had the courtesy to sit down and discuss the matter with me before you took so radical a step."

It was finally occurring to me that she was here for some other purpose altogether. "You're upset about something else."

"Fritz is gone."

"As of when?"

"I'm not sure. We only realized he was missing a short while ago and then it was by a fluke."

"What fluke?"

"I had five checks sitting on my desk, already endorsed and ready to be deposited. I know they were there Thursday afternoon because I was making calls and I remember seeing them. This morning, they were gone. I asked Hollis and he had no idea where they'd disappeared to. In fact, he thought I'd gone to the bank and I assumed he had."

"You're talking about this past Thursday, the twenty-eighth?"

She nodded.

"When did you last see Fritz?"

"Well, that's just it. He's been spending weekends with friends. Since his release from CYA, he's been very testy about my asking where he's going or where he's been so I make a point of not inquiring. When I noticed his bed hadn't been slept in the past three nights, I paid no attention. I went over to the bank this morning and talked to one of the tellers. It seems Fritz showed up with a deposit slip, putting seventy-eight thousand in our savings account and taking back twenty-five thousand in cash."

"The bank will do that?"

"Ours did. The total on the five checks was a hundred and three thousand dollars, so his taking a portion in cash wasn't unusual."

"What if the checks hadn't cleared?"

"It wouldn't have made any difference. We keep over five hundred thousand in that account."

I said, "Wow. How much interest do you earn on savings like that? One percent?"

"Hollis likes to keep some of our assets liquid."

Half a million in liquid assets seemed like a lot to me, but I didn't want to stop and argue the folly, which was off-topic.

Meanwhile, she was saying, "Ordinarily, the bank would have put a hold on the money for a few days, but the teller knew the twenty-five was covered because she looked it up. We've been customers for twenty years and we've never had a problem. The teller knows me, knows Hollis, and knows Fritz. There didn't appear to be anything irregular."

"Wasn't a signature required for the twenty-five in cash?"

"My signature was already on the deposit slip. He forged it."

"He must have done a damn fine job of it."

She stiffened slightly, but let the comment go.

"When did he make the deposit?" I asked.

"Friday morning. He made a point of taking the cash in twenties and hundreds."

"Do you remember seeing him after that?"

She shook her head. "Neither of us do."

"What about clothes or personal possessions? Did he pack a bag?"

"We keep luggage in a storage area on the ground floor. I haven't had a chance to check. His closet is always crammed, so there's really no way to tell if he took anything or not. The bank teller remembers he had a backpack. Maybe red or black, she wasn't sure."

"Well, a close guess at any rate. Does he have a valid California driver's license?"

"He hasn't had time to apply for one. His expired when he was incarcerated."

"What about a vehicle? Are yours accounted for?"

"We have two and, yes, both are in the underground garage. He must have gone on foot."

"Unless someone picked him up."

"True."

I was on the verge of stating the two obvious possibilities: either Fritz had generated the blackmail scheme and had finally taken the payout into his own hands, or the extortionist had communicated instructions about how the money was to be delivered and Fritz had acquired the cash and handed it over to the blackmailer, thinking that would put an end to it.

"You have a theory?" I asked.

"I know he was feeling desperate. Hollis and I should have been more supportive. I can see that now."

In my view, their "support" was what had gotten him in trouble in the first place, but I didn't think she'd want to hear that. "Do you have any idea where he might have gone?"

She shook her head in the negative.

"No close relatives?"

"Not in the area and none who'd take him in without talking to us first."

"What about friends? You said he's been spending weekends with friends. Have you contacted them?"

"I don't know who they are. He never mentioned anyone by name."

"He didn't leave a contact number in case you needed him?"

"I know it sounds ridiculous, but we were so relieved to think he still *had* friends we didn't press him for the particulars."

"Does he have an address book?"

"I found one that predated his time at CYA. Most of the names and phone numbers are out of date."

"How many did you call?"

"Five or six. I drew a line through those if you'd like to see."

She retrieved her handbag from the chair next to her and opened it. She reached in and pulled out a 4-by-6-inch address book with a Led Zeppelin album cover on the front. The black-and-white image showed a rigid airship shaped like a cigar, with the back end in flames. "The ones I tried were disconnects or had been reassigned," she said as she passed the address book across the desk to me.

Fritz's handwritten entries were done in a clumsy fashion, with smudges and cross-outs that made them barely legible. In a quick flip-through, the only name I recognized was Iris Lehmann's and I didn't believe her number would have been the same. I placed the address book on the desk in front of me. "What's your current thinking? Will you file a missing person's report?"

"I don't think he's *missing*. He's simply gone. I'm hoping you can track him down."

"But I'm no longer an employee."

"I thought we went over that. You misunderstood."

"Not to argue the point, but I don't see how you could have been any clearer. You said I was fired and I took you at your word."

"Well, then I suppose I should apologize."

"That would be a start," I said. I waited, thinking she would offer an apology, but she seemed to believe the mere mention was as good as a deed well done. I put a hand behind my ear, indicating that I was waiting to hear from her.

"I hope you can appreciate the bind you're putting

me in if you refuse to help," she said. "Under the circumstances, I can't hire anyone else without confiding the topic of the extortionist to yet another outside party."

"Then you better hope Fritz comes home on his own."

She seemed flustered. "That's all you have to say?"

"What did you expect?"

"I thought you'd be willing to help."

"And I thought you'd be offering an apology, so I guess neither one of us is getting what we want. Would you like to try again?"

Lauren cleared her throat. "I'm sorry you misunderstood."

"You can't be sorry for *my* behavior or mental state. You can only be sorry for your own."

She was quiet for a moment, as though trying to translate the concept into her native tongue, which apparently wasn't English. "I'm sorry I butted in. I won't do that again. I'd appreciate it if you'd agree to help."

"First, let's see if you really have a problem. If he's been spending weekends with friends, that might be the simplest explanation. Call me tomorrow morning if he hasn't showed up by then."

"And the missing money?"

"Let's handle one thing at a time."

I was not much in the mood to get beat up in my women's self-defense class, but I made myself go anyway. It's all too easy to let these things slide. If I missed one class, I might as well kiss off the rest. At three thirty, I made a quick trip home, where I changed into my workout clothes and picked up my gym bag. By four, I was seated cross-legged on one of the floor mats with my fellow students, listening to our instructor's introductory remarks.

On the subject of self-defense weapons, we were advised that in most states it's legal to carry Mace as long as the container is 2.5 ounces or less.

She said, "It's important to remember that criminals

don't operate by such a tidy set of rules. Actually, it would be hard to imagine a rapist complaining to the police about your failure to comply."

This netted her a laugh. She went on to remind us that we should recognize and avoid dangerous situations, bypassing dark and deserted areas, walking with others, parking near streetlights, moving with purpose and confidence. This wisdom had been drilled into me before. It was all common sense, but it was amazing to me how often we overlook the obvious. The problem is that it's almost impossible to live in a state of constant vigilance. The sustained spike in blood pressure alone would condemn you to an early grave. So what were we meant to absorb? An awareness of the perils unique to womanhood: rape and physical assault at the hands of strangers and acquaintances alike. The majority of rapes are perpetrated by men we know, a sad cause for reflection when embarking on the dating scene. I counted myself wise to confine my love life to cops and other law enforcement worthies to whom I could at least recite the relevant penal code.

Having paid big bucks for the class, we were gifted with a pinch light and whistle attached to a key ring so we could summon assistance if set upon by thugs. The whistle was tiny and emitted a high-pitched shriek in a range doubtless only heard by dogs, but it was better than trusting ourselves to yell for help. Early on, we'd practiced screaming in an exercise designed to attune us to someone approaching from behind. One of us would walk and a faux-assailant would come up from the rear, closing the distance with stealth. The minute you became aware of your potential attacker, you were supposed to turn suddenly and scream at the top of your lungs. I did a fair job of it, but most of the others could barely manage a squeak. One woman said she was worried about hurting the guy's feelings if she misunderstood his intent.

We spent the remainder of the hour in a series of exercises—simulated kicks and punches, which were designed to tax and strengthen our hard-worked muscles.

As had been true the week before, I was quickly drenched in sweat and panting for breath. The last thirty minutes, we engaged in combat with the well-padded opponents hired to acquaint us with the rapid response necessary when attacking and being attacked. At the end of the class, I showered under blissfully hot water, feeling energized and buoyed by the exertion. I knew that within thirty minutes, my body parts would begin seizing up to the point where I could barely lift my arms. I drove home, hoping I still had ibuprofen on hand.

Back in my neighborhood, I found one of those miracle parking spots that so seldom come my way. I was only four doors from home when I locked my car and hit the sidewalk. Up ahead, I heard the gate squeak and looked up to see Pearl in her wheelchair, trying to get through the opening, with her one wheel catching against the fence support. She was banging at it with one of her crutches as though it had attacked her and she was having to fend it off. I'd never seen her in such a snit. Once she lurched free, she came barreling down the walk toward me. Her arms were moving fast and her wheelchair tilted slightly at a crack in the sidewalk where a tree root was pushing up. I thought she'd topple over and lie there with her wheels spinning ineffectually. Instead, she nearly plowed into me.

I said, "Hey! Slow down. What's the matter with you?"

"I'm mad is what's the matter. You never seen a temper tantrum? Because this is what they look like where I come from."

"What's made you so mad?"

"Not a what. It's a who."

"Who are you so mad at?"

"Henry, who else? And I'm not just mad, I'm furious!"

"Why?"

"Because I messed up. I wisht he'd never encouraged me to bake because I can't get it right. I don't know why I even bothered to try."

"I don't get what happened."

"I'll tell you what happened. I put together this cake

and baked it exactly like the recipe said. The whole middle sunk, and when I cut into it? Nothing but goo."

"Aren't you supposed to touch the center of the cake and see if it springs back before you take it out of the oven?"

"So now you want to *criticize*?"

"Sorry. What did Henry say?"

"He said his oven temperature was off, but he was bullshitting so I wouldn't be upset. Said he'd have the gas company come out, but he was just being polite."

"Henry wouldn't do that. If the oven temp is off, the same thing would happen to him, so of course he'll have it looked at. Even if you made a mistake, so what? Don't you ever fail at anything?"

"No, I do not. And you want to know why? Because I hate feeling like this. Feeling like this is the story of my life and it stinks. I remember in grade school when I couldn't do arithmetic standing at the board and I couldn't spell for shit. Eight years old and I never been so humiliated in my life. I told my mama how bad I felt and you want to know what she said? She said, 'Now, Pearl. That is the wrong way to look at things. You're not all that smart, so you ought not to expect so much of yourself. You do the best you can with what God give you and in your case it's not enough to worry about.' "

I laughed. I couldn't help it. "Would you listen to yourself? Your mother was a moron. There's nothing wrong with you. You don't like doing a bad job and neither do I. Who wants to feel stupid, incompetent, or inadequate?"

"But you can do all kind of things."

"No, I can't. I can do a few things well enough. Everything else, I try to avoid. Once in a while I learn something new in spite of myself, but that's about it in the way of my accomplishments."

"Name one new thing you learned."

"I learned to pump my own gas."

"Well, that's ridiculous. You didn't know how to pump your own gas?"

"So now you're criticizing *me*?"

"Well," she said, grudgingly. And then she couldn't seem to think of anything else to say. "Anyways, I'm off to Rosie's. She said I could help in the kitchen, peeling taters for which I'll get paid. Miminum wage, but I can't complain."

"You mean minimum wage?"

"That's what I said. Miminum wage."

"Well, there you go then. Gainfully employed."

Henry's back door was open and Killer was asleep on his mat, forcing me to step over him to tap at the screen. By now, I knew Killer was nothing but a big old baby, but you don't want to startle an animal that size when it's deep in the throes of a doggie dream. The other rule is you don't want to get between a dog and what it wants to eat. That can make them cranky. Henry was in his rocking chair with his Black Jack over ice and the newspaper open in front of him. When he heard the knock, he called out, "Unlocked," which I took as permission to enter.

He seemed both surprised and pleased to see me, setting his paper aside so he could get up and give me a dignified hug, which didn't involve a lot of body contact. He's eighty-nine to my thirty-nine, but we both know what it means to be circumspect.

He said, "Anna stopped by earlier and confessed that she's the one in a family way, so I owe you an apology."

"No, you don't, but I accept anyway. What a scene. I was never so astonished in my life."

"I can just imagine. That Robb woman's behavior was so *unseemly*. And now all of them are embroiled in an impossible mess," he said. His cheeks were tinted with embarrassment. "Pardon my bad manners. I should have offered you a glass of Chardonnay."

"Thanks. I'd love one. Also a couple of ibuprofen if you have any on hand. I'm fresh out. I just finished a self-defense class and I'm hoping to head off a full-body lockdown."

Henry returned to his rocking chair and folded the paper away. I was soon supplied with good white wine and over-the-counter pain meds, which generated a lengthy conversation about Ned Lowe and my dismay at learning he'd been living in the office crawl space under my feet. This reminded him to show me the new alarm panels, duplicates of those I'd had installed at the office.

"What's Lucky up to?" I asked. "I didn't see him as I was passing through the yard."

"He's gone off to Harbor House to sign up for a bed. He lost his when he was thrown out for drunkenness, which means he got sent to the end of the line. I don't know how long it takes to work your way back up the waiting list, but he's doing what he can," he said. "I don't suppose you ran into Pearl as you were coming in the gate."

"Actually, I did. I gather she had a massive cake failure that threw her into a snit."

"The woman has quite a temper. I tried to explain, but she said I was patronizing, so I gave it up," he said. "At any rate, my present concern is your cousin Anna. What will she do?"

"I was just about to ask if she'd said anything to you."

"She asked what I'd do in her place, but I refused to be drawn in. That's not a decision she should make in haste, but from what she says, she's running out of time. You've met her siblings up in Bakersfield?"

I nodded. "Ethan and Ellen. Both are married with three kids each and Anna looks on their lives with horror."

"Is that your opinion as well?"

"Not at all. I saw Ethan with his kids and thought he was a good dad—just the proper mix of freedom and supervision. The problem is he's a talented musician who's missed out on the career he wants. There's just no way for him to balance family life and the requirements of the road. I'm sure a lot of people manage, but he isn't one. Ellen, I don't know about. The point is, Anna views parenthood as a fatal trap."

"Well, it's too bad she doesn't have a friend who

could serve as a good example. A positive role model might make all the difference."

Henry made supper for us: a green salad and cheese omelets with fresh herbs. I didn't realize how much I'd missed him until I found myself back in the thick of conversation with him, catching up on life in general. I was home by nine. Before I did anything else, I got out my gun cleaning kit and sat at the kitchen counter. Once I was satisfied that it was immaculate and in good working order, I wrapped it in a clean cloth and locked it in the trunk at the foot of my bed. Then I crawled between the covers with every muscle in my body aching, but my heart at peace.

28

THE BLOWUP

June 1979

The drive up the pass took twenty minutes, not long at all when you felt like you were a million miles from town. As the road wound up the mountain, Santa Teresa was visible below, diminished to a distant crescent with the Pacific Ocean cradled in its curve. A marine layer hovered on the beaches, looking smoky and insubstantial. Just shy of the summit, Troy made the left turn onto Horizon Road, which threaded along a mountainous terrain that felt isolated and remote. The few houses they passed were set well back from the road on heavily wooded lots with little open space to spare. In places, vehicles were lined up nose-to-tail along the berm, attesting to the popularity of the area despite the fire hazard.

Sloan kept an eye on the house numbers, pointing out Austin's when she spotted it on a metal mailbox posted near the road. Troy pulled his pickup into an empty spot, wheels tilted slightly against the hill. A few yards down the road, she could see Bayard's car parked in much the same way, left front and rear tires hugging the slope. In front of Bayard's car, she saw Poppy's Thunderbird, and beyond that, Stringer's van. Troy and Sloan trudged up the steep gravel driveway. Toward the top, much of the timber had been cleared, leaving generous expanses of open space under a bright sunny sky. Austin's mother's station wagon sat on a parking pad out front.

The Browns' cabin was constructed with an exterior of half-logs, as if built by pioneers, though the house was probably fewer than twenty-five years old. She caught sight of the shake roof, which was doubtless fire resistant. Two stone chimneys flanked the main structure and a wide front porch was furnished with rustic bentwood chairs. The front door stood open and music was audible, emanating from the rear.

As she and Troy passed through the living room to the kitchen, they could see through the oversize sliding glass door that the parcel was flat and large enough to accommodate a swimming pool with stunning views down the mountain to the coast. The pool decking was Saltillo tile and sported a large stone barbecue at one end. An oversize Weber grill sat next to it. Kids were milling around the pool. Half the chaises longues were taken and the air smelled of Coppertone, pool chemicals, and an occasional whiff of dope.

Sloan watched Fritz cannonball off the diving board, raising a tsunami of splashes that had the girls shrieking and ducking to protect their hair. A boom box blasted the Beatles album *Help!* Patti Gibson and Steve Ringer, better known as Stringer, were dancing barefoot on the concrete apron at the deep end of the pool. Sloan recognized two sophomores, Blake Edelston and Roland Berg, neither of whom she knew well. Bayard was smoking a joint. He smiled at Sloan and then chugged down his drink from the same cup he always carried, his perpetual bourbon and Coke.

On the far side of the pool, Austin sat on a green metal glider in his bathing suit, already a gorgeous red-brown under his suntan oil. His old girlfriend Michelle, in a hot pink T-shirt and a snug pair of navy blue OP shorts, sat on a stray cushion at his feet, looking every bit the acolyte. She had an enormous tangle of dark curly hair that fell across her shoulders. She put a proprietary hand on Austin's thigh, giving Sloan a wide-eyed look. Apparently, the two were back together, which might have been what had put him in a charitable mood. As he rolled a joint, he glanced up at Sloan with a smile that seemed friendly enough to make her think he was sincere about the truce. Maybe she'd bury her suspicion regarding his authorship of the anonymous note. Better to let their antagonism dissipate without adding further fuel.

The beer keg sat in the shade against the back of the cabin. An oversize plastic punch bowl sat on a nearby harvest table, the virulent pink contents surrounding an island of solid ice. There was also a bucket full of ice cubes and a stack of clear plastic cups. Iris was manning the punch bowl in a black bikini, her skin already darkly tanned. Sloan was guessing she lay out in her backyard most weekends, soaking up the sun. Fritz tossed back punch with the same abandon as everyone else; anything to feel like one of the gang.

Iris ladled a cup of punch for Sloan and offered a second to Troy. "Joy juice," she said, "unless you'd rather have beer."

"This is fine," Sloan replied.

"I'm a beer kinda guy myself," Troy said and grabbed an empty plastic cup.

Iris polished off the punch she'd poured for Troy and then paused to light a cigarette, probably thinking she looked sophisticated for a fourteen-year-old. All Sloan could think about was Iris splayed out on the pool table while a wobbly handheld video recorder made a pitiless visual record of her disgrace.

Sloan took a sip of her punch. The alcohol content was almost overpowering, with a faint suggestion of fruit. She made a face. "What's *in* this? Yuck."

"All natural ingredients except for the red food coloring. Vodka, pink lemonade, and sloe gin, whatever that is. The strawberries are organic. Very wholesome."

"I don't see strawberries."

Iris peered into the bowl. "Oops. Guess I forgot. Oh well. I leave it to your imagination."

"Not my business, but are you going to be okay up here? Poppy told me you were supposed to be spending the night with her."

Iris made a dismissive gesture. "My parents are at a day-long retreat. Tantra yoga. Unfolding their spiritual natures by screwing their brains out. They won't be home until after dinner."

"Just be careful."

"Totally."

Sloan crossed the patio to a spot near Austin and stood watching him roll another joint, which he stacked with its mates in a vintage cigarette case.

"I see you got here all right," he remarked.

"This place is great. When you said 'cabin,' I was picturing Abraham Lincoln."

"Nothing so crude. Have a look around if you want."

"Thanks."

She took her punch and went into the kitchen. She was unaccustomed to drinking, but she didn't want to appear uptight. She was also ever so slightly tense in Austin's company and the punch was helping her relax. Groceries had been unloaded and the counters were covered with packaged hamburger buns, potato chips, onions, condiments, paper plates, and plastic ware. The sink was packed with ice, soft drinks and bottled water nestled in the depths. The six-burner propane stove looked like it had never been used. In the background, she could hear the Beatles singing "Yesterday."

The living room had been furnished with two big upholstered couches and assorted comfy-looking side chairs. The coffee table was plank, in keeping with the fantasy of frontier life. Sloan took in the high-gloss cherry paneling, the rag rugs, and louvered shutters painted a soft blue. A wood-burning fireplace was central to the side wall, with ample firewood stacked up on the stone hearth. The interior of the house smelled of wood smoke and the inevitable touch of mold.

Off the wide hallway, she saw bunk beds in one guest room and a full-sized bed in each of the other two. The second wood-burning fireplace was located in the master suite, which was more luxurious than many she'd seen in Horton Ravine. As she passed the master bedroom, Poppy emerged from the bathroom in a red halter-top bathing suit, shoes in hand, her street clothes folded neatly over one arm. Her skin had the creamy texture of silk with a tracery of blue veins showing through. In strong sunlight, she'd burn in half an hour and be left peeling for a week.

"Hello again," Poppy said.

"Hey, when I asked for a ride, I wasn't thinking about the fact that Iris rode up with you. How's she getting home?"

"Bayard's taking her, last I heard."

"Great." Sloan cast about for something more to say, but she and Poppy had lost the capacity for small talk. "Anyway, I'll see you out by the pool."

She closed herself in the bathroom, where she changed into her bikini, already wishing she were somewhere else. One curious side effect of the shunning was that it had left her feeling detached. She understood now how easily loyalty could be dispatched and how little most relationships meant. She left her clothes on a chair in the master bedroom and tugged at the bottom of her bathing suit. The bikini, while flattering, left more of her exposed than she was comfortable with. She crossed the hall and moved through the living room and kitchen to the patio.

Fritz stood in the shallow end of the pool, water up to his waist. "Hey, Troy! Catch this!"

He used his clenched hands to squirt a stream of water at Troy, who stood on the diving board poised to go in.

The water caught Troy in the face. Fritz's hyper braying cut through the cheers as Troy dove in, his body slicing the water with scarcely a splash. Austin watched Fritz with a barely concealed contempt. Fritz was a sophomore, one year behind them at Climp, and his showing off was typical of his immaturity. Bayard had once suggested Fritz had a crush on Austin. At the time, she hadn't given much credence to the claim, but she was aware of how often Fritz stole quick looks at Austin, like a kid hoping for his mother's approval.

Sloan watched Austin fire up a joint, sucking in the smoke, which he held for a count of ten. When Austin got stoned, he turned nasty and she hoped she wasn't going to be the target of his caustic remarks. As sweet as Austin had been during their brief romance, withering judgments came more naturally to him.

She put her drink down on the edge of the pool near the deep end and sat down, dangling her feet in the water as she watched Patti and Stringer making out.

From behind her, Poppy appeared. "Can I have some of that?" she asked, pointing at her punch.

"Sure, have it all. It's too strong for me."

Poppy took the cup, downed half the remaining pink punch, and made a face much as Sloan had.

Sloan edged off the side of the pool into the water. She turned her body and held on to the side briefly before she sank. She drifted toward the bottom, loving the silence, the isolation, and the escape. The water was chilly and she pushed off the concrete bottom and crossed the pool under the surface, doing the breaststroke. She'd have to find another ride home. No doubt about it. She couldn't sit in a car with Poppy for even twenty minutes if Poppy was going to wheedle for information the way she did at the house. For now, she seemed to have dropped the subject, but who knew how long that would last?

None of this was worth all the bad feelings. Sloan decided that as soon as she got home, she'd destroy the tape. Since it had surfaced, all the demons in hell had been freed. Now it was time to force them back into the box. If Austin reneged on the agreement, she'd find a way to deal with it. In the meantime, she couldn't imagine Troy or Iris owning up to their behavior, but if one of them had an attack of conscience and confessed all, she could still claim she hadn't seen that part of the tape. Who was going to contradict her?

When she reached the far side of the pool, she pulled herself out of the water and plopped down on the edge. She grabbed a towel off the chaise behind her and mopped her face. She wrung her hair out and tucked the waterlogged strands behind her ears. Stringer and Patti Gibson had gone into the house. Betsy Coe and Roland danced to the Beatles' "Ticket to Ride." Poppy be-bopped in their direction and joined them to make it a threesome. Good spirits, good energy, good bodies; all of them young and in perfect health.

In her peripheral vision, Sloan caught sight of a wiggling bare foot. Someone said, "Steal my towel? That's not nice."

She turned and saw that Bayard was stretched out on the recliner. "Sorry. I didn't see you there."

"Invisibility's my middle name."

Impulsively, she said, "Can I run something by you? This is in confidence because I may be dead wrong . . ."

"Oooh, I like it. Sounds juicy."

"Well, it may or may not be. On the drive up, Troy mentioned that his being caught cheating had knocked him out of the competition for the Climping Memorial Award."

"No big surprise."

"That's not where I was going. What occurred to me was that I got knocked out of the competition as well. Everyone is convinced I wrote the note and I'm sure the faculty's been keenly aware that I was being shunned for it. They're the ones who vote. None of them said anything, but I can tell by the way they look at me, like 'Too bad, kid, but you deserve it.' Know what I mean? I'm tarred with the same brush as Troy and Poppy, but for snitching, which is worse. Cheating, you only hurt yourself; snitching hurts everyone involved."

"Hey, don't worry about it. That's over and done."

"I don't think so. Just listen to me. With Troy and me out of the competition, who do you think benefits?"

Bayard's smile faded and he blinked. "Austin."

"Right, and he's the one who turned the whole class against me."

"Got it."

"You think I'm off base?"

"Hey, it makes sense to me. What are you going to do?"

"There's not much I can do without proof, and I don't see how that's possible. I was just curious if you'd see my point."

"Absolutely."

"Is there any way you could give me a ride home? Poppy was supposed to take me, but I'd rather go with you. Only problem is, I have to leave early to take care of Butch."

"Sure. Iris can go with Stringer. He's got room for her in his van." He patted the edge of his chaise. "Come sit. You look tense."

She got up, pulled the towel around her shoulders, and took a seat beside him. "Austin's not exactly restful company."

"Don't let him get to you. He only has as much power as you give him."

"Ha. Don't I wish," she said.

Austin appeared from the kitchen and crossed to the punch bowl. "You want the rest of this? I'm starting a new batch."

"Fine by me," Sloan said.

"I'm on hold," Bayard said.

"Well, that's a first."

Sloan said, "Austin? I have to go pretty soon. I left Butch out in the yard."

"Why don't you call that neighbor lady, Mrs. Chumley. She has a house key, doesn't she?"

"Well, yeah. For emergencies."

"So have her bring Butch in from the backyard. She can make sure he has food and water and you'll be there in a little while."

Sloan wasn't happy with the idea, but she didn't want to raise any objections. She'd have Bayard take her as soon as they could find a way to slip out.

Austin picked up the bowl and carried it to the kitchen.

Sloan got to her feet, murmuring, "I really ought to help."

"Right. We don't want it to look like we're conspiring out here."

Sloan made her way into the kitchen in time to see Austin tilt the last of a fresh bottle of vodka into the punch mix, which was now a garish green. Through the doorway, she caught sight of Fritz sitting on the floor in the living room, still wearing his damp bathing suit. He flicked through television channels with the remote, pressing buttons repeatedly, apparently to no effect. "Hey, Austin. You got batteries for this thing?"

"End table drawer. Don't see any, you're out of luck."

Stringer stuck his head around the door from the hall. "Any hope of food? I'm starving to death and Patti just puked up a pint of pink bile."

"I'm on it," Austin replied.

He tossed the empty vodka bottle in the wastebasket under the sink and went out the back door. He paused as he passed Michelle, who was lounging facedown on a chaise, her bare back shiny with suntan oil.

He said, "Yo! Grab the burgers while I fire up the grill."

She looked up, irritated. "I'm a guest. I don't know my way around this place."

"Neither does anyone else so figure it out. Jesus, get a clue. You're not pretty enough to be useless."

"Thank you so much." She made no move. Austin stopped in his tracks and stared at her. She rolled her eyes unhappily, but she did push herself up from the chaise, securing the strings of her bikini top as she stood. She crossed to the kitchen, murmuring, "Shithead."

Austin's head whipped around. "*What* did you say?"

"Nothing. I am fetching the meat. Will there be anything *else,* your highness?"

"Clear the big table while you're at it and have Betsy bring out the condiments. We can serve ourselves inside and then eat out here."

He crossed to the free-standing Weber barbecue, fueled by a propane tank. He lifted the lid, picked up a wire brush, and scraped the grill. Then he turned on the burners and lowered the lid to allow the interior to heat.

Troy ambled over to his side. "You need help?"

"Keep an eye on this while I go get oil for the grill."

Sloan watched the exchange through the open kitchen window, aware of Michelle behind her removing a platter of meat patties from the refrigerator. Michelle put the patties on the counter, picked up a knife and cutting board, and reached for an onion.

On the patio outside, Iris appeared as Austin approached the kitchen door. She reached out, slung an arm across his shoulders, and hung on to him, her weight dragging him down. He struggled for balance and when he to tried to shrug her off, she let out a long wordless note of complaint.

Annoyed, he said, "Get off me. What's the matter with you?"

"Come on, Austin. How come you're never nice to me?"

"Has it sunk into that pea-sized brain of yours that my girlfriend is here?"

"Pooh on Michelle. Don't you think I'm cute?"

"Like a tarantula. You give me the creeps."

She said, "Well, I'd do anything for you."

"I'll bet," he said and pushed her away.

"I'm serious."

As Iris ambled toward the grill, she stumbled and grabbed a lawn chair, then fell into it, laughing at herself. "I am so shit-faced."

Troy looked at her with concern. "Chill out. You're making a fool of yourself."

She put her hand over her eyes. "Who asked you?"

"I'm offering you a piece of advice. Austin is bad news for someone as fucked up as you. Your reputation's in the toilet as it is."

"I can take care of myself."

"Yeah, right. We've seen ample evidence of that. You think he won't take advantage?"

"I'm in love with him."

"You are not."

"I am."

"Well, keep it to yourself. If he finds out, he'll rope you into something good for him and not so good for you."

"Shows what you know."

Sloan listened to the exchange with a sense of doom. Iris was reckless and out of control. One day it was all going to catch up with her. She tore open a package of hamburger buns and then opened the package of paper plates. She counted out a dozen and placed them on the counter, along with a stack of paper napkins. Austin crossed to the stove, opened the cabinet above it, and grabbed a container of olive oil.

"How're you doing?" he asked. "You need anything?"

"I'm good. You have a serving spoon for the potato salad?"

"I'll find you one." He disappeared into the walk-in pantry.

Iris wandered in, clearly unsteady on her feet. She leaned on the kitchen table and eased herself carefully into a wooden chair. "Where'd he go?"

"Who?"

"Austin."

"He's busy. He's about to cook the burgers," Sloan said irritably. Given her mother's constant state of inebriation, she had no patience for drunks.

"I knew that."

Fritz appeared from the living room. "Hey, look what I found."

In his right hand, he held a small-frame automatic pistol.

Michelle glanced at him with alarm. "Shit. Where did that come from?"

"It was in the drawer. Man, this is one gnarly weapon. What is this, a Smith and Wesson?"

Austin emerged from the pantry with a fistful of serving utensils. "No, you moron. That's my dad's Astra Constable. We sit out here and target-shoot, picking off squirrels."

Stringer said, "The neighbors don't complain?"

"The gun club's a mile down the road. People fire off guns all the time."

Stringer reached for the gun while Fritz pretended to sight down the barrel. "Hey, put that thing down. Are you nuts?"

Fritz held it up and away, trying to retain control.

Austin looked at the two of them. "Cool it, Stringer. It's not loaded. Here. Gimme that thing." Fritz surrendered the Astra to Austin, who popped out the magazine and held it up as though performing a magic trick.

Fritz said, "Now can I see it?"

"I don't know, Fritz. You think you can handle it?"

"Is there a trick?"

"Yes, asshole. You have to take off the safety. Don't you watch cop shows? And quit waving that thing around or you'll shoot yourself in the foot. Put it back in the drawer before I shoot you myself."

Fritz returned to the living room, pretending to fire the weapon while he made mouth noises. He opened the end table drawer and put the gun back where it had been.

There was an uptick of laughter from the patio, where the Beach Boys sang, "Fun, fun, fun till her daddy takes her T-Bird awa-hay."

Poppy scooted in, talking over her shoulder. "Thanks a bunch, guys. I love you too."

She caught sight of Austin, who handed her a cup of green punch. She seemed to focus in on him. "So what's the story on the video?"

Austin's expression became watchful, like a fox in the presence of a rabbit. Sloan froze where she stood. Blake and Roland came in from the patio, roughhousing, unaware of the stillness that had suddenly settled over the room. Troy, entering the back door, caught the dead quiet and stopped in his tracks.

Austin said, "What video are you referring to?"

Poppy said, "The one half the kids in class are buzzing about. A smutty sex tape."

"Why don't you ask your friend Sloan?"

"I did. She hasn't seen it yet."

He smiled. "Well, that's bullshit. Of course she has.

We're currently in negotiations to return it to its rightful owner."

"Which is who?"

"Me," Austin said. "The project was my idea."

"My equipment," Fritz hollered from the living room. "I want credit."

"Shut up, Fritz. You're an idiot."

Poppy's smile faltered. "What's it about?"

Austin said, "The film? It's a cooking show using Crisco, which is the new hot ingredient."

Blake and Roland burst out laughing and Fritz's high-pitched chortle sounded from the living room.

Poppy was still smiling, but it was clear she was desperately unsure of herself. "Why are you all cracking up? Come on, fellas. Let me in on the joke."

Roland said, "You're too uptight."

"I am *not*."

Austin said, "Roland doesn't know what he's talking about. He hasn't seen it, either, so don't feel bad. The title is 'Pool Cue: A Love Story.' It's the Troy and Iris Show."

Iris did a seated bump-and-grind and nearly tumbled out of her chair.

Troy spoke up from behind Poppy. "Why don't you drop it?"

She turned, blinking rapidly, her cheeks hot with embarrassment. "Drop what?"

"You know what."

"What's Austin talking about, 'The Troy and Iris Show'? I want to know what you did."

"Would you just quit it with the third degree? I'm not accountable to you."

"I never said you were. I asked about the tape."

"Why do you care?"

"Because you told me you loved me. You gave me your ring."

Austin snorted. "Shit, Poppy. You sound like the lyrics to a bad song."

"He did."

"Well, give the damn ring back. Obviously, Troy doesn't care enough to tell you the truth. You want me to 'share' or would you rather hear it from him?"

"Hear what?"

Troy made a low moaning sound and banged his head against the wall. He looked to Sloan for relief, but she couldn't maintain the eye contact.

Poppy said, "Hear what?"

Irritably, Troy said, "Okay, I banged her. Iris. What the fuck, Poppy. You don't own me."

The animation drained from Poppy's face. Where she'd been tentative and wounded, pushing for a reply, she now turned to stone. She did a slow pivot until she was looking straight at Sloan, still standing at the sink.

She crossed the distance between them in two steps and slapped Sloan across the face. The impact made a wet smacking sound that startled everyone. There was dead silence. Sloan was so stunned, she didn't react. Poppy slapped her again and only then did Sloan lift a hand to her cheek in wonder. "Jesus, Poppy. Why piss all over me? I didn't screw your boyfriend. Iris did!"

Poppy would have slapped her a third time if Austin hadn't grabbed her wrist.

"Cool it," he said.

"You cool it, asshole!" Poppy snapped at him. She turned to Sloan. "You should have told me the truth. You're supposed to be my friend."

"Iris is your friend, Poppy. I'm the one you dumped."

"I will never forgive you. Never. You knew all the time and you let me walk into this. You can get your own damn ride home."

Poppy snatched up her clothes and her purse. As she passed Iris, she paused. "You're pathetic," she said and then she moved on.

In silence, Iris watched her leave the cabin, her expression forlorn.

29

Tuesday, October 3, 1989

Tuesday morning, I arrived at the office to find Iris Lehmann and her fiancé, Joey Seay, sitting in a ten-year-old VW bug parked out front. As soon as I pulled into the drive, the two got out and proceeded to my front door. After a brief exchange of greetings, they stood by while I went through my ritual of unlocking the door and disarming the system, after which I ushered them into my office. The mailman had shoved a handful of bills and catalogues through the mail slot. I leaned over and swept up the pile and set it on my desk. I gestured for them to take a seat and then went around my desk and settled in my swivel chair. "Would you like coffee?" I asked.

Iris sat with her arms crossed, refusing to look at me. "I don't have time. Joey has to drop me off downtown so I can open the store."

"Up to you," I said.

I couldn't help but note the differences between them. His complexion was speckled red from the healing of old acne scars that probably undercut his confidence as a teen. His ears weren't comically large, but otoplasty wouldn't have been out of the question. I was again struck by the worry lines that had been etched across his forehead. I could imagine him at ages five, ten, and fifteen with the same burdened look. His outfit had that odd air of stunted youth. He wore tattered running shoes and his jeans were cinched with a brown leather belt taken down to the last hole. His long-sleeved T-shirt had wide horizontal stripes in red, yellow, and green. I wondered how seasoned construction workers felt about his management skills, given that he was half their age and seemed even younger.

Iris wore a vintage outfit that consisted of a long navy-blue silk skirt with a long-sleeved, high-necked blouse. The stand-up collar was edged with ruffles and was made of a cotton fabric referred to as "lawn" in the few romance novels I'd read. Lawn is lightweight, known for its semi-transparency, which here translated into a garment that covered her bosom primly while at the same time revealing and emphasizing her voluptuous flesh. Where Joey looked like a kid who suffered from arrested development, Iris was as ripe as a peach. I couldn't help but notice his eyes straying to her cleavage with a giddy look of disbelief. How a boychick of his unsophisticated demeanor had been granted access to such riches probably had him lying awake at night, marveling.

Iris said, "Joey's stepmom showed me your business card. When you came into Yesterday, you claimed you were a journalist. Now I find out you're a private detective."

"I understand why that might not sit well—"

"*Might* not sit well? Are you kidding me? You lied!"

"I did and I'm sorry about that. I was looking for information and I couldn't think of any other way to get it."

"Well, how nice for you. I guess you think that justifies dishonesty, but I don't think there's any excuse for misrepresenting yourself."

"I'm sorry, Iris. If I'd known you, I'd have tried a straightforward approach, which might have been better for both of us."

"Better for you maybe . . ."

Joey put a consoling hand on her arm and his tone was mild. "Babe, she apologized. Let's not get sidetracked when that has nothing to do with why we're here."

She shot him a look, but seemed to accept his point. Clearly, he knew how to handle her and I gave him credit for a maturity that wasn't visible on sight.

Both of them now seemed ill at ease. It was Joey who broke the ice. "Reason we're here is something came up and my stepmom thought we should tell you."

"I'm all ears," I said before remembering that his protruded like the sideview mirrors on a car.

He turned to Iris. "You want to talk or you want me to?"

"I'll do it," she said. She still seemed sulky and out of sorts, but at least she'd finished berating me. "What happened is I thought I saw Austin Brown a couple times last week."

"Really. When was this?"

"First time was Tuesday of last week when me and Joey were playing pool at the Clockworks over on lower State Street. I was lining up a shot and I happened to glance to my left and I saw Austin in the other room. Just a flash, but I knew it was him."

"How did you know?"

"Have you seen pictures of him? You don't forget a face like his. He's a good-looking guy. He has those honed cheeks and the slight smirk, like he's better than the rest of us. He'd grown his hair long and he had on these mirrored sunglasses, but when he saw me, he took them off and we locked eyes. I was so flustered I missed my shot and when I looked up again, he was gone."

"You think he wanted you to see him?"

"He didn't make any effort to conceal himself. On the other hand, if I hadn't looked up when I did, he might have walked right on by."

"What do you think he was doing at the Clockworks?"

"We used to hang out there in high school. Not me so much after I dropped out of Climp, but a lot of kids. He might have gone for old times' sake."

I watched her, trying to make sense of what she'd said. "Seems odd to me."

"Why?"

"It's just not very smart of him. He succeeded in vanishing for ten years. Now suddenly he's back and he walks into a place where he could be recognized?"

"It's the other way around. Austin always acts like he's in charge, like he knows what he's doing. Maybe he didn't expect to see me, but when he realized I had seen him, he had to make it seem like his idea. Something he'd done on purpose instead of being caught out."

"I can understand that," I said. "You mentioned seeing him more than once."

"The other time was Friday. He was in a car that passed me on State."

"This past Friday? You're sure of that?"

"Friday's the day I go to the bank. I was on my way when he went by."

"He didn't see you?"

"He was looking the other way."

"He was driving?"

She nodded.

"Anyone else in the car with him?"

"He had a passenger, but I couldn't get a good look at him from where I was. I thought it was Fritz but I could be wrong about that."

"What time of day was this?"

"Must have been just after lunch because I had to close the shop for twenty minutes so I could make a deposit at that Wells Fargo at the corner of State and Fig."

"You're sure it was Austin?"

"Not a hundred percent, but pretty sure," she said. "If I hadn't just seen him on Tuesday, I might not have noticed him at all."

"Curious," I said.

Joey said, "You going to tell her the rest of it?"

"I guess," she said, reluctantly. "That day you came to

the store, you didn't ask if I'd seen Fritz, but I had. When he got out of CYA, he called Stringer—Steve Ringer—and said how great it would be if Steve would get some of the old gang together. Stringer's roommate is this other friend of ours named Roland Berg so they invited a few of us over. Joey didn't go because he didn't know anyone from Climp."

"Who else besides you?"

"Patti Gibson. She's married now and her husband came with her. And let's see. Betsy Coe and Michelle and me. Bayard, of course. Blake Edelston was invited, but I ended up leaving before he got there."

"Troy?"

"Not him. He doesn't have much to do with the kids from Climp these days."

"So how'd it go?"

"The party? It was boring. I don't have anything to say to those guys. I went to be polite and because I was curious, but that didn't last long."

"How did Fritz seem to you? You think prison changed him?"

"He was as obnoxious as ever. He has this laugh that gets on my nerves. Around Climp kids, he was always self-conscious and sort of out of it. He still is."

Joey, Iris's prompter in the great play of life, said, "You want to tell her what he said?"

She looked at him blankly.

"About the blackmail demand," he said.

"Oh, right."

"You know about that?" I asked.

"Everyone knows. You mentioned it when you came to the store, acting like a fake reporter," she said, unable to resist the dig. "The minute Fritz heard about the scheme, he was on the phone bitching about the twenty-five thousand; pissed because his parents wouldn't pay. He complained to everyone."

I said, "Ah. So that's why you were all so well-informed. And here I thought the matter was private."

"Nothing's private with him. He never mastered the art of keeping his mouth shut."

"Did he voice an opinion about who he thought was behind the scheme?"

"He didn't, but if you ask me, it sounds like something Austin would do. He liked to have something to hold over your head so he could make you do what he wanted."

"You think that's why he came back?"

"I wouldn't be surprised. He was always hostile toward Fritz, so why not put the squeeze on him?"

"Speaking of Fritz, when did you talk to him last?" I asked.

"I forget exactly. Sometime last week."

Joey said, "Bayard invited us over for a swim and Fritz was there."

Iris said, "Then he called back all in a lather because the extortionist left a message on his parents' answering machine. He mentioned Austin's name himself, so he was under the same impression I was."

I shook my head. "I'm not sure I understand what's going on."

"Then we're all in the same boat," she said.

Joey stirred restlessly. "Anyway, that's about all there is. I don't mean to rush this, but we both gotta get to work."

"Well, I appreciate your coming in," I said. "If you spot Austin again, would you give me a call?"

"We can do that," Joey said. As he stood up, he reached over and shook my hand. "Sorry to have to run. Appreciate your time. Nice seeing you again."

"Same here," I said.

The minute they were out the door, I put in a call to Lauren McCabe.

When I identified myself, I could hear her voice deflate. "I was hoping this was Fritz," she said.

"Still no sign of him?"

"None. You mentioned filing a missing person's report, which Hollis thought was a good idea. He went down to the police station this morning."

"Good. I'm glad. It's a wise move."

"You said if Fritz hadn't put in an appearance by now, you'd help."

"Of course, but I'll do this my way. If I make a mistake, that's on me. If you interfere, then I'm out."

"Agreed, as long as you explain your terms to Hollis," she said. "He thinks he should be running the show. I understand your point, and while I'm willing to give you full rein, he might not be as agreeable. You don't want me to step out of your way only to have him step in. Right now, he's furious with me."

"Why?"

"He says he should have been allowed to handle this from the start."

"Last I heard, the two of you were in agreement. What would he have done differently?"

"He'd have pretended to accept the terms and then confronted the extortionist before he paid."

"What if the extortionist settled on a money drop at some remote location? Most blackmailers aren't going to agree to meet face-to-face. They want the cash. They don't want you knowing who they are."

"Hollis would have insisted or no deal."

"Come on, Lauren. That's ridiculous. For all we know, the extortionist would have turned him down cold and put the tape straight in the mail to the DA."

"Then he'd have gotten nothing. No money at all."

"You're assuming money's the motive."

"What else could it be?"

"Making you suffer. Ruining your lives. Something along those lines."

"Oh dear."

"I shouldn't have said that. Sorry. I'll be there as soon as I can."

I hung up, grabbed the mail, and shoved it in the outside pocket of my shoulder bag. I was up and crossing the room when the phone rang. As usual, I was tempted to let the call go to the answering machine, but just in case it was Lauren again, I picked up.

"Kinsey, it's Erroll."

I walked back around the desk and sat down. I could feel my heart give a hard thump. "How's Phyllis? Is she okay?"

"We're hoping so. Sternberg put her in a medically induced coma."

"This is your friend the neurosurgeon?"

"Sorry, yes. Tom Sternberg. He says when the brain swells in the wake of an injury like this, the pressure can starve some areas of oxygen. Swollen tissue can also be injured when it pushes against the inside of the skull. The point is to reduce the electrical activity and slow down the brain's metabolism to minimize the inflammation. He'll know more as they bring her out of it. For now, she's stable and that's about as much as we can expect."

"Will she recover?"

"No guarantees, but he's optimistic," he said. "Something else has come up and this news isn't so good. Ned came back."

"To the condominium? When?"

"Yesterday afternoon."

"How do you know it was him? Dumb question. Skip that. How'd he get in?"

"He still had her keys. He waited until I went off to work and let himself in. I might not have known about it except that I hired a company to come in and clean blood off the carpeting late in the day. When I unlocked the door to let the crew in, I could see he'd torn the place apart."

"The locks hadn't been changed?"

"I notified the property management company and asked them to send a locksmith, but the guy didn't arrive until this morning and by then, the damage was done."

"Why would Ned come back? That's a big risk."

"He went through the moving cartons he hadn't hit before."

"All of them?"

"Looks that way. He was systematic and took his sweet time this round."

"Shit," I said.

"You haven't told me what he was looking for."

"He believes his ex-wife has the box of souvenirs he collected from each of his murder victims. What he needs is his ex-wife's alias and her current location. Phyllis mentioned jotting the information on a slip of paper she'd tossed in a moving carton."

"How did Ned get wind of *that*?"

I went back through events, explaining how I discovered not only where the fugitive had been holing up, but how he'd managed to tap my phone. "He actually installed an extension so all he had to do was lounge in the dirt down there, listening to every word I said." I filled him in on Ned's threat to burn me out and how I'd blasted him through the vent opening.

"Well, that explains the mess he left. He stayed long enough to change the dressing on what must be a nasty wound. He went through a bottle of hydrogen peroxide, gauze pads, and adhesive tape, and then he stole her Valium and prescription pain pills and left the empty bottles in the trash. Apparently, he can't resist showing how clever he is . . ."

"Could you bring Detective Altman up to speed on this?"

"That's the next call on my list."

30

When I reached the McCabes' condominium, Hollis was home. He'd gone over to the police station, where he filed the missing person's report on his son, and then called his secretary to tell her he wouldn't be in. The three of us sat down in the living room. Just in case the forthcoming conversation wasn't going to be difficult enough, Lauren hadn't told Hollis she'd fired me. When I repeated the terms I'd laid out for my continued employment, he had no idea what I was talking about. We spent ten minutes sorting out the details, which seemed to make Hollis cranky. What a surprise.

Lauren was busy smoothing things over. "You'll want to see his room," she said. "Maybe you can figure out where he went."

Given that I'd never stepped a foot in Fritz's room, I couldn't see the point, but we were all now on our best behavior and I was pretending to be agreeable.

Lauren showed me in, saying, "I'll leave you to look around."

She left, closing the door behind her. My guess was that she and Hollis would engage in a low-level argument, probably a continuation of the one sparked by the discovery that Fritz had forged his mother's signature and walked away with twenty-five thousand in cash. Their murmured conversation in the living room had a rising and falling tone to it that reminded me why I'm so happy to be single.

Fritz's room was not what I expected. I'd tagged him as spoiled and overindulged, so I'd assumed he'd have the best of everything and lots of it: his own phone and answering machine, a television set, stereo components, cameras, tennis rackets, skis, a surfboard, skateboards, guitars, and whatever else a young lad like him might consider essential. I was right about the phone and answering machine and wrong about everything else. His room was as plain as a jail cell, which made a certain amount of sense. Lauren was right about his closet being crammed, but only because she and Hollis had moved every article he owned before he went off to prison. The hangers were packed together so tightly, it was hard to determine what was there, let alone what he might have removed. Most of the garments had all the sophistication of a fifteen-year-old's taste, roughly his age when the legal bombshells started going off in his face. His life had come to an abrupt halt for eight years and now that he was home, all the items of clothing he owned were outdated, out of style, and probably too small.

No books, no school texts, no magazines, no photographs, no artwork, no records, no cassettes, no Sony Walkman, no personal correspondence. No trash in the trash can. There was nothing out of place because he had so little in the way of possessions. In the bathroom, I saw his safety razor, his deodorant, his toothbrush and toothpaste arranged on the glass shelf above his sink. In the shower, his Mickey Mouse soap-on-a-rope dangled from the shower fixture. In the medicine cabinet, a bottle of aspirin and an unopened box of assorted Band-Aids. To me, it didn't look like he'd left with any of the usual toiletries. As for changes of clothing, I had no way to guess.

I circled his room again and studied the phone and his answering machine. No indication he had messages, but I pressed Play nonetheless. A mechanical fellow wholly without enthusiasm assured me Fritz had no messages. I opened and closed his desk drawers but found nothing of interest. To demonstrate how thoroughly an investigator of my caliber proceeds in such matters, I got down on my hands and knees and peeked under the bed. I also inspected the underside of drawers in his chest of drawers, the interior and the back of the toilet tank, and the space between his mattress and his box spring. For the first time, I felt sorry for him. Not that he needed my pity or my dismay, but I knew now how small his life had become.

When I emerged from Fritz's room, Hollis was standing at the wet bar, fixing himself a drink. It was two in the afternoon, which for all I knew was the usual cocktail hour for him. "So, Sherlock, did you find any clues?" Hollis asked. "Any secret messages written in invisible ink?" The jocular tone barely disguised his belligerence.

"I don't need secret messages. Either he was delivering the twenty-five thousand to the extortionist or he was taking it for himself," I said.

"Of course he was taking it for himself," Hollis snapped. "Are you just now figuring that out? Lauren can't accept the fact, but it seems obvious to me."

"All he had to do was ask," she said. "We'd have given him the money if we knew it meant so much to him."

"We wouldn't have given him a cent! Kid gets out of prison and thinks he's entitled to a lump sum? For doing what?"

I closed my eyes briefly, wishing I could click my heels and be somewhere else. This was exactly the reason I didn't want to work for these people.

Hollis turned to me. "It would have been nice if you'd come up with the insight before the kid ripped us off."

"She did," Lauren said, blinking back tears. "I didn't want to hear it."

"Why are you getting all emotional? Big boo-hoo. Do we have to go through this again?" he said.

I raised a hand. "All I did was suggest the possibility. In the meantime, it doesn't look like he left with any of his personal belongings. Certainly not with his toiletries, which suggests he didn't expect to be gone long."

"Well, at least now you're earning your keep. That's a refreshing turnabout," he said.

"I can do without the sarcasm, Hollis, if you don't mind," I said. I'd already been fired once, so being fired a second time was of no consequence. Turned out there was no danger there because both of them ignored my comment.

"We should have gone to the police in the first place," Lauren said. "Fritz has taken matters into his own hands and he's going to make a mess of it."

"It's already a mess!" Hollis said.

"I don't think it's too late to talk to law enforcement," Lauren said. "He'll just have to take what's coming to him. Here we are, trying to protect him and we're only making matters worse."

"How can it get worse? Fritz has already stolen the money. We don't even know where he is."

My gaze settled on the answering machine that sat on a side table inside the arch between the foyer and the living room. "Mind if I check that?"

"What for? If there were messages, the light would be blinking," Hollis said.

"I'm interested in the old ones," I said. "Iris came into my office this morning to report seeing Austin twice this past week. She also mentioned that the extortionist had left a message for Fritz on your machine. I checked the one in his room and there's nothing on it."

I glanced at Lauren and she shrugged, giving me the okay.

I crossed to the machine and pressed Play. The mechanical butler who handles these matters assured me there were no new messages. He went on to say, "You have ten old messages."

As I continued to hold down the Play button, the machine said, "Message one." There was a beep. *"Lauren, sweetie, this is Florence. I'm afraid we're not going to be able to make it Tuesday night."*

Florence was explaining why she and Dale couldn't make it when Lauren cut in, saying, "You can erase that."

I dutifully pressed Delete and the mechanical butler started again at the beginning of the amended sequence. "Message one." Beep. *"Mr. McCabe, this is Harley at Richard's Auto Care. Your Mercedes is ready. Let us know if you want the shuttle to pick you up."*

I looked to Hollis, who frowned impatiently. "Erase," he said, gesturing with his drink.

I deleted the message and pressed Play. We went on in this fashion through seven more old messages, none of which were significant. The last was as follows: *"Yo, Fritz. Hope you recognize this voice from your past. Enough with the bullshit excuses. It's pay-or-play time. I want that money, so you better find a way to get it. I'll pick you up at the corner of State and Aguilar Friday at noon. If you're not there, good luck, pal. Your life's going to get very, very tough."*

Hollis's expression shifted from impatience to dismay. "Who the hell is that?"

"Austin is my best guess," I said. "The second time Iris saw him was Friday around noon, driving up State. She thought he had a passenger, but she couldn't see who it was. The timing would have coincided with the instructions about Fritz being downtown."

"You're saying Austin's behind this?" Lauren asked.

"Looks that way."

"Do you think he's had the tape all this time?"

Hollis said, "Who cares? Either he's had it or he knew where it was and came back to collect. Whatever the case, that dumb cluck son of yours has just handed twenty-five thousand bucks to a fugitive, so you can kiss that cash good-bye."

"It's not about the money," Lauren said.

"You say that now, but that's not what you were saying when this business came up."

"You think you haven't changed *your* tune? If we'd talked to the FBI in the first place, we wouldn't be in the trouble we're in."

"I don't know where you get that. If we'd gone to the authorities, Fritz would be in jail."

"You don't know that and neither do I," she said.

"Well, at least we wouldn't be out the twenty-five grand. We could have used that as a retainer for a hotshot defense attorney to get us out of this."

I said, "Hey! The bickering isn't going to get us anywhere. I'll need a recent photograph of Fritz. I'll show his picture to ticket agents at the bus station, train station, and the airport and see if anyone remembers selling him a ticket."

In the car on my way home, I reviewed their discussion about the time frame for the pivotal call, which might have come in at any point in the last ten days. Neither of them was in the habit of checking messages. Fritz had made his trip to the bank Friday morning and hadn't been seen since. It looked like the extortionist was Austin Brown. I wasn't convinced, but I really had no reason to doubt the report. The point was Fritz met someone Friday at noon and it was Tuesday afternoon now. If they'd left town together, they had a four-day head start. How far would twenty-five thousand take them? Austin didn't strike me as a guy who'd share, so he'd probably dump Fritz before too much time had passed.

I circled my neighborhood twice and found a parking spot a block and a half away. On the walk to the studio, I decided I'd better carve out time for my three-mile jog. I bent down and plucked the afternoon paper from the sidewalk as I let myself through the gate. On the front page, there was the same black-and-white photograph of Ned Lowe I'd seen on the STPD bulletin. The recap that ran below the picture summed up Ned's criminal history.

Authorities are hunting for a California man they say assaulted and severely injured a Perdido resident before fleeing the area on Saturday, September 23. Identity of the victim is being withheld pending notification of her kin. Ned Lowe, 55, was last seen on Monday in downtown Santa Teresa, where he emptied a can of gasoline against the side of a bungalow in an attempt to set fire to the structure. Evidence suggests that he had been living in the crawl space under the small office building for a week before his presence was discovered. The occupant fired shots that are believed to have struck the fugitive shortly before he escaped on foot. Lowe is wanted in connection with the deaths of five teenaged girls in California, Nevada, Arizona, New Mexico, and Texas over the past six years. He is also a person of interest in the death of his first wife, Lenore Redfern Lowe, in Burning Oaks, California, in 1961.

The California Highway Patrol said Lowe is believed to be driving a stolen 1988 red Oldsmobile Cutlass Supreme with a California license plate LADY CPA. Lowe is described as Caucasian, 5 feet 11 inches tall, and weighing 195 pounds.

That should turn up the heat, I thought.

It bugged me that the manager of the condominium hadn't acted swiftly to change the locks on Phyllis's apartment. From what Erroll said, Ned had worked his way through every moving carton she had on hand and had then torn up the rest of the place. Seemed logical to assume he hadn't found what he was looking for. If he had, he'd have hightailed it out of town on his way to find Celeste. Assuming she still had his souvenirs, of course. The press had alerted the public to the dangers of this man on the loose. Between that and his festering gunshot wound, he'd be looking for another place to hole up.

I changed into my sweats and walked to Cabana Boulevard, where the bike path paralleled the beach. I chunked my way through the first half mile, feeling rusty and unenthusiastic. My muscles were still in a state of shock from my self-defense class the day before. The afternoon was a pretty one with temps in the low seventies and a breeze whipping up whitecaps out on the ocean. For the time being, I set aside the specter of Ned and focused on another problem.

In my conversation with Henry, he'd brought up an interesting point, that being that Anna's views of motherhood were, in part, the function of her exposure to parental attitudes that were largely negative. Her brother, Ethan, and her sister, Ellen, had six children between them. Ellen seemed to be happily married, but her life was weighted down by exhaustion. I hadn't met her three kids during my brief time in Bakersfield, but from what I'd seen of her, she wasn't radiant with maternal love. Ethan's marriage was less than ideal, and while I respected his parenting, the presence of his children put a damper on his pursuit of his career. In a little Bakersfield bar, I'd watched him perform, accompanying himself on the guitar while he sang. The transformation was stunning. I could see that being confined to Bakersfield would limit his chances of being picked up by an agent or a record company. As far as I knew, Anna had neither talent nor ambition, but she had dreams of a better life, and to her way of thinking, children were nothing more than an impediment.

It occurred to me that my friend Vera, with her five gorgeous, well-behaved kiddy-winks, might be the perfect role model for Anna to contemplate while she pondered her choices. When I finished the run, I showered, dressed, and then put in a call to Vera, explaining the situation.

"I'd love for Anna to see you in action," I said. "She equates motherhood with the end of life as we know it. She actually talks about loading her coat pockets with rocks and walking into the river. Not that we have one around here . . ."

"Got it. No problem. Round her up and bring her

over by five. The twins should be home from school by then—"

"Wait a minute. Scott and Travis are in school? That can't be true. The twins are only six months old."

"I'm being facetious, dear. If you'll remember, you didn't meet Abigail until she was a year and a half."

"But I met the twins months ago! I knit both of them those booties with the teddy bears on the soles."

"So you did and they were adorable. I had no idea you possessed such homely skills. Anyway, Neil is on call tonight, so he won't be home till late and dinner's anything we choose. Get here in the next hour and she can witness feeding time. It's better than the zoo."

I locked up and then trotted the three doors down to Moza Lowenstein's house, where I knocked on the door. When Moza appeared, I remembered she was not only hard of hearing, but still under the impression I was soon to be great with child. I didn't have time to set the record straight. "I'm looking for Anna. Is she in?"

"She's taking a nap."

"At this hour? It's nearly dinnertime. Was she up late last night?"

"I don't know what she ate last night."

"Why don't I go rouse her myself?" I said as I proceeded down the hall.

"I wouldn't do that if I were you," she said, but I was already halfway to Anna's room. Moza followed me, looking on uneasily as I knocked on her bedroom door, then opened it and stuck my head in. "Hey. We have a dinner date. I want you to meet a friend."

Anna sat up in bed and pushed a tangle of dark hair away from her eyes. She wore an oversize tatty T-shirt in a robin's-egg blue, which of course looked fetching on her. "Is this a joke?"

"I don't have a sense of humor, Anna."

"Who's the friend?"

"Vera Hess. She lives in that gray Victorian house next door to Cheney's. You've probably seen her."

"The big blonde," she said. "She intimidates the shit out of me."

"Oh pooh. She's great. You'll love her to pieces. Now, come on. You even have time to shower if you make it quick."

When we arrived at Vera's back door, it was close to five thirty. I knocked once and let us in. Vera doesn't believe in guests knocking or ringing the bell because it forces her to drop whatever she's doing and come running. Her three older children, Peter, Meg, and Abigail—ages five, three, and almost two, respectively—were in the kitchen, seated at a little white wooden table with matching chairs. The twins were in their infant seats nearby, both of them asleep, their dark hair faintly damp. All of them were clean and scrubbed, already in the kind of pajamas you've seen in children's catalogues featuring sleepwear no ordinary mortal can afford. They were eating their dinner, which in the case of Peter, Meg, and Abigail consisted of grilled cheese sandwiches and cups of tomato soup, my personal favorite.

Vera does have "help," I have to be honest about that. Mavis was at the stove tending the soup, which was close to simmering and smelled divine. Vera was in charge of the grilled cheese sandwiches. Anna and I sat at the counter looking on. I could see why Anna would be intimidated. Vera was a force of nature and seemed to do everything well. I'd worked with her at California Fidelity Insurance in the "olden" days when she was single, smoked cigarettes, and drank bottles of Coca-Cola she kept in a little cooler behind her desk. She'd tried to fix me up with her now-husband, Dr. Neil Hess, a charming general practitioner whom she felt was too short for her. I could see they were smitten with each other and I confess I played Cupid, which mostly consisted of Vera being furious with me in the ladies' room at work because she thought I'd been flirting with Neil.

"How's it going?" she asked Anna.

"Not well," Anna said.

"Kinsey filled me in on your situation. She thought

you ought to see motherhood in action, so here it is," Vera said.

I raised a tentative hand, wanting to protest. I hadn't expected Vera to take so direct an approach. I pictured subtlety, Anna gradually taking in Vera's competence and her love of her job. Vera had had her children comparatively late in life and she'd adapted to motherhood as though she'd been born with a gift. I thought Vera would be the perfect antidote to Anna's view of babies as poisonous. Vera's children were beautiful, cheerful, good-natured, and cooperative. When they finished their dinner, the older three took their plates and bowls to Mavis at the sink, handing them over with a pretty "Thank you." This wasn't as obnoxious and syrupy as it sounds.

Vera produced crayons and coloring books and the three sat down again and began to scribble vigorously. Peter was industrious, Meg precise, and Abigail was the clown. I was watching them with frank appreciation, so it took me a moment to tune into what Vera was actually saying. "Oh yeah. Most of the time they drive me nuts. You can imagine having the lot of them age five and under. I'm lucky I get a shower in every third day. This is them being good, which I'm happy to report occurs sometimes as often as once a week. Wait until one of them comes down with a cold. Then they're all sick as dogs, including me and sometimes Mavis. Right, Mav?"

Mavis said, "Amen."

"I don't know your feelings about termination," Vera went on, conversationally. "What's your current thinking?"

"I'm still debating," Anna said.

"I can offer you an alternative," Vera said. "I was hoping to have one more, but I'm getting a little long in the tooth and Neil's not that happy with the idea of me being as big as a house again with milk squirting out of my jugs. Good news is he's not opposed to adding a kid, so if you decide to go through with the pregnancy, you might consider the notion of open adoption."

"Give the baby up?" Anna said.

"To the perfect family, which you're looking at. Next door to Cheney, so you could see the baby as much or as little as you want. My kids get a sister or brother out of the deal and everybody's good."

"I don't know," Anna said with uncertainty. "I hadn't even thought of that."

"It's a possibility to factor in," Vera said, ever practical. "Travis and Scott will be fifteen months old by the time yours comes along. The age difference is ideal."

I raised my hand again. "Vera?" I said, cutting into her proposal. "Jonah has a say in this, don't you think?"

Vera waved dismissively. "Men don't care about these things."

"Well, he does," I said. "He's already got three great kids and he's crazy about them. He's nuts about Anna and he's looking forward to having one with her." I hadn't spoken to Jonah on the subject, so I was making this up, but it sounded right.

"Forget Jonah. How much do you think he'll pitch in? Nada. So let's focus on Anna. The choice is hers. That's where we started, with you telling me she was going to load her pockets with stones and jump off a bridge."

"You told her that?" Anna said with a sudden look at me. "I can't believe you'd mention it."

"You're the one who said it," I remarked defensively.

"I was joking!"

"Sorry." I could feel the heat mount in my cheeks. I couldn't believe the abrupt right-hand turn the conversation had taken.

Vera said, "Don't sweat it. I've felt that way myself early on. You'll go through all kinds of emotions. Eventually things work out. Jonah might not be as opposed as you'd think. I mean, he knows us. Might be a win-win for everyone while he sorts himself out with Camilla. Change your mind, it's no big deal. All I'm saying is, consider it when you're weighing your options."

"No, I like that. I appreciate your perspective," Anna said.

Shortly after that, Mavis took the three older children

upstairs to the playroom while Vera, Anna, and I ate our sandwiches and soup. Vera and Anna were chatting delightedly while I tried to remember the point at which my plan had gone so far wrong. It always comes back to the notion of doing a good deed, which I've known for years is the definition of disaster in the making.

31

Wednesday, October 4, 1989

One good thing about a town as small as Santa Teresa: even with 85,000 souls, there's only one bus station, one train station, and one airport with a total of six gates. Armed with a photograph of Fritz, I made a number of brief stops, consulting with Greyhound ticket agents, ticket sellers at the train station, and desk clerks for Delta, United, American Airlines, and USAir, none of whom recognized Fritz as someone they'd done business with in the past week. I would have paid a visit to the two fixed-base private operations, but I doubted Fritz would carve out a chunk of his hard-won cash to charter a flight. Just to be thorough about it, I had a quick chat with five of the taxi drivers in the queue waiting for an airport fare. None of them recognized Fritz's photograph. Once I was back in the office, I'd run off a batch of fliers that I'd address to the remaining twenty. It was possible Fritz had left town by car in the company of Austin Brown or, if he were traveling alone, he might have hitchhiked his way to parts unknown. The long and short of it was that I didn't turn up a trace of him.

I went back to the McCabes' at eight that night. This time, Lauren was in her robe and slippers, looking like an invalid. Hollis was fixing himself a drink and automatically poured me a glass of high-end Chardonnay. I rendered a verbal account of what I knew. Then I said, "You mentioned earlier you didn't have relatives in geographical range."

"I have a brother in Topeka, but we haven't heard a peep out of him since Fritz went to jail," Hollis said. "Look, Fritz has all kinds of friends. They threw a party for him when he first came home. He's been staying with his pals on weekends. He's a popular boy. You can't tell me nobody has a clue. Surely he said something to one of them."

"I'll check with Troy and Iris first thing in the morning," I said.

Lauren said, "What about Bayard?"

"He's on my list."

"The sooner the better," she said. "Do you think it would help to put a notice in some of the papers? Los Angeles and San Francisco, for instance?"

"I doubt it. If he left voluntarily, he's not going to be checking the personal ads to see if you're sending messages."

"What do you mean, 'if he left voluntarily'? Are you suggesting he's been kidnapped?" she asked.

"He hasn't been *kidnapped*," Hollis said irritably. "The kid's loaded. He's walking around with a pocketful of dough. Chances are he's gone to Vegas and blown the whole wad by now."

"It's not productive to speculate," I said. "The Santa Teresa police will circulate his photograph and the circumstances surrounding his disappearance. When it comes to tracking him down, they're your best shot."

"I can see you have a lot more faith in the police than I do," Hollis said.

* * *

For the umpteenth time, I sat in my car and went over my notes, using my little penlight for illumination. When at an impasse, my general policy is to start over from the beginning and hit all my sources a second time. I fanned out a handful of cards facedown and picked one at random. Bayard's name had risen to the forefront and I headed for his house in Horton Ravine. It was, by then, nine fifteen and I wasn't sure how advisable it was to call on folks at that hour. I didn't think anyone would be in bed, but they might be in their jammies, engrossed in their favorite television show. The day was over. Not many welcome an intrusion of any kind, let alone one from me.

When I rang the bell, Ellis responded. He was barefoot, in sweatpants and another tight white T-shirt, this one without writing on it. I said, "I apologize for the hour, but something's come up with regard to Fritz and I was hoping to speak to Bayard."

"His masseuse is here, but he should be free in ten or fifteen minutes. I'll tell him you're waiting."

"No hurry," I said. "Mind if I use the bathroom?"

"Third door on the right," he said, and then proceeded down the hallway into another wing of the house. I confess I took my time, pausing to open other doors along the corridor. Really, I couldn't help myself. If Ellis didn't want me peeking, he should have said so. Coat closet, bedroom, bedroom, linen closet.

I found the bathroom, which featured an Egyptian motif. The padded walls were covered in a fabric printed with mythological creatures and a profusion of stylized blossoms. There were lithographs of human figures rendered flat with their arms stiffly bent and their pointy feet turned sideways. A dressing table extended along one wall, the surface an elaborate inlay of wood veneers. The dressing table stool had a cane back and a brocade seat in tones of blue and gold. Lions' heads and lotus leaves were carved into the uprights. It was all surprisingly tasteful. I picked up and sniffed at the collection of perfume bottles, but I didn't dab any of them behind my ears. I was certain Ellis would have picked up evidence of the pilfered scent the minute we were in the same room.

I availed myself of the facilities just to keep up an honest pretense. Then, with a tiny bit of time on my hands, I had a look around. I noticed a door on my right, which I opened, of course. I found myself in a guest room with matching blue everything: carpet, drapes, bedding, wallpaper. There were no knickknacks in sight and the two drawers I peeked into were empty, ready to accommodate weekend visitors. Of interest was the large wheeled split duffel and an expandable four-wheeled packing case closed and standing at the foot of the bed. Open on the bed was one soft-sided carry-on and a hard-sided case of a size that could probably be shoved into the overhead bin. The contents in one bag—shirts, sweaters, and two pairs of trousers—were neatly folded. The clothing in the other gave off a distinct air of carelessness and haste. I'd have been willing to bet that the first belonged to Ellis and the second to Bayard, who probably didn't have the patience to do much better. I was surprised he hadn't turned over the entire packing chore to Ellis. All of the luggage was new and still bore tags denoting their special capacities, exclusive features, and whopping prices. The black leather carry-on bore a tag that sported a monogram, BAM. Bayard Something Montgomery. Arthur. Allen. Axel. I admired the royal blue cashmere sweater he'd packed. He'd added his headset and his Sony Walkman, both of which I was sure would come in handy when he reached his destination.

I tiptoed back into the bathroom, where I washed my hands noisily and then stood for some moments trying to figure out what to dry them on. I don't know why rich people do this. It's so inconsiderate. The pristine white linen towels were the size of dinner napkins and if I used one, my paw print would have compelled the housekeeper to send them off to a special laundering service at god knows what cost. I chose my jeans, wiping my hands on the back sides where the damp spots would hardly show. I'd have to make a point of not sitting down.

When I returned to the living room, Ellis was back.

"Bayard says you can wait in the library where you'll be more comfortable. Can I bring you something to drink?"

"No, thanks."

He left me alone in the library, which was like a massive treasure trove of trouble to get into. I limited myself to the stack of unopened mail in Bayard's inbox, a quick search of his address book, and a study of the note he'd made on the top sheet of the scratch pad, adorned with his monogram. The first line said AA with a circle around it and a question mark. Was he contemplating Alcoholics Anonymous? That would be a big step. Below that, he'd written 8760RAK. The combination of letters and digits suggested a California license plate. I found a clean sheet and duplicated the notes, removed the page, folded it, and slid it into my pocket, leaving the original where it was. I took a seat in a chair on the other side of his desk and was thus able to look entirely innocent when Bayard finally made his appearance in a white terry-cloth robe.

He must have come straight from his massage. I could smell the oil on his skin, which had also encouraged his hair to stand on end. "How're you doing? Sorry to make you wait."

"Not a problem," I said. "I owe you an apology for showing up this late without calling first."

"I'm a night owl. This is not late."

He went around to the far side of his desk and took a seat. "If you're here to tell me Austin's back, I know. Fritz says he left a message on his parents' answering machine."

"Word travels fast."

"Stringer called and told me the same thing. He'd heard it from Iris, though she didn't mention where she saw him."

"The Clockworks. This was last Tuesday night. She

and Joey were playing pool and she was lining up a shot when she caught sight of him. Then she spotted him again Friday driving up State Street. She couldn't say for sure that Fritz was in the car with him, but that was her impression."

"Really. Friday's the last time I saw Fritz, as a matter of fact."

"Morning or afternoon?"

"He showed up Friday morning. I had a dentist's appointment at ten thirty and I was annoyed with him for hanging around. He was so giddy and hyper, I thought he was on drugs."

"What was he so excited about?"

"He wouldn't come right out with it, but typical Fritz. Either he tells you everything before you ask or he stalls and hints and drops snippets until it's the same as telling the whole story. That's him keeping a secret."

"What was it in this case?"

"He pulled some fiddle at the bank that put twenty-five grand in his pocket. He'd already told me how he meant to do it, but I didn't think he'd have the nerve."

"You can imagine how thrilled his parents are," I said. "Did he tell you what he planned to do with it?"

"I assumed he'd decided to pay the blackmailer, which I thought was a mistake."

"How'd he get over here when he doesn't have a driver's license?"

"He'd taken his mother's car, so he must have been driving without one. Ask me, he should have kept right on going."

"Why is that?"

"Because Austin vowed to get even. That came out at the trial. He swore he'd kill anybody who ratted him out. Fritz was the one who snitched on him. Ergo, Austin was out to kill Fritz."

"Ten years seems like a long time to wait."

"What choice did he have? Fritz was in prison until four weeks ago. How's anybody going to get to him there? Unless Austin had a pal at CYA who'd do the job for him, he'd have to postpone his satisfaction until Fritz was free."

"True. So why did he come to see you?"

"He wanted me to go with him when he went to meet the guy. I had already turned him down by phone, so he was trying the personal approach. I didn't think he should go at all and I certainly wasn't going to make it easier."

"How did you leave it? Did he intend to meet Austin alone?"

"I guess. Unless he managed to con someone else into going with him."

When I got home, I took copious notes, which did little to relieve my stress. This business was getting to me and I needed a change of pace. First thing the next morning, I went into the office, where I called Diana Alvarez and invited her to lunch. I'd decided to take her to the Edgewater Hotel, which I hoped would intimidate her sufficiently to put a dent in her glossy façade. I had an idea I was hoping to sell her and I wanted to take control. Before I could finish voicing my proposal, she cut in, saying, "I have a better idea. We'll go Dutch. I have a standing date on Thursdays and you're welcome to join me. You pay your way and I'll pay mine."

"I know what going Dutch means, Diana," I said. "If you have a date, I wouldn't want to interfere."

"No danger of that. I'll meet you in the parking lot at Ludlow Beach, right there at the end by the picnic tables. Make it eleven thirty. Any later and we'll be out of luck."

"Sounds fine," I said.

How had she managed to get the upper hand?

I had an awkward history with Diana Alvarez. Her brother, Michael Sutton, had walked into my office some months before, hoping to hire me. He'd read an article in the paper written on the anniversary of a kidnapping in Santa Teresa many years before. A three-year-old named

Mary Claire Fitzhugh had been snatched from her backyard in Horton Ravine and he'd had a sudden memory pertaining to her fate. He was convinced that, when he was six, he'd stumbled across the two kidnappers burying Mary Claire's body in the woods. The two men were, in fact, the pair who'd demanded fifteen thousand in ransom, which I thought marked them as amateurs. Granted, the twenty-five grand the McCabes' extortionist was asking was more, but the principle seemed the same.

I'd managed to track down the location Michael remembered, but then his estranged sister, Dee—a.k.a. Diana Alvarez—had come into my office bearing proof that he was wrong about the date and therefore couldn't have seen what he claimed to have seen. What he'd actually witnessed was the two men burying marked bills from a "practice" kidnapping that went off as planned, but netted them money they couldn't spend. When the kidnappers tried again, the crime hadn't gone well and the second little girl had died.

Prior to that, Michael Sutton had come under the influence of a therapist who worked on repressed memories of sexual abuse. She'd convinced him that he'd been victimized by his father and his brother. In the end, he'd recanted, but the family had been destroyed by his accusations and thereafter he was radioactive, at least where Diana Alvarez was concerned. That early encounter with her had set the tone for our relationship, which got off to a bad start and was just now beginning to right itself. From my perspective, her one redeeming quality was her fashion sense, which I'm embarrassed to admit I mimicked from the first. Now I wore flats and black tights, miniskirts, and turtlenecks when I wasn't decked out in the usual jeans and boots. As a badass private investigator, I was never going to admit this to a living soul, but fair is fair.

When I pulled in and parked in the picnic area at Ludlow Beach, I discovered that Diana's standing date was with a guy who ran a food truck, selling the nastiest, finest, most succulent, and decadent hot dogs you ever ate. The line of avid customers was already halfway around the parking lot and it was only because she was pushy that we managed to find a spot near the front of the line. I insisted on paying and then the two of us discussed the virtues of Coneys versus corn dogs, beef versus pork, New York–style versus Chicago, half-smokes versus bratwurst, and organic versus nothing, as we were both morally opposed to the notion of organic foods of any kind.

We sat across from each other at a picnic table, variously moaning and exclaiming as we bolted down our weenies loaded with mustard, ketchup, onions, pickles, and hot peppers. It took us three paper napkins apiece to clean up afterward. My choice would have been to stretch out on the grass and nap, but it seemed unprofessional. By the time I broached the subject of the Sloan Stevens shooting, I was surprisingly nervous. I barely got the first sentence out when she cut in.

"I told you my editor's not interested," she said.

"Pitch the idea somewhere else," I said. "I'm not talking about a news story. This is feature-length, maybe two or three parts. Listen to this. The kids involved haven't turned out well. It's like Sloan's death tainted their lives. Go back and tell the story from the beginning, when Iris Lehmann stole the test. That act set everything in motion and the consequences are still reverberating all these years later. You know Margaret Seay will give you all the help you need. She's got the transcripts from both the grand jury and the trial, and those contain a wealth of detail."

She stared at me for a moment.

I could see she wasn't buying it. I didn't realize it mattered to me until I studied her face and realized she wasn't sparking to the notion of taking up the cause. I said, "You're the one who said it has all the elements. Youth, sex, money, betrayal."

"Well, that's true," she said. How could she disagree with something she herself had said?

"The repercussions of a crime like this go on and on. Look at the lives it's already touched, and it's not over yet."

Her expression shifted. "Oooh, I think I'm getting this. When you first called about Fritz McCabe, you didn't mention why you were so interested in the facts of the case."

"Yes, I did. I told you I wanted to talk to the players."

"Because you'd been hired to investigate something, right?"

"Maybe."

"What was it?"

I had to hand it to her, she was a bird dog on point when it came to a story. She zeroed in on the heart of the matter and I knew she wouldn't let it go until she was satisfied with the answers, which was what I was counting on. "I'd rather not go into it," I said. "The issue's confidential."

"Then why are we having this conversation? Why talk about it at all?"

"Fritz McCabe is missing. His father filed a police report yesterday morning. Some of the facts will come out anyway and you asked me to keep you informed about developments."

"Well, you've got my attention. Developments such as what?"

"Are you aware that Iris Lehmann is engaged to Sloan's stepbrother Joey?"

"I didn't know that, but it strikes me as strange."

"Well, me too, but love relationships often seem strange to me. The point is they came to my office Tuesday because she claims she saw Austin Brown twice last week."

"Why would he come back?"

"Good question." Clearly, the story wouldn't make sense until I gave her the relevant information. "Off the record?"

"Absolutely."

"It looks like he's behind an extortion scheme. This is in regard to the footage on the sex tape someone shot around the same time Sloan was killed. He's threatening to send a copy to the DA unless the McCabes pay up." I sketched in the details, including Fritz's trip to the bank and his walking off with the twenty-five thousand in cash.

"What's his motive coming up with a scheme like that?"

"I suppose because he needed the twenty-five grand. His life's a mess. He thought he'd be a hot-shot attorney. Instead he's out there somewhere doing god knows what. Surely, it wasn't the future he imagined for himself."

"Which feeds back into your suggestion that Sloan's murder has had life-altering effects."

"Exactly," I said. "Same is true of Troy. As far as I can tell he's a good kid, but prison set him back on his heels and he may never recover his balance."

"What about Bayard?"

"He's an idle drunk living on his inheritance. He's currently shacked up with his daddy's widow, who must have been half Tigg's age. Then there's Poppy Earl. She was Sloan's best friend until Iris Lehmann came along. She's writing a screenplay about the murder, hoping to make her personal fortune."

"I get it," Diana said. "I'd have to think about it. I know a couple of magazine editors who might take a flier on it."

"Here's my opinion for what it's worth," I said. "Go high or go home. Don't try dinky little regional publications. Think *Vanity Fair*. That caliber."

"Wow. You *are* ambitious about this." She reached for her handbag. "I'll make some calls and get back to you."

I raised a hand. "One more thing. I need to say something about your brother Michael."

Her tone was flat. "No deal."

"Just let me say this. You don't have to respond. Believe me, I know about family rifts and I'm not asking you to change your position."

I waited, and when she didn't get up from the table and walk off, I went on. "He was a mixed-up kid and I know he did irreparable harm to people you love, but in the end, he was trying to do the right thing."

She was silent for a long time and I was about to concede defeat and let the matter pass when she took a deep breath and released it.

"Fair enough," she said.

32

Thursday, October 5, 1989

Home again, as I made my way through the squeaky gate, I could hear Lucky wailing. I thought his dog must have died, but when I reached the backyard, I saw Killer staring him in the face transfixed, wagging his doggie tail. What an amazing beast he was, with his short black coat, tawny yellow lion ruff, and a face the size and shape of a bear's with the added oddity of an orange dot over each eye. Lucky was beside himself and Pearl was running short of patience. "Would you listen to yourself?" she said.

I looked from one to the other. "What's up?"

"This lug got his bed back at Harbor House."

I put my hands on my cheeks. "Oh no!" I said, as though the news were tragic. I was about to carry on, but a look at Lucky's face showed such misery, I couldn't bear to tease him. "Sorry. I was being stupid. Why is that a problem?"

"They won't let me bring my dog."

"What's Harbor House gonna do with a dog?" Pearl snapped. "Next thing you know, every panhandler with a borrowed pup is gonna want to bring it in. It'd be like a kennel with all the barking and dog poop. The homeless deserve better."

I looked from her to Lucky, saying, "I thought you told me he'd been with you twelve years."

He sniffed and rubbed a teary eye with a knuckle. "Since he was six weeks old."

"So if Harbor House put up with him for that long, why not now?"

"Dog was never at Harbor House," Pearl said scornfully. "That's against the rules. Lucky comes to town, spends one night at the shelter, and sneaks Killer into bed with him. He's drunk . . . I'm talking Lucky, not the dog. House manager spots the dog and escorts both to the door. That's when Lucky turns around and tears the place apart."

To him, she said, "Would you quit your bellyaching? *I'll* keep the dog. He's better company than you are anyway. He don't fart at night."

I let myself into the studio and sat down at my desk. It was while I was pawing through my shoulder bag, looking for my index cards, that I came across the mail I'd stuck in the outside flap earlier. I extracted the handful and did a quick finger walk. I'd received checks from two different clients, both of them slow-pays. That cheered me up no end. The rest of the collection was the usual crap except for one plain white number ten envelope with a Perdido return address. When I opened it, I found a fold of white paper with a telephone number in the 406 area code and the name Hazel Rose, someone I'd never heard of. I couldn't remember ever calling anyone with a 406 prefix and I had no idea what part of the country it was associated with.

I opened my bottom drawer and grabbed the telephone book. Up front, in the pages devoted to community services, emergency numbers, government offices, and public schools, there was a handy-dandy map of the

United States, with the progression of time zones displayed in pastel colors, and the many and various area codes indicated state by state. Starting on the West Coast, in the Pacific Time Zone, I ran a finger down the page, zipping past Washington State, Oregon, California, and Nevada. I moved on to Mountain Time and quickly came across 406, which covered the whole of Montana, where I knew absolutely no one. I took out my atlas of the United States and flipped through the alphabetized listings until I came to Montana, which was sandwiched between Missouri and Nebraska. From the itty-bitty print in a box to one side, I learned that the population of Montana was over a million and a half souls spread out across approximately one hundred and forty-five thousand square miles. I was now in possession of many facts about a state I'd never visited, and I still didn't have a clue about Hazel Rose. I went back to the return address, which looked familiar now that I was seeing it again. When the answer popped into my head, I said the word "Ah!" in a jolt of recognition. This was Phyllis Joplin's new home address in the condominium complex where Ned Lowe had lain in wait and beat the shit out of her. Hazel Rose had to be Celeste Lowe's alias. Her new location must be somewhere in Montana, which didn't narrow it down that much. Ned had torn into Phyllis's moving boxes searching for the information, which she'd had the foresight to put in the mail to me.

I sat and thought about it briefly and then picked up the handset. Then I put it down again. Ned had managed to tap the phone at my office, so why not here as well? I took apart the handset and studied the interior, which appeared to be clean. Before I crawled around on the floor, eyeballing the baseboards in search of spike mikes and related eavesdropping devices, I hauled out the small-band receiver I'd purchased years before from RadioShack. I unearthed the gadget at the back of my top desk drawer and then hunted down fresh batteries. I swept the area until I was satisfied there wasn't a transmitter planted on the premises, and *then* crawled around on my hands and knees. One can't be too careful about these things.

I went back to the fold of paper and punched in the number I'd been given. After six rings, the call was picked up by a machine on the other end.

Nothing. No voice message and no instructions. Just that silence followed by the sound of the beep.

I said, "Hello. My name is Kinsey Millhone. We met at your home in Cottonwood six months ago. This number was given to me by a mutual friend who's recently suffered serious injury. I'd appreciate it if you'd return my call. You don't need to mention your name or location, but it's imperative that we talk."

I recited my home phone number twice and then hung up. For all I knew, Celeste had been standing right there listening to me. I'd have to wait and see what she decided to do in response to the news that I'd passed along. In the meantime, I hid the fold of paper in my bra, where I knew it would remain undisturbed. Sorry state of affairs, isn't it?

I had no choice but to turn my attention to the job at hand.

I checked my notes for the contact information Margaret Seay had given me for Steve Ringer, Roland Berg, and Patti Gibson, whose married name I didn't have. I noticed that Steve and Roland shared an address in a singles development in Colgate. I hit the 101 and headed north. Iris had mentioned their throwing a homecoming party for Fritz, so I deemed them a likely source of information regarding his current whereabouts.

The two-story apartment buildings must have gone up in the sixties. The units on the second floor boasted high, slanted rooflines, punctuated by skylights. The stucco structures were arranged in groupings of four, each with laundry rooms, a workout center, and an enormous resort-style swimming pool in the center. Ground-floor units had patios sufficient to accommodate impromptu parties. Given the warm autumn afternoon, many louvered windows had been cranked open and music spilled out onto the balconies, most of which were furnished with Weber grills, lawn furniture, bicycles, and houseplants. Wet bathing suits were strung over the wrought-iron railings and whiffs of marijuana drifted out of every third door. Parking was generous. No pets allowed. The Santa Ynez Mountains formed a hazy backdrop to the north.

I was surprised by the number of residents in evidence. This was early afternoon and my guess was that employment consisted of waitressing and barkeep jobs that started at eight in the evening and went on into the wee hours. The apartment where Steve Ringer and Roland Berg lived was in a building that overlooked the freeway. Passing traffic mimicked the ebb and flow of the Pacific, with copious exhaust fumes added.

I climbed to the second floor and knocked on the first door, which was opened by a tall, thin fellow in flip-flops and a ratty knee-length green chenille robe, with his hair in a ponytail and an embarrassingly thin goatee. He was in the process of blowing his nose vigorously on a tissue. I placed him in his midtwenties. It was the nut and bolt in one ear that triggered the flash of memory.

I pointed at him. "You're the guy from the camera shop."

He shook his head in the negative as though I'd accused him of ditching school. "I called in this morning and Kirk said take the day off. He doesn't want us coming in to work if we're sick."

"I'm not the health police. I met you a couple weeks ago when I came to the store and asked about duplicating a tape."

He pointed back at me. "The exhibitionist."

"That was work-related."

"I'll bet."

"I'm a private detective. Kinsey Millhone," I said.

I held out a hand as though to shake his and then thought better of it. He'd already held up both his hands as though at gunpoint, declining to expose me to his upper respiratory woes.

"You can come in if you like, but we're better off out here," he said, honking into his tissue again.

I caught a glimpse of orange shag carpet. I suspected the kitchen appliances would be avocado green. "Fresh air works for me," I said. "Are you Stringer?"

"That's right."

I handed him a business card. "I'm hoping to track down Fritz McCabe. He's been spending time with friends and I was hoping you'd know who."

"That's us," he said. "He was here a couple of weekends, but that got old fast. I read in the paper he's out of prison and suddenly he's on the phone, dropping these not-so-subtle hints about getting the old gang together again. This was a couple of days after he got back."

"You had a welcome home party for him."

"Strictly his idea. Roland and I weren't all that thrilled about picking up the relationship. I feel sorry for the guy, but that doesn't mean he can attach himself like a barnacle. Kid's a basket case, you know? Okay, so on one hand, he's been in prison and he's Mister Tough-Guy. Mister Know-It-All. On the other, it's like he's still fifteen years old and completely out of it because he's stuck back in time. I didn't like him much to begin with and I thought it was pushy asking us to pitch a party for him. Talk about a weird vibe. None of us had a good time. It was just so freaking awkward, but what were we supposed to do? He put us on the spot. We agree to it once and he takes it for granted he can latch on for life. Next thing we know, he's spending nights on our couch."

"Did you see him this past Friday?"

"Briefly. Is there a problem?"

"A big one. Fritz was last heard from on Friday. There hasn't been a peep out of him since."

"Well, I saw him Friday afternoon. Thursday morning, he called, kind of like he was expecting an invitation. I told him we were busy and then he asked if he could crash here anyway and I said, 'No, dude, you can't.' I mean, shit. The guy can't take a hint. I said maybe some other time, just putting him off, and then told him Roland was waiting for a call, so I had to go. He called again Friday morning, all jazzed, because he'd actually gotten his hands on the twenty-five thousand bucks."

"So I heard. He intended to pay the extortionist?"

"I guess so, but next thing you know, the story's changed. He shows up at my door and there's this big switcheroo. Fritz says it was all a misunderstanding. The guy didn't intend to play hardball. He needed the money and couldn't think of any other way to get it. Fritz was stoked and told him he'd be happy to help out. He's acting like it's a short-term loan the guy promised to pay back in a couple of weeks."

I stared at Stringer like he'd grown a second head. "Are you serious?"

"I'm just telling you what he told me."

"That makes no sense. Was this someone he knew?"

"Sounded like it to me. I mean, it must have been, right? You wouldn't lend twenty-five grand to some schmo off the street."

"He didn't tell you who it was?"

"Nope."

"Did you ask?"

"Why would I ask when I didn't give a shit? I was happy to have him off our hands."

I found myself squinting, trying to make sense of this unexpected turn of events. "The extortionist was supposed to pick him up downtown. So is that how he got to your place?"

"Absolutely. The guy drove him out here. He and this dude were going camping at Yellowweed, which was why he stopped by—to borrow a sleeping bag."

"He didn't have one of his own?"

"He did, but he didn't want to go back to his place in case he ran into his mom and dad."

"That's nice of him. They've been worried sick," I said. "You know what? I don't like this. How did we get from blackmail to a chummy little camping trip?"

"I don't like it either, now you mention it. Especially if no one's heard from him since. That area up near Yellowweed is isolated. If Fritz thought there was any danger, why would he go?"

"Maybe the guy came up with the proposal about a camping trip to get him to cooperate."

"Could be," he said. "You've met Fritz, right?"

"Shortly after I was hired."

"Not meaning to diss the guy, but he's pathetic. He'd do anything if he thought he could get you to like him. Know what I mean? He's one of those people who doesn't believe anyone would take advantage. To him, it feels like friendship. Understand, I didn't lay eyes on this so-called pal of his because he waited in the car. I'm judging from what Fritz said."

"What if this was someone he knew in prison? That might explain his being so cheerful. Might have been a guy released about the same time he was and now he's trying to jump on the gravy train. Either that or it's someone from Climp."

"If it was one of the kids from Climp, why be so secretive?"

"Maybe he was being secretive because he knew you knew the guy."

Stringer shrugged, not really interested. "Anyway, he needed a Coleman stove and lantern, so I let him take mine. I'm being sarcastic, saying, 'Sure you don't want my tent?' And he says oh no, they have one. So I go, 'What the hell are you going to do up at Yellowweed?' He's looking at me like I'm nuts and he says, 'What do you think? A doobie and a twelve-pack.' A doobie? We haven't called 'em that for years. I don't want to pick a fight with the guy. He just irritates me. At least lending him a bunch of stuff was better than having him hang out."

"What about Roland? Could he have heard from Fritz?"

"If he had, he would have mentioned it."

"Fritz still has your camping gear?"

"Yeah, but I wasn't using it anyway. I'm hoping he'll get it back to me, but if not, no biggie."

I stared out toward the horizon, thinking about what he'd said. In the distance, along the ridge where the Santa Ynez Mountains spilled into the valley beyond, I saw birds riding the thermals, circling like dark specks.

"When's the last time you ran into Austin Brown?"

"Gotta be ten years. Dude's been gone since Fritz shot off his big mouth and blabbed to the police."

"Iris Lehmann thinks she saw him twice last week."

"No way. What's she talking about? He might be a badass, but he's not a fool. Cops would pick him up in a heartbeat."

"Why would she make a claim like that if it wasn't true?"

"She's a flake. What she says doesn't mean shit and never did."

I said, "Well, I appreciate the information."

"Anytime."

As I turned to go, an issue popped to mind. To this day, if pressed, I couldn't identify the impulse that made me ask because this wasn't a matter I'd given conscious thought to. "One quick question," I said.

"Sure."

"You were one of the kids at Margaret Seay's house the day Sloan's room was emptied, right?"

"Yes."

"Who found the tape?"

I could see him process the query, which seemed to have taken him by surprise.

"Nobody. No one came across anything. The police had already been through her room, so there was nothing to find."

"Are you sure about that?"

"Sure, I'm sure. What made you ask?"

"Simple assumption, I guess. That was shortly before Fritz was released."

Cautiously, he said, "Okay, but I don't get the connection."

"I thought the tape came to light that day. There were six of you and I can't believe someone didn't set up a whoop at the discovery."

"No whoop. No discovery. Scout's honor," he said, holding up his right hand as though to attest to his honesty.

I had no choice but to accept his account, but I was having trouble adjusting my mental picture. From the outset, I'd taken for granted the fact that the blackmail scheme had been set in motion by the discovery of the tape. Either the tape wasn't discovered that day or Stringer knew nothing about it.

Feeling unsettled, I trotted down the stairs to my car. My immediate concern was Fritz's whereabouts. He reminded me of Pinocchio. As clever as he thought he was, he was gullible, likely to fall into bad company. If his goal was to be liked? Hand over twenty-five thousand bucks and see how popular you are. From his perspective, he'd solved the problem. Once the twenty-five grand was paid, that would be the end of it. He could call it a loan if he liked, but his chances of getting the money back seemed minuscule. Not that it would matter to him. He was probably having fun. He'd outmaneuvered his parents, outwitted the bank, and everything had gone as planned.

It was time to see if I could run him to ground. Being a big fan of the obvious, I decided to start up at Yellowweed since that's where he was headed at last report. As a place to transact off-grid business, the abandoned campsite was isolated and therefore offered privacy. If Fritz had gone up there with this guy on Friday, why hadn't he come home? Maybe the original plan was to get him up there and relieve him of the money. The guy must not have realized how pointless cunning was when Fritz was so eager to hand over the cash.

I stopped off at a service station and topped off my tank on the way to the 101 and then I headed for the pass. As I wound my way up the mountain, I could see the turkey vultures wheeling in the sky overhead. I counted four of them, their wings held in a shallow V, occasionally tipping from side to side, which caused the flight feathers to look silvery in the late afternoon light. The turkey vulture forages by smell, which is apparently uncommon in the world of birds. Flying low to the ground, they're capable of picking up the scent of gasses that herald decay in dead animals. The turkey vulture feeds on carrion, looking at road kill as life's perpetual banquet.

I parked at the side of the road, pulling my Honda in

close to the rising hillside. This must have been roughly the spot where Troy had parked his pickup truck the night Sloan was killed. I started the climb. The Boy Scout camp at Yellowweed had been deserted for years. The trail was overgrown and I was probably wading through poison ivy that would net me a nasty rash later on. The signs along the trail were faded, some posts broken off at the midpoint, leaving a ragged bouquet of splinters. As is usually the case, the hike made me conscious that I was out of shape. The aggravating thing about exercise is that it prepares you solely for the one you're engaged in. Biking, hiking, running, or lifting weights—the activity conditions you for that activity, but not necessarily for anything else.

At the summit, where the ground leveled out, I stopped and took stock. At first glance, I had no way to guess if Fritz and his pal had been here. Visitors usually accessed the area by way of the old gravel road, which in drought conditions such as ours would yield no tire prints. A fine haze of dust had settled on the scrub brush, but it might have been there for months. I counted eight more vultures congregated in the trees, which were otherwise bereft of leaves. The dry weather had created a premature change of season and the foliage had dropped without ceremony.

The vultures occupied the lower limbs of a stand of trees fifty yards away. Branches sagged under their weight. Some hopped awkwardly across the bare ground, picking their way as far as the foundation of one of the cabins leveled long ago. Two of them waddled on flat feet, making hissing and grunting noises, as graceless as penguins on dry land. One stood with wings spread, drying his feathers, his legs streaked with white as though he'd defecated on himself. It was clear the meeting had been called to order, but the minutes hadn't been read. The buzzards had gathered in anticipation of a tasty snack, but nothing was forthcoming. In consequence, they seemed ill-tempered and out of sorts. I kept an eye on them, hoping they wouldn't regard me as a canapé.

On closer inspection, I could tell someone had been

here recently. Wood had been gathered and piled to one side. I could see the remnants of a campfire that had been doused with water. When I checked with my bare hand, the ashes were cold. There was a flattened spot where a tent had been erected. The tent stakes had been driven into the hard ground in the shape of a hefty square. Various scuffle marks suggested that the tent had been taken down and stowed in some form. I'm not a camper, so I don't really know how these things are done. A palm frond had been used as a makeshift broom before it was tossed aside. A fine sweep of dirt formed a fan shape, but there was no way to judge what had been there before.

A large plastic trash bin had been dragged into the clearing. Someone had tossed in a plastic grocery bag loaded with empty baked bean cans, the packaging for hot dogs, and an empty cellophane wrapper for the hot dog buns. They'd rounded out this wholesome repast with a bag of Fritos, also depleted. I was starving to death and found myself staring wistfully at the wrappings from a packet of moon pies.

I walked the periphery of the campsite. No empty beer cans. No rolling papers or joints. I wasn't sure what they'd done to amuse themselves. A number of the old cabins had been bulldozed and the construction debris had been used to fill the old swimming pool. The concrete rim looked like the edging for an Olympic-sized flower bed. I could almost hear the nine-year-old boys shrieking as they did cannonballs off the side. The "fill" was a treacherous-looking tangle of old fencing and broken-up lumber where the cabin remnants had been pushed into this final resting place. There must have been an argument about the virtues of removing the rubble versus leaving it where it was, but since the twice-abandoned campground wasn't slated for further use, economic imperatives had prevailed. The pool was tucked in among the ancient trees, so the sunlight wouldn't have penetrated far and the surface of the water would have been subject to slime where falling leaves rotted.

Some of the underbrush had been broken off or crushed underfoot. The raw pith indicated that a vehicle might have been driven across it recently. In the meantime, the buzzards kept a close eye on me. One of them, with a great flapping of wings, managed to become airborne and two others followed suit. What worried me was the occasional whiff of dead dog. This might have been a deer carcass, but I didn't think so. The odor wasn't directional. I turned this way and that but I couldn't pinpoint the source. This was now Thursday and Fritz had been missing since the previous Friday. I peered down the steep hillside. Maybe twenty-five yards down the slope, I saw a crumpled form. It looked like someone had fallen down the hill and now lay in a clumsy tangle, dead to the world.

Gingerly I sidestepped my way down, trying to keep my balance as the loose dirt slipped out from underfoot and traveled in a mini-avalanche in advance of my approach. When I reached the form, I realized it was a discarded sleeping bag, empty to all appearances. I peered closely at the opening where the zipper was caught in a fold of fabric. No bullet holes or dried blood. I left it where it was. Impossible to tell how long it had been there. I made the return climb, sending a shower of additional dirt down the hill.

When I reached the top, I stood in the clearing and did a complete 360 turn. I could have been smelling sewer gas, but it occurred to me that a campground like this, in the midst of a wilderness, couldn't be connected to the city sewer system because the logistics would have been impossible. Which suggested a septic tank. Septic systems are meant to be as inconspicuous as possible. Once they're installed, the grass grows back, time passes, and few visual cues remain. I crossed to the ruins of one of the cabins, circled the foundation until I located a four-inch pipe at the point where it surfaced outside. I figured the septic tank would have to be ten to twelve feet from the nearest structure, so I paced off twenty-five giant steps and began to walk. Seven minutes later, I located a rectangle of concrete, easily five feet by eight. Here, the smell was strong enough to activate my gag reflex. I used the hem of my T-shirt to cover my mouth and nose. This filtered the odor to some extent. There was a single 4-by-4-foot concrete lid in the center of the rectangle that bore an enormous iron ring. One try and I knew the cap was too heavy and awkward to manage on my own.

One of the vultures sailed down within range and landed on the concrete with a series of hops. He tilted his head, peering at the source of the smell, and then fixed me with a black and beady eye. His head was small in proportion to his body, red in color, his long neck bald. I've been told the paucity of feathers works to the bird's advantage when so much of his time is spent with his head in the bellies of dead animals. He made an aggressive feint in my direction and I backed away step by step.

I returned to the highway on the old gravel road, carefully making my way down the hill. I returned to my car and drove as far as the nearest scenic turnout, where I'd seen a call box. I punched in 9-1-1 and talked to a dispatcher, detailing where I was, what I knew, and what I suspected. Then I waited for the first patrol car to arrive. Though I wouldn't have confirmation for another few hours, Fritz McCabe wasn't far away.

33

THE DRAWING OF STRAWS

June 1979

Bayard stood at the sink with a dish towel tucked in the waistband of his jeans. It was close to nine and the party was winding down. The kitchen window had been closed, but he could still smell the light perfume of chlorine from the pool. Darkness would soon settle over the patio, erasing the day. Austin had flapped open an oversize plastic garbage bag, into which he shoved used paper plates, plastic ware, soft drink cans, crumpled napkins, and leftover food. Most of the time Austin played King of the Hill, happy to be regarded as the man of the hour. School was out and he told everyone his parents had offered him the cabin for the party. Bayard had his doubts. More likely it was Austin's idea and he'd failed to tell his good old mom and dad that he was entertaining. Now he was busy covering his tracks, erasing every vestige of the gathering. Austin, for all of his braggadocio, was a chickenshit at heart.

Bayard was nicely drunk, his inebriation buffered by the dope he'd smoked, each balancing the other in terms of their effect. The alcohol made him loose. The cannabis made him mellow. Bayard never got falling-down drunk and he was never out of control. This bunch of high school yahoos drank and smoked to excess and they were all over the place, passing out, puking, laughing like hyenas, munching down everything in sight. Or in the case of Patti Gibson and Stringer, getting it on in one of the guest rooms. Bayard's thoughts flitted to his dad's diagnosis and the most recent test results. Things were not looking good. They'd done a CAT scan with contrast and Maisie said his dad's insides lit up like a Christmas tree. Bayard shut the door on that idea. Certain subjects he didn't like to visit even in the privacy of his own head. Especially matters related to his father's death.

He'd learned to toss painful issues into little boxes with the lids nailed shut; this when he was five years old and his parents got divorced. Even at that age, he recognized the jeopardy he was in. He was the focus of the hostilities—not his person, but the fact that he was Tigg and Joan Montgomery's only begotten son. They quarreled, through their attorneys, over legal custody, physical custody, visitation, child support, schooling, and every other decision that was made from the moment they separated. He was pulled this way and that, loyal to one parent at the expense of the other, which generated its own anguish. *Into the box with that one,* he thought. Sometimes he knew how good it would be when one or the other of his parents died, which would, at least, cut the agony by half. In his father's case, it looked like his wish was coming true. Recent revelations had threatened his financial expectations and he still hadn't decided what options he had, if any. For now, he'd medicated his rage to a manageable level.

Stringer came into the kitchen, in the process of rounding everyone up for the drive back to town. "Where's Iris?"

"On the couch last I saw," Bayard said. He turned and

verified her presence in the living room. "How you doing?" he called though the open door.

"I think I'm going to be sick," she said.

Stringer said, "Well, do it somewhere else. I'm outta here and I don't want you barfing in my van. You with me, Michelle?"

"Sure."

Austin said, "What the fuck, Michelle. You're taking off? This place is a mess. You can't just walk out and leave me with this."

"I told you I had a curfew. I don't go with him, how'm I going to get home in time?"

"What a load of crap! It's still light outside. What time's your curfew, nine o'clock? Hold your horses and I'll take you. I told you I would."

"Sure. When and if you ever get around to it."

Stringer stuck his head in the front door. "Hey, Michelle. You coming or not?"

"Hang on just a second, okay?"

Stringer disappeared.

Michelle said, "Austin, I really have to get home. Bayard's doing dishes and the trash has been dumped so what more do you want?"

"I want this place cleaned up. Bring in stuff from the patio and gather up all the soggy towels so I can start a load. Ten minutes more is all I ask."

Michelle was annoyed, but she seemed resigned. "Shit. Let me get my purse. I left it in Stringer's van."

Austin lifted the plastic bag, which was bulging with trash. He tied the plastic strands in a knot and put the bag by the back door. He turned his attention to the kitchen counter, which was littered with condiments. He replaced the cap on the ketchup, recapped the mustard, and placed both in the refrigerator.

Troy came into the kitchen. He'd changed from his bathing suit into jeans and a white T-shirt. "Where's Michelle off to?"

"She left her bag in Stringer's van. She's coming back."

"Man, I don't think so. She got in the van and they all took off."

"Stringer did?"

"Right. Him, Betsy, Patti, and Roland Berg. They couldn't wait to get out of here. Rats deserting a sinking ship. They probably thought you were going to ask them to pitch in for the keg."

"What about Blake?"

"Him, too. I saw him scoot over to make room so Michelle could crawl in the back."

"Damn it! She said she'd help."

Troy said, "Apparently not, pal. I guess she didn't want to get into an argument."

Fritz wandered into the kitchen, dressed except for his feet, which were bare. "Anybody seen my shoes?"

"In your hand," Austin said.

"Oh, yeah. Thanks."

"You know what? This is the last of my parties you're invited to. Go hang out with those bullshit sophomore friends of yours."

Sloan, coming into the kitchen from the patio, caught this exchange. She was still in her bikini and flip-flops and she carried a stack of empty punch glasses that she tossed in the trash. "Why are you on *his* ass? He didn't do anything."

"He doesn't have to do anything. He gets on my nerves."

"Give him a break. You don't have to put him down in front of everyone."

"What's your problem?"

"I'm just tired of your being such a shit to everyone."

"What, now you're the champion of the underdog? Fritz can look after himself. He doesn't need you coming to his rescue."

"Don't turn this into a pissing contest, Austin. I'm asking you to get off his case. And mine, too, while you're at it."

"And I'm asking you to shut your big mother and butt out."

Sloan suddenly laughed. "Oh my god, did you hear what you just said. You said shut your 'big mother' instead of shut your big mouth. Talk about a Freudian slip. That's hysterical."

"Ha . . . ha . . . ha," Austin said, giving each word emphasis. "And by the way, where's the tape? The deal was you'd bring it with you."

"I forgot."

"I'm tired of talking about this. Why don't you go put on some clothes, Miss Porky Pig. I can't believe you'd wear that bikini and leave all your fat hanging out. It's obscene."

Troy said, "Hey!"

Sloan's smile died. "That was in bad taste, even for you."

"Oh, lighten up. Can't you take a joke?"

Sloan said, "I'd tread easy if I were you. Keep in mind the fact that you want something from me. I don't want anything from you."

"What's that supposed to mean?"

"It means, oops, I told a fib. I don't have the tape at my house. I left it somewhere else. I'll give it to you as soon as I get it back."

"And when would that be?"

She shrugged. "Your guess is as good as mine."

"Well, who has it? You have no business giving it to anyone else."

"But I did."

"What are you trying to pull?"

"I'm training you to be nice. I know it's an alien concept, but I'm sure you can learn. The deal was treat me nice or no tape."

"The deal was no more shunning."

"No, Austin. That was your claim. You called off the shunning voluntarily. You said it was a done deal. You said if I gave you the tape, we'd be square."

"Right."

"So you didn't say you'd go on treating me like shit. That's not going to work."

"You know what? Trying to control me is a bad idea."

"Just give it some thought."

"Give what some thought?"

"Being nice. Now if you'll excuse me, I'll go put some clothes on my porky self."

"About time, you oinker."

Sloan left the kitchen and moved into the living room, headed for the master bedroom, where she'd left her clothes.

Austin said, "What a bitch. Did you hear that? What makes her think she can threaten us?"

"What threat? Why do you push everything to such extremes?" Bayard asked, annoyed.

Austin moved into the living room and opened the end table drawer. He took out the Astra and checked the magazine. "She still has the tape, doesn't she? Or did she give it to you?"

"She didn't give me anything," Bayard said. "What are you so pissed off about?"

"Don't you get it? She won't cooperate unless I eat shit."

Troy said, "She asked you to be nice. Why is that so hard?"

"Listen, you halfwit. She's gaming us and I won't put up with that. Time to put the pressure on. She wants to go home, she'll have to hand over the tape or it's a no-go."

"She can't hand it over if she doesn't have it," Troy said.

Austin closed his eyes, his patience sorely tried. "I guess I didn't make it clear. No more stalling. She should have brought it with her. I told you to make sure she had it, didn't I?"

"I asked her when she first got in the truck and she told me she didn't have it. What was I supposed to do, make her get out and walk? You didn't say anything about forcing her to do anything."

Austin said, "You should have insisted. You should have made it clear we meant business."

"What are you talking about? Even if I'd insisted, she could have refused. I have no control over her."

"You know something, Troy? You're weak. I should have known better than to trust you with this."

"Fine. I'm weak. Now what?"

"Now I'll take care of it."

Bayard said, "Why don't you drop it, Austin? For god's sake."

Austin stared at Bayard and slowly lifted one finger in the air. "One phone call."

Bayard dropped his gaze. "Don't."

"Don't what? I'm telling you what I'll do if you cross me."

"Fine. Have it your way," Bayard said darkly.

"My plan exactly. We take her up the mountain and keep her there until she figures out we're serious." He found the extra magazine and slid it into his jeans pocket.

Bayard looked over at Iris, who rose from the couch and walked hurriedly toward the master bathroom, her fingers pressed to her lips. He shook his head and then shifted his attention to the handgun. "What's that for?"

"Insurance."

Troy said, "No, man. I'm not doing this. I'm outta here."

"What about you, Fritz? Are you bailing on me, too?"

"No, I'm in. I mean, I don't want to hurt anyone . . ."

"'I don't want to hurt anyone,'" Austin said in a mewling tone. "You know your problem, Fritz? You're a fucking faggot."

"I'm not."

"Then prove it. Take this and shut your trap."

"I don't want it. I don't know what to do with it."

"Really. I thought you were having such a good time with it." He imitated the sounds of gunfire that Fritz had been mouthing earlier. "How about this? We'll draw straws. Guy who gets the short one takes the gun."

Fritz said, "What straws?"

Austin crossed to the fireplace, where a stack of newspapers and long wooden matches had been left near the pile of logs. "We'll use these. There are four of us, right? So we'll pull four and I'll break one and then I'll line 'em up behind my back." He took four long wooden matches from the box.

Troy said, "One chance in four. Not very good odds."

"Not so. It means three out of the four of us don't have to worry. Hang on."

He turned aside and Bayard heard the faint snap of a wooden match. Austin turned back. He held out his hand, with four wooden matches lined up evenly above his thumb and index finger. "Who wants to go first?"

"I'll go," Troy said. He chose one of the matches and pulled it out from between Austin's fingers. It was clearly a long one.

Austin smiled. "Lucky draw. You're off the hook. Who's next?"

"Me," Bayard said. He studied the remaining three matches, hesitated, and then pulled one. Again, it was a long one.

Austin laughed, amused by the tension he'd generated. "Down to you and me, Fritz. Have a go and best of luck."

He held out the matches, pretending to steer Fritz from one to the other of the remaining two.

Fritz picked one and pulled. The match was two inches long.

Austin put the remaining match in his pocket and held out the gun. "You gonna take this or not? If you're chickenshit, that's fine with me. I'm not going to pressure you."

Fritz said, "I'll take it."

"Are you sure about that?"

"I drew the short straw. Everybody saw that."

Bayard found himself looking at Austin's left hand, wondering why he'd done such a smooth job of tucking the remaining match out of sight.

Austin was still watching Fritz closely. "Short straw doesn't commit you. You can tell me to stuff it if you don't like the deal."

"I'm good. Gimme the gun. I'm cool with this."

"Attaboy. You'll do fine." He turned toward the hall and then turned back to Bayard. "Go find out what's taking Sloan so long."

Bayard left the living room and crossed the hall to the master bedroom. The door to the bathroom was open and Iris was sitting on the floor by the toilet, her cheek resting on the rim. The air smelled sour. He paused in the bathroom doorway, watching her. "This doesn't bode well."

"I don't feel good."

"You don't look so hot, either. Are you done?"

"I think so." Iris put a hand on the vanity and pulled herself to her feet. She lowered the lid on the toilet and flushed it. Then she leaned over the sink, turned on the water, and rinsed her mouth.

"Your parents have any idea where you are?"

She shook her head. "They signed up for this marital retreat to deal with some of the stress I caused them by getting kicked out of Climp. They're supposed to get home tonight, but they weren't sure what time. I told them I was spending the night with Poppy, but if they call to say hi, then what? She won't lie for me now, after what went on. My parents are already furious. What am I gonna do if they find out I'm not at her house?"

"Has it occurred to you that you have no business being here in the first place? This is a bad environment for a girl like you."

Iris turned off the faucet and placed a hand towel against her face, dabbing off water. "What's Austin need a gun for? That's what I don't get."

"It's all bull. You know him. He does shit for effect."

"So everything's all right?"

"Of course. All Sloan has to do is tell us where the tape is and we can get this over with."

"Do you think we should call the sheriff?"

Bayard laughed. "What for?"

"To make sure no one gets hurt."

"Seriously, Iris. Are you going to call the sheriff's office and have some deputy show up? Austin would shit a brick. I don't think his parents have any idea he invited us up here. Last thing he needs is some cop at the door. We got enough booze and dope up here to land us all in jail. Is that what you want?"

Iris hesitated, her face pale. "I'm worried about Sloan."

"Well, don't. You just worry about yourself."

"Bayard, this is scaring me. There's no telling what Austin might do."

"You want him to turn around and fix his beady eye on you?"

"No."

"What then?"

"I want to do what's right."

"Then go ahead and call the cops, but don't say I didn't warn you," he said. He turned and did a visual search of the bedroom behind him. "Where's Sloan? I thought she was in here."

"I didn't see her. I've been puking my guts out."

"She didn't come in to get dressed?"

"I don't think so."

"Where'd she go then? Her clothes are right where I saw 'em earlier. And isn't that her gym bag?"

"I guess. Maybe she left. She might have gone out the front door."

"Fuck."

Bayard returned to the living room. Fritz had tucked the gun in his waistband and Bayard was already worried the fool would shoot himself.

Austin looked up, expecting to see Sloan.

Bayard said, "She's gone. Iris thinks she might have left by the front door."

Iris appeared in the doorway behind Bayard. Austin was still focused on Bayard. "What the fuck is wrong with you? What are you standing around for? You guys get out there and round her up. Can't any of you think for yourselves?"

Troy was exasperated. "Okay, so we round her up. Then what?"

"Then we take her up to Yellowweed and have a chat."

"Why do we have to drive up there?" Troy said. "Why not have a chat here and then we can get the hell home?"

"You'll get home, dude. No sweat. I have something to show her so she'll know we're serious."

"What are you going to do, strip her clothes off and leave her up there?" Troy asked.

Austin laughed. "Not a bad idea. I like that."

Bayard shook his head, staring at the floor. "You know what? This is all more trouble than it's worth. Why don't we just bag the whole idea and get out of here? We can pick her up along the way."

"What the hell's the matter with you?" Austin said. "We're all in trouble as long as she has that tape. Just find her and bring her back. We'll go up the mountain, smoke a little dope, and negotiate."

"And that's it?" Troy asked.

"I want us to get this settled. You think I like being a shit? Well, I don't. I'm trying to work this out so it's win-win."

"That would be a first," Troy said.

"Don't start on me, Troy. I'm doing my best, okay?"

Troy studied him for a moment while Austin looked him steadily in the eye.

"Okay," he said. "We'll swing by and pick you up as soon as she's in the truck."

"Thank you."

As the three of them trooped out the front door, Iris sent Bayard an imploring look. Her face was dead white and she looked like she was on the verge of bursting into tears. She might be right about making that call to the sheriff's office. He debated about going back to re-open the subject, but she'd already turned away.

He went out on the front porch and zipped up his sweatshirt jacket, which wasn't nearly heavy enough to protect him from the mountain cold. Dark had descended at some point during the last hour and the temperature had dropped sharply. Troy'd had the presence of mind to bring a leather jacket. He pulled the truck keys from his right pocket and opened the door on the driver's side. Bayard went around and got in on the passenger side.

Fritz said, "Where'm I supposed to sit?"

"In the truck bed, fuckhead," Bayard said. He didn't like any of this, but he wasn't sure what to do about it.

He thought Troy was in his camp, sensing that the situation was already out of control.

Once the three reached the road, Fritz clambered up into the truck bed while Bayard turned in his seat and slid back the glass in the rear window.

Bayard said, "You okay back there?"

"Yeah, but it's cold as shit," Fritz said. He crossed his arms tightly against his body and put his face close to the space created by the sliding glass window like some eager pup going on his first road trip.

Troy started the truck and made a slow, easy U-turn on the two-lane road. "Why don't we just tell Austin we never saw her? How's he going to know?"

"We can't leave her alone out here," Bayard said. "What if something happened to her?"

"Like what?"

"She could get hit by a car or picked up by some weirdo."

"Better than dealing with Austin."

"If we lie about it, Fritz will blab," Bayard said. "Kid can't keep his mouth shut."

"Hey, I'm right here! I can keep my mouth shut."

Troy said, "There she is."

They'd only driven half a mile when the headlights picked her up on the side of the road, where she trudged doggedly. She was still wearing her bikini, but she'd buttoned a man's flannel shirt over it. Instead of flip-flops, she'd shoved her feet into size twelve men's dress shoes, which looked incongruous. She'd lifted all the items from the closet in the master bedroom. As the truck approached, she glanced back and stepped off the road.

Troy pulled up close to her and looked across Bayard in the passenger seat. "We got worried about you," he said.

"Bullshit. Austin sent you as soon as he figured out I was gone."

"True," Troy replied.

She began to walk again, not looking at them. Troy idled along at her pace.

"I'm not going back," she said.

Bayard rested his right arm on the open window. Wind roughed his thatch of dark hair, which lent him a childish air of innocence. "Come on, Sloan, just do it. Come back and talk to him. He'll never give you any peace until you kowtow to him."

"You ought to know," she said. She held up one finger, indicating that she understood why Bayard was doing Austin's bidding.

Fritz said, "What's that mean?" He held an index finger up as Sloan had.

"It's no concern of yours."

Sloan had stopped in her tracks. Troy brought the truck to a halt. The road was quiet except for the truck engine huffing. Exhaust fumes mingled with the scent of bay leaves. Bayard was hoping she'd decided to return to the cabin with them.

He said, "Get in the truck. Please. You can't walk back to town dressed like that. It's ten miles in the dark and it's dangerous. Make your peace with Austin and we'll give you a ride home."

She turned and faced him directly. "No deal. I've had it with him. He's a fuckin' bully and he wants me to knuckle under, which I won't."

"Why infuriate the guy? You know he doesn't react well to stuff like this," he said.

"Who cares? He thinks he can push me around? I'm not going to do it."

Fritz swung himself down from the truck bed, using his left hand in a surprisingly graceful move. "Maybe this will help," he said. He had the gun in his right hand, which trembled with the unfamiliar weight.

"Oh, for god's sake," Sloan said. "Don't point that thing at me."

"Yeah, Fritz. Cut it out," Bayard said. He opened the passenger-side door and stepped out on the gravel berm.

Fritz backed up a step, gesturing with the gun. "Get in, Sloan. I'm serious. Austin told us to bring you back and that's what we're doing." He turned the gun on Bayard. "Get in the back. I'm riding up front with her."

"This is a nice development. You're acting just like him," she said.

"That's exactly right. You think I'm a dope? Now I'm a dope with a gun, so maybe you could show me some respect," he said. "Get in!"

Sloan exchanged a look with Bayard, but she did as she was told.

Bayard hauled himself up into the truck bed.

With the gun still trained on Sloan, Fritz got into the passenger seat so she was wedged between him and Troy at the wheel. "Make a U-turn and let's go."

Troy shook his head in disbelief. "I think I can manage to drive without help. Is it all right with you if I back up and do a K-turn instead?"

"Do it any way you like," Fritz said.

Troy put his right arm on the seatback and turned so he could see through the rear window. He made the turn, shifted from reverse into first, and headed back the way they'd come.

The four of them rode in silence. Bayard sat in the truck bed with his legs stretched out in front of him and his back against the cab while he kept his eyes on the road. Fritz was right, it was cold in the truck bed with the wind whipping in from all sides. Fortunately, they didn't have far to go. When they reached the cabin, rather than parking at the road, Troy turned left into the rugged driveway and trundled up to the parking pad just outside the cabin.

Austin had apparently heard the rumble of the truck and he appeared on the porch, zipping himself into a puffy black parka. Iris appeared in the open doorway behind him. She'd hauled a comforter off one of the guest beds and wrapped it around her like a cape.

Austin came down the porch steps and crossed to the driver's-side door. "What have we got here?" he asked when he saw the players in their new configuration.

Troy said, "Your boy Fritz is now calling the shots, so to speak."

Austin seemed amused. "Will wonders never cease?"

Troy said, "So now where?"

Austin hoisted himself into the truck bed and settled beside Bayard. He leaned toward the sliding panel in the rear window, directing his instructions to Troy. "I told you, Yellowweed. Go back to the 154 and take a left."

For the second time, Troy put the truck in reverse and swung around until he was facing Horizon Road. Bayard turned his head toward the cabin and fixed his gaze on Iris, who hadn't moved. This sequence of events felt weird. He had no idea what Austin intended to do, but it couldn't be good. He locked eyes with Iris and lifted a hand, making a gesture as though he were talking on the phone. He wasn't sure if she picked up on it or not. The last he saw of her she was still in the doorway, silhouetted against the living room light.

Once the truck was out of sight, Iris stepped into the cabin and closed the door, shivering uncontrollably. She could feel sobs bubbling up and she made a small humming sound, trying to get control of herself. What did Bayard expect her to do? Why would the guys take Sloan up to Yellowweed unless it was for something bad?

She thought about Bayard's gesture. What did that mean? First, he'd told her to look after herself. He said Austin would be furious if the cops showed up. Was he now urging her to call for help? What if she made the call and meanwhile Sloan and Austin settled their differences? Austin would never forgive her.

She was in trouble enough as it was. She eyed the phone, torn by indecision. Better to do *something*. How long was the drive to Yellowweed? Time was running short. She took out a tissue and blew her nose. She dashed tears from her face and picked up the handset. What did it matter if one more person was mad at her? She punched in the number and waited, sniffing quietly to herself. As soon as she heard the man who picked up the line, she began to weep. In a squeaky little girl's voice, she said, "Daddy? Can you come get me?"

34

Thursday, October 5, 1989

I waited well outside the crime scene tape, leaning against a boulder that had initials and rude remarks scratched onto its face. A wide area had been cordoned off for a systematic search. The deputy who'd arrived first in response to my call was in command until the investigator appeared and assumed responsibility. An hour had passed and it was getting dark. The mobile crime lab was on hand, having labored up to the area on the long, winding two-lane road of gravel and cracked asphalt. The county coroner's car was parked to one side. Two deputies from the sheriff's office were present and I caught sight of Cheney Phillips conferring with a plainclothes detective, who was probably his counterpart in the Santa Teresa County Sheriff's Office. Meanwhile, the crime scene techs picked and sifted their way through every square inch of the physical surroundings, aware that once the tableau was deconstructed, there would be no way to re-create it.

Those of us not directly engaged in the tagging and bagging of evidence were encouraged to wait on the highway below, where a flat gravel apron provided space enough for four vehicles, mine among them. As chilly as it was, I was happy to return to my Honda, still parked on the berm. I opened the trunk and took out a sweatshirt that I pulled over my turtleneck. I slid into the driver's seat, fired up the ignition so I could keep the heater running in an attempt to keep warm. I was hungry, but there wasn't any point in complaining or expecting relief. I found a cherry Life Saver at the bottom of my shoulder bag and called that dinner.

Passing cars slowed so that drivers and passengers could peer out at us, wondering what we were up to. In my rearview mirror, I saw Cheney make his way down the access road and walk along the berm in my direction. When he was close, I got out of the car. "What are you doing here? I thought this was the county sheriff's turf."

"I could ask the same thing of you," he said. "Larry Burgess called me as a courtesy because I took the missing person's report from Hollis McCabe. He tells me you're working for the McCabes."

"That's correct."

"Whatever job you started with, this is now a homicide investigation, which takes precedence over any confidentially agreement you might have with them."

"You're not going to get any argument from me," I said. "But could we do this sitting in my car? I'm freezing my ass off out here."

"By all means."

Ever the gentleman, he opened my car door on the driver's side and then walked around to the passenger side and slid in. He said, "Go."

I took a deep breath and went. It was a relief to lay out the whole long tale, which I proceeded to do. He knew about the tape, but wasn't aware that it was back in play again after disappearing for ten years.

"When the demand note first arrived in the mail, the McCabes called Lonnie Kingman and he referred them to me," I said.

"It didn't occur to you to bring us into it?"

"Of course it did, but the McCabes were adamant."

Cheney said, "I know public perception would have it otherwise, but we're trained to handle situations like this. If we'd known what was going on, we might have been able to help."

"The issue was confidential. I was under no obligation to make their situation known to you. I saw the bind they were in and I understood their desire to keep it quiet. If you'd seen the tape, you'd understand as well."

"I feel sure we'll see it now."

"No doubt," I said.

I talked him through the chain of events, including the people I'd interviewed and the bits and pieces I'd picked up along the way. For the purposes of simplicity, I omitted a few of the minor characters, including Poppy Earl's father and stepmother. I'd provide further details when and if the need arose. Cheney was a quick study and I didn't have to spell out the particulars. He'd taken out a notepad, jotting down the occasional date or reference point.

I went on. "Last Thursday, the extortionist left a message saying he was tired of excuses and wanted his money. He said he'd pick Fritz up at State and Aguilar at noon on Friday. If Fritz didn't show up with the cash, he was in big trouble, or words to that effect."

I paused the narrative long enough to explain the fiddle Fritz pulled at the bank. "That's how he managed to get his hands on the twenty-five thousand. It looks like he met the guy as instructed."

"Foolish move on his part."

"Very," I said. "For what it's worth, there's talk that Austin Brown is back."

"Who told you that?"

"Iris Lehmann and her fiancé came into my office. She said she'd seen him twice the week before. Tuesday night at the Clockworks when she and Joey were playing pool, and again on Friday around noon when she was going to the bank. That sighting, he was driving up State right around the time of the proposed pickup."

Cheney said, "I'd be interested in hearing it from her. Go on with your story."

"Anyway, Lauren McCabe came to see me this past Monday because she realized Fritz hadn't slept in his bed for the previous three nights. By then she knew he'd forged her signature, which she was prepared to overlook. The pickup must have gone as planned and this is where things get bizarre. The way I heard it, the extortionist did an about-face and told Fritz the threat of blackmail was the only way he could think of to get his hands on some cash. The two stopped off at a friend's place to borrow camping gear. Fritz was in a chatty mood by then and he told his friend he offered to lend the guy the money, which the fellow promised to repay."

"Who's the friend who told you this?"

"Fritz's high school buddy Steve Ringer, commonly referred to as Stringer. He and another classmate have an apartment in a singles complex in Colgate. Iris and Poppy Earl both claim Austin vowed to eliminate anyone who betrayed him, which would be Fritz McCabe in a nutshell. Something changed. I have no idea what. Maybe the cash sweetened the guy's disposition. Whatever it was, by the time Fritz and his pal stopped off at Stringer's place, he'd gone from anxiety to good cheer. Fritz said they were coming up to Yellowweed and that's the last anyone saw of him."

"What about his companion?"

I shook my head. "He made a point of waiting in the car and Fritz didn't refer to him by name. I think he must have known him or he wouldn't have felt comfortable coming up to a place as remote as Yellowweed."

"I take it Fritz had the cash with him at that point."

"As far as I know," I said. "There's no sign of it now?"

"Nope."

"Well, I don't think robbery was the motive, if that's what you're thinking. Fritz came up here fully intending to hand over the money."

"Maybe he changed his mind."

"Always possible."

Cheney stared out the window, watching the passing traffic while he thought about what I'd said. "Someone will have to put together a time line."

"I can tell you one stop Fritz made. Friday morning, he paid a visit to Bayard Montgomery."

"You got this from him?"

"I did. I was in the process of working my way through witnesses again to see if there was anything I missed. He says Fritz showed up at his place and asked if he'd come with him when the extortionist picked him up downtown. He'd already asked once, but Bayard thought it was a foolish move and he wanted no part of it."

Cheney closed the notebook and tucked it into the inside pocket of his coat. I had the feeling he wanted to chide me for my part in the whole disaster, but what would be the point?

He shook his head. "I have go to the McCabes' and tell them. That's a conversation I don't want to have. I don't know how many times I've had to deliver the bad news."

"Fritz has been positively identified?"

"Pending confirmation by one or both of his parents. You want to come?"

"I don't, but I will." I didn't want to deal with the McCabes any more than he did, but someone had to tell them. "When?"

"Now's as good a time as any. Why don't I follow you in my car? We'll drop yours off at your place and take mine."

Driving down the pass, I could feel the dread thrumming in my chest like a swarm of bees in a chimney flue. There were probably fifteen of us by now who were aware of Fritz's fate. His parents weren't among the numbered, but they would be soon.

Home again, I parked and locked my car, then popped

my head into Henry's kitchen and told him what was going on. There wasn't much to say about the situation, but I wanted him to know where I was.

Cheney drove us in his spiffy little red Porsche, which for the first time didn't generate appreciation for his financial status as the son of the moneyed class. His father owned the Bank of X. Phillips, which was only one aspect of the family fortunes. In my mind, he was so closely associated with the Anna Dace/Jonah Robb debacle that I nearly asked him for an update, which would have been irrelevant given the circumstances. I was worried I'd be chided for introducing Anna to Vera, an impulse that had sparked the offer of an open adoption.

We left the car in the parking lot behind the condominium and walked through the covered gallery that led from the Axminster Theater to the street beyond. We passed the box office, which was dark now, and made a left turn. The condominium entrance was three steps away on State Street. Cheney and I went through the gate at street level and trooped up the stairs. I stood back while he knocked. Hollis came to the door in an immaculate three-piece suit. The minute he saw us standing there, he seemed to stiffen. "Lieutenant Phillips. This is unexpected. I take it you have news."

"Not good news," Cheney said. "Mind if we come in?"

"Sorry. Please do. I should tell Lauren we have visitors."

From behind him, Lauren spoke up. "I'm here, Hollis. Who's this?"

Hollis said, "Lieutenant Phillips. He was the one who took my report about Fritz being gone."

Cheney introduced himself to Lauren using his first name, which made the encounter seem less formal.

Lauren, in a nightie with a shawl wrapped around her shoulders, had already sunk into a chair. She remained seated and the look she pinned on Cheney was haunted before the first sentence passed his lips. From her perspective, as long as she wasn't told her son was dead, he could be alive and safe.

Cheney said, "I'm sorry to have to tell you this, but Fritz was found up at Yellowweed. It looks like he's been dead for days."

I noticed Cheney had deleted the detail about the septic tank. Dead is dead and there was no point in mentioning that final indignity.

Hollis had retreated behind the wet bar, where he braced himself as though the glittering array of liquor bottles and crystal glassware could form a force field that would protect him from harm.

Clearly, both he and Lauren were prepared for the worst. His stiff posture and Lauren's stricken expression signaled that any show of sympathy would be rebuffed. Cheney fleshed out the circumstances without going into the harrowing details. After all, what did it matter that the body was dumped in a septic tank and covered with dirt and leaves? What possible difference could it make that in the days since he'd died, nature had gone to work dismantling his remains?

Hollis said, "You're positive it's him?"

"We had his photograph on the missing person's flier. In his wallet, there were additional pieces of identification. We'll need one of you to drive out to the morgue at some point and confirm the fact, but there's really no chance of error."

Lauren said, "How . . ." She paused and cleared her throat. "How did he die? And please, no sugarcoating."

"This hasn't been confirmed by the medical examiner, so it's not for publication . . ."

"Of course not," she said.

"It looks like he was shot twice at point-blank range. I doubt he had warning and I'm sure he didn't suffer any pain. We found his sleeping bag where it had been tossed down the hill. No shell casings and no weapon. That's as much as we know at this point. We'll do everything we can to find the person responsible."

Their reaction to the news was muted and they responded with a conversational acceptance. They didn't seem surprised. Hollis went through an explanation of what had gone on in the past few weeks. Lauren offered the occasional correction or comment, but neither exhibited distress. Hollis had been stripped of his anger and hostility. Lauren's hopes had fallen away. Neither one of them could marshal defenses of any kind. Wearily, she covered her face with her hands, but she didn't weep. He remained on the far side of the room, silent for once. He didn't resort to pouring himself a drink. I'll credit him for that.

Hollis said, "His friends will be devastated. They're young and I'm sorry they have to deal with this. He hadn't been home a month, barely time to renew those old bonds."

His words defined the gap between reality and his view of his son. Hollis and Lauren spoke as though Fritz had friends who held him in high regard, which I knew to be untrue. They believed Fritz had been made whole again, that he'd paid for his moral shortcomings and returned to them a wiser man. This was the fiction they lived with, the fable that kept them afloat. I could see how they'd been functioning for years. Fritz was the center of their world. Even the friction between husband and wife had Fritz at its core. His participation in the killing of Sloan Stevens had set the family on a downward spiral and nothing had gone right for them since. Sloan's death had upended the delicate family balance and toppled their expectations. They'd tried to right themselves. They'd done what they could to integrate their errant son into the world he'd left. In truth, Fritz was already out of control and the threat of blackmail had swept away any chance of regaining their equilibrium. This was what they had come to, this loss. Their money and social status didn't render them immune.

Even now they didn't sit together. They didn't touch. They didn't even make eye contact. They would deal with the finality of their son's death in their own way. There was no right or wrong to it. I wasn't a touchy-feely person myself so I didn't fault them for their chilliness, which was in keeping with what I knew of them. I didn't picture them turning to one another for comfort or solace. Fritz's actions had driven a wedge between them and his death would trigger the final blow. It might take six months or a year, but in the end Lauren and Hollis would sever their ties and struggle forward on divergent paths. I was looking at the end of a marriage, the final flicker as that last wee ember winked and went out.

Hollis asked Cheney a few questions, but his curiosity seemed disconnected from any emotion. The conversation shifted to clerical matters: when the ME would perform the autopsy, how soon the results would be made available. Hollis asked about the procedure for reclaiming the body and Cheney told him he could contact a funeral home and have them take care of the details. Hollis mentioned a memorial service, but he wasn't discussing it with Lauren. This was his musing about trivia as it occurred to him. She hadn't moved except to place her cupped hands over her nose and mouth as though recycling her own air was the only hope she had of surviving the suffocating disaster that had erupted in her living room.

The air seemed weighted, as though the forces of gravity had accelerated and we were all anchored to the earth. I thought it was Cheney's place to break the spell, but he seemed to want to keep himself available. The Santa Teresa police are sensitive to occasions like this when a different skill set is required. Neither Lauren nor Hollis gave any sign of recognition, but I appreciated the reservoir of patience Cheney offered.

Finally, he said, "Is there anyone you want us to call?"

Lauren shook her head. "I can't think of anyone. Can you, Hollis?"

"My brother, I suppose, but not at this hour. We can address the subject tomorrow when we have a better sense of where we stand."

Lauren smiled briefly. "I think we should let you go. We appreciate the courtesy of the visit. These can't be easy calls to make."

•

By the time Cheney dropped me back at Henry's, I was so exhausted I could barely see. I've noticed that my homecomings of late have been marked by the unexpected, but for a change, it was quiet. I let myself in the gate. Henry's house was dark and the pup tent was zipped tight so I assumed we were all home and safely tucked in for the night. I let myself into the studio and took a quick look at my answering machine. Nothing from Celeste. I stifled my disappointment. It hadn't even been one full day since I'd called and left my number. For all I knew, she would never contact me, and that was her prerogative.

I locked the door and was on the verge of securing the chain when a horrendous ruckus went up in the backyard. Killer was loose and on some kind of rampage. Apparently, the dog had managed to dig his way out from under the tent. He was still barking savagely as I stuck my head out the door. I reached for the light switch in haste. With one flick, the whole rear portion of the property was bathed in hot light. Henry must have been at Rosie's because under ordinary circumstances, uproar of this sort would have brought him out his back door like a shot, wielding the baseball bat he brandishes to protect hearth and home. No sign of Pearl either, which meant she was probably at Rosie's, too.

Killer lunged at the fence in a frenzy. I'd never seen him in this state. Even on our first meeting when he was holding Henry and Pearl as virtual hostages, his aggression hadn't been this pronounced. There was no point in calling him down. He ran parallel to the shrubbery along the property line, throwing his body at the barrier that separated him from the object of his hostility. I thought about Ned Lowe. How could I not think of Ned? In moments of alarm, in moments when I was on high alert, during times when my interior radar picked up danger of any kind, Ned Lowe was always at the core.

The dog's wrath subsided, leaving him in an agitated state. He circled the yard, his nose close to the ground, making a high whining sound. Occasionally, he barked for effect. I sat down on my step and waited for his circuit to bring him in close. I held out a hand, babbling nonsense, while he trotted back and forth. He was still fulminating and incensed, but he'd probably already lost track of what had set him off. Heart still banging, I fetched a flashlight. I approached the fence, sweeping the wide band of harsh light from side to side. I didn't venture out into the alley and I didn't turn my back on the dark, but I was confident Killer would attack anyone who tried to cause me harm. Satisfied that all was well, I returned to my front door.

I didn't want to leave him alone in the yard, so I invited him in. Gingerly, he stepped over the threshold. This was apparently the most mystifying event in his entire life. He sat at attention, holding his big shaggy head still as he studied the interior. He could probably smell Ed the cat, but surely he was accustomed to him by now. With some uncertainty, he wagged his tail, after which he allowed me to pet and praise him. I filled a bowl with water and marveled at what a mess he made while he was drinking his fill. Afterward, he moved to the door.

He checked to make sure he had my attention, and then he whined softly and scratched at the wood. It was possible he needed to go out and pee on one of Henry's trees, but it seemed more likely he was worried about his dolly. I let him out and he trotted here and there until he found her. He picked her up carefully in his teeth and toted her inside. He deposited her on my living room floor and proceeded to lick her from head to toe. Before I locked up for the night, I left a note on Henry's back door and a second note pinned to the tent, advising them that Killer and his baby had been invited for a sleepover that night. It was the best rest I'd had in recent memory.

35

Friday, October 6, 1989

Friday morning, while I ate my Cheerios, my phone rang. I crossed to the desk and picked up the handset.

In response to my greeting, there was silence.

Ordinarily, calls at this hour involve a lot of heavy breathing on the other end and my usual response is to activate a tinnitus-inducing air horn and then hang up. In this case, I waited, my senses sharpening. "This is Kinsey."

"You left me a message."

A woman's voice, and I thought it safe to assume this was Ned Lowe's ex-wife Celeste, though I was feeling so protective of her that I redacted her name from my mental directory.

"I did, and thanks for returning my call."

"What happened to Phyllis?"

"Ned pounded the shit out of her trying to track you down. He failed, but he hasn't given up."

"How's she doing?"

"She's in the hospital and the care she's receiving is excellent. Her doctor seems optimistic."

"Thank god for that. Ned's still on the loose?"

"I'm afraid so."

"You know I stole the keepsakes that tie him to those poor girls he killed, which is why I'm being so paranoid. I won't feel safe until the package is in the hands of the police."

"I'm with you on that. How do you want to go about it?"

"I can't risk putting his souvenirs in the mail. Too many things can go wrong. These may well be the only tangible items that connect him to those killings."

"What about entrusting the package to the closest law enforcement agency in your area—"

"No, no," she cut in. "Documents get lost. Evidence disappears. Some detective ends up with the package on her desk and sticks it in her bottom drawer because she doesn't know what else to do with it. I can't take that chance."

"You've given this more thought than I have, so you tell me."

"I'm willing to fly to Santa Teresa. I've checked and there are flights available on four different airlines, connecting by way of five different hubs. Once I set up the reservation, I'll call with the details and you can pick me up at the airport. I want you waiting outside where I can see you."

"I can do that. And then what?"

"You'll drive me to the police station and I'll deliver the package to the officer who's been working the case. Lieutenant Phillips?"

"That's right. He'll be thrilled."

"Let's hope so. Afterward, you can return me to the airport and walk me to my gate. Once I'm through security, I should be fine."

"When?"

"Tomorrow, if you're available."

"I'll make myself available. You're talking about Saturday," I said.

"That's right."

"Do you remember what I look like?"

"I do. What about you? Will you recognize me?" she asked.

"Unless you've altered your appearance."

"I'm the same."

"Me, too. I'll wait to hear from you."

"I'll call as soon as I have the tickets in hand."

I hadn't leveled with her about how Ned had picked up Phyllis's new address and I was happy she hadn't asked. If pressed, I'd have felt honor-bound to lay out the whole creepy account of his camping under my office, with access to every call I made. I'd done what I could to tighten security since then, well aware of how relentless he was in the pursuit of his goal. He wanted his trinkets, and if he was thwarted, he'd go after one of us instead. Better me than her. I still had a score to settle with him in any event.

When I reached the office, I put a call through to Cheney at the Santa Teresa Police Department. When he picked up and identified himself, I said, "Do you have a few minutes?"

"I was just about to call you and ask the same thing. You want to pop over to my spacious cubicle?"

"Why don't we meet somewhere in between?"

"The sunken garden at the courthouse?"

"Perfect. I'll see you there."

The walk took roughly six minutes. Coming from my office, my route had me passing the police station and I half expected Cheney to join me as I crossed Santa Teresa Street at the light. The courthouse takes up an entire city block, with the sunken garden tucked away in the lee of the main structure, which boasts a tower that once housed the county jail. The architectural style of the original courthouse was Greek Revival, but that building was severely damaged in an earthquake in 1925. Construction of the current courthouse, built in the Spanish Colonial Revival style, was started in 1926 and completed in 1929, two months before the stock market crashed. The thick white walls, red-tile roof, deeply recessed windows, and wrought-iron grilles are typical of many Santa Teresa buildings of that era. Charles Willard Moore, a prominent architect, called it the "grandest Spanish Colonial Revival structure ever built."

I settled on the wide stone steps, which were chilly in the shade of the two-story building behind me. The drought had browned out most of the sweeping lawns, but the palms, while stressed, seemed to be holding up well. From the right, I watched Cheney cross the grass, his head bent, his hands in his pockets. He looked up and when he saw me, he smiled and lifted a hand. I tried seeing him as I would if I hadn't known him for so many years. Height, five foot eleven, medium build with curly brown hair. I wondered if Anna's report was true, that he was learning to finish projects. It seemed odd that the disconnect between his intentions and their manifest completion had bothered me so much. During our romantic entanglement, I remembered being irritated by rooms half-painted, perpetual drop cloths down so long they resembled wall-to-wall carpeting. It annoyed me that door and window hardware was always missing, the floors littered with electric drills and nail guns. Now I couldn't imagine reacting at all, which said more about me than it did about him. I was a neatnik and a control freak, traits that others don't find restful as a rule.

He settled on the step beside me and we exchanged pleasantries.

"You have news for me?" he asked.

"More like an update."

I laid out the circumstances under which I'd picked up Celeste's alias and her out-of-state phone number. I was forced to loop back in time and include a quick summary of my original call to Phyllis, Ned's eavesdropping, and the beating he'd administered in his attempt to get his hands on Celeste's contact information.

"You've talked to her?"

"I left her a message and she returned my call this morning. She's prepared to deliver Ned's souvenirs. Her plan is to fly in tomorrow. I've agreed to pick her up at the airport and drive her to the station. Once she's handed over the package, I'll take her back to the airport and put her on a plane."

"All of this to avoid Ned?"

"Absolutely. The man's a maniac. Both of us credit him with supernatural powers. Somehow he's managed to drop off the radar again. I don't know how he does it."

"He'll surface at some point. He can't run forever, and how many places can he hide? If you're lucky, his suppurating wound will throw him into sepsis and he'll die before sundown."

"This is giving me a stomachache," I said. "What did you want to talk to me about?"

"I'll get to that," he said. "First, I think we should talk about Anna's situation. I know you were convinced the two of us were having an affair."

"I was *not*."

"Yes, you were."

"You don't owe me any explanations," I said.

"Just let me say this. I felt bad about the deception, but it was the only thing we could think to do until we knew where things stood."

"Fine. I understand. Not to worry."

"Come on. It bothered you. I could see the looks you were giving us."

"I wasn't giving you *looks*," I said.

He smiled. "Are you being defensive or indignant?"

"Is there a difference?"

"Big one. Defensive is I'm dead right and you're denying it out of embarrassment. Indignant is I'm dead right and you're pissed that I saw right through you."

"Indignant then, or maybe both."

"I can make it up to you. I have information. This will probably appear in the paper anyway, but keep it to yourself. Burgess is a bit of a hardass."

"Scout's honor."

"One of the evidence techs came across a handgun up at Yellowweed. It was in the scrub off the beaten path, so it looks like the shooter tossed it."

"Thinking it wouldn't come to light?"

"Not sure. It's an Astra Constable."

"The one that killed Sloan?"

"No doubt in my mind. We'll know for sure when ballistics have been run. Probably killed Fritz McCabe as well."

"That gun's been missing for years."

"Right. Seems pointed that it would magically reappear, just when we're beginning our investigation."

"It's good news, though, isn't it? To finally have the murder weapon?"

"Theoretically," he said. "Three possible explanations. The shooter dropped it, tossed it, or planted it."

"What if someone else had the gun and dumped it?"

"Make that four possibilities."

"You think it's Austin."

"I'm not ruling him out, but I don't get it. If he's the extortionist, why kill the golden goose? I don't like the timing and I don't like the convenience of the Astra dropping in our laps."

"I thought the gun was registered to Austin's dad. Have you talked to him?"

"Burgess is doing that. He'll claim ignorance."

"Well, you know he didn't go up there and shoot anyone," I said.

"What bugs me is the motivation. You're the one who said it wasn't robbery."

"Not if Fritz was happy to hand over the money. His pal Stringer is convinced he knew the guy. I wondered if it might be someone he knew at CYA."

"That's worth looking into."

"You said 'if' this was the extortionist. Who else might it be?"

"If I knew the answer to that, I wouldn't be sitting here." He held up a finger. "One more item of note. ME found traces of a white powder on Fritz's clothing. No idea what it is yet, but they're working on it."

"Powder as in cocaine?"

"No point in guessing. The lab report should get back to us sometime today."

My office phone rang as I was unlocking the door. I was in my usual panic about entering the alarm code in the twenty seconds allotted, which is ample unless you feel you're working against the clock. I successfully achieved entry and reached my desk on the fourth ring. I picked up the handset in haste and identified myself.

"Kinsey, this is Erroll."

I said, "Oh lord. Is everything okay?"

"Sure, sure. I'm sorry to scare you. Phyllis is doing fine. She tires easily and she has a long way to go yet, but she's in good shape compared to where she was. Thing is, she wants to see you. She's been asking for the past two days and made me promise I'd call. Any chance you can get down here?"

"I've got time this afternoon. Any idea what's bothering her?"

"All she says is she wants to talk to you."

For much of the drive to Perdido, I let my mind go blank. The day was typical of California: clear blue skies, temperatures in the seventies, a light breeze that scuffed at the surf, kicking up a spray as fine as dust. The five offshore islands were clear enough to count the ridges on the range of hills: Anacapa, Santa Barbara, San Miguel, Santa Rosa, and Santa Cruz make up the Channel Islands National Park, which offers hiking, camping, snorkeling, kayaking, and bird-watching—all activities that had so little appeal, I'd cut my wrists first. San Miguel, in particular, has thirty-mile-an-hour winds that render the place especially hostile—or so I've heard, never having made the trip. None of the islands provide water, goods, services, public phones, indoor toilets, or overnight accommodations. Visitors are expected to bring all their own food and supplies. Why is that fun?

The twenty-six miles sped by while I entertained myself with foul thoughts. I was reassured by the uniformed woman posted outside Phyllis's hospital room, but nothing prepared me for the sight of her. She seemed shrunken. Her dark hair was wispy and unkempt, which a hospital stay would do for anyone. Her veins could have been applied with pale blue transfer tissue on arms that were painfully thin. She had an IV line in her right arm and her left in a cast. Her left eye was still so swollen she looked like the prize fighter who'd just lost in the ring. I could see the bony substructure of her badly bruised left cheek, which might never be smooth again.

The nurse cautioned me to keep my visit brief.

I pulled a chair close to the bed and held Phyllis's hand, which was as cold and as light as snow. "What's going on, babe?"

Her voice was raspy from disuse and the wired jaw caused her to speak through clenched teeth. "I told Ned. When he beat me."

"Told him what?"

"Sent you Celeste's name and location. Thought I was lying . . ."

"Ah. Which is why he came back to the condo to search the remaining boxes."

She nodded as best she could. "Worried sick," she murmured.

"I am, too. Turns out he set up housekeeping under my office and jerry-rigged the phone so he could listen to my calls. That's how he picked up your address. It never occurred to me he'd found a way to breach my safeguards. Happily, I managed to fire several shots at him, nicking him at least once if his shrieks were at all indicative."

"He wants Celeste."

"I'm aware of that. I've already talked to her and we have a plan in place. She's flying in from an unknown location. As soon as she has reservations, she'll let me know what time her flight gets in. I'll meet her and then take her to the police station, where she'll hand-deliver the evidence to Lieutenant Phillips, who's in charge of the case. After that, I'll take her back to the airport and send her on her way."

"Dangerous."

"I understand your concern, but I don't see how he could get wind of it. She's being extremely cautious."

"No, no. Tell her don't come."

"That may not be possible, but I'll do what I can."

On the return drive to Santa Teresa, I wondered if there was really any way to effect a change of plans. I had no idea where Celeste was coming from or where she'd pick up her connecting flight. My only hope was to catch her before she left. The minute I got home, I went straight to the phone. My message light was blinking and I pressed Play with dread. One sentence: "Arrive 1:15 on agreed date."

I retrieved the fold of paper from between my boobs and punched in her number. The line rang and rang and rang. This time there wasn't any reassuring beep to indicate that I could leave a message. I let the line ring fifteen more times and then I hung up. So much for warning her off or canceling her trip to Santa Teresa. I could feel my stomach churn. Phyllis's anxiety was contagious, but I couldn't see where the plan could go wrong. Wherever Ned was holed up, I didn't see how he could intercept either one of us. We'd just have to keep moving forward and hope for the best. As plans go, "hoping for the best" is not a good one.

36

IRIS AND JOEY

Friday, October 6, 1989

Joey, barefoot and in his robe, brought in the morning paper and tossed it on the counter between the kitchen and the living room. He continued into the bedroom, where he'd strip and take his shower. In the kitchen, Iris poured a cup of coffee as the toaster popped up. She put the toast on a plate, buttered it, and carried it to the table, snagging the folded newspaper before she sat down. She opened the *Dispatch*, took one look at the front page, and screamed. She jumped up, the chair tipping dangerously before it righted itself.

"*Joey!* Oh my god, oh my *god*!"

Joey appeared in the doorway in his boxer shorts. He was accustomed to her hysteria and wouldn't address the shrieking until he knew what she was going on about. "What?" He knew he sounded faintly annoyed.

She pointed at the paper.

"What!"

"Fritz is dead. Look at this. He was found yesterday up at Yellowweed. He was shot to death."

Joey said, "That can't be."

Her hand shook as she held out the paper. He sat down and scanned the article, then opened the front section to the continued coverage on an inside page.

Joey said, "Jesus. This is terrible. Wonder what happened?"

"We're screwed. This is the end of us. Oh my god," she said. She sank into a chair, white-faced. She crossed her arms, hugging herself. "What do we do now?"

Joey said, "Hang on a sec."

He read the article again carefully. "This is bad. Poor guy."

"Should we turn ourselves in?"

Joey frowned. "What for? We didn't kill him."

"But what if they pick up on the blackmail and trace it back to us?"

"Why would it occur to anyone to look at us? He's a pal. We're his best buds. How're they going to trace anything?"

"I don't know, but suppose they do. Maybe it's better to go to them before they come to us. If they link us to the blackmail, we'll be prime suspects. The only suspects."

"Calm down. Just settle down and let's take a look at this. Sure, we *knew* about the blackmail. Fritz told everyone, so that in itself wouldn't be significant."

"They have the message you left. That's your voice on the machine."

"They don't know that. It could be anyone. Austin, for instance."

"What if they trace the call?"

"They can't trace a call from a recording," he said, though he was not at all sure of it. Technology was a wonder these days. No telling what forensics could do.

Iris leaned forward and hung her head between her knees as though she might pass out. "It's over. We've had it. If we don't go to them and they figure it out, how's it going to look? Like we're guilty of murder!"

"But we're not. We didn't do anything. Paper says

he's probably been dead for close to a week and we were nowhere near Yellowweed. We don't even own a gun, so how could it be us?"

"He called us at home. Remember?"

"But we didn't see him. We didn't connect up with him. We ate dinner at my stepmom's. She can vouch for us."

"What if they pull phone records? How are you going to explain his call?"

"We don't deny the call. I'll tell 'em how it went. He said he was going to meet the guy and wanted us to come along—"

"Why would he ask us?"

"He was nervous. He needed moral support. We told him not to do it and he got pissed off. That's all it is. That's as much as we know. We advised against it. We told him not to do it. We had no idea he'd actually *meet* the guy. Right?"

Her mouth trembled and her faced tightened into an unbecoming mask.

Joey put a hand on her shoulder. "Hey, babe. It's okay. Don't go all wonky on me."

He hunkered down beside her and rubbed her back, offering consolation, which he knew was falling on deaf ears. "Hey. Look at me."

He waited until she managed to get control of herself. She breathed deeply. She patted herself on the chest and looked at him.

Joey snagged a tissue from the box on the end table and held it out. She took it gratefully and blew her nose.

Joey went on. "We didn't do anything. We're in this together. We didn't know he was dead until this morning's paper. Isn't that the truth?"

She nodded.

"We go to them and then what? They don't have any reason to think we're involved. There's nothing that ties us to Yellowweed. Margaret will vouch for us and it's the truth. If we admit to the blackmail, all we've done is expose ourselves to scrutiny."

He studied her face, which had the haunted look of the doomed.

Iris finally nodded, calmer but still anxious. She twisted the soggy tissue in her hands. "What if they figure it out?"

"What if they don't?"

"How is it going to look if they find out we sent the note and the tape? What if you left fingerprints—"

"I didn't. I was too smart for that," he said. "Anyway, if we have to, we'll admit that much and say we didn't follow up. We dropped the whole thing because we knew we'd made a mistake. What's the worst that could happen?"

She shook her head mutely, imagining hideous possibilities that she didn't dare verbalize.

"The worst is if we pipe up and confess, which would make it look like we're guilty when we're not. We backed away. Remember that? Okay, so we're guilty of threats, but that's not against the law. Well, it *is* against the law, but shit. We didn't *kill* anyone. You gotta trust me. You trust me?"

Iris nodded, miserable.

Joey placed his hands over hers. "Here's the deal. We go about our business like nothing's wrong. Anybody asks us, we read about it in the paper, and of course we're devastated. He's a friend of ours and we feel terrible, but that's all."

"I don't want to go to work. I can call in sick—"

"No. Out of the question. That would not look good."

"I can tell Karen I'm upset because my friend was killed. She'd understand."

Joey shook his head. "We do what we always do. Business as usual and it's nothing to worry about. We'll see how the day plays out and we'll talk about it again tonight. Can you manage that?"

Iris nodded, her eyes pinned on his like a pup in obedience training.

Joey dropped her off downtown and she opened the shop. She put her purse under the counter and turned to the mirror on the wall behind her, leaning close so she could assess her reflection. She looked bad: no makeup, her eyes swollen from weeping, her hair straying out of the combs she wore. She paused to rearrange two combs and a barrette, which helped a bit. She sniffed. She took a big breath and let it out, emitting a soft sound . . . leftover grief, not for Fritz but for the trouble they were in. How could the authorities find out? She and Joey hadn't *done* anything. Okay, a note demanding money, which for all anyone knew could have been a joke.

She heard the bell jingle over the front door.

The man who entered was in his late fifties. He wore a dark sport coat with a red polo shirt under it. He looked like an aging athlete . . . tennis or golf . . . because the outdoor activity had tanned his skin to a warm brown. Receding hairline, his forehead speckled with irregular spots of sun damage. The fringe of gray hair that remained was cut close. He reminded her of her Uncle Jerry, same age, same build. She was her uncle's favorite.

He let his gaze travel around the store, taking in the racks of vintage clothing, the glass showcases filled with additional merchandise. She knew the air in the shop had a distinct scent to it. He wandered in her direction, in no particular hurry. When he was close enough, she saw that his dark lashes were so long it looked like he'd bought them at a drugstore and glued them into place. His lips were thin and formed a wavy line that suggested he was capable of smiling though she saw no other evidence of it. Maybe he was buying something for his wife. She checked his left hand. No wedding ring, but old guys didn't always wear them.

"May I help you?"

"You're Iris Lehmann?"

She thought, *Shit, not this again.* Instantly, her smile became flat and fake, which she hoped wasn't obvious.

He removed a leather case and exhibited his badge: a star with seven points and a circle in the center. A banner read "Lieutenant" with "Deputy Sheriff' on the top half of the curve and "Santa Teresa County" on the lower half. There was some sort of raised image in the center, but he tucked it away before she could determine what it was. He said, "Detective Burgess. County sheriff's office."

Her stomach sank. If he was here to ask about Fritz, the blackmail scheme was bound to come up. Her mind went blank. Her lips felt like they were stuck together. How would she react if she had no direct knowledge?

"May I help you?"

She winced. She'd just asked the same inane question.

"Hope so. We're contacting friends of Fritz McCabe . . ."

"I read about him in the paper. It's horrible what happened. I was shocked."

"Sad to lose someone so young," he said. "I can imagine what you must be feeling." He watched her as though he imagined many other things as well, none of them favorable to her. She realized he'd taken out a pocket-size spiral-bound notebook. She watched him flip to the first blank page. "We're trying to piece together his actions in the days before his death. Do you remember the last contact you had with him?"

"Well, mm, let's see . . ." She looked up as though trying to recall their last conversation. "I believe we spoke to him last week. By phone. We didn't see him. This is my fiancé and me. We live together so when Fritz called, Joey talked to him."

"What day was that?"

Iris shook her head in the negative and then decided it would be more realistic if she added a detail. "I'd say Wednesday or Thursday. Toward the end of the week. I don't think it was Friday. Joey took the call."

"You have any idea what they talked about?"

"I don't. Maybe you could ask Joey. Or I can ask and get back to you."

"He didn't fill you in on the subject of the conversation?"

"I had to get to work so there wasn't time."

He flipped back a page or two as though to refresh his memory. "You know about the blackmail business," he said, stating it as a given.

She hesitated. "I knew a little bit about it, but not a lot. I mean, not the details."

His frown was barely perceptible. "I was under the impression Fritz broadcast the information to all his friends. I'm surprised he'd leave you out."

"No, no. He *told* us, but then he made us all swear we'd keep it to ourselves. I don't think I should talk about it, out of respect for him."

His smile seemed thin. "I appreciate your discretion and I'm sure he would, too." There was a pause. She thought he'd finished speaking. Then he said, "On the other hand, with him gone, those same restraints wouldn't apply, would they? Especially when the facts might shed light on his death. If you think I'm out of line, just say so. I don't want you to talk about this if you're uncomfortable."

"Why would I be uncomfortable?"

"I don't know, Iris. You tell me."

"I'm fine. This is fine. Go ahead."

"You mentioned Friday. Can you tell me how you spent the day?"

She blinked. "I don't remember. I probably came to work as usual. We must have done something, but I can't recall. I could ask Joey. Really, I don't know about any of this. I wish I could be helpful, but I can't think of anything."

"What about Friday night?"

Iris shook her head. "Sorry, I'm drawing a complete blank."

"I understand you spotted Austin Brown a couple of times last week. Why don't you start with that?"

Iris wasn't prepared for the change of subject, but she could see the pit she was digging for herself. The Austin sightings were pure fabrication. "I'm not sure it was him. I can't swear. I don't want to be quoted in case I made a mistake."

"What about the blackmail scheme? How much were you told?"

Back to that again.

"Not much." She licked her lips. Her mind went blank again. Obviously, she and Joey knew far more about the blackmail scheme than anyone else. So how much knowledge would seem reasonable for an innocent bystander?

"Take your time," he said.

She cleared her throat. "We knew a copy of a tape was sent to the McCabes along with the note. Fritz told us that."

He shook his head, his smile weary. "The infamous tape. Creeps into the conversation everywhere you turn and why is that?" The question sounded rhetorical, but he was looking at her as though he expected a reply.

"No idea. Really."

He made a note. "But you did know the tape was the leverage in the extortion scheme."

"Everyone knew that."

"What do you think made the tape so dangerous that someone would be willing to pay thousands to keep it away from the police?"

"I wouldn't know. I never saw it."

Mistake, mistake. Of course she'd seen it. The minute Joey found it behind the vent cover that shielded the heater opening in the boys' bathroom at Margaret's house. She'd seen it six times if she remembered correctly. There she was, lolling about big as life, naked with her tits splayed flat, completely out of it, and sloppy drunk while Fritz and company assaulted her with whatever came to hand.

"Not a problem," he said mildly. "We'll be screening it later. The chief might hold it for the squad meeting first thing tomorrow morning. Fritz didn't tell you anything about the subject matter?" He watched her, his pen poised.

She flicked a look to his notebook, trying to see what he'd written so far.

How could she answer a question about subject matter? She couldn't claim ignorance when he'd be seeing it himself. The notion of him watching Troy go at her, his back turned to the camera, buttocks squeezing together every time he thrust himself into her. Jesus. And Fritz standing by, twisting his imaginary mustache while he held up the can of Crisco? How many officers would be sitting there? Why not rent out a theater and charge admission?

She felt her cheeks flame. He'd been there three minutes and he'd already backed her into a corner. She'd never been so frightened in her life. She knew how these things went. You said one thing and you couldn't go back later and say something else. Contradict yourself and everyone assumed you were lying. "Do I have to answer questions like that without an attorney present?"

His brown gaze settled on her squarely. Now she had his full attention. So much like her Uncle Jerry. This man had the same gentle air about him, except now he sounded puzzled and disappointed. "Why would you need an attorney? This is a preliminary chat. Information gathering. We can halt the conversation right here if you think the implications would be damaging. Something going on I don't know about?"

"I don't want to talk to you."

He closed his notebook and slipped it into his pocket. He took out a business card and handed it to her. "How about I'll catch up with you later? Call me if you change your mind. I appreciate your time. You take care."

As soon as the door closed behind him, she picked up the phone and punched in Joey's number at the construction trailer. The secretary picked up and said he was out on a job site and wouldn't be back until noon. Iris left a message for him to call her and then she burst into tears. This was only going to get worse. What the hell would happen to them?

37

THE EXECUTION

June 1979

Trudging up the mountain path in the dark, Fritz felt sick, wondering how the situation had spiraled so far out of control. Somehow he was caught up in the thick of it when the quarrel wasn't even his. If Austin had a bone to pick with Sloan, how had the rest of them been sucked in? Austin already thought Fritz was an idiot and the judgment made him act like one. It was like his mom telling him what a bad driver he was. The minute she got in the car with him, he'd do something stupid, like back into a garbage can. She didn't have to say a word. From that moment on, he'd catch a tire on the curb going around a corner or he'd be looking somewhere else when the stoplight turned yellow and she'd gasp, brace herself on the dashboard, and point at the oncoming car he was unaware of.

Troy had been smart enough to go on strike. He'd driven them as far as the trailhead and then refused to accompany them further. Fritz wasn't crazy about the expedition himself, but it was probably too late to protest. Even if he had the courage, what was he going to say? Austin would never let him off the hook. At the party, Fritz had tossed down five glasses of pink punch and two of green and had barfed it all back up while pretending to go outdoors to take a leak. Now his head was pounding and if he weren't so afraid he'd make a fool of himself, he'd hike back down to the road. He and Troy could ditch the others while Austin did whatever he did. It would doubtless entail humiliation of some kind for any fool unlucky enough to be present. Fritz would have given anything to be able to stretch out in the truck bed and put his jacket over his head, but it was easier to keep on walking, looking for the perfect moment to stand up for himself. Right. Like *that* was going to happen.

He could hear the others scrambling up the trail behind him. Austin carried a flashlight, but its primary purpose was to guide his own passage, leaving the three of them to cuss and complain. The uneven path was little-used, with fallen branches snapping underfoot. He focused on the irregular terrain, working hard to maintain his balance. He wasn't in good shape, so he was panting heavily and he'd broken a sweat.

"I used to go to camp up here when I was a Boy Scout. I don't know what we're doing, man. Place is a shit hole," he said.

"Shut up, Fritz." As usual, Austin's voice was loaded with contempt.

"I'm serious. Ask me, this is stupid."

"No one asked you."

A moment later, Fritz stumbled and the gun went off. He'd squeezed the trigger involuntarily, but of course Austin was all over him, getting right in his face. "What's the matter with you? Put the safety on! You could have killed one of us."

"But—"

"Don't say 'but' to me, you ding-dong."

Fritz turned away, but Austin cuffed his shoulder.

"Hey. Don't turn your back on me. I gave you an order and I expect acknowledgment. Put. The. Safety. On."

"You said take the safety off. You took it off yourself when we were at the cabin." Fritz knew his voice was shrill, but he was tired of being blamed for everything.

"Does this look like a cabin to you?" Austin yelled. "This is the fucking wilderness. We're climbing a trail in the dead of night. You fall down with the safety off and you'll shoot yourself, assuming you don't shoot one of us first. Here. Gimme that."

Austin yanked the Astra from his hand and made a big display of securing the trigger lock.

Fritz thought Austin's action was far more dangerous, grabbing the weapon and pointing it every which way. At least Fritz had kept the barrel aimed at the dirt path so when the gun as good as fired itself, he wasn't pointing it at anyone.

Sloan had yelped once when the gun went off, but aside from that she'd been quiet. Fritz figured she'd adopted the same attitude he had. Best to shut up and do as they were told or the situation would only get worse. If they played along, maybe the whole deal would blow over and they could all go home.

They reached the mesa, where nature had flattened the ground to form an enormous clearing. The cabins, as well as the old assembly and dining halls, had been abandoned years before and the county was in the process of bulldozing the dilapidated structures and using the detritus to fill the old swimming pool, which had been drained but was still considered an attractive nuisance. An excavator had been parked near a dumpster, where some of the shattered lumber had been piled. In the few buildings that remained standing, the windows were boarded over; porch planks rotted through. Even in its heyday, the structures were "rustic," which is to say badly heated and poorly lighted. Fritz still shuddered when he remembered the wolf spiders: big, very black, and very fast. By night, it was cockroaches. After lights-out, when the boys were settled, one of the older campers would yell, "Death Trap!" and flip on the light. Insects of every size and description would dart off while everyone else banged at them with tennis shoes. Another way they amused themselves was to toss lighted cherry bombs in the septic tank.

Fritz and Bayard were both winded from the climb and Austin wasn't in much better shape. Sloan was the only one who responded to physical exertion with exuberance. The four of them stood there, chests heaving, while Austin flashed his light across the wooden buildings. Everything looked dead except for the weeds and poisoned ivy, which seemed to be flourishing. It reminded Fritz of a movie set where a special machine had been used to spray fake cobwebs across the doorways. Austin crossed to the semicircle of dirt in front of the assembly hall. The makeshift amphitheater was used by campers when they gathered for nature talks. Crudely constructed benches, usually stacked in front of the dining hall, could be dragged into service. Fritz always stood at the rear so he could disappear once the program was underway.

A low mist drifted across the landscape, but the sky was crystal clear above them, stars everywhere. On the far side of the mountain range, a dull glow formed a fan shape against the night sky—light pollution compliments of the city of Santa Teresa. It was cold and Sloan, in her makeshift outfit, crossed her arms to keep warm. They were all waiting for their cues while Austin extended the silence for maximum dramatic effect.

Fritz tucked his hands in his armpits for warmth and flicked a look at Bayard. "I don't like this."

"Me, neither."

Austin picked up on the complaint. "Bayard, you know what? I don't care if you like it or not."

"I'm with him. I don't want any part of it. You let Troy beg off so why not us? This isn't even our deal," Bayard said.

Austin's tone turned liquid, soft and seductive. "Are you refusing, pal?"

Bayard said, "Come on, Austin. Let's dispense with the horseshit and get the hell out of here."

Austin said, "I'm not done yet."

"Yeah, well, we are."

Austin ignored him. "Hey, Sloan. What do you think this is?"

He angled his flashlight beam to illuminate a trench three feet deep and six feet long. A shovel and a pickax rested on the loosely packed soil nearby. He shifted the flashlight beam to a spot under his chin, which threw his features into sinister shadows. It was something kids did at night to spook each other.

"Like you're so scary," she said.

"I asked you a question. What do you think that is?" He returned the beam to the trench.

Sloan put a hand to her cheek. "Gee, Austin. I don't know. It looks like someone dug a hole in the ground."

"Why don't you lie down in it and see if it's your size?"

"Not funny."

"You don't think so?" he asked. "I think it's a riot."

"You have a twisted sense of humor."

"But a strong sense of fair play."

Sloan laughed. "Is that how you see yourself? A guy with integrity? A man of honor? Because I know better and so do you."

Austin said, "You know, I'm sorry now I dated you. I can't remember what I was thinking."

"Maybe you were thinking I was such a pig I'd be grateful for the attention."

"Good one. That did cross my mind now you mention it," he said.

"Let me tell you what crossed *my* mind. All this bad blood between us goes back to the infamous cheating incident when somebody wrote the note to Mr. Lucas. You claimed I was guilty when you knew damn well I wasn't."

"You were the one who got on her high horse when you heard Poppy and Troy intended to use the stolen test answers. You begged them not to do it. Next thing you know, Mr. Lucas gets a note spilling the beans."

"You wrote that note."

Austin laughed in disbelief. "I did? Where'd you come up with that screwball idea? I think you've been smoking too much dope."

"How about this? There are five juniors up for the Albert Climping Memorial Award, including you, me, and Troy. Once Troy's caught cheating, he's out of the running. Then you point a finger at me, which puts me out of the running as well. The teachers are supposed to be unbiased, but it's their vote and once they hear the rumor about me, my goose is cooked. You're the one who benefits."

"Are you forgetting Betsy and Patti?"

"They're not serious contenders. They're window dressing, which you know as well as I do. Troy and I are your competition and you can't stand to lose. You want that award so badly, you'd do anything."

"I can't believe you're accusing me."

"Well, I am."

Austin's voice dropped. "Take it back."

"No. Nuhn-un. No can do."

"Are you out of your mind? First you threaten me with the tape and now you pull this? You can't accuse me of shit like this."

"I just did. What do you think, Bayard? Does it sound reasonable to you?"

Bayard looked from Sloan to Austin. "Actually, it does. I never thought of you as a tattletale until Austin made his claim."

"Fritz?" Sloan asked, turning to him. "What's your inclination? Is Austin guilty or innocent?"

"Hey. I want no part of this," Fritz said. He laughed uneasily, hoping Austin wouldn't rope him in any further.

Austin leaned down to the dirt piled up near the hole he'd dug. He grabbed a handful of soil. "Eat this."

Sloan laughed, incredulous. "I'm not going to eat that. You eat it."

Austin grabbed Sloan by the hair and yanked her head back. He lifted his fist and tried to force dirt into her mouth, but she shifted her head so the dirt tumbled to the ground. Sloan made a sound in her throat and Fritz felt his heart start to bang in his chest. It was clear Austin hadn't pictured this part of the confrontation. He probably imagined himself prevailing, stronger, quicker, and more dominant, but Sloan had a will of her own. She was accustomed to contact sports and she wasn't afraid of impact. She kicked at him, a swift, savage delivery with the toe of her hard-soled shoe striking him in the shin. Fritz backed up a step, not wanting to get caught in the cross fire.

Bayard had both hands in front of him, gesturing downward as though he could diminish the conflict by sheer dint of will. "Hey, come on. Don't do this. Let it go. Let's everyone just calm down, okay?"

Fritz was spellbound, paralyzed by indecision. Violence was usually directed at him by reason of his father's temper and his quickness to strike out. His automatic response was an accelerated heartbeat, which is what happened now. Fight or flight were two options, but Fritz was in the habit of rolling over and playing dead.

A silence fell as Austin and Sloan fought on with a series of grunts and the occasional cry of pain. Sloan was getting the best of him, but Austin was tough in his way and not one to give up. The two paused. Sloan was panting, blood trickling from her nose. Field sports had taught her to fight hard and she wasn't afraid of pain. Austin assumed in a pitched battle with a girl, he'd have size and weight on his side, but Sloan was strong and well-muscled. And she was mad. Austin was sweating with the effort. He reached down for a broken limb and smacked it against a rock. The branch splintered, leaving a gaping wound of raw wood. He was upping the ante, ratcheting up the game. Sloan backed up and then got a running start, heading straight at him at full speed. She lowered her shoulder and plowed into him before Austin could put up a defense. She was on her feet in an instant and when he regained his balance, she shoved him hard. He went down on his butt and Sloan started to run.

Austin screamed, "Fritz!"

Sloan reached the near side of the clearing where a tangle of construction debris provided screening. Fritz didn't have time to think. A wonderful clarity sharpened his perception. The darkness limited the visual information coming to him, so all he had to work with was the sound of her running. He felt expansive, puffed up, all instinct with no time to reflect. For a moment, he was free of self-consciousness, free of worry, free of any concern about other people's opinion of him. He knew this was what combat felt like: intense, immediate, and base. Austin seemed to fade, Bayard disappeared, and Fritz was left with a thrilling sense of the present. Sloan pounded into the woods.

Fritz could see that she'd disappear within another ten or fifteen steps. His hands were shaking so hard the gun nearly flipped out of his grasp. He pushed off the safety and chambered a round. He held the gun in both hands, doing a fair imitation of a police officer facing a thug. He fired, bearing down with his trigger finger so the bullets sprayed the underbrush, cutting a line as though someone were trimming brush with a weed whacker. In the darkness, he could hear Sloan running and he followed the sound of her crashing across the terrain, gasping now and then as though she might have tripped. He could hear her humming with fear and sorrow. He zeroed in on the noise, anticipating her path. She didn't even know enough to zigzag like they did in the movies, dodging bullets, as though that were possible in real life. He wasn't thinking about what he did, only that he was suddenly competent, filled with a feeling of power. There was a brief shriek and then he heard her hit the ground. Silence after that. He turned to Austin with a flash of triumph. "Whoa, baby! We did it, man."

Exhilarated, he looked at the Astra in wonder. "Wow! This thing has power. Did you see that? I thought it would jump out of my hand. That is so cool." He whooped with excitement, reveling in his accomplishment. He glanced at Austin, expecting an "Attaboy!"

"Shit. What did you do that for? Now we're screwed."

Caught off guard, Fritz stared at Austin with bewilderment. "You told me to shoot."

"I did not! I wanted you to stop her, not shoot her. Now get out there and find her and we'll see how bad she's hurt. Here, take this." He passed Fritz the flashlight and gave him a push.

"I couldn't have hit her. I was just 'bang, bang, bang,' you know? I don't think I scored."

"What, like you won a stuffed monkey? You better hope not."

"But she's faking, right?"

"Would you get out there and find her! Shit, I can't believe you're this incompetent. What are you looking at me for? Go see if she's okay."

Fritz turned on the flashlight. The beam was strong and seemed to wash all of the color from the landscape. He was hyped. Adrenaline flooded his system and he felt charged with excitement. It was an energy he'd never experienced before, what he imagined cocaine or heroin must be like. His whole body felt light, like he'd levitated, like he was outside himself looking on. Austin was nothing. He was nobody. Fritz was larger than life.

His heart thundered in his ears. He crossed the clearing, following the path Sloan had taken. She was faking, pretending to be hit as a ruse to persuade him to quit firing. She was fast and he had no experience with a firearm. She could be easing through the underbrush at that very moment, slyly moving herself out of range. He wasn't even sure how he'd find her in the dark.

He waded into the bushes, which were dry and thick, snagging on his pant legs. The ground was cushioned with pine needles, a dense carpet of rotting plant material that slowed his progress. He was almost sure Sloan pretended to be hit so he'd quit shooting. That's what he'd have done in her place. He saw the low-hanging tree limbs snapped off and broken branches she'd trampled as she ran. He came across an empty shoe she must have lost in her haste. This was a pair she'd stolen from Austin's father; probably didn't fit right to begin with.

He came to a foot with a cotton sock. Her right leg.

He moved the beam upward. He was relieved there was no blood though her bare leg looked very pale, with a harsh scratch across her calf. Hips and torso. He shone the light in a sweeping arc that illuminated the white of her flesh, half concealed in the overgrown vegetation. All he saw was blood and bone and the wreckage of her face where the bullet had torn into her.

She lay twisted, the lower portion of her body resting on its side, the upper portion flat on the ground with her arms spread wide. Much of the left side of her jaw was gone, a great, gaping burst of torn flesh with mangled teeth, like a goofy grin. She must have turned her head to the right because it looked like the bullet had ripped along her jawbone, taking everything in its path. Her jaw and cheek were raw meat, dirt clinging to her face, stuck to her flesh like mud.

For a moment, he stood and blinked, uncomprehending.

He couldn't think how to undo this.

Could he be blamed when he hadn't meant to do it? Would they understand how unlikely it was that he could hit a moving target when he fired? It was just a crazy accident—a tragedy. Something that happened in the moment with no conscious intent on his part.

"Austin?" Fritz could feel his voice break. Though his lips had moved, no sound came out. He coughed once and cleared his throat. "Austin?"

Austin's voice came back, laden with annoyance. "What's the matter with you? Shine a light over here. I can't see jack shit."

Fritz redirected the flashlight beam, pushing back the underbrush so Austin could find his way. He heard trampling in the underbrush behind him. Austin thrashed over the rough ground as Fritz had done moments before.

"Where?" Austin said.

Fritz moved the beam. Austin caught a glimpse of Sloan in the harsh beam of light, a tangle of long dark hair showing blood at the roots. He moved the light to Sloan's ruined face.

Austin said, "Oh, Jesus, man." He started shaking his

head. "We are so fucked." He turned on Fritz in a fury. "What the hell have you done?"

Fritz dropped to his knees beside her, blinking. "It was a mistake. I didn't mean to hit her. What are the chances I would hit her? I don't know anything about guns."

Austin said, "All right. Shit. What's done is done. Let's just get this over with. Gimme a hand here."

"I don't want to touch her!"

Austin stared at Fritz, his expression dark with disdain. "This is your mess. I'm not doing this on my own. Get in here and help!"

"I didn't do it on purpose. You know that. It was just my dumb luck, right? You yelled and I started shooting, but how did I know she'd take a bullet in the face like that? You yelled and I just started firing—"

"I didn't tell you to kill her, you stupid shit. Did you hear me say that? Did I say anything at all about shooting her?"

"She was escaping. You yelled and I fired because I thought you wanted me to."

"I'm not going to stand here and argue with you. We have work to do. Get Bayard over here. You have put us in a world of hurt with this."

Fritz seemed transfixed.

"What are you waiting for? Get Bayard!" Austin screamed.

Fritz scrambled through the bushes and burst into the clearing just as Troy appeared, coming up the trail from the road below.

"What's up?"

Bayard turned to Fritz. "What's Austin screaming about? Where's Sloan?"

"Back there," Fritz said. "She got caught by a bullet when she ran."

"What do you mean, 'caught'? Like you shot her?"

"I didn't mean to," Fritz said. His voice broke and he knew he was babbling because what would happen now? How would they explain? "I don't even know how the safety came off. Austin yelled at me about that and put it on himself. You saw him do it, right? So when she started running, the gun shouldn't have fired at all . . ."

Austin appeared behind Fritz. He was focused on Troy. "Go back to the truck and bring another shovel. We have a job to do."

Bayard said, "You dug this hole, assuming we'd have a body on our hands?"

"No, Bayard. That would make it premeditated murder, wouldn't it? Like I planned it all in advance, which I did not. I figured it would be expedient in case we had to bury the gun."

"Why would we have to bury the gun if we didn't use it?" Bayard asked.

"What's with you and all the questions? Take my word for it, okay?"

"I'm just curious. If Fritz wasn't supposed to shoot her, why dig a hole?"

"Why are you quizzing me about a hole in the ground? Fritz is the one who plugged her, and you know what? I don't hear a note of regret out of him. Now go back in there and drag her out. And make sure you don't leave anything of hers behind."

Troy said, "Shouldn't we find a phone? We could call for an ambulance. It might not be too late."

"Yeah, well, it's very late where she's concerned. Bring her out here and put her in the hole. Troy, you bring up the other shovel. Let's be efficient about this. We'll get her out of sight and no one will be the wiser."

Later, it would seem to Fritz that time skipped forward, a herky-jerky leap from moment to moment, with big pieces missing when he tried to reconstruct events. He and Bayard hauled her through the brush, dragging her by the feet, which was hard work. Sloan was big and she seemed to weigh a ton, this whole inert slab of a person they were having to maneuver through the dark. The two made a concerted effort, towing her backward over the rough ground. Her hair trailed across the terrain in a long stream, picking up dead leaves and dirt. Her feet and ankles felt warm to the touch and Fritz felt a spurt of hope that she wasn't as badly injured as he thought. His gaze kept straying to the left side of her face, where her teeth had been shattered, leaving a gaping wound that only the dead could have endured.

Once in the clearing, they rolled her in the hole, and when Troy got back with the shovel they took turns tossing dirt in on top of her. Troy was crying. Fritz realized he was weeping as well. Bayard sat on the ground with his back to them, rocking back and forth, murmuring to himself while Austin popped the magazine out of the Astra and reloaded it. Fritz watched him uneasily. Maybe Austin meant to kill all of them. Shoot 'em down and push them into the same hole.

Austin's tone was conversational. "So here's the deal. We were together at the cabin, just hanging out and drinking beer. It was a pool party. A few people went home. We stayed to clean up some and then we drove down the mountain together."

"What do we say about Sloan?"

"She came with us, of course. She needed a ride because Stringer left without her, so we put her in the truck with us and dropped her off downtown. Then we say we went to my house and shot some pool and watched TV. She was fine last we saw her."

"Is anybody going to believe that?" Bayard asked.

"Why wouldn't they?" Austin asked. "We're not killers. We're just a bunch of stupid kids. If the cops should ask, all we did was goof around until we finally hit the sack around midnight. We admit to smoking dope because that sounds like we're being candid."

"We did do that," Fritz said.

"My point, you ass."

Fritz was white-faced. "Why would they talk to us at all?"

"Because we're friends of hers. We were all at the same party. Of course they're going to ask us if we know where she is."

"What if someone saw her out on the road?" Fritz asked.

"Didn't happen. She missed her ride, so she stayed at the cabin until we could give her a lift back to town."

"Then we're in the clear?" Fritz asked.

"I didn't say that. We're on shaky ground and we have to hang together. Cops are tough and they're wily. We gotta keep our mouths shut."

"I won't say a word. That's for sure."

Austin shook his head. "All we have to do is stay calm and stick to the story. Any one of us cracks, it's all over and I can promise you this. You 'fess up, you're dead. You got that?"

"What do we do now?" Fritz noticed a tremor in his voice that made him sound weak, even though moments before he'd felt indomitable.

"What do you think we do now? We go back and keep our fucking mouths shut. I just got done saying that. For starters, no one except Iris knows we came up here with her. When Stringer and Michelle and all of them took off, Sloan was fine, right? Last anybody saw of her, she'd had a little too much to drink and she was sleeping it off. What happened was she sobered up and asked us to take her back to town. We said sure. The four of us dropped her downtown, the corner of State Street and whatever. We're the only ones who know different and all we have to do is get our stories straight, tell the truth as we know it, and stick to that."

"Won't someone report her missing?"

"Like who? Her folks are out of town. Maybe she went to a movie or met a friend somewhere. None of our business. She asked us for a ride into town and we were happy to oblige."

"What if someone finds the body?"

"What are you talking about? No one's going to *find* her. Why would anybody even think to look up here? Isolated, rugged. It's off the beaten path. If the coyotes get wind of her, then aren't they the lucky ones. Dig her up and cart her off, bone by bone. Nothing left to identify. The only trick is to keep calm. We're innocent. We didn't do anything. She asked us to drop her off and we did. End of incident. Someone asks us, we're as worried as everyone else."

"But, Austin, they're dismantling this camp. Look at all the machinery. There must be guys up here every day."

"That's why we buried her, schmuck. She's four feet down. We pack the dirt, maybe leave the excavator on the spot so no one sees the ground's disturbed."

"What about the cops?"

"What about them? The average cop is denser than a load of manure. Barely anything going on up here," he said and tapped his head. "They'd like you to think they're smart, but what are the percentages? You think they solve even half the homicides that come their way? Guess again. Case gets cold and they're on to the next, bumbling along the same as always. Just don't let anybody shake your confidence. We back each other up. Even if they interrogate us separately, all you have to do is button your trap and what proof do they have? Other kids at the party will swear the same thing. Last they saw Sloan, she was doing great. Meantime, if one of you breaks down and blabs? I will kill you."

Bayard said, "What about the gun?"

"Shit. Good point," Austin said.

He looked at Troy, who backed off a step, saying, "No way. I'm not touching that."

Austin pushed the gun into Bayard's hand. "You take it. I can't afford to have it on me if I get picked up."

Bayard said, "I don't want the fucking thing. What am I supposed to do with it?"

Austin said, "Give it to Iris and tell her to hold on to it."

"Until when?"

"Until I say so."

Bayard started to protest, but Austin held up a finger.

"Fine," Bayard said, annoyed.

Austin said, "Any questions?"

He looked from Fritz to Bayard to Troy, but no one said a word. "Okay, then. We're set. End of story. Just hang tight and we'll be fine."

38

Friday, October 6, 1989

I ate a brown bag lunch at my desk. I'd packed it with care, the "entrée" being one of those peanut butter and pickle sandwiches I'm so fussy about. Whole grain bread, Jif Extra Crunchy, and Vlasic or Mrs. Fanning's Bread'n Butter Pickles. In a pinch, dill will do, but never sweet. My practice is to cut the finished product on the diagonal and then wrap it in waxed paper that I still fold the way my Aunt Gin taught me. I'd added two Milano cookies and, being ever so dainty, I included two paper napkins, one to serve as a place mat and one for dabbing my lips.

I had just finished arranging the items on the desk in front of me when I heard a tap at the office door. I got up and crossed to the outer office, where I peered around the door frame. Troy waved at me through the glass. He wore his dark blue Better Brand coverall, so he'd apparently come from work. He waited patiently while I went through the disarming and unlocking process. Once I let him in, I didn't bother to lock the door. If Ned burst in, Troy would make short work of him. He wasn't tall but he had a brawny look about him, a red-headed fireplug of a guy. As a bonus, he was twenty-five years old, which gave him the advantage over Ned except in the matter of craziness.

He followed me into my office.

"Have a seat," I said. "Aren't you supposed to be at work?"

"This is my lunch hour. I ate in the truck driving over. Spilled crap all over myself."

I sat down and indicated my spread. "Mind if I go ahead?"

"Have at it."

"What's up? I thought you were mad at me."

He flashed his teeth, which were crooked but very white. "I got over it. 'What's up' is I saw the article about Fritz in this morning's paper. They found the Astra Constable at the scene."

"Quite a coincidence, don't you think?"

"Not so. I called Stringer and had a long chat with him. He told me about Fritz stopping by to borrow camping gear and how goofy he acted. I think I know how the gun ended up at Yellowweed."

I was surprised. "Well, that's interesting. You should probably be talking to Detective Burgess at the county sheriff's office."

"No way. I know Burgess and he's a shit. He hassles me every chance he gets," he said. "And don't start naming five other cops I should be talking to. I want to talk to you."

"Fine."

I picked up my sandwich and took a bite, making an effort not to moan. What a combination: the peanut butter salty, soft, and crunchy; the pickle tart and crisp. I might not have been as subtle as I thought because he pointed, saying, "What the hell *is* that?"

"Peanut butter and pickle."

"Have you ever eaten one before?"

"Many times and I've lived to tell the tale. Want to try?"

"Sure. Sounds like something my boys would like."

I passed the remaining half sandwich across the desk to him and watched as he bit off a corner. He chewed and nodded to himself. He divided the remainder into two parts and ate one while I looked on with alarm. I hadn't meant to surrender more than a bite, but it was too late to protest.

"Not bad," he said.

"You have a theory about the guy who took Fritz up to Yellowweed?"

I watched him polish off the rest of my sandwich.

Still chewing, he pointed at me. "See, that's your mistake. You're assuming it's a guy."

"Ah."

"What Stringer described is how Fritz acted around girls. Ask anyone who knew him and they'll tell you the same thing. He got all giddy and gushy and made a fool of himself."

"You have a particular girl in mind?"

"Iris."

I heard the skepticism in my voice. "Based on what?"

"Well, I'll tell you what it's based on. The night when Sloan was shot? The four of us are up at Yellowweed. This is Austin, Fritz, Bayard, and me. Austin tries to palm the gun off on me and I go, like, 'No way!' So he hands Bayard the gun and tells him to pass it on to Iris to hold for him. He said he couldn't afford to have it in his possession if he got picked up."

"You're saying *Iris* shot Fritz? That seems unlikely."

"Not as unlikely as you might think."

"What's her motive?"

"She hated him for what he did to her."

"Why would she hate him and not you?"

"Because I apologized. I asked her to forgive me, which she did. The two of us are square."

"How do you know she hated Fritz?"

"She's in a support group for victims of rape and sexual assault. She's talked about him for years and she's always bitter."

"I thought those sessions were confidential."

"Hey, come on. Women gossip. They can't help themselves. Doesn't matter what's going on or how solemnly they swear not to say a word. They're barely out the door before they're on the telephone, spilling the beans. That's how women bond. Scary, isn't it?"

"You know someone who was in the group with her? Is that where this is coming from?"

"Let's don't get into that. Just trust me, I know what I'm talking about."

"Iris claims the tape was all a joke."

"And you're convinced it's a bullshit cover story. You think we sweet-talked her into going along with us, which is exactly what we did."

"Why would she agree?"

"To keep tabs on Fritz. Around us, she picked up a steady stream of information. Where he went, what he was up to. We didn't see her as the enemy and she didn't appear to be a threat. If she'd let on how pissed off she was, we'd have cut her out of the loop. You want to blackmail someone, you want the barriers to come down. You don't do anything to indicate how hostile you are."

Restlessly, I shifted in my chair.

Troy held up a hand. "You're about to ask why I think she's the extortionist. Not just her. Her and that jug-eared fiancé. Look at it from their perspective. Fritz gets out of prison and starts a whole new life. He's got his mommy and his daddy and access to a boatload of money. Meanwhile, according to Fritz, he's paid his debt to society and he's home free. Iris and Joey don't have two nickels to rub together. You should see how they live. Apartment the size of a bread box. Twenty-five thousand could make a hell of a difference, especially since they wouldn't have to work for it. Wouldn't pay taxes on it, either."

"I did wonder about that, with the wedding coming up. Iris has class. I can't picture her getting married on a shoestring."

Troy said, "Another motive for her killing him, if you want to put icing on the cake? Fritz was a blabbermouth.

He's constitutionally unable to keep a secret, so if he found out Iris and Joey were behind the scheme, he'd go straight to the police."

"Even though the tape might expose him to further charges?"

"He'd probably figure it was worth the risk. He'd own up to the crime from his callous youth in exchange for police protection."

"If I tell Cheney Phillips what you've just told me, would you be willing to talk to him?"

"Sure, if you keep Burgess out of it. It's his case, isn't it?"

"Technically, but it's not like there's a pissing contest between Burgess and the Santa Teresa PD."

When Troy was gone, I sat and pondered the conversation. I thought about Margaret Seay's contention that revenge doesn't have to be an eye for an eye, just comparable or equivalent. Fritz had "despoiled" Iris sexually and now she'd despoiled him by putting a couple of slugs in him. As retribution goes, that seemed a bit severe, but if her future mother-in-law had fed her a steady diet of bloodthirsty talk, Iris might have felt justified in just about anything she did. As is always the case, I had to subject Troy's theory to scrutiny as well. Since he'd pointed a finger in the name of good citizenship, I had to question his motive. Might have been to deflect attention from himself.

It seemed easy enough to double-check the truth of what he'd said. I grabbed my jacket, my shoulder bag, and my car keys and headed out the door. Take for granted that I locked up properly, okay? I drove to Bayard's house in Horton Ravine. I rang the bell, and moments later Maisie opened the door. She had her hair pulled back in a ponytail. She wore electric blue running shorts and a tank top, with a lightweight headphone set resting around her neck. Her arms and legs were tanned and shapely, suggesting weight lifting of an intensity I tend to avoid. What surprised me was the complete absence of makeup, which at first made her look unfinished and washed out. This impression was quickly followed by the realization that without the foundation, blusher, mascara, and eye shadow, she was actually much prettier.

It was clear she hadn't expected to see me. "Oh. I thought Ellis forgot his key."

"I'm hoping to talk to Bayard."

"He's on a call with his broker. I'll tell him you're here."

"No hurry," I said. I noticed that the two suitcases I'd seen in the bedroom on my earlier visit had been moved to the foyer. She caught my gaze as it drifted from the luggage back to her.

"Bayard and Ellis are going on a trip while I pack my things. I have a moving van coming first thing Monday morning."

"You and Bayard are splitting up?"

She seemed amused. "You think it's me Bayard's interested in? Good luck."

"I assumed the two of you were romantically involved."

"He's my stepson. He's ten years younger than I am. What do I need with a pip-squeak whose alcohol consumption is out of control? Time to move on in life. I told him I'd rented a place in LA and next thing you know, he's leaving town himself. Probably trying to save face."

I was already worried I might not have another opportunity to pick her brain. "Would you mind if I asked a couple of questions about Sloan?"

She made a gesture that signified her consent.

"You were in the picture when she was killed."

"I was."

"I understand Tigg was supportive of Bayard."

"He made a deal with the DA, didn't he?"

"But that might have been more about his pride than protecting Bayard."

"The truth is Tigg mistreated Bayard. He and Joan fought over him like two dogs over a bone. He was just a little kid and they tore him apart. Do you know what kept him going? He knew in the long run he'd inherit Tigg's estate, which he considered just compensation for all the shit he put up with."

Bayard approached from the corridor in chinos, a white polo shirt, and deck shoes without socks. "Thank you, Maisie, for minding my business for me. If I need sympathy, I'll give you a call."

She turned on him. "I don't have much sympathy for you, Bayard. I'm all played out. Your life was tough, I'll grant you that one, but you put yourself where you are. You don't like it, then straighten up your act."

"Good counsel from someone who's never worked a day in her life. You think your advice is so sterling, hang out a sign. Maybe someone else will take you seriously. I don't. It's been a pleasure doing business with you."

"I wish I could say the same," she snapped.

The look that lingered between them was, for the first time, intimate, possibly because they were finally putting their cards on the table. Maisie crossed to the front door. She adjusted her earphones, activated her CD player, and let herself out.

"Sorry about that," Bayard said. His apology was a move designed to shift me to his side, as though Maisie's candor had embarrassed us both. Not so from my perspective, but I didn't think I should say so to him.

"Good I caught up with you," I said. "I understand you're going out of town."

"Just for the weekend. Palm Springs. I'm hoping to fine-tune my golf game."

I was hoping he'd be sober enough to hold a club. "When do you leave?"

"Late tomorrow afternoon. Ordinarily we'd drive, but in the interest of saving time, we decided to fly."

"Could I ask a quick question? I may not have occasion to talk to you again."

The notion of never seeing me again seemed to improve his mood.

"You want to come into the living room and have a seat?"

"I'm fine here. This really won't take long."

He gestured carelessly. "I heard about Fritz, so you can save the condolences for someone else."

"You weren't a fan?"

"He was an irritating little shit, so no love lost. I'm sorry for what happened, but I can't say I'm upset."

"You're aware the Astra Constable was found up at Yellowweed?"

"The police must be thrilled."

"Do you remember what happened to the gun after Sloan was killed?"

"Vividly. This was still up at the site while Austin was coaching us on our alibi. He tried to foist it off on Troy, but Troy was having none of it so then he turns to me, like I'm the lucky recipient. I don't want the damn thing. He says all he wants me to do is pass the gun to Iris to hold for him. I mean, how weird is that after what happened to her?"

"And she agreed?"

"She never had the chance. Once Sloan's body was found, the police were all over us. Of course, they were all over everybody else as well, but the focus quickly narrowed to the four of us. We might have gotten away with it, but let's face it, we were amateurs. Austin and I managed to keep our composure, but even early on, it was clear Fritz would crack."

"What about Troy?"

"He's a Boy Scout at heart. If Fritz rolled over, so would he. Anyway, before I had time to give Iris the gun, Austin showed up and asked to have it back. He said he was hitting the road and needed it for protection. He also wanted to keep the weapon out of the hands of the police because it was registered to his dad and he didn't want his father implicated."

"How soon after that did he leave?"

"Don't know, but I doubt he hung around long. Within days, word was out that Fritz had broken down and confessed everything. Austin's ass was grass. Mine, too, of course, but Fritz painted him as the mastermind. There was no way Austin could tap-dance his way out of that."

I stared at the floor, wondering if he was leveling with me. Somehow, I thought not. "Any idea where he went?"

"He didn't mention a destination. The less I knew, the better where he was concerned."

"And you haven't heard from him since?"

"Not a peep."

In the car again, wending my way out of Horton Ravine, I passed Maisie as she ran along the road. She was some distance from the house, so she'd made good time. I drove another hundred yards beyond her and pulled over on the berm. When she reached me, I rolled down the window. "I'm not sure we finished our conversation. Is there anything else you want to say?"

She placed her hands on the roof of the car and supported herself for a moment while she caught her breath. I could see sweat collecting in the creases in her neck. "Talk to Sloan's mom."

"About what?"

"Her bio-dad."

"I'll do that," I said. "Why are you willing to help now and not before?"

She smiled. "At this point, what do I have to lose?"

39

I made a U-turn and drove back into the heart of Horton Ravine. It was a gorgeous day, sunny and mild with a sky irritatingly empty of clouds. You could check the radar sweep from San Francisco to San Diego and you wouldn't see even the smallest green freckle that might signify r-a-i-n. I parked the car in Margaret's drive and made my way up the walk, wondering how she felt now that she'd been robbed of the object of her bloodthirsty fantasies. I had just reached the porch when the front door opened and a kid came out, closing the door behind him. He was a carbon copy of Joey Seay—same jug ears, same furrowed brow. He stopped when he saw me.

"Are you Justin?"

"Yes. Who are you?"

I held out my hand. "Kinsey Millhone," I said.

"Got it. The private detective."

"So true," I said. "Mind if I ask you a couple of questions?"

"Is there any way to avoid it?"

"Not really. This will be quick."

"Good, because I'm due at work. What do you want?"

"I understand you were here the day Sloan's room was emptied."

"Me and some other kids."

"In the process, did one of you come across the infamous tape?"

"Nope."

"Isn't it possible one of the others found it and didn't say anything to you?"

"Nope."

"How can you be so sure?" I said, sounding slightly cranky.

"Me and Joey found it the year we were living here, right after Sloan died. It was like a scavenger hunt. We knew it was somewhere on the property, but we didn't know where. I was actually the one who found it."

"Where was it?"

"There was this bathroom between our two bedrooms. She'd removed the heater vent set into the kickplate and she'd slid it in there."

"What happened to the tape?"

"Nothing. Joey hung on to it with the idea that one day he'd find a use for it."

"That turned out to be fortunate."

"Well, yeah. First day at Santa Teresa High School, who does he run into but the chick spread out on the pool table?"

"Lucky for him. And here they are years later, about to get married."

Justin shrugged.

"Your stepmother's a fan of patience."

"Sure, if you want to even the score."

"Really? Was it that important to Joey ten years after the fact?"

"He loved Sloan. She was a goddess to him. Fritz McCabe was a twerp and deserved everything he got."

"And he's dead now."

"Good news. We didn't have anything to do with it."

I rang the bell and she opened the door moments later. Behind her in the hall, Sloan's now ancient companion, Butch, made his way painfully to her side. Maybe in his dimming memory, he still held out the hope that one day Sloan would be there. He was a sad old guy and I felt my heart break all over again at his optimism.

Margaret brightened when she saw me. "Oh, Kinsey. Please come in. Something's come up and I was wondering who to talk to. Maybe you can help."

"I'll do what I can."

This time, instead of leading me into the living room, she walked me through to her study at the back of the house. This room was a jumble: big rolltop desk piled high with paper—bills, correspondence, catalogues, newspapers. To one side of the desk, there was a table topped by a typewriter. On the rolling chair, she'd balanced six fat accordion-style folders with ragged index tabs. The bookshelves were helter-skelter, some books lined up properly, some flat, many leaning drunkenly on adjacent volumes. There was an enormous stack of last year's Christmas cards on a side table and an upright metal stand was stuffed with documents, so many files jammed in together that I doubted the device served its purpose, which was easy access. She'd struck me as being neat, tucked in, and conservative, and the disorder here seemed out of character.

Today she wore a red shantung pantsuit, a dramatic contrast to her black hair, which fit her head like a feather bathing cap. Her only jewelry was a necklace of gold beads, graduating in size from the small ones near her throat to larger ones at the outer rim. Her black-rimmed glasses lent her a serious air. "Sit anywhere you find room," she said as she settled in her wooden swivel chair.

There were three other chairs in the room, all in use. I did a quick survey, trying to determine which pile would be easiest to move. I chose the magazines, but to my dismay, once I set them on the floor, they slid sideways in an avalanche of glossy paper.

I took a seat, saying, "Why don't you tell me what's going on?"

"A detective from the sheriff's department stopped by the store this morning to talk to Iris. She was terribly upset. She'd just read about Fritz in the paper and she hadn't absorbed the shock of it. Up pops this fellow asking where she and Joey were the previous Friday night, as though they might be implicated in the murder."

"Was this Detective Burgess?"

"Yes, him. She mentioned the name, but it went in one ear and out the other."

"He's just starting his investigation, so this is routine. Right now, he's assembling a picture of Fritz's life—friends, old classmates, and acquaintances. He'll be talking to a lot of people, asking whether Fritz had enemies and that sort of thing. If Iris and Joey were good friends of his, there shouldn't be a problem. Did she say why she was so distressed?"

"Well, that's just it. She drew a complete blank when he questioned her. He asked how much she knew about the blackmail scheme and she didn't know how to reply. Fritz had confided the details in the strictest confidence and she didn't want to violate his trust. His parents might still be determined to sweep it all under the rug."

"Extortion is the last thing on their minds at this point. They're trying to come to terms with their loss. Aside from that, I'm sure Detective Burgess understands how flustered some people get when dealing with law enforcement. Honestly, he's a nice man and I'm sure he didn't mean to frighten her."

"It's just that he caught her by surprise. She worried if her answers were incorrect, she'd have painted herself into a corner later on."

"If she tells the truth, why would it come to that?"

"That's how it seems to me, but she doesn't know anything about the law or police procedure. She wondered if she should have an attorney present as a safeguard, but when she asked, he looked at her like she'd just admitted she was guilty of something."

"He was probably surprised she raised the issue in the course of a simple conversation."

"You don't know if it was simple or not."

"True enough," I said.

"The fact of the matter is, she and Joey were with me Friday night because I asked if they'd paint Sloan's room. It looked very shabby once the furniture was gone and I thought it was time to freshen it up. Joey went to the paint store and bought the supplies they needed, including paint trays and rollers. I have the receipt showing the date and time of the purchase. Later, after they'd worked for a couple of hours, I ordered pizza for the three of us. I have that receipt as well."

"Those should come in handy if Burgess asks. I'm not sure I'd volunteer the information."

"Why not?"

"He's not accusing her of anything at this point. It sounds like she overreacted."

"Perhaps, but I thought you might talk to him for us and clarify her position."

"That's not a good idea. All it would do is make him wonder why I was sticking my nose into his business."

"What if he comes back and asks something else? What is she to say?"

"She can talk to an attorney if it would make her feel better."

"She and Joey don't have money to spare, but I suppose I could spend a few dollars."

"You might not even have to do that," I said. "Most attorneys will offer an initial consultation to determine if your problem is a legal matter they can help you with."

"Thank you. I'll remember that. It doesn't sound so alarming when you put it that way. At any rate, I should have asked what I could do for you instead of launching into this whole long tale."

"Don't worry about it. It's natural for you to be concerned."

"I appreciate your understanding."

I realized I could probably go on like this with her for the rest of the afternoon. I'd comfort, reassure, and inform. She'd be grateful and thank me again. That way I could postpone having to pry into her personal business. "I'm interested in Sloan's biological father."

Margaret, unexpressive to begin with, seemed to turn to stone.

I leaned forward. "Margaret, listen to me. Just listen. What possible difference could it make after all these years? She's gone. She won't suffer any shame or embarrassment. I understand you feel protective, but I don't see how it could matter."

"Why do you want to know?"

"Because it all connects. It has to," I said, though the idea hadn't occurred to me until I opened my mouth and said so.

"How?"

"I don't know how. Look at it this way: the players have been the same all these years. Bayard, Fritz, Troy, Austin, Poppy, and Sloan. Sloan dies. Austin disappears. Troy and Fritz go to prison, and when Fritz gets out, he ends up dead within weeks. These events are not random."

I could see her considering the claim. I saw something flicker in her eyes and I wondered what piece of the puzzle she held. "Who is the guy?"

She shook her head once, like a horse shooing off a black fly.

I leaned forward and took her hands. "Just tell me."

"Tigg Montgomery," she whispered.

I sat back. The answer was unexpected and I considered the obvious implications. "You're telling me Bayard and Sloan were siblings? He's her half-brother?"

"Yes."

I waited while she clasped and unclasped her hands and then she went on.

"I worked for him. This was before Joan divorced him, so the pregnancy would have put him in jeopardy financially. Santa Teresa was unsophisticated in those days. He was highly regarded, a pillar of the community, and I was his employee."

"It must have been difficult."

"It was hard. He was the love of my life and I couldn't fault him for wanting to conceal the situation. I'd have done anything for him."

"Thus the years of silence," I said.

"I promised I'd keep quiet. In return, he promised to provide for her. Near the end, when he realized how sick he was, he came to me and said he'd make good. He intended to divide his estate between the two."

"Did Bayard know this?"

"Tigg told him, but I have no idea what his reaction was. It must have come as a shock."

"What about Sloan? Did she know?"

Margaret shook her head. "I didn't want to tell her until I was certain Tigg would come through for her. Why get her hopes up when it might not come to pass? Why open the door if she couldn't walk through? He put it off. He delayed. Maybe he got so sick, he wasn't thinking straight. Maybe he was ambivalent or changed his mind. How would I know? I didn't want her hopes dashed, which they would have been. I believe he was sincere. I think he meant well, but he didn't act quickly enough. The new will was drawn up, but he died without signing it."

"What was the age difference between Bayard and Sloan?"

"Two years."

"I thought they were in the same class at Climp."

"They were. Bayard was held back a year because of behavioral issues."

"And when Sloan died?"

"Bayard blamed himself. He knew he should have stepped in. There were many opportunities to intervene and he did nothing."

"But when Sloan died, all the money was his again, right?"

"It didn't matter. Nothing mattered except the fact that he let her die when he could have prevented it."

"Why were you so bitter about Fritz?"

"He was Austin's instrument. Austin wanted her dead

because, in his mind, she'd wounded him. She hadn't actually done anything but he didn't see it that way. Fritz was a puppet. There was no reason for him to do what he did, except to please Austin. Bayard hated Austin, which is why he testified at the trial."

"But that was to get himself off the hook, wasn't it?"

"Both were true. He settled a score and he protected himself. There's nothing wrong with that."

"And now that Fritz is dead, where does that put you?"

"If he'd taken responsibility, things might have come out differently."

"That isn't what I asked."

"Where it puts me is I'm glad he's dead. I wished it on him. I may go to hell for it, but I don't care."

"Did you have a hand in his death?"

"No, but I wish I had."

"You have a hard heart."

"You may discover you do as well," she said. "Meanwhile, do you want to know how I know there's a god? Because he answered my prayers."

Well, that was a depressing conversation. I drove home, pondering the meaning of it all without understanding any of it. Sloan's death seemed to be the sorry culmination of random elements—paranoia, miscues, rage, passivity, herd mentality, and poor judgment among them. Fritz's death had a different feel to it. I believed he was killed for a reason, while she was killed for no reason at all. Bad luck as much as anything. I didn't think his killing was predicated on hers, but there had to be a link between the two. At least that was my current working theory and one I needed to test. I'd have to talk to someone who was present back then and perhaps understood the larger picture. Lauren McCabe came to mind.

I drove into town and left my car near the Axminster Theater, then walked through the covered passage that led from the parking lot. The McCabes' condominium appeared at my immediate left as I emerged onto the street. Lauren and Hollis had learned about their son's death less than a day ago and I imagined their apartment filled with friends, offering support, sympathy, and casseroles. When I reached the top of the stairs, however, there were no signs of life. The front door was ajar and there was a stillness pouring out of the place like smoke. I pushed the door open, saying, "Lauren?"

There were no lights on. The interior, which had seemed simple and uncluttered, now seemed diminished. The absence of artificial lighting lent the living room an air of coldness and abandonment. No fresh flowers. No cooking smells. No voices.

"Lauren?"

It felt intrusive to be present without someone greeting me. I knew from my first visit where the library was located and I knew that Fritz's bedroom was the first door on the left. I thought about going as far as his room, but I was reluctant to infringe on their privacy. I didn't hear anyone approach, but I sensed movement in the corridor and Lauren appeared. She was barefoot and the clothes she wore looked like she'd selected them from a pile on the floor.

I said, "There you are. I'm sorry to barge in uninvited. I thought maybe you'd have people here."

She shook her head. "We're on our own. Hollis is napping and I'm wandering around thinking I should be doing something. I don't blame people for avoiding us. There's nothing in the etiquette books to cover situations like this. What do you say to a mother whose son has been murdered? What comfort can you offer a father who's lost his only child? It's awkward and difficult and people think of reasons to stay away. They tell themselves we'd prefer to be alone. They'll remember how undemonstrative we are and think we'd doubtless protect our solitude. In some ways, that's correct. I find it hard to deal with people I don't much like."

I'd actually told myself much the same thing, thinking that if I tried to hug or console her, she'd rebuff me. I don't particularly like to be hugged myself, especially in a social setting where there's no reason whatsoever to promote physical contact beyond a handshake. Most of the time, people are just going through the motions anyway, pretending to be happier to see you than they actually are. "Isn't there someone you'd like me to call?"

"Well, that's just it. I can't think of anyone. A friend will come to mind and I'll realize I haven't spoken to her in a year. This is hardly the time to offer an invitation. I tried calling another friend, someone I was close to in the past. I found out she died two months ago and no one thought to tell me."

"What about Hollis's brother? You've mentioned him."

"Their relationship is strained. Really, it's quite superficial. Having him here would be a burden. They don't get along and I'd be stage-managing their bad behavior, which is something I can do without. I'd have to think about meals and entertainment and small talk. You can't have people in from out of town and then leave them to their own devices, even if the occasion is a death."

"I can see your point," I said. "The question may seem odd, but have you heard from the extortionist?"

"No and I don't anticipate contact. If this is someone who knows us, then he's probably heard about Fritz's death. Even if he doesn't know us, surely he'd be keeping tabs on us and he'd be aware of what's happened. Anyway, Valerie did stop by and I thought that was lovely."

She made the reference to Valerie as though the name would mean something, which it didn't. Then I remembered that Valerie was the cleaning lady I'd encountered in my initial meeting with her.

I thought I should tell Lauren why I was there, but I wondered if it would seem callous if it was business as usual for me while she was trying to cope with her son's death. This was probably one of the finer points of good manners that she was referring to. "This may not be a good time for you, but I have questions and I don't know who else to ask."

"Why don't we sit?"

We moved into the living room, where she took a seat at the end of the sofa and I settled in the upholstered chair nearby. "Were you aware that Tigg Montgomery was Sloan's bio-dad?"

"Yes. He talked to Hollis about his options—whether to own up to it or keep the information under wraps. There might have been a middle road, but none of us could think of one. Tigg was extremely conservative. His values were strictly Old Testament. Adultery was prohibited, as he believed it should be, even though he was a party to it. He decided to keep it quiet, which I didn't particularly admire, but he was Hollis's boss and I knew better than to speak up."

"Eventually, Bayard found out. How did that happen?"

"Tigg told him. When he had the new will drawn up, he thought it would be unfair to have Bayard find out about the changes after he was gone."

"What was Bayard's reaction?"

"He was angry at first. He looked at Tigg's money as his reward for being a good boy and putting up with the brutal emotional gamesmanship he was subjected to as a child. The notion of cutting his payoff in half didn't sit well at first. Then he realized how much he loved and admired Sloan. He'd been raised as an only child and suddenly he had a younger sister. It shed a whole different light on the situation."

"You think he was sincere? He wasn't just covering?"

"I can't answer that. I thought he was fully reconciled, but he's always been good at guarding himself."

"You said Tigg was extremely conservative. How did he feel about Bayard's being gay?"

"He didn't know. The rest of us were aware of it, but he seemed to have a blind spot. He was rabidly homophobic, so if he found out, he'd have cut Bayard off without a cent."

One call. I thought about Austin's warning about one call, his harping on it. That's what it was about, Austin's threat to pull the rug out from under Bayard. One more piece of the puzzle had locked into place.

40

Saturday, October 7, 1989

I didn't sleep well. I found myself turning this way and that, thinking some as-yet-undiscovered position would be sufficiently comfortable to invite unconsciousness. Instead, with one eye on the digital clock, I watched the minutes flick by. If I slept at all, it was in brief increments, at least until the wee hours when I fell into a deep pit of dreams. I woke at nine, feeling groggy, startled that the time had gotten away from me. It was Saturday and it was light out, so in theory I could have gotten in a run, but I didn't want to. I was anxious about Celeste's arrival, uneasy about the fact that Ned had dropped out of sight again. I didn't see how he could interfere with the plan, but Ned had the built-in cunning of a psychopath and he'd show up when least expected.

I showered. I dressed. I ate my bowl of cereal. I drank two cups of coffee, which woke me up as I'd hoped, but also fed my apprehension. I felt heavy and full of dread, little flickers of fear like heat lightning dancing along my spine. Celeste's plane got in at 1:15. Just to be on the safe side, I'd leave for the airport at 12:30, which meant I had roughly three hours to kill. I went next door to Henry's, where the back door was open and the screen unhooked. I could smell freshly baked cinnamon rolls. I tapped and he told me to come on in. Anna was sitting at his kitchen table, which was taken up with two sheet pans onto which she was dolloping cookie dough with a small ice cream scoop. Now that I knew she was pregnant, she seemed Madonna-like, bathed in serenity. It had been two weeks since her condition was made known and already she seemed rounded and ripe, her skin aglow.

Henry sliced the crusts from a loaf of white bread and he had a bowl of egg salad at the ready. He'd already prepared small homemade buns with butter and country ham, small leaves of baby endive with a dab of blue cheese at the tip of each. There were six trays of finger sandwiches covered in Saran wrap. Peering closely, I could identify anchovy butter and radishes, thinly sliced cucumber with cream cheese, sharp cheddar and chutney—all specialties of his. He'd arranged cupcakes, petit fours, and tiny cream puffs on three silver platters, again protected from the drying air with clear plastic wrap.

"I'm catering a tea party for Moza Lowenstein," he said in answer to my unspoken question.

Anna said, "I'm invited because I live there. Now that I have a little peanut on board, I'm ravenous. I eat everything, all the time. I can't stop myself. You want to see a picture?"

"Sure."

She took a 4-by-6 black-and-white photo out of her pocket. The image was fuzzy and looked like somebody had been making snow angels in the background. In the center of this colorless world, there was a creature that might have been left behind by an alien space-craft: big head, body curved in a soft C, thin limbs, transparent skin, tethered in place by a gray rope.

"You've decided to keep the little tyke," I said.

"Well, I don't know about that. I've decided to see this through and hope for the best."

I said, "I'm operating on the same plan. Are we screwed or what?"

"I have no idea what you're talking about."

"Just as well. May I have a cinnamon roll?"

"Help yourself," Henry said. "There's still coffee if you'd like."

"Why not? I'm a nervous wreck anyway."

"What's going on?"

"I'll tell you when it's over with." I crossed to the coffeepot, took a mug down, and filled it. "What time's the tea party?"

"Four. If I know Moza, she'll bring out the cooking sherry and the ladies will go on until the wee hours."

"No husbands to feed?"

"These are widows. They all have little dogs that they bring in their purses, with tiny cans of dog food. One has trained her pup to do its business on indoor potty pads with fake grass so she doesn't even have to take him outdoors. She just folds up the mat, seals it in a gallon-sized plastic bag, and she's good."

"These can go in," Anna said.

Henry opened the oven door, reached over, picked up the two trays of raw cookie dough, and slid them in. He set a timer and went back to his finger sandwiches.

I said, "I'm surprised Pearl's not here."

"One of her homies thought he saw Ned Lowe and they've gone off on the hunt."

"Well, I hope she uses good sense. She has no clue how dangerous he is." I finished my coffee and put the mug in the dishwasher. "You need help?"

"We're covered here, but thanks."

"I'm going to try to find something useful to do."

I let myself out and returned to the studio. I made a trip to the supermarket, where I stocked up on life's essentials, toilet paper being primary. Home again, I unloaded my bags and put everything away. I'd used up forty-two minutes, during which I'd gone from being worried to being bored. I lay down on the couch with a paperback mystery and read until I fell asleep two paragraphs later. I woke at 12:25, which I took as a good omen since it allowed me just enough time to brush my teeth, avail myself of the facilities, and head out to Colgate.

The Santa Teresa Municipal Airport was built in the 1940s and most nearly resembles a modest hacienda, complete with stucco exterior, red-tile roof, and magenta bougainvillea. The baggage claim area looks like a carport affixed to one end. There's a coffee shop on the second floor, and a grassy courtyard below surrounded by a glass-topped wall so that you can watch planes take off and land. I positioned myself twenty feet from the main entrance, in full view of five of the six gates.

Within minutes, I saw a little commuter plane wobbling toward earth in the final moments of its descent. I knew from previous flights that the landing would have a rocky start, with the ups and downs of a roller coaster, passengers fingering their rosaries and trying not to scream. The wheels touching down would chirp like sneakers on hardwood flooring.

Passengers began to trickle into the terminal, some with rolling suitcases trailing behind, some on their way to baggage claim. Celeste was one of the last to emerge. I'd assured her that I'd recognize her, but I hadn't been entirely certain. I'd met her once six months before and most of the image I retained consisted of an oval face, pale hair, and dark eyes. Also, the demeanor of a prisoner of war recently released from captivity. Life with Ned Lowe had deadened her. At the time I encountered her, she'd reduced her personality to a shadow as flat as a photo mounted on a piece of cardboard. Anything more animated would attract Ned's attention and, shortly after that, his ire.

Celeste spotted me and raised a hand in greeting. She looked like she'd been rehydrated, her exterior plumped up by confidence. Hers wasn't a type A personality, so she'd never be a firebrand, but she moved as though a spark had fanned to life in her. She wore a lightweight brown tweed coat. She carried a briefcase and had a purse hooked over one shoulder with a leather strap.

"Hey, how are you?" I asked, holding out my hand for her to shake. I'd avoided the use of her name, still censoring myself lest Ned picked up a faint whiff of her presence in town. "You have luggage?"

"Just this," she said, indicating the briefcase.

"Have you had lunch?"

"Maybe afterward. I'm nervous."

"Me, too."

As we proceeded to my car in the short-term parking lot, both of us scanned the area for signs of Ned.

"I really don't think he can get to us," I said.

"Are you armed, by any chance?"

I shook my head. "My H&K is locked away at home. If I'd thought about it, I'd have carried it. Last contact I had with him, I fired off three rounds. If my line of sight had been better, I'd have crippled him for life."

"You shot him?"

"Nicked is more like it. His hip or his thigh, but whichever it was, it made him howl. Later, he used the keys he'd stolen from Phyllis to let himself back into her condominium. He applied first aid, leaving behind bandages that suggested a festering wound."

"Love it. I am so proud of you," she said.

The drive into town was without incident. I was careful not to ask any personal questions on the theory that the less I knew, the better. When we reached the police station, I parked on the nearest side street and walked with her to the front steps. Both of our heads swiveled from side to side.

Once in the lobby, I relaxed. Ladies and gents in uniform, decked out with deadly weapons, create a sense of safety I treasure. The desk officer called Cheney in the Detective Bureau and he appeared shortly thereafter and accompanied us to his desk. I watched Celeste hand over the envelope containing Ned's trinkets and then I excused myself and went back to the lobby to wait while she told him what she knew. The gasoline receipts Ned had saved would serve as a road map of his travels and might yield as-yet-undiscovered victims.

The meeting went on longer than I'd anticipated and I became more antsy as the minutes rolled by. Celeste hadn't given me her departure time and I had to trust she'd keep an eye on the clock. Finally, at 4:10, Cheney appeared and I crossed the lobby to the desk.

"Where's Celeste?"

"Visiting the ladies' room. She says you're taking her straight to the airport and she wanted to be prepared in case time was short."

"What time's her flight?"

"Five fifteen."

I checked my watch again. "That's cutting it close."

"Trust Providence," he said.

Behind him, Celeste appeared. "Are we okay here?"

I said, "Fine. But we have to hustle. It's twenty minute to the airport as long as we don't run into traffic."

Cheney and Celeste shook hands. The "thanks and appreciation" exchange was hurried along by my shifting from foot to foot. I'm a stickler about arriving an hour before flight time and we'd already cut that in half. Celeste was apparently one of those people who don't mind showing up after the airplane door is closed and requires a lot of banging to gain admittance. Many airlines won't oblige the tardy passenger once the door is shut. If she missed her flight, it would mean hours of chitchat while we hung out, waiting for a seat to open on the next available flight.

We trotted back to my car. I turned the key in the ignition and pulled out of my parking spot before she had a chance to fasten her seatbelt. I clicked mine into place when we reached the next intersection. I headed down Fig to Chapel Street, where I turned right and drove the six blocks to Arroyo, which I knew had a freeway on-ramp. We were third in line to merge and the stream of cars had slowed to a stop. It's pathetic to see a grown woman weep over traffic, so I was forced to control myself.

Celeste murmured, "Sorry. I should have wound up my meeting a bit quicker."

If she was seeking absolution, I wasn't going to give it to her.

Five minutes later, we eased into the northbound lane. The vehicles in the two lanes to my left had turn signals on, telegraphing an intention to ram right into other motorists if they didn't make way. I saw drivers casting about desperately, trying to find recourse as the poacher came ever closer to sideswiping the car with the right-of-way. We were all going to be out of our cars exchanging insurance information if we didn't play nice. I thought the traffic jam must be the result of an accident ahead, but there was no sign of a fire truck, an ambulance, or a patrol car with flashing lights.

Eventually, the car in front of us moved forward as the car in front of that car opened the gap by a car's length. Suddenly the bottleneck yielded and we were on our way. I kept to the speed limit, not willing to risk a moving violation. One off-ramp went by. Two. Three. Two miles further on, I left the 101 and crossed back over the freeway at the top of the ramp. Smooth sailing at that point, which didn't relieve my tension. I checked my watch. It was 4:35 and we had two miles to go. The distance didn't bother me so much as thinking ahead to parking, locking the car, and the walk to the terminal, where she'd have to stand in line for her boarding pass and then pass through security. These were not always speedily accomplished.

By now, Celeste was as anxious as I was, which at least eliminated small talk as we focused on our progress. I took the off-ramp for Airport Boulevard. When I hit the straightaway, I did a quick search for a traffic cop and seeing none, I poured on the gas. I approached the entrance to short-term parking, snagged a ticket from the machine, and moved forward almost before the arm was fully up. She got out of the car as I was parking and she was already making her way to the terminal entrance when I caught up with her. The tight schedule had at least erased Ned from our consciousness.

We hurried through the front doors and she took her place at the United Airlines ticket counter. The wait was mercifully short, since every passenger with a grain of sense was checked in by now and waiting at the gate. The absence of luggage saved us forty-five seconds, though the desk agent did shoot Celeste a quick look, wondering if she was up to no good. I caught the fellow's eye, circled a finger at my temple to denote craziness, pointed at her, and mouthed "This is my sister," as if that made a difference. He slid her boarding pass across the counter and I walked her the fourteen feet to security. Once she was on the other side, she waved, indicating that she felt safe and I was free to go.

I took a minute to survey my surroundings on the off chance that Ned lay in wait and might hurdle over the X-ray machine and seize her by the throat. Again no sign of him, which generated a moment of hope on my part that he was already suffering the fever, difficulty breathing, low blood pressure, fast heart rate, and mental confusion of sepsis. I confess I didn't wait for her plane to take off. I left the terminal and returned to my car. The traffic pattern at the airport is such that a departing vehicle is made to circle back, passing the terminal entrance a second time before accessing the exit lane.

It was because of this very quirk that I spied a taxi pulling up at the curb. Bayard Montgomery emerged from the backseat on the right and Ellis got out on the left. Bayard wore a black leather jacket and what looked like a black chauffeur's cap with a shiny patent-leather brim. Ellis was in a white dress shirt with a red sweater across his shoulders, the empty sleeves folded together in front as though holding hands. The driver allowed his taxi to idle while he got out and walked around to the trunk to help remove luggage. He unloaded the large wheeled split duffel and the expandable four-wheeled packing case I'd seen in the foyer at Bayard's house. After that, he removed the soft-sided carry-on, two medium hard-sided cases, a rolltop backpack, a leather travel tote, three matching pieces of soft-sided luggage in graduating sizes, a garment bag, and an overnight case. This did not look like a weekend in Palm Springs.

Bayard's travel plans were none of my business and I was close to completing the roundabout and returning to Airport Boulevard when I felt myself squint. I checked the rearview mirror, watching the redcap load the pieces on his cart. I veered into short-term parking a second time and searched for a space. None. Not one. I went around twice, hoping to see taillights that indicated someone was pulling out, but there was no movement. I could be doing this for another twenty minutes while Bayard and Ellis were doing who-knows-what. I found a no-parking lane with diagonal stripes to announce the unsuitability of the space for my purposes. I parked and got out of my car, locking it behind me.

In the terminal, at the American Airlines ticket counter, I saw Bayard take possession of their two boarding passes. He had his soft-sided carry-on and he joined the security line while Ellis went into the gift shop. I watched him buy several fatty snacks, two magazines, and a travel neck roll filled with organic flax. I bent to study something in the window as he walked away with his purchases and headed for security. Bayard had already secured two seats in the waiting area. I glanced at the signage and realized the flight they intended to board was a commuter plane to Phoenix, Arizona. Bayard had mentioned Palm Springs and I could feel my head tilt like a puzzled pup's at the change in plans.

I had no way to approach them in the area where they were seated since they'd already been through security screening. I was not a ticketed passenger and I wouldn't be allowed past the first checkpoint. I got as close to them as I could and called Bayard's name. Seven people turned around to look.

When he lifted his face, I gave him a cheery wave. I gestured for him to join me and he made a comment to Ellis. Thanks to my highly developed lip-reading skills, I saw him saying, "Shit. Go see what she wants."

Ellis said, "Why me?"

Bayard said, "Never mind. I'll do it."

He got up, trying to match my smile with one of his own.

I said, "Hey. I didn't expect to see you here. I was just dropping off a friend."

"Small world," he said, offering no encouragement.

"Off on your weekend jaunt?"

"Yep." He pantomimed a golf swing.

"I thought you said Palm Springs. This flight goes to Phoenix."

"Last-minute switch," he said. "Our flight was canceled, so we decided on Phoenix instead."

"I'm sure the golf is every bit as good," I said.

"And the hotel rates are better."

"Everything works out for the best," I said.

He replied, "Nice seeing you," and returned to his seat. He sent me a faint smile when he was settled again, lest I think his departure was rude. I waved again and turned on my heel.

Now what was I to do?

As I passed the American Airlines ticket counter, I felt a mental nudge. On the scratchpad in Bayard's library, I'd seen AA with a circle around it. My first association with AA was Alcoholics Anonymous, but American Airlines was probably closer to the truth. I slid a hand in my pocket, congratulating myself on my habit of wearing the same jeans four days in a row. I pulled out the note I'd made: 8760RAK. Maybe not a license plate. The American Airlines check-in line had picked up a host of travelers, so I moved to the United desk.

When the ticket agent looked up as though to check me in, I put my finger on the RAK. "Do you recognize this?"

He glanced down. "It's an airport code."

"What airport?"

"Marrakech-Menara Airport. Morocco."

I nearly laughed. "Really? You can fly from Santa Teresa all the way to Marrakech?"

As though to a simpleton, he said, "Uh, yes. That's possible in this postmodern era of international travel.

All you need is thirty-four hours' flying time and three to four thousand dollars for the seat."

"And 8760 is the flight number?"

"You'd have to check with American on that."

"What's the routing?"

"Ask them," he said, not about to extend warm public relations to a rival company.

I walked back to the American Airlines counter and took my place in line. There were three people ahead of me, and as is true of lines in your local bank, these were all customers with "issues" that required long discussions with the ticket agent, frequent references to the computer, head shakes, and more discussion. I checked the departures monitor on the wall behind me and saw that the Phoenix flight was leaving in twenty-six minutes. This is just about the same amount allotted for early boarding, passengers with children, the feeble, and infirm. I leaned sideways and stared at the ticket agent and when he looked up, I pointed to my watch. He was singularly unimpressed with the urgency I hoped to convey. Two minutes later, that passenger left the desk and the next woman in line took his place. I heard the preboarding announcement for the Phoenix flight and shifted restlessly from foot to foot. The woman left and the ticket agent made quick work of the two passengers in front of me.

When I reached the head of the line, he moved a small metal sign to the middle of his station. Next window please.

"Oh no, no, no. Please. I just have a quick question . . ."

"Union rules," he said primly.

"Fine. I honor that. I appreciate everything the union does for you. All I need to know is the routing from Santa Teresa to Marrakech."

He blinked and began to rattle off the information. "Phoenix, Philadelphia, Madrid, Marrakech. Phoenix, Philadelphia, Chicago, Madrid, Marrakech. Phoenix, Detroit, Madrid, Marrakech. Phoenix, London, Madrid, Marrakech. Phoenix, London, Casablanca, Marrakech. Phoenix, Chicago, JFK, Madrid, Marrakech. Regardless of the route you choose, you'll be flying into Madrid or Casablanca. I don't know about the latter, but from Madrid, there's only one flight to Marrakech and that's 8760."

"Thank you."

I did a 180 turn, looking for a public phone. I saw one next to the door to the ladies' room. It was currently in use. A woman in heels, wearing a chinchilla coat, was deep in conversation. I crossed to the phone and stood behind her, hoping she'd pick up on the hint. She was heavily perfumed, I noticed now that I was in range of her. She didn't even look around at me. I stepped to one side and stared at her. She noticed me then and turned protectively, placing a hand over the mouthpiece so I couldn't hear what she said. I checked my watch pointedly. I tapped my foot. I moved into her line of sight again and did the rolling-hand gesture that means hurry the fuck up. No dice.

I took out my wallet and removed two bills. I leaned close to her ear. "Lady, I will pay you twenty-five dollars to get off the phone right this minute."

Startled, she looked at me and then at the twenty and the five I held in one hand. She snatched the bills and said to the party on the other end, "I'll call you back."

I said, "Oh, wait. Excuse me. Do you have a quarter?"

She sighed heavily, but found one in her coat pocket and placed it in my open palm.

And with that, she was gone.

I dialed Cheney's number at the police department, wondering what I'd do if he didn't pick up. Four rings later, he snatched up the handset, saying, "Phillips."

"Thank god. I'm so happy to hear your voice."

"I've been trying to reach you— "

I said, "Wait, wait. Me first— "

Cheney was so enamored of his news that he charged right on. "Remember, I mentioned the white powder Fritz picked up on his clothing? The ME identified it as quicklime, so we went out to the crime scene and took another look at the septic tank. Know what we found? Under the fill dirt and construction debris where Fritz was dumped, there was a second victim. Somebody had covered the body with about eight pounds of quicklime and probably half a dozen containers of drain cleaner. The common perception is that the two in combination will dissolve a body over a period of time, but the truth is just the opposite—"

I said, "Cheney! Enough."

This went unheeded as he continued his forensics revelation. "Quicklime slaked with water will cause a small degree of superficial burning, but the heat from the chemical reaction will mummify the body. Slaked lime absorbs moisture from tissue and the surrounding soil, and prevents putrefaction. You'll never guess who it is."

Someone on the public-address system was saying, "Will the owner of a dark blue four-door Honda report to the short-term parking and claim your vehicle?"

I said, "It's Austin Brown."

Dead silence. "How did you know that?"

"Bayard Montgomery killed him because he threatened to call Bayard's father and tell him that Bayard was gay. Tigg was wildly homophobic and would have cut him off without a cent."

"Where's this coming from?"

"Don't worry about that. Bayard and his boyfriend, Ellis, are out here at the airport about to board a flight to Phoenix. Their final destination is Morocco, which I bet money has no extradition treaty with the US."

Another brief silence. "You're right."

"Will the owner of a dark blue four-door Honda please return to short-term parking or your vehicle will be towed."

I said, "Shit, my car's being towed."

I caught movement out of the corner of my eye and looked over at the departure gate as the gate agent picked up her microphone.

"Ladies and gentlemen, American Airlines Flight 5981 to Phoenix, Arizona, is now ready for boarding. We'd like to invite passengers with small children, those with disabilities, or any others who might require additional time to proceed to gate four."

I watched Bayard and Ellis rise from their seats and gather their belongings. Bayard picked up the black leather carry-on I'd seen in his guest room. Ellis crossed to a trash receptacle and tossed in some candy wrappers, then returned to his seat and picked up the plastic bag containing articles he'd purchased in the airport gift shop. He found his tote and hefted it. He patted his pocket for his boarding pass and then remembered it was in the outside pocket of his tote. He retrieved it and checked his seat number. Passengers were already forming an orderly line, with first-class ticket holders at the head. Bayard had saved Ellis a place about three passengers back and the two chatted while they waited.

"Cheney, they're boarding. It's American 5981 to Phoenix."

"Got it. I'll take care of it. Just stay where you are. I'm putting a call through to airport security."

I dropped the handset in place and crossed to the gate. The gate agent invited first-class passengers to board. The first gentleman in line handed his boarding pass to the gate agent. She ran it through her machine, smiled at him, and handed it back. He moved through the gate and through the exterior door to the tarmac beyond.

I was standing there thinking, *What if the security phone line is busy? How long is it going to take for Cheney to convey the urgency of the situation?* I spotted the airport security officer who stood by the X-ray machine, chatting with another airline employee.

At the gate, the second gentleman reached the head of the line and handed over his boarding pass, which was screened and returned. Bayard and Ellis shuffled forward a couple of steps.

I took a quick look at the entrance. Naturally there was no sign of a police presence outside the terminal. Apparently no messages were being conveyed to the hefty security officer, who'd now folded his arms while he settled in for a comfortable chat with his pal.

Bayard handed his boarding pass to the gate agent. Carry-on in hand, he moved through the gate and then waited for Ellis to clear the barrier.

I crossed to the officer and said, "Excuse me."

He didn't seem to hear me and didn't interrupt his conversation.

"Excuse me, sir, but someone just stole my carry-on."

Now that I had his attention, I pointed at Bayard. "See that fellow in the black leather jacket with the chauffeur's cap? His companion's in the red sweater. I put my carry-on down in the gift shop, and when I turned around it was gone."

"You have a way to identify it?"

"Yes, sir. I do. The bag has a leather tag with my monogram. BAM. My name is Barbara Ann Mendelson. If you'll check the contents, you'll find my blue cashmere sweater along with a headset and my Sony Walkman."

He looked at me and then looked back at the gate. "Which gentleman is this?"

"Right there, just going out on the tarmac. Black leather jacket and black chauffeur's cap with a black patent-leather rim. The fellow with him has on a red sweater and he's got a shopping bag from the gift shop."

He said something into the radio affixed to his shoulder. He listened and then made his way into the waiting area, moving very quickly for a guy who carried that much weight. He made a statement to the gate agent, who stepped aside to let him pass. Even from inside the terminal, I could hear him say, "Sir. Can I have a word with you?"

Other passengers moving toward the plane divided to form a stream passing on either side of them.

At first, Bayard didn't seem to realize he was being addressed. A man nearby touched his arm and pointed at the officer, who was already repeating his request. Bayard stopped. Ellis was ahead of him, approaching the exterior rolling stairs leading up to the aircraft, when he realized Bayard wasn't close behind. He spotted the security officer, frowned, and returned to Bayard's side. There was a three-way conversation, the officer making it clear there was a problem in the works. Bayard made a response, but didn't persuade the officer of his need to board the plane. Ellis started to kick up a fuss but Bayard waved him down, probably thinking a show of cooperation would speed them along. The officer repeated his request and the three of them walked back to the boarding gate.

I decided to make myself scarce just in case the security officer intended to ask for a full accounting of the theft from Barbara Ann Mendelson. I went through the front entrance and intercepted the tow truck before the driver could position himself for the removal of my vehicle. I don't know how I persuaded him of my innocence, but with frequent reference to Lieutenant Phillips, and by citing the ongoing investigation of Fritz's death, I somehow extracted my car before it was hauled off to the impound lot.

I slid behind the steering wheel and took a moment to collect myself.

Traffic was still slow and I made the drive home reconciled to the time it would take. Once in my neighborhood, I found a parking spot, got out of my car, and locked it. I let myself through the gate, rounding the corner of the studio as I moved into the backyard, slowing my pace. I'd been greeted by so many unexpected sights recently that I leaned forward for a quick look before committing myself. Ned's attack came from behind. I felt his fist in my hair. He yanked hard. I raised my hands and clung to his wrist to prevent his scalping me. He dragged me sideways and my feet flipped out from under me. He maintained an iron control by the simple expedient of his grip on my head. I was scrabbling backward as swiftly as I could in the face of his forward motion, which kept me off balance until he'd towed me out of range of the street. I couldn't avoid a sharp intake of breath, which was part surprise and part pain. I managed a brief moment of equilibrium, which he offset by hooking a foot behind my leg. I dropped, but only until he hauled me around so we were face-to-face. His complexion was gray and the strand of hair that fell across his face was oily, suggesting weeks without a shower. His breath on my face was hot and moist and stinking. He was jabbering at me, words and phrases that scarcely made sense, not that clarification was necessary. He'd come back to finish the job of killing me, which I sincerely hoped to prevent. I heard a quick noise that I knew was a switchblade triggered into play.

Belatedly, I registered Killer's presence. He reclined between the open tent flaps, happily licking a 3-by-6-inch Styrofoam tray. He'd torn a piece of plastic wrap to shreds and gnawed off bites of Styrofoam that were now strewn on the dirt around him. His preoccupation was puzzling except for the certainty he wasn't going to help. My immediate salvation came in the form of Pearl White, who'd rounded the corner of the studio on her crutches.

She was saying, "Bad news about Ned. He got away again—"

At that point she spotted me and stopped in her tracks. Ned had forced my head back around until I faced her, my mouth open, no sound coming out. He had the blade against the base of my throat, where one swipe would do the trick.

"Well, son of a bitch. I guess we know where he's at," she said. And then shouted, "Killer!"

The dog rose to his feet, his Happy Meal forgotten, though a chunk of Styrofoam still dangled from his mouth. He had enough latent mastiff and Rottweiler in him that a deep vein of canine ferocity had leaped to the fore. The ridge of hair went up along his back and the low rumble emanated from his chest. Over countless generations, his breeding had rewarded assault as a survival strategy. Unfortunately, domestication held equal sway and he was stricken with what was clearly a moment of doggie consternation. Which was stronger, the drive to protect his mistress, fighting to the death, or his enthusiasm for the amuse-bouche? Pearl and I exchanged a quick look, both of us counting on his baser instincts.

I heard a squeak from his throat and looked over in time to see him surrender to a gargantuan yawn. He lowered his head, which I hoped was the prelude to an unprecedented display of viciousness. Instead, his upper body continued sinking until his legs buckled under him. Killer rolled gently onto his side and slept. Ned had apparently laced a pound of hamburger with a sedative and Killer had obliged the man by wolfing it down. The sight of the dog was absurd and Ned laughed. It was in that moment of inattention that Pearl made her move.

She crossed the distance between us with remarkable speed for someone of her massive proportions with a broken hip contributing to her physical condition. He was unprepared for the aggression he'd unleashed. She swung one crutch and delivered a blow to the side of his head. He wasn't stunned so much as surprised. She brought the same crutch down on his wrist. His grip on the knife loosened and it flew off to his right. Pearl stepped forward and aimed the tip of the crutch at his Adam's apple. Ned made a sound like a cat coughing up a hairball. She tossed the crutch aside temporarily and embraced Ned and me in a bear hug of such magnitude that the three of us toppled sideways into the pup tent, which collapsed under our combined weight.

Ned popped up first, fueled by outrage and fury. Pearl had trouble getting to her feet. He snatched a heavy fold of canvas and tightened it over her face. While I worked to free myself from the voluminous tenting, he straddled her and bore down, cutting off her air. She flailed. Without traction or leverage, she had a hard time bucking him off, but she finally succeeded. Her hip must have been giving her excruciating pain because I heard a quick cry of distress as she lumbered to her feet. Ned had turned his attention to me and we grappled without much effect. The quiet was punctuated with quick gasps and inarticulate grunts. Some of the sounds mimicked sobs, but none of us wept. I pulled myself upright, shoved him back, and kicked him on his injured side. He toppled, howling with agony.

Pearl struggled to hold herself upright while racked with pain. For a moment, none of us moved. In this orgy of violence, this was the moment when we might have paused for a postcoital smoke.

The interval was short-lived. Ned scrambled forward and tackled her around the knees. She fell on one side and he sat astride her, his weight sufficient to immobilize her. Desperate for a weapon, I grabbed the chain used to tether Killer to the tent stake. I whipped the chain over his head and around his throat, crossing one hand over the other to tighten the noose. He thrashed and then jerked forward abruptly, which flipped me over his body and onto the ground.

Pearl snatched up one of the fallen crutches and delivered a sharp thrust to his solar plexus, then plowed into him before he could regain his balance. She whacked him twice in the side of the head with the support end of the crutch. He dropped to his knees and groped the dirt around him, searching blindly for the knife. His fingers made contact and he swung his arm in an arc, prepared to plunge the weapon into any portion of her he could reach. She caught his hand midair and they arm-wrestled for control. She sank to her knees, bringing her face to a point level with his. The two strained. Her arm was shaking from the effort. In this, the two were equally matched, his upper-body strength pitted against her bulk. There were a solid twenty seconds of stasis. Then Pearl growled low in her throat and prevailed, forcing his hand down, pinning it to the ground.

I crossed the yard, closing the distance between me and the garage. I jerked Henry's shovel free from its designated location and swung it like a baseball bat, blade parallel to the ground and traveling at a speed that made the air sing. If I'd caught him in the neck, I might have severed his head. As it was, he raised an arm and deflected the blow. The sharpened edge sliced his shirt and cut deep. Blood welled in a fast-spreading blossom of bright red.

I was charting the progression of pain that threatened to overwhelm me. What our self-defense instructor hadn't spelled out was how focused such a fight could be and how debilitating. Pearl dragged herself to her feet again. Her face was a hot red, and sweat was pouring down her cheeks. He scuttled to a point a few feet away from her, creating a neutral zone in which he could rally his forces. He stood up again, calling on reserves of strength that surprised me. His right arm was of little use to him now. He was sweating heavily and his renewed blows lacked conviction. When he paused to assess the situation, Pearl gathered herself and drove at him, her fist back. When she connected, there was a sound like a waterlogged bag of cement dropped from a height. He went down like a board, as stiff as a 2-by-10. She landed in the middle of his back. I was on my feet by then and I put my hands on my knees, winded and panting from the effort.

My lungs burned. My energy was depleted. I noticed bodily injuries, but couldn't remember how or when they occurred. I glanced at Pearl's face, which was a mask of bruises. One eye was black, one tooth was missing, and a cut at the corner of her mouth oozed blood. She'd positioned herself in the middle of Ned's back, and gravity was sufficient to hinder the rise and fall of his chest.

She said, "Shit. I think I broke my hip again, but right now I'm numb and it doesn't feel like nothing."

She bounced a couple of times and I heard an *oof* of air escape Ned's lungs. She bounced again, though she winced as she did so. "What's this here? What I'm doing. You're a smart girl. I bet you know."

"As a matter of fact I do. It's called 'compressive asphyxia,' which is mechanically limiting expansion of the lungs by compressing the torso, hence interfering with breathing."

"Hence. I like that. I'm setting here bouncing on Ned, hence making it impossible for him to draw breath. That's what he did to them little girls, isn't it?"

"That was his method of choice," I said. "He also pinched their noses and mouths shut, which probably speeded the process, a flourish referred to as 'burking.' "

"How long does it take?"

"Pearl, sweetie, before we go on, let's just get one thing straight. You do know you're killing him."

"I get that," she said.

"Well, I'm not sure it's smart. Suppose one of the neighbors heard the ruckus and dialed 9-1-1? Barring that, Henry will be home shortly and he'll call them himself. If the police find you like this, your actions won't look good."

"You let me worry about that."

"You don't think your actions are extreme?"

"Are you seriously going to set there and argue mercy for this guy?"

"No."

"Then shut your pie hole and let me get on with it."

She looked down at Ned, her expression almost affectionate. "You know what I love best about my queen-size self, Ned? Turns out I can squash you like a bug."

She rapped her knuckles on the top of his head. "You still with us? You don't have to say nothing, but if you could move one finger, then I'll know you're still on board."

She studied his right hand first and then checked his left. "There you go. Good boy. He moved his pinkie," she remarked in an aside to me. Then to him, she said, "I want to make sure you're awake for this because I have one final word of advice. You don't never want to mess with women, son. They will take you *down*."

EPILOGUE

So here we are in March of 1990, five months after the events that make up the bulk of this report. Jonah is currently in the process of divorcing Camilla, who clings to him like a barnacle. Anna's baby is due in two weeks and she still hasn't quite decided what to do. She's trying to talk me into taking the little tyke, but I reminded her I had my hands full with Killer and Ed, the cat. Besides which, I'm not exactly a maternal type, though I suppose I could fake it in a pinch.

Phyllis Joplin, Ned's ex-wife, has recovered from his vicious attack on her. She's since moved to a community with tight security and she's begun to sleep through the night without jumping at every sound. The two of us don't have much in common except for the psychopath we shared for a time. I doubt we'll ever be close friends but we have drinks together now and then, during which we make a point of not discussing him.

The medical examiner attributed Ned Lowe's death to compressive asphyxia—the same method he employed in killing an unknown number of young girls. Pearl should have been held accountable, but when she was questioned by the homicide detective, she looked him straight in the eye and said, "Well, hon, he knocked me out cold and I fell on top of him completely unconscious, inadvertently squeezing the life out of him. You can't even imagine how terrible I feel." That was the position she took and she refused to budge. She wept so noisily at that point, the detective had to hand her a tissue and leave the room. Under the circumstances, he decided to accept her explanation as adequate. I've searched the California penal code and nowhere is there mention of penalties for sitting on a man to death.

As of this moment, in the interests of rehabilitating her reputation, she's employed at Rosie's restaurant part-time and she's officially apprenticed herself to Henry, working toward certification as a baker, which will take her another two and three-quarter years. Assuming she has the patience.

For my part, having watched Pearl crush the life out of Ned, you might wonder if I feel badly about the manner in which he died, suffering as he did. Nah. Not even a little bit.

In most states, crimes of extortion (including blackmail, bribery, and ransom) are generally considered felonies, punishable by fines, imprisonment, or both. Iris was so rattled by her conversation with Detective Burgess that she called the number on his business card and said she had to talk to him. She knew Joey would disagree with her, so she proceeded without consulting him. Once at the station, she confessed the whole sorry mess. She hated implicating Joey, but she felt this was their only hope of getting out from under the burden of what they'd done. The fact that their scheme was never carried to completion worked in their favor, and while the two were charged, they were given probation and served no jail time. The district attorney figured Iris had suffered enough with the disclosure of the sexual assault video after the copy they'd sent to the McCabes ended up circulating around town. Lauren would never admit she was responsible, but she needed some small measure of satisfaction in the wake of Fritz's death. Iris and Joey got married and moved to Arizona, where he's opened a satellite office of Merriweather Homes, his father's construction company.

It was Iris who told me about Fritz's claim that he knew the perfect hiding place for a body, a boast he made in the course of Bayard's pool party. At the time, he made no specific reference to the septic tank, but he'd attended camp at Yellowweed several summers in his youth. He told her that after the campgrounds were closed, he and his pals would go up there, remove the concrete cover, and have pissing contests, cackling as the streams of pee arced into the hole. He reported this to his mother as well, thinking she'd be amused. She was not, but she did confirm my theory about the matter when I asked.

In reconstructing events, my guess is that when Fritz and Bayard reached Yellowweed, his impulse would have been to open the septic tank and show Bayard the space to demonstrate how coffinlike it was. I can't even imagine what he thought when he looked down and saw Austin's desiccated body in the pit. He probably didn't have time to assess the implications before Bayard fired off the shots that killed him, after which his body was shoveled in on top of Austin's. The two might never have been found if not for the turkey buzzards and my keen sense of smell.

Bayard was arrested at the airport. His boyfriend, Ellis, was in no way implicated in his crimes, and from what I hear, he returned to the house, packed up the rest of his belongings, and left the state. On the advice of his attorney, Bayard refused to be interviewed by the police and never admitted any responsibility in the deaths of Austin Brown and Fritz McCabe. For those of us who knew the story, it was no big leap to conclude that he'd killed Austin to prevent his telling Bayard's father about his sexual preferences. In this day and age, there's no shame in admitting to being gay, but Tigg Montgomery had an aversion to homosexuals and would have cut Bayard off without a cent if he'd known.

Though this is unconfirmed, my hunch is that Bayard killed Fritz to avoid exposure in Austin's murder, finishing a story that began ten years earlier. After a painstaking investigation by the DA's office, Bayard was charged with both homicides. At the end of a lengthy and contentious trial, the jury brought back a verdict of not guilty, saying the prosecution hadn't persuaded them of Bayard's guilt beyond a reasonable doubt. I'm not saying justice is for sale, but if you have enough money, you can sometimes enjoy the benefits of a short-term lease.

Respectfully submitted,
Kinsey Millhone